Magic & Murder in the Holler

The Arcane Codex Book 1

Sara J. Lilienfeld

SJL CREATIVE

Ebook ISBN: 979-8-9929365-2-0

Paperback ISBN: 979-8-9929365-0-6

Hardcover ISBN: 979-8-9929365-1-3

Book Cover by Ashton M. Smith Designs

First edition 2025

For anyone who feels a little out of place no matter where they are, even if they can't exactly pinpoint why.

Balance in all things, particularly in witchcraft, is to be maintained as mandated by the laws of nature and the edicts of the Moranaa Dessis. Any feat attempted without reciprocity risks the destruction of all.

-Article II of The Arcane Codex, 1346, by author unknown

PROLOGUE

1998

"Knife, candle, herbs, matches. Am I missing anything?" Adeline Coburn muttered to herself as she glanced at the items spread out on the floor of her bedroom. She cross-checked the spell and accounted for all of the listed ingredients.

Turning back to her mirror, she finished pulling her dark brown hair into a ponytail and smoothed out a wrinkle in her work uniform. She hated the blue gingham dress and white apron that made her look like a waitress from the 1950s, but Lou, owner of Lou's Diner, preferred a classic look. The first time her twin, Elijah, saw her wear it, he said she reminded him of a shorter, meaner Judy Garland. She punched him in the shoulder in response.

Adeline hadn't wanted to become a waitress any more than Elijah wanted to become a miner, but the diner and the coal mine were the only places near Evarts hiring when the twins graduated eight months ago. Harlan County, Kentucky didn't have many jobs for two eighteen-year-olds with high school diplomas.

The sounds of her brother getting ready for work drifted down the hall and reminded her that she was running out of time to cast the protection spell before he left the house. She couldn't risk that it wouldn't take.

She took a seat on the floor and placed the candle directly in front of her, and surrounded it with yarrow and black walnut ash. She lit the candle and pricked her finger with the ritual knife beside her. She let a few drops of blood fall onto the flame before closing her eyes.

"I call upon the strength of my ancestors and hope they hear my plea." The room around her became a few degrees warmer and the smell of wet grass filled her nose. "Keep Elijah safe down in the mine. He doesn't have my Gift, but he is a son of the hills. Do not allow—"

"What the hell are you doing?" Elijah asked from the doorway.

The feeling of comfort evaporated, replaced with goosebumps on her skin. She opened her eyes and turned towards the door as he walked into the room. She shoved down her panic at the interruption as she met his hazel eyes. "What does it look like I'm doing? The same thing I've done every day since you started working at the mine. The same thing Mama'd be doing if she were here: using my Gift to try and protect you."

"If John walked in and saw you—"

By some miracle, the twins had managed to keep Adeline's Gift a secret from their father for their lives. Adeline didn't care now. Practicing witchcraft openly was a risk, but one she'd happily take. Any peril was worth keeping Elijah alive.

"He's passed out on the couch after he stumbled in at two this morning," Adeline said with an eyeroll. "I doubt a tornado siren could wake him. Regardless, with the way this house creaks, and how heavy his gait is, I'd hear him coming."

"Still, I don't need you trying to protect me. My job's not danger—"

"Mining might be safer than it was a generation ago," she raised an eyebrow and pursed her lips, "but that don't make it a safe job. I'll take the risk of getting caught if it keeps you safe." She surveyed the spell components surrounding her. The candle was lit, so the spell had started, but how far into its recitation had she gotten? "Damn! You made me lose track of where I was." She turned to her brother. "What was I saying when you cut in?"

"I only caught a few words, but it sounded like you were almost done."

It wouldn't hurt to repeat the ending of the spell again, in case she missed something. She closed her eyes once more. "Please grant me this boon and protect Elijah from the dangers of the mine." She blew out the candle and stood up.

Elijah seemed to be at a loss for words as he turned and walked out of the room. Adeline put her spell supplies away and headed downstairs a few minutes later.

She stopped in the doorway of the kitchen as the prone form on the sitting room sofa let out a loud snore. She froze, as did Elijah, until they were certain their father wasn't waking up. She sent a glare towards the sitting room before walking into the kitchen.

"Remind me why we don't just kick Johnny out?" Adeline asked. "Or why you won't let me turn him into a newt?"

"Because you don't know that spell, and his check keeps the lights on. It's about all he's good for." Elijah grabbed his belongings. "We've almost got enough money to get out of here. Don't lose sight of that." He looked around as he patted his pockets. "Do you need me to drop you off at the diner? It might be too warm to walk."

"No, Dinah's gonna give me a ride." The other waitress lived down the road and often gave Adeline a lift to work, since she had to pass the Coburn house to get to the diner anyway.

Her brother snagged his lunch pail as he walked towards the door, and a pit opened in Adeline's stomach. Goosebumps formed on her skin and her hands grew clammy. Without intending to, she shot out her hand and grabbed Elijah by the wrist as he walked past her.

"Addy—"

"Don't go. Please." She cleared her throat. "Don't go into that mine. Not today. Call in sick. Tell them there's a family emergency. Make something up. It doesn't matter what lie you tell, but don't go there."

"Miners don't get sick days." He released his arm from her grip. "It'll be fine."

"No, it won't. You don't – I'm telling you, don't go down into that mine. I've had this feeling all morning that … She's had enough."

"Who?"

"The mountain. She's tired of being torn apart."

People spoke about Evarts—the mountains, valleys, and woods that made up the holler they called home—as if it were a stagnant thing, but Adeline and others with her Gift understood it was a living, breathing entity with a soul and a mind of its own. If the dread she felt was any indication, the mountain was done being ripped apart by coal mining.

Elijah stared at her for a moment, as if he wanted her to say more, before shaking his head and walking out of the house.

Adeline stood at the kitchen window and hoped her protection spell would be enough, that the ancestors would answer her plea. She'd lost her mother; she refused to lose her brother. She didn't care what it might cost her down the line to protect him today.

She remained there, watching the horizon, until Dinah arrived to pick her up for her shift at the diner.

***

Between serving customers and her cleaning tasks, Adeline's day was so hectic that she barely had time to worry about Elijah until she had clocked out. The unsettling sensation she'd had all morning subsided a little before noon, and she'd barely even noticed due to the diner being unexpectedly busy. She hadn't forgotten the feeling, though, and its equally mysterious resolution nagged at her until she'd finished her work.

When she arrived back home, she saw Elijah's pick-up truck in the driveway and noticed John's was gone. She let out a sigh of relief; her brother was safe, and she wouldn't have to deal with her father.

"Elijah," she called as she stepped inside, but received no response.

Bluegrass music voice twanged from a radio somewhere in the house. She began to search the ground floor and found him at the kitchen table, staring at the wall. Three empty beer cans lay on their sides next to his lunchbox. "I hope this isn't the start of a new habit. Don't turn into our daddy."

"It's just to take the edge off." He opened another beer and took a swig. "You were right."

"Right about what?" She sat down at the table and pulled her hair out of its disheveled ponytail.

"I guess news must not have spread yet. Something happened at the mine today. I shouldn't have been down there." He met her gaze as he cleared his throat. His eyes were unfocused, like he wasn't seeing her. "The mountain nearly came down right on top of me. The whole shaft caved in as Wyatt Dunn and I stepped out into the daylight."

Adeline opened and closed her mouth a few times, struggling to find something to say. "I'm glad you made it out."

"Not everyone did. At least, it sounded like some of the men might've gotten trapped."

"How many?" She leaned forward.

"Don't know. All the boss said was that a few haven't been accounted for. I can't remember who was next to me when I was down in the hole and the shaking started, whether I ran past someone on the way out ..." He took another swig and his gaze settled onto the table in front of him. "The rock around me started shuddering, everyone was shouting, and the next thing I knew it's like the holler itself started talking, telling me to run."

"You heard something deep down in the mine speak to you?"

"Nothing was calling out to me from the dark; it was all in my head." He tapped a finger against his forehead. "It sounded like Mama, and that's the only reason why I listened to it." He pushed his metal lunch pail towards his sister. "Here."

She raised an eyebrow and tentatively reached for the container. "Why are—"

"Open it."

She unhooked the latch and lifted the top to find a bunch of wadded-up bills held together in stacks with rubber bands. "I don't understand. What is this?"

"Those are my wages for the past few months. It's enough money to get you out of here. It was the only place I knew John wouldn't look, since he's allergic to honest work."

"I still don't—"

"Word of the collapse is gonna spread, and folks are gonna want someone to blame. I don't want that someone to be you."

"Why would anyone blame me?"

"Wyatt Dunn asked me if the rumors about Mama's family were true and if you've been practicing witchcraft. He didn't outright say you caused the cave-in, but he sure as shit implied you're a witch." That kind of speculation was a dangerous thing around Evarts, especially after any kind of tragedy or unexpected death. People thought of so-called granny witches, women passing down home remedies and herbal cures from their mothers, as harmless. True witches, the ones with a real Gift, were another matter. Superstitions and old wives' tales made folks see them as evil and twisted monsters to be feared and eradicated, and not simply ordinary people with a rare talent.

"And you denied it, right?"

"Of course I did. Told him he didn't know what he was talking about. So, he brought up the rumors about Aunt Eve and what happened to her after word got around that Gavin Slater's death might not have been natural. Wyatt's threat was clear, and when people start looking for someone to blame, you'd be an easy target. If word starts to spread about you possibly being a witch or consorting with dark forces, or however it might get twisted, they'll come after you. It's better if you're not here, should they come looking."

"What about you?" she whispered. "We had a plan; we're both supposed to get out of here. I can't just take your money and run off."

"That's exactly what you're gonna do. You need this chance to leave more than I do. No one's gonna try to start shit with me, but you're a different story." He took another drink. "I'll be fine. Take the money, start somewhere new, and don't come back."

"I'm not leaving you here, stuck in this house with John." She clenched her jaw. "Running away isn't the answer."

"Eve thought the same thing after Gavin died, and they killed her for it. I buried Mama. I helped bury Eve. Don't ask me to bury you too." His voice became thick, and he blinked a few times to keep the tears from escaping his watery eyes. "Addy, the only reason I was gonna leave was that Mama would've wanted me to keep an eye on you, but you don't need me. You never did. It's not like I'm giving up a lot of opportunities by staying here, either." He cleared his throat. "I know you got into UK and turned it down because of me."

"Eli ..." She let out a sigh.

"You should've left as soon as you graduated. I know Mama always said you had to stay, but I think even she'd want you to go if she were here, after everything that's happened."

"Are you sure about this?" she asked, her voice thick with emotion.

"Yes. You should've left a long time ago."

**

A week later, Adeline was settling into her apartment in Tennessee. She used her landlady's phone to call Elijah that night.

"How's it been up there?" Adeline asked as soon as he picked up the phone.

"I want to hear about what you've been up to first," he said. "Where are you calling from?"

"I'm down in Tennessee. I found a cheap apartment and a community college where I can take some classes. My landlady's letting me use her phone. Your turn."

"Well, our dear old daddy didn't realize you'd left until three days after you were gone. And I went up and told Mama's family about you leaving, like you asked me to. Some of them weren't happy about it."

"That's not what I meant and you know it. You insisted I leave because you didn't think I was safe. What's been happening? Is everything okay? Are you safe?"

"I was never in danger," he sighed. "But no one's shown up with torches or pitchforks. Rock Ridge released the names of the three miners who didn't survive the cave-in: Fred Blevins, Jeremiah Lee, and Peter Blackburn."

"That's a shame." Evarts was a small town, so all three names were familiar. While Adeline didn't know Jeremiah personally, she knew some of his relatives. She'd babysat Fred's son on occasion and knew Peter from school.

"Yeah, it's sad. Peter was getting ready to propose to his girlfriend and every-thing." Elijah said. "But the rumors have started, so you shouldn't come back for at least a few years. Just to be safe."

CHAPTER 1

2014

"I heard witches from your part of the world perform human sacrifices on the equinox," Lena Payne said, looking at Adeline with interest and a bit of malice in her green eyes. "Is that true?"

Adeline nearly spat out the lemonade she was drinking as she glanced around and saw that Lena wasn't the only witch waiting for an answer. "Her part of the world," as if Appalachia was some foreign locale. The invitation to the Seattle coven's autumnal equinox party had been unexpected, and she hadn't accepted the invitation as eagerly as they probably anticipated. In the sixteen years since leaving Evarts, she hadn't celebrated a single solstice or equinox, and her life wasn't any worse for it.

Lena tapped a manicured finger against her glass as she waited for an answer. Her eyes scanned Adeline from head to toe, taking in her affordable yet formal navy top and black jeans, which stood out compared to the colorful and pricey dresses most of the guests wore. The invitation hadn't stated a dress code, yet Adeline had still violated it.

"No, Lena. We don't do human sacrifices," she said, biting back her vitriol. "Someone would start to notice eventually."

Adeline hadn't paid much attention to the broader supernatural world when she was growing up, but she knew better now. If witches out in Harlan County had sacrificed people regularly, others would have noticed and involved the local Guardians at the very least. The idea was laughable. Adeline had to use nearly every drop of her self-control not to snap and tell Lena and the whole coven how stupid the question was.

"Well, how do you celebrate the occasion, then? What passes for a good equinox party out in ... a more rural area? You've seen our celebration." She gestured to the mid-century modern kitchen around them with its cool grey tones and lack of clutter. It, along with the rest of Lena's spacious house, resembled something straight out of a magazine.

"We don't." Adeline's mother had always noted the day and once or twice had made a different dessert, but that was the extent of the observance.

"What? You don't celebrate the equinox? What about the solstices?" another witch asked. Adeline thought the woman's name was Emily, but she couldn't remember for sure.

She saw that every other woman in the room was waiting for her answer, even those who'd ignored Lena's rude question. "No, we don't observe those either."

Adeline didn't view herself as especially interesting, yet her comment caused the other witches to study her like something they had never seen before. If it hadn't felt so demeaning, she might have laughed at their expressions.

"How can you not celebrate them? They're the most important days of the year for our magic—"

"For your magic, yes. But not mine." One of the few things she missed about Kentucky was being surrounded by true magical peers. None of the witches she'd met since leaving home understood much about her Gift or how it differed from their own. "I don't draw my power from the stars. The movements of the sun, the moon, and the earth don't influence my abilities."

"Doesn't every witch draw from the cosmos?" Lena asked with a smirk. She seemed desperate to embarrass Adeline or catch her lying. "I mean, every witch I've ever met does."

"Most witches do, but not all," Molly Adams said from the doorway.

Adeline felt a rush of relief as the blonde witch, and the only coven member she considered a real friend, walked into the room. "Adeline's magic works differently from ours, as I told everyone when I invited her."

"I thought you just meant she used different spells, or that her rituals were some variation of ours." Lena turned back to Adeline. "Are you sure you're a real witch?"

"I couldn't deny it if I wanted to."

"Prove it."

"Fine, but this will be my only demonstration. I'm not some kind of show-off." Adeline twisted a ring on her right ring finger, one she'd inherited from her mother, back and forth a few times. She wiggled her fingers and the glass in Lena's hand shattered. For a moment, she thought she smelled the apple crisp her mother made every fall. Several witches startled at the noise. Lena's jaw dropped, as did a few others. "I guess I'm a real witch. Sorry about the glass."

Adeline swayed, but caught herself by leaning against a counter before she fell over. Spots appeared along the edge of her vision. The spell, minor as it was, had taken more energy out of her than she'd expected.

"How did you do that? You didn't say a spell or anything."

"Witchcraft. Like Molly said, mine doesn't work like yours." Adeline watched the assembled witches. Some seemed intrigued by what she'd done, while others seemed wary. "Thanks for the invite, but I'm going to head home now. Good luck with your ritual this evening."

She exited the house and was unlocking her car when she heard someone call her name. Looking up, she saw Molly walking over.

"Hey, I'm sorry about Lena. She's always been a bitch, but I didn't expect her to do something like that. The others aren't that bad. Come back inside and stay a bit longer. No one else is going to try and start anything."

"Because they're too scared to. I broke that glass without a word, half of them thought I used to sacrifice people, not to mention—"

"Wait, back up. They think you sacrificed people? Why would they think that?"

"I don't know." Adeline resisted the urge to cross her arms in frustration. "Because they hear a twang in my voice and decide I'm an ignorant, uncivilized hillbilly with backward ways. Because my witchcraft comes from my blood, not the stars. I don't care what they think or why they think it, but I'm not going to stand around and be insulted." Molly didn't reply, and Adeline barreled on. "Why did you invite me to this party anyway?"

Her friend shifted back and forth on the balls of her feet. "I know you don't have a coven out here and thought you might miss it. Miss having a community."

"Seattle's supernatural community's not exactly small."

"But this is the only coven in Seattle." Molly pointed behind her at the house. "I know it's different magic, yours and ours, but I invited you because I thought having a coven to connect with might make you feel less alone."

"Who said I felt alone? Because I don't, and you don't need to worry about me." Adeline had made her choices. They may not have been the best, or left her in a great position in the world, but she had chosen this path and accepted the consequences.

"You're far from home, surrounded by people you say don't understand you. I still don't fully understand how your magic works, and you've tried explaining it to me like five times. You have friends, sure, and colleagues from working at the Alliance, but no real community. Not like I do, or the vampires, or any other faction."

"Oh, I have one. My community's waiting for me back in Kentucky, if I'm ever desperate enough to go back there."

"You said you moved here for work." Molly frowned. "What do you mean 'desperate enough to go back'? It's your home."

"It is. I love it—the hills, the woods, the colorful sunsets deep in the mountains that don't seem quite real." The vast and clear night sky, with too many stars to count. The smell of bourbon and earth that clung to everything. The dilapidated houses with peeling paint and rusted-out cars by the side of the road. The way everything in sight looked old and worn out. Faded billboards promising salvation and radio preachers ranting about damnation. The whispers and judgmental looks that followed her and her mother.

Adeline shook herself and focused her attention on her friend. "I moved away for a reason. I appreciate your intention, but let's face it. I don't belong with those women in there. Or in a place like this." She gestured to the affluent neighborhood around them. "I don't think I've ever stuck out as much as I do around your coven."

"We're still friends, right?"

"Of course! Lena's a nightmare, but you didn't do anything wrong." She paused and forced herself to relax a little bit. "Just ... I don't think you should invite me to any more of your coven events."

"Lena's going to demand I never invite you again, so that's a moot point."

"And I'm *very* torn up about that." Adeline rolled her eyes.

"I'd come with you if not for the ritual. I know you don't celebrate it, but happy equinox," Molly said before heading back into the party.

Adeline picked a maple leaf off the bottom of her shoe as she slid into her car. Spinning it by the stem, she studied it briefly and considered what had happened inside when she broke Lena's glass. Her power had been diminishing over the years, but she'd never felt drained like that. Why had one spell tired her out?

She pushed some of her Gift into the leaf, hoping to change it from its current reddish hue to a bright green. It was an arduous process, but slowly she restored it to its summer vibrancy. She let out a relieved sigh; her post-spell exhaustion appeared to be a one-off incident.

Once she was finished, she spun her mother's ring around her finger a few times as she considered what she'd do if the experience repeated itself. Over two thousand miles away from home, the ring was one of the few things she possessed connecting her to the hills and hollers where generations of her family were laid to rest.

***

Adeline arrived back at her apartment a little before the sun had fully set, and the fading light of the day painted the sky over the Puget Sound a kaleidoscope of colors. An alarm she'd set for herself that morning went off, so she started her computer in order to tune into the livestream that would be starting any minute. The fall equinox meant the Chancellor of the Pacific region would be giving an address. She had learned over the years that it was smart to watch it, even if very little of what he said was of interest to her.

After a few minutes of watching the countdown on the screen slowly tick down to zero, James Horton, the Chancellor, appeared on screen sitting on a plush tan couch with a handful of people milling around behind him. He was a white man in his early sixties, and the little hair he had left was completely white. His mood seemed jovial as he spoke to someone off-screen, inaudible with his microphone muted.

After a few moments, the movements in the background came to an end. His microphone came on, his smile turned forced, and some of the light in his eyes went away. He cleared his throat.

"I want to wish a good evening and a blessed autumnal equinox to everyone, on behalf of myself and my family. It's my hope that each and every person watching had the opportunity to celebrate the day with their community and their families. This is an important time for many of you, and the coming months will mark a variety of holidays and celebrations in both ordinary human society and within our world. I know I speak for myself, as well as the Stewards of Alaska, California, Hawaii, Oregon, and Washington, when I say the summer of 2014 was a productive one. I also want to apologize to those watching from Hawaii for having to watching this address while they eat dinner. I'm sure they'd rather be tuned into something more entertaining."

The men and women behind him laughed politely.

"I'd like to take a moment to highlight some of the things this region has accomplished in recent months. In Alaska, we saw the reconciliation of two werewolf packs who had been at odds for three generations." Polite claps sounded from off-screen. "California and Hawaii both saw increases in community engagement." More polite claps. "Last, but certainly not least, Washington and Oregon had the largest growth in population in recent years."

Adeline smiled in spite of herself. Some of the people she worked with wouldn't be happy that a population bump was the only thing the Chancellor mentioned about Washington. She could practically hear some of them ranting about it.

"As summer comes to a close, we must continue looking to the future, as always. It's my goal to create a more cohesive and robust method of communication between states so information can be quickly and more easily disseminated. This is the first step to having a network between regions, which is something the Chancellors, the state Stewards, and a number of Guardians have been working on for years. This network would allow for more communication and collaboration across the country."

Adeline continued to watch but tuned out most of what Horton was saying. Hearing about the communication infrastructure and his other proposals didn't interest her. The livestream ended after an hour. Not two minutes after it ended, her phone rang.

"Hello?"

"How pissed are your bosses going to be over what Horton said about Washington?" Molly asked her. "Haven't they been making the drop in supernatural-involved crime a big deal?"

"Some of them have, and I'd wager they're livid right now." The only reason the Alliance existed in the first place was because supernatural activity in Seattle had nearly exposed the hidden world to humans a few decades earlier. "I don't know why they expected a pat on the back for it. Or for the Alliance to get a special mention."

"A reduction in crime is a good thing."

"I don't disagree. But he's not going to mention it because a drop in crime means it's been a problem in the past. The Chancellor's a politician, as is the Steward. They care about crime when it benefits them, and mentioning it now doesn't do them any good. I bet you fifty bucks Seattle's lower crime rate doesn't come up until one of them runs for reelection."

"You're the most cynical person I've ever met. Have I mentioned how much that worries me?"

"I come by it honestly." When Adeline was young, politicians came to eastern Kentucky every four years, hoping to pander to the folks living there. They made all kinds of promises to grow the economy, to create better and safer jobs. Little ever came of it, and she'd learned early not to put stock in a politician's words. Actions were the only thing that mattered. "If you think I'm bad, it's a good thing you've never met any of my relatives."

"Not for lack of trying," Molly reminded her. "Why didn't you introduce me to them the last time they came for a visit?"

"The timing didn't line up." For Adeline to introduce her family to Molly, her family would need to come visit. Elijah was too busy, her parents were dead, and her more distant relations likely had no interest in travelling so far to see her. "I have to go. The next few days are probably going to be rough."

"I wish you luck."

Adeline could've gone to sleep. She should've gone to bed early and tried to get as much rest as she could. Instead, she grabbed a bottle of bourbon and poured herself a glass. She wasn't scheduled to work in the morning, so there was no harm in staying up a little later than normal.

"Happy equinox to me and my coven of one," she said to the empty room. "Many happy returns or whatever the toast is." She drank half of the glass in one swallow.

CHAPTER 2

— • —

Adeline jolted awake to the sound of someone pounding on her door. Her alarm clock showed it was a little after nine in the morning. She'd fallen into bed around one, expecting no commitments today. Yet, to someone, it seemed she was running late. Thankfully, she woke up hangover-free.

"Just a second."

She jumped out of bed and started running a brush through her hair as she walked over to her closet. The only reason someone would come by unannounced was for something work-related. After staring at her clothes for a few minutes, she grabbed the black dress pants she'd worn the day before last off of the floor and tugged them on. She pulled a plain blue blouse over her head and smoothed out the wrinkles.

Another knock rang out as she crossed the apartment to answer the door. "What?"

"Guess you didn't see my message. I got a call from Bill," Dominic Scarlis said, leaning his five-foot, eleven-inch frame against the doorjamb of her apartment. Both his blond hair and blue suit were pristine. Her partner of nearly two years had an annoyed expression in his brown eyes and let out a huff when she gave him a blank look. "I sent you a text. We got word of some kind of siren-creature operating by the waterfront. Since people like you are immune to them, we're the lucky Guardians dealing with it."

She didn't take the bait he'd thrown out about people like her. Maybe he meant witches, maybe he meant women. Neither would've surprised her.

"A siren, in Seattle." Something about his wording seemed cliche. "A rusalka, then." She unplugged her phone from where it was charging by the door. She had a text from Dominic, saying he was on his way, along with two missed calls from Elijah, as well as a voicemail.

"Aren't they the same thing? What does it matter what I call them?"

"It matters because rusalki actually exist. Sirens don't."

"I don't care what they call themselves." He rolled his eyes. "There aren't any in Mississippi, so you probably think they're exotic or special, but no one else cares."

Adeline let her comment that she was from Kentucky, not Mississippi, die on her tongue. In Dominic's eyes, the distinction didn't matter since she was from "the South," and he assumed everyone living there was backward anyway. Yet, anytime someone assumed he was from Washington, and not Colorado, he saw it as a personal insult. She briefly wondered if Mississippi had rusalki since it was along the Gulf Coast; it wouldn't be uncharacteristic for the water spirits to settle there.

A meow from her couch brought Adeline back to reality. "I'll feed my cat, and we can go." Her grey tabby cat, Whiskey, moved from her sleeping spot on the couch and stretched. The animal spotted Dominic and bolted to the bedroom to hide. "If I can get her to come out."

"You've got five minutes." He grabbed the doorknob. "Why's your familiar still scared of me?" He closed the door without waiting for her response.

"She's just a cat, but she can tell you're awful," she told the closed door. She wished she had a familiar, but they had been made up by non-witches centuries ago, and the stereotype stuck. "Oh, come here, sweetie. The scary dog man is gone now."

Luring Whiskey out from under the bed took a few minutes. Dominic seemed to be in a rush, but she didn't feel the need to hurry. She wasn't at his beck and call. He'd wait for her or deal with the rusalka on his own. Either option was fine with her.

***

"Did you see the Chancellor's speech last night?" Dominic asked Adeline as soon as she closed the door of his sedan.

"Yeah, I did."

"Can you believe that shit? All the work the Alliance has done over the last few months, and he can't spare ten seconds to acknowledge it. What does he bring up? Population growth. I knew Horton wasn't going to thank me personally—others would've gotten upset if he had—but mentioning the Alliance, at least, wouldn't have been hard."

Adeline peered out the window so he wouldn't see her trying to control her laughter. He thought he deserved to be thanked? For what, doing his job? They hadn't saved anyone's life or averted some major catastrophe. All they'd done was cover up supernatural activity so humans didn't notice any odd occurrences. She wondered what planet Dominic was living on where he thought he deserved praise.

"Everyone in the office is pissed about it, including the management. Especially the senior management."

The car fell silent when she didn't react in shock after hearing the conceited leaders of the Alliance were angry that their egos hadn't been validated.

"So, this rusalka. What do we know?" she asked as he took a turn and they drove through downtown Seattle. "How'd she wind up on our radar?"

"About two o'clock this morning, Seattle PD got called to break up a bar fight at a club by the waterfront. A couple of guys were beating the shit out of each other. When the cops finally got them down to the station, both men said the fight was over this girl they'd just met. Each man said there was—"

"Something about her that they couldn't describe, but they were instantly drawn to. She was too beautiful to put into words, or impossibly interesting." Every account of the rusalki she'd read cited an irresistible allure that drew victims in and lowered their guard.

"Maybe not in so many words, but that was the general idea. Bill sent me a recording from one of the interviews, and the victim sounded pathetic. I'm sure the other guy's in the same state. Falling over himself over some woman like she's that special. I bet she's not even really that hot." He rolled his eyes.

"The Alliance doesn't want a repeat of last night. Gabriel's concern is that the longer the woman stays at large, the more likely humans are to notice something strange happening. We have to find her before this turns into a bigger issue and winds up on someone more powerful's radar."

"All this worry over one bar fight."

"She used her powers on humans in public, and there might be footage of it. That's two of the Alliance's rules broken, minimum. That one bar fight could lead to the exposure of the rusalki's existence."

"And if they get found out, then humans are going to start to wonder what other myths are true. They'll start looking for proof of other supernatural creatures, putting every supernatural being in the city at risk." Adeline nodded knowingly. "But that's a pretty big 'what if' scenario."

"Not big enough. She could get all of us killed."

Adeline thought Dominic was blowing things out of proportion, given how quick he was to assume the worst-case scenario would happen. Before she could ask why he seemed so unsettled, he stopped outside a small shop. The worn-out sign offered fortunes and palm-reading. She frowned at the familiar storefront. "Why are we here?"

"The rusalka escaped during the excitement last night. One victim couldn't describe her at all, and the other claimed she was brunette and the most gorgeous girl he'd ever seen, which is beyond useless. I don't have a way to track her down." He waved towards the building. "We need Tatiana's help, unless you've got a better idea."

"I don't." Leaving the rusalka alone to see if what happened was a fluke wasn't currently an option.

He walked into the shop, and Adeline followed. The scent of sage and other herbs permeated the air inside the building. She had no idea how Dominic's heightened senses could stand such strong smells. She found it difficult to breathe or even think amid so many powerful scents until her nose adjusted.

"I have been expecting you," Tatiana Petrova called. She stood behind the counter with a dark red shawl wrapped around her frame and her eyes fixed on the door. Her greying brown hair was pulled into a bun, and she wore a long, flowy skirt and loose-fitting blouse, both light blue.

"That's hilarious." Adeline crossed her arms.

Tatiana narrowed her eyes, causing her crow's feet to become more pronounced, and for a moment, she looked as old as she claimed to be.

"What's next? Do you see a tall, dark stranger in my future?" she continued with a raised eyebrow.

"No, but I'm happy to discuss what I have seen," Tatiana leaned forward. "Would you like me to give you a reading?"

"Why? So you can tell me—"

"Ladies, you're both pretty and we're not here to gossip," Dominic said with an eyeroll. "Tatiana, we need your help with—"

"You want me to help you find the rusalka you're looking for. The girl responsible for the brawl last night," Tatiana cut him off. "As I said, I was expecting you." She motioned to the chairs sitting at the round table where she did her readings and began to walk towards them. "Sit, both of you."

Once the two were seated, she lifted a small cinched bag from the table. The contents of the pouch clinked against one another as she dropped it in front of Dominic. "Pour these out onto the table."

"Can't Adeline—?"

"All witches impact my abilities to some extent. Adeline, for reasons that wouldn't interest you, throws off my reading quite substantially."

Adeline huffed. "Not this again."

Tatiana ignored her. "I've never had an issue with reading done on werewolves. Toss the stones onto the table." She leaned back and watched as he lifted the bag, opened it, and unceremoniously dumped the contents onto the table. "Let me see what I can divine."

Adeline had no idea what Tatiana could possibly glean from the way a dozen or so small stones scattered across the table, but the clairvoyant was engrossed in them so she must be seeing something. If Tatiana was a fraud the truth would have come out already, and Adeline and Dominic wouldn't have come.

After a few moments of Tatiana studying the stones, Dominic studying Tatiana's reactions, and Adeline studying the wallpaper, hoping time would move faster, Tatiana cleared her throat.

"The woman you're looking for can be found at Battery Street and Third Avenue currently. Though I cannot say how long she will be there." She raised her head. "I need to speak with Adeline alone."

Dominic opened his mouth to argue.

"The reason why is none of your concern, nor would it be of interest to you. The sooner you leave, the sooner I can finish telling her what I need to, and thus the sooner you can be on your way."

Dominic stood and left the shop, slamming the door behind him. Once he was gone, Adeline and Tatiana fell into a staring contest until Adeline spoke. "What? I don't have all day." She crossed her arms over her chest.

"Dominic is incredibly dismissive towards you." She smiled conspiratorially. "He will regret that in time. I hope I get to witness it."

"Is that what you wanted to tell me? That he'll get what's coming to him, so I shouldn't hex him or anything?" she scoffed. "He isn't worth my time, so I wasn't planning to. If that's all, I'm going to leave before you start with your normal BS."

"Is your disdain for clairvoyants in general, or am I the exception? It's been years. You know by now that I cannot control what I divine."

"You can't help what you see. However, you don't have to share what you see with people. I never asked you to read me. I never *wanted* you to. I didn't need to hear some cryptic crap about how I don't belong here two seconds after meeting you." During their first meeting, Adeline had felt isolated enough in Seattle, twenty-five hundred miles away from everyone she knew, including witches who understood her unique type of witchcraft. Hearing that she shouldn't be there from someone as respected in Seattle as Tatiana was had been painful.

"I never said you didn't belong. I said your destiny lies to the east and you were avoiding it. It does, and you are. In the interim years, nothing of what I said has changed."

"I've been a little busy, if you haven't noticed."

"Your work as a Guardian can be done by another. Your destiny is yours alone. You cannot outrun it any more than the rusalka you seek can escape her fate."

Adeline stood up. "Well, destiny will have to wait." Homesickness hadn't driven her east in the sixteen years since she left Kentucky; destiny wouldn't either. "I've got a rusalka to question." She walked to the door. "This was fun. Let's do it again in about fifty years."

"Destiny won't have to wait for long." As the door was closing, Tatiana seized the last word. "You will thank me for this once you understand why it has to be this way."

***

Dominic and Adeline drove in silence from Tatiana's shop to the location she had given them. Adeline tried her best not to think about the cryptic things the older woman had said. She didn't know, and wasn't interested in trying to guess, what Dominic was thinking. She wasn't in the mood to hear him bitch about wanting a different partner. He told anyone who would listen that she was holding him back from his true potential. When she'd pressed him on it, the one time that comment became too much for her to let slide, he couldn't tell her where he expected to be by now or how she was holding him back from supposed greatness.

One apartment building stood at Battery Street and Third Avenue. The search shouldn't be hard or take too long. It was an older building, and the neighborhood was fairly quiet, so there was little concern about a random bystander seeing something they shouldn't.

"So, what's the plan?" Adeline asked as they exited the car.

"What do you mean 'what's the plan?' We do our jobs. The Alliance wants the rusalka brought in before she attacks anyone else and gets someone killed, so we bring her in. Be ready to cast a spell or whatever it is you do." He walked into the building without looking back.

"Yeah, fat chance of that." With so many miles between Adeline and the resting place of her ancestors, her strength wasn't what it had once been. The exhaustion after her demonstration to Lena yesterday betrayed how depleted her magic had become. No one in Seattle knew of her waning power thanks to luck, a few tricks, and plenty of lying by omission. She could recoup her power by going back to Kentucky, but it would be far too easy to stay among the comforting hollers and familiar accents if she returned. "I hope she's not even home."

She and Dominic alternated as they knocked on different doors, trying to find the rusalka as they made their way through the building. Most tenants weren't home, and the few who were expressed annoyance at their day being interrupted. Adeline went to knock on the door of Apartment 704 when Dominic held a hand up.

"Don't." He signaled to the door. "It's her."

"How do you know?" she whispered back.

"Because unlike you, I actually know what I'm doing. I can hear her in there. She's talking to someone about what happened last night." He nudged her out of the way so he was standing directly in front of the door.

"Okay. Knock on the door then."

"Or, we skip the pleasantries." A beat passed and then another. "She's being reckless. She's a threat to all of us. She may as well be confessing to the police."

He knocked the door off its hinges and stormed into the apartment. Adeline stayed in the doorway, stunned by his actions. Two people jumped up from the couch. One was a brunette woman around twenty wearing athletic gear. The other was a muscular man with dirty blond hair who looked a few years older than the woman. He wore a suit with his jacket thrown over a chair. The pair had similar features: blue eyes and sharp cheekbones. Adeline guessed they were siblings.

"What the hell did you just do to my door?" the woman yelled. "Who are you?"

"My name's Dominic Scarlis. I work for the Alliance. They'd like a word."

"The Alliance of what? What's going on?"

"Don't pretend like you don't know. You're not fooling anyone. I'm here about what you did to those two men last night at the bar. And in front of humans, no less."

"Dominic, what the hell?" Adeline yelled. They hadn't confirmed the woman was a rusalka yet, nor had she tried to attack. Why was he being so aggressive?

He faced her. "Stay out of my way if you don't plan to be useful, Adeline."

"Lucy, run," the blond man murmured before launching himself at Dominic.

Dominic was ready for his attack. Using his enhanced strength, he quickly maneuvered the man into a sleeper hold and knocked him out. "This isn't your fight. You should've stayed out of it."

"Oliver," Lucy cried, before glaring at the man in front of her. "What did you do to my brother?"

"Your brother tried to get in my way. Like I said, the Alliance wants a word." He dropped Oliver onto the couch and started to stalk towards her. "You need to come with us."

"I don't know what you're talking about." She backed away from him. Her eyes caught Adeline's as she looked around frantically. "Last night, I-I didn't mean to do that. I didn't know I could do that. I—"

"That's awfully convenient," Dominic said.

"Please, you have to believe me. I didn't want to hurt anyone. I—"

"Even if you're not lying, which I doubt, it's too late." He started to close in on the girl.

"Wait," Adeline called out, stepping into the apartment. "Maybe we should hear her out before we do anything."

"Of course you want to listen to her," he sneered. "You always want to handle problems by talking."

"Look at her. She's not some crazed killer or meticulous schemer. She's scared." She saw Lucy start to back further away from them, out onto her balcony. "She said she didn't know—"

"It doesn't matter! There's nothing to hear out. There are rules and she broke them. My orders are to bring her in. Otherwise—"

"She doesn't deserve to die over a mistake." The Alliance monitored all supernatural activity in the city, but they didn't have unlimited power. They weren't the final authority. Their rules weren't the Arcane Codex, despite how often the organization acted as if they were. The girl in front of her seemed confused and scared, not dangerous or conniving. If she had malicious intent, she would've used her abilities by now. She hadn't done anything to warrant an aggressive approach, yet Dominic had become confrontational before he even entered the apartment.

"And, if she comes quietly, she won't have to. Assuming last night's events were a mistake, which I find unlikely." He turned his attention back to the rusalka. "What's it going to be?"

"Get out! Both of you," Lucy took her phone from her pocket with trembling fingers. "Or I'll call the police."

Adeline tried to think of a spell, any spell, to utilize to defuse the situation or prevent Dominic from making it worse. She came up empty. Her only idea was to set him on fire, and that wasn't the best plan. She was more than two thousand miles from her ancestors; her magic was so drained that she couldn't cast any powerful spell even if she thought of one.

"Wrong answer."

He rushed at Lucy. She moved backwards, not taking her eyes off him. When her hips hit the railing of the balcony, her momentum caused her to fall backwards over the edge. She let out a surprised scream. Dominic tried to grab her arm, but missed as she fell.

Adeline rushed over to join him on the balcony, but Lucy had already hit the ground. She lay face down in the pool of blood forming beneath her, limbs spread out. The street felt miles below them, yet the crimson blood was vibrant enough to see from the seventh floor. Adeline couldn't look away from the sight. Her brain was still trying to process what happened when she realized Dominic was shouting at her from only a few inches away.

"Why the fuck didn't you do anything to stop her from falling?"

"What?" She tore her eyes away from the pavement below.

"All you had to do was cast a spell, keep her from moving, and we could've brought her in. But you didn't. You stood there and did nothing. No. Less than nothing, since you wanted to let her off and kept saying we had to talk to her," he scoffed. "Just my luck that I got stuck with a useless witch."

She wished she'd set him on fire a minute ago. "I'm not the reason she fell! She was trying to get away from you!"

"Don't blame me for your weakness." He stalked out of the apartment.

Oliver started to stir from his spot on the couch. He sat up and glanced around. "What happened? Where's Lucy?"

"It's—I'm sorry." Adeline rushed off before he could respond. She didn't think she could handle breaking the news of his sister's death to him.

By the time she made it outside the building, the police had arrived. Some neighbors and a few passersby were murmuring about what happened. Dominic and, more importantly, his car were nowhere to be seen.

"Dick."

***

Adeline moved on autopilot for the next few hours. She barely recalled getting back to her apartment or changing into sweatpants and an old t-shirt as her mind kept playing and replaying the interaction with Lucy. Deaths were fairly rare in her work, though this wasn't the first one she'd witnessed. When she came out of her fog, she was seated on her couch, petting Whiskey. With her cat curled up beside her, she decided to listen to the voicemail her brother left her that morning. It couldn't make her day worse.

Elijah had called her a few weeks ago and said he needed to tell her something. When she'd returned his call, he had seemed distracted, but didn't mention anything important or tell her why he'd asked her to call. In the past week, though, he'd called multiple times and left messages. The number of calls was odd, and the tone of his messages was starting to concern her.

"Addy, there's something ... You need to come back home," Elijah said before letting out a sigh. "Something here's not right. I can't explain it, but – If you won't come back, at least call me. We need to talk."

A pit opened in her stomach, but a knock at the door interrupted her as she was about to dial Elijah's number. She opened it to find Bill Wong, her boss.

"Do you have a moment to talk?"

She stepped to the side and held an arm out, inviting him in. His greying hair and wrinkles made him look grandfatherly, but his shrewd expression and the fact he was dressed in a black suit, like he'd come from the office, told her that this wasn't a social call. "Do you want a cup of coffee or something?"

"No, thank you." He took a seat on her couch while she poured herself some coffee. "Dominic told me what happened with that rusalka."

"I'm sure he did." She placed her coffee pot down a little too forcefully before turning to face him. "Let me guess, he blamed everything on me."

"Perhaps not everything. But he said you wanted to hear the girl out and wouldn't use your magic to prevent her from escaping. So, he had to intervene, which led to the rusalka falling to her death. That makes today's events mostly your fault."

"Of course that's what he said. Otherwise, he'd have to take some of the blame for what happened," she said through clenched teeth. "You know, there's a reason he doesn't have a pack. I don't blame the other wolves for rejecting him. He's just out for himself." She took a sip of her coffee. "Yes, I wanted to hear what the girl had to say. Because she was scared and two strangers, including an unreasonably pissed-off werewolf, had just stormed into her home and attacked her brother before demanding she come with them. She didn't seem to know what the Alliance was or what she'd done. She – Forget it."

"No, finish what you were saying." Bill leaned forward. "She what?"

"She didn't even seem to know she was a rusalka. And now, she's dead." She paused. "If Dominic had stopped for a second, if we'd talked to her, maybe she—"

"Wouldn't have done it again? That's wishful thinking. She was a rusalka. What happened in that bar was what's in her nature. She wouldn't have stopped.

No one can outrun what they are. Even if she could, you know the rules. She should've gotten in touch with the Alliance last night and not tried to run."

"She'd have to know the Alliance existed in the first place, which she didn't seem to. And the Alliance's rules aren't the Arcane Codex." The rules the Alliance was so adamant about everyone following had gotten someone killed, someone who didn't need to die. The Arcane Codex, the centuries-old supreme laws of the supernatural world, was intended for the opposite outcome. "I'm thirty-four and I'm older than most of the rules you're talking about. They can easily be changed if the Alliance wants to amend them."

"They could, but we both know that won't happen over this incident."

The apartment fell silent. Lucy could've been innocent. If her death wouldn't change the rules, what would?

"I know that's not all you came to tell me. Otherwise, you could've told me tomorrow at the office."

"No, you're right. It's not." He gazed out of her window. "Dominic went over my head. He talked to Gabriel before he talked to me about what happened."

Adeline gripped her mug tighter, her fingers turning white. "Let me guess. He convinced Gabriel that he needs a different partner. One who's not as 'useless' as I am." She took a sip of her coffee to calm herself slightly. "At least, I think that's the word he used. It might not have been 'useless'. It might've been 'weak.'"

He cleared his throat, but still didn't meet her gaze.

She leaned forward in her chair, eyeing him. When he finally looked into her eyes, there was a tiny bit of fear in his.

She continued speaking. "He thinks I'm holding him back, but he's forgetting that I have more knowledge and experience than him." She relaxed into her seat. "Anyway, he wants a different partner and he's convinced Gabriel, so you're splitting us up." As a Senior Guardian, Bill couldn't circumvent Gabriel, the Head Guardian. "Who's my new partner going to be?"

"No one. We'd like you to resign," he said in an even tone. "The Seattle Alliance needs Guardians with more conviction than you. People who won't let emotions get in the way and risk our world being exposed. Those are Gabriel's words, not mine."

Dominic was duplicitous and self-serving, but he wasn't stupid. Gabriel had never been fond of Adeline. The day she'd met him, he had made his distrust of her known, and his opinion hadn't changed in the subsequent years. He'd finally found an excuse to get rid of her, even if his reasons were flimsy.

"I want to listen to what one scared girl has to say, and I'm putting our entire world at risk? If that's all it takes for the Alliance to dump me, fine."

"It's not just about what happened today. There's also what went down back in March when you killed that vampire."

"He was feeding on a fourteen-year-old girl," she bit out. "I don't regret it. My actions were justified, and I'd do it again."

"Well, the rest of his vampire enclave, including his sire, have spent months insisting it wasn't your place to do that. His sire claims it was her infraction to punish, and you overstepped your authority. Estelle's a prominent member of the community, and you, to put it bluntly, are not. Additionally, threats have been made. The kind that the leadership won't ignore."

"What threats? Did she say the vampires weren't going to pay their dues?" She rolled her eyes. Every supernatural faction made contributions to keep the Alliance operating, though some threatened not to pay whenever they were unhappy with the organization. "I hope she knows that won't work."

"Estelle—the whole enclave really—have threatened to go over the Alliance's heads due to what happened to make sure justice is served. All the way up to the Moranaa Dessis, if they have to."

"Of course they did."

Vampires were dramatic, and Estelle's tendency to be theatrical was extreme nearly to the point of farce. If complaining to the Alliance wouldn't get the vampires what they wanted, they'd take it up with the Washington Steward, or the Pacific Chancellor above him. Appealing to the Moranaa Dessis was excessive, but if any community was going to try it, it would've been them.

The Moranaa Dessis were shrouded in such mystery that few people knew what to believe about them. No one could agree on who or what they were, what the term meant, or why they were the ultimate authority over the supernatural world. Adeline only knew what little the Arcane Codex said about them, and that the board of supervisors, the Alliance's senior leadership, was scared of them.

"You parting ways with the Alliance is in everyone's best interest."

Adeline wasn't stupid. Her resignation benefited Bill, Gabriel and their bosses much more than it helped her. She was out of a job either way. If they fired her, they'd have to explain why to their superiors, which could lead to scrutiny. If she resigned, they skirted the issue.

"Consider this conversation my resignation, effective immediately."

"The standard transition period is—"

"Accept my immediate resignation or tell Gabriel to file the paperwork to fire me." She wouldn't stay where she wasn't wanted, and she had no interest in spending two weeks working at a job with people who thought so little of her. "Either way, I'm parting ways with the Alliance today."

"Okay. I accept your resignation, but I'm sorry to see you go." Bill's expression was earnest, and she wanted to believe he was genuine. "I'll make it official in a few days, once heads have cooled a bit. I hope you understand."

"That's fine." Her phone rang. Elijah was calling again. It was late out in Kentucky now. She remembered the tone of his earlier message. "I'll be leaving Seattle." Her lease would end in a little over a month, and she had no reason to stay here. "I've been thinking about moving on. I never intended to stay here as long as I have."

"Oh." He raised an eyebrow. "Well, I suppose it's for the best then."

She walked over to the door and held it open. "Tell that to Lucy Radassi."

"Who?" he asked as he got up from the couch and exited her apartment.

"The rusalka." She slammed the door behind him. "Of course you don't know her name. You'd have to care about what happened to her. I should hex all y'all as a parting gift." Her cat came and rubbed against her leg. "Well, not you, of course, Whiskey. You've already been hexed with being so sweet and beautiful."

If anyone working for the Alliance asked her for a favor anytime soon, they'd be in for a big surprise. She had a long memory, and forgiveness wasn't her strong suit.

She started another pot of coffee, which she drank as she packed. Since her apartment was tiny and most of the furniture came with the place, it wouldn't take her long.

CHAPTER 3

— · —

Adeline left Seattle three days after Lucy Radassi's death and started driving east without a final destination in mind. Even if she had one, she doubted Whiskey would do well traveling by air. The long drive gave Adeline plenty of time to think and decide what her next step would be.

On the first day of her drive, she was halfway through Idaho when she missed a call from Bill. She pulled over at the next gas station to call him back.

"Hey, Bill. Sorry I didn't pick up earlier. I was driving," she said. "What's going on?"

She hoped the slight twinge of excitement in her voice wasn't obvious to him. A few days ago she'd been willing to resign, but now the idea of starting over somewhere seemed daunting. If the Alliance's leadership changed their minds and wanted her to stay, she'd be tempted to consider an offer. It was unlikely to happen, but there was a chance.

"I don't agree with the decision to ask you to leave. You were great at what you did and one or two incidents don't change that," he paused, "—but the choice was out of my hands after Gabriel became involved."

"I figured. Is that why you called earlier? To tell me the decision is final, despite you disagreeing?" She held back a bit of her anger. Empty platitudes were useless to her and she hated her time being wasted. Bill didn't agree with letting her go, but she doubted he'd fought with Gabriel or anyone above him to keep her around. His comments did nothing to help her now, and she wasn't interested in sympathy.

"No, I thought that was clear when we talked. I'm calling because I made some calls this morning. I know people working all over the country. You're from Kentucky, right?"

"Yes, I am." An uneasy sensation filled her body.

"There's an office of Guardians in Big Stone Gap, Virginia, not far from the Kentucky state line. They're in the Southeast Chancellor's territory. Steve Kresler runs that office; he's an old friend. I told him you were looking for a fresh start away from Seattle and a new job. I didn't tell him why. I don't know if your fresh start means a new line of work, but Steve said his office could always use extra manpower." He waited a beat. "They operate a little differently than how we do things, but it's something. Like I said, you were good at your job, and you didn't get a chance to tell anyone your side of the story."

"I'll think about it."

Bill had been a good boss, but Adeline knew why he'd done this. He felt guilty about her leaving and thought helping her find a new job elsewhere would soothe his conscience. She found herself wondering how many other former Guardians had left of their own accord and how many had been put in her position.

"The option's there, but there's no pressure."

"Like I said, I'll consider it." She fell silent for a few seconds. "And it was nice of you to make some calls on my behalf."

Rustling on Bill's end of the line and muffled voices overlapped her last few words. She pictured him covering the receiver with one hand as he talked to someone else. She waited for him to either hang up or start talking again.

After about thirty seconds, Bill spoke again. "Sorry about that. What were you saying?"

"I said it was nice of you to call Steve Kresler. Please send me his contact information." She saw no harm in setting up an interview with Steve even if she didn't take the job. It gave her a destination, in any case. She'd call when she was closer to Kentucky.

"You're welcome. Oh, I'm supposed to remind you that you'll need to return to Seattle if there's an inquiry into any of your cases. And we ask that you fully cooperate if the need for one arises."

"I wasn't planning to do otherwise on the off-chance that happens." The timing of his reminder was suspicious considering how recently everything had unfolded. "Are you expecting there to be an inquiry?"

"No, no. We're not. It's not a worry of ours," Bill answered a little too quickly. "I mention it because you've already left the city and we didn't go through the normal off-boarding process we undergo when someone leaves the organization. This is all normal procedure. I'm afraid I have to go now. I hope things work out, and please keep in touch."

"That was weird, right?" Adeline glanced over her shoulder at the cat in the backseat of her car.

Whiskey let out a meow as she batted at a suitcase zipper with her paw.

"You're right. I should see what that's about before we start driving again."

It took Adeline a few minutes of searching on her phone to piece together why Bill and the rest of the Alliance might be worried about an inquiry. Oliver Radassi was a deputy district attorney. If he wanted answers about his sister's death, he could make things rather uncomfortable for the Alliance.

"Oh, if there's an investigation, I'll happily tell Mr. Radassi anything he wants to know," she muttered as she started the car. "You're going to beg me to stop talking before too long."

***

On the second day of her drive, as she crossed into South Dakota, Adeline started to feel a slight tingling sensation in her fingers. As she drew closer to Kentucky over the following days, the tingle grew stronger and developed into a noticeable itch.

When she crossed the border into Kentucky, everything snapped into sharper focus. The world seemed brighter. Colors were more vibrant. She could see and hear better than only hours before. The itch she'd felt over the last few days turned into a pulsing beneath her skin, begging to be released.

She passed through the bluegrass state, skirting Harlan County, and arrived in Big Stone Gap, Virginia late in the afternoon. After meeting with her new landlord at the bungalow she'd rented, she unpacked her car and let Whiskey out of her carrier. She changed into black slacks and a white blouse and left to meet Steve Kresler for the interview they'd arranged. She hadn't loved her job in Seattle, but wasn't willing to throw away a guaranteed job in Virginia either.

The address brought her to a free-standing building on the edge of town. The sign advertised a private investigation firm: Kresler and Co. Investigations. In Seattle, the Alliance operated under the guise of a community outreach organization. She'd heard of other fake business being used as a front for Guardians elsewhere. A cover story as a team of private eyes seemed like a weak front, but she didn't know how much scrutiny it faced. It was a rural area, and perhaps no one gave the business a second thought. When she was younger, Adeline certainly wouldn't have noticed anything odd about a random business claiming to have been established a few generations prior.

Adeline stepped inside, where the majority of the space was taken up by a large open room set up like a bullpen. Six desks faced one another with three on their side, allowing for a walkway in the middle. Towards the back, there was a private office and what looked like a conference room. Two of the desks to Adeline's right were occupied.

A woman in her late thirties was seated at the desk closest to the door, writing something down on a notepad. She had medium-brown skin, a heart-shaped face, and black hair pulled into a bun. She wore a blue pantsuit and didn't look up when the door opened. The desk next to the woman was empty, but a white man in his late twenties or early thirties with light brown hair sat at the desk furthest from the door. He had a triangle-shaped face with a thin, flat nose and wore a grey Henley. His head shot up when the door closed behind Adeline, and his blue eyes locked with hers.

"I'm looking for Steve." Adeline cleared her throat and spoke. "My name's—"

"You must be Adeline," a white man in his mid-fifties said, coming out of the office. "Steve Kresler, nice to meet you." He shook her hand. "Come on in."

He led her into his office while calling over his shoulder. "Jakob, Rebecca, you can head home. You'll meet Adeline tomorrow, assuming she accepts the job."

As she sat down opposite Steve, she could feel Jakob's piercing gaze on her back. She fought the urge to turn around and see if he was staring at her or if she was imagining it. "Bill didn't say what he told you about me. Only that he'd called you."

"He didn't say much, truth be told. Just that you worked for him as part of some alliance-thing out in Seattle, but decided to move here." He leaned back in his chair.

"Move back, actually. I was born and raised in the area." To avoid fidgeting, she placed her hands in her lap. "As for work, I worked for him as part of the Seattle Alliance of Supernatural Species."

"The name is ... well, I don't know how to say it politely." He grimaced.

"It's not the most subtle or creative, I know. Most people called it the Alliance."

"And what is that? He didn't explain."

"A special office of Guardians, focused on the Seattle-area only." She leaned back in her seat, relaxing a bit. "There were issues keeping the supernatural world under wraps a few decades ago, or so I've been told. Once things were better under control, the Washington Steward wanted more structure and oversight for the city."

"Interesting." Steve looked skeptical. "Around here, Guardians report to me. I report to the Steward of the relevant state, and they answer to the Chancellor. The Moranaa Dessis are above him, though they stay out of things for the most part." He crossed his arms. "How was Seattle different?"

"More bureaucracy, mostly. Guardians report to the Senior Guardian for their department, who answers to the Head Guardian. The Head Guardian reports to a board of supervisors, and the board reports to the Steward."

"Departments sound unnecessary." He scratched his chin. "What was your job?"

"If a supernatural being, or community, were causing a problem and threatening to expose our world, I had to find them and remind them what the Codex and other rules say."

"That was your whole job? Waiting around for people to act up? Nothing else?"

Adeline brushed her ponytail off her shoulder before answering. "At first, I was handling a wider scope of assignments. After a few years, it turned into only dealing with folks skirting the line and bending the rules." She hoped she wasn't coming across as defensive.

"That's not how things work around here. I don't run my office that way," he said, leaning forward to rest his forearms on his desk. "We can't wait around for issues to arise and then act. Don't get me wrong, we still enforce the laws in the Arcane Codex, but I'm of the opinion that the spirit of the law matters more than the literal words."

"Good. Things in Seattle were ... I found I had different priorities than others." The Alliance's top priority had been secrecy. They didn't care who died or was hurt, as long as the supernatural world remained secret. "Though I grew up not far from here, I didn't learn about any of this stuff until after I left home. My family tended to keep to ourselves." It wasn't until after college that she learned the Arcane Codex existed, let alone Guardians or the like. "So, when you say 'out here' what does that mean? How big of an area are you responsible for?"

"There isn't a set-in-stone border or anything. Generally, we're responsible for everything between Roanoke, Virginia and Lexington, Kentucky, east-to-west, and from the Ohio-Kentucky border down to Knoxville, north-to-south. Bigger than Seattle, I imagine. People are spread out pretty far, though, and each faction has its own unofficial territory. We don't know how many supernatural individuals, since we've never done a count."

Bigger than Seattle was an understatement. Geography wasn't Adeline's strong suit, but by her mental math, the area was five times the size of Seattle.

By her logic, that meant five times as many supernatural beings in the area. This office only had at most seven people, including her, to keep track of a few thousand.

While she was pondering that, she almost missed Steve's next question.

"Did you leave Washington because of a conflict between you and the Alliance? Your differing priorities?"

"Partially, but I was also ready to move on." She would elaborate if asked, but wasn't going to volunteer extra information if she didn't have to. "Is there anything else you want to know?"

"Not really, truth be told. Salary's gonna be a step-down from what you were making out west. I'll be up front about that, but this area's also not as expensive." He went over a few more logistical things before stopping to look at his watch. "It's getting late, and you're probably still getting settled. The job's yours if you want it. If so, I'll see you tomorrow morning."

"Sounds good."

***

Adeline stopped to pick up Chinese food on her way home. When she walked into the house, she waited to see if a fluffy grey tail would come around the corner, but her cat didn't appear.

She changed into yoga pants and an old t-shirt as she debated calling Elijah. Her brother needed to know she was back, but as she hovered her finger over the icon to call him, she didn't tap it.

No, she should go see him in person. He deserved that much after she'd been away for this long. It was too late to drive out to Evarts. She'd stop by to see him in the next few days.

After finishing her fried rice, Adeline took a seat on the floor of her new living room and cut open the first cardboard box she could reach, which turned out to be full of grimoires. She closed the box and carried it into her bedroom. Having spell books in plain sight was a recipe for trouble.

The next few boxes consisted of random items, non-magical books, and clothing. She unpacked and put those away with little fanfare.

When she found another box of spell books and spell ingredients, she hid the contents as she unpacked. Some items were easy to explain, like herbs or dried flowers, but others would seem out of place, like animal bones, non-native plants, and certain stones.

"If all else fails, I'll just say I'm into healing crystals and spirituality," she told herself. "Unless that makes me too eccentric. I'd rather not be the town weirdo. Again."

As she worked and began to turn the bungalow into more of a home, she considered Steve's job offer. She had to take it, seeing as she didn't have another option at this point.

After an hour and a half of unpacking, she noticed Whiskey had come out of her hiding spot. The cat wandered around the living room exploring the open boxes before jumping onto the couch. She graced Adeline with a sleepy yawn and a few blinks of her yellow eyes before curling up and falling asleep.

Adeline was unpacking her last suitcase when her phone rang. The number was unfamiliar but it had a Seattle area code. It was eight at night on the West Coast, so she answered the call. "Yes?"

"Hello, Adeline," Tatiana said. "Bill Wong gave me your number after I needled him for a few days."

"Of course he did, and of course you did," she scoffed. Her last conversation with the clairvoyant replayed in her mind. One of the comments she'd made, Adeline had initially dismissed, but it seemed terribly sinister in hindsight. "You're a real bitch, you know that?"

"There's no need for name-calling."

"Yes, there is. You could've told me that rusalka was going to fall to her death. I could've stopped it. You could've – Is your name even Tatiana Petrova?"

"No, but Tatiana Peters doesn't have the same ring to it. You shouldn't be surprised to hear that a great deal of what I do is performance. When people go to a fortune teller or want their palm read, they expect to see an older woman with a foreign name or a vaguely eastern European accent. The accent is too cliche for my tastes, but there were several Petrovas in my family history. My great-grandmother was a Tatiana Petrova," Tatiana said, "As for the girl, her death was already in motion before you entered my shop. Nothing you could've done would've prevented what happened to her."

"I don't believe that. I refuse to."

"Of course you don't, because if I'm telling the truth I could also be correct about many other things I've told you over the years."

"I'm not in the mood to argue with you about fate, so tell me what you want."

"I understand you no longer work for the Alliance."

"Yeah." She gripped the phone tightly. "Lucy, that's the rusalka's name by the way, fell to her death. Dominic blamed me, and others believed him. So, congratulations; I've left Seattle and you got your wish. I'm back east, where I grew up. I hope you're happy."

"It wasn't my wish, and I'm indifferent to the workings of fate. Returning to your birthplace is vital to fulfilling your destiny, and just as you couldn't have prevented Ms. Radassi's death, your return was inevitable." Tatiana paused. "I expected you'd be happy to be home. Why aren't you?"

"I left for a reason. I stayed away for as long as I did for a reason. Don't pretend you care about any of that now. You haven't said why you called, or why you're so invested in what I do with my life, for that matter."

"Curiosity on both fronts. I knew you left Seattle, but I wasn't sure where you had gone. I wish you luck. You—"

"Don't say something cliche like I'm going to need it." Adeline rolled her eyes.

"I wasn't planning to say that. I don't know if you'll need luck or not. As I told you many times, witches throw off my readings. I cannot see your future."

"You can't see my future, but you know my destiny? That doesn't make sense."

"I've never claimed to be omniscient. I see your destination, but not the road you must travel to reach it."

"You're so full of shit, and I'm tired of hearing it. Goodbye."

She ended the call, hoping this would be the last time she heard from Tatiana or anyone with the Sight. Clairvoyants gave her a headache.

CHAPTER 4

— • —

W hen Adeline returned to the Guardian office the next morning, Rebecca and Jakob were already there, as was a Latino man she hadn't seen the day before. He appeared to be in his early forties, with a square face and warm, brown eyes. Jakob sat at his desk, while the other two stood in front of the empty desk next to him. As soon as she entered the building, all three sets of eyes shifted to her.

"Can I help you, ma'am?" the unknown man asked.

Adeline fought the urge to cringe. During her time in Washington, she'd grown used to people using "ma'am" exclusively to address much older women. She wasn't sure if she was under or overdressed in her business casual outfit of black slacks, a navy blouse and blazer, and ballet flats. Rebecca and the unidentified man wore suits, but Jakob wore a dark grey Oxford shirt and black jeans.

"She's our new coworker, Ned," Rebecca said before Adeline could answer. "I didn't get a chance to introduce myself yesterday. I'm Rebecca Cooper." She held out a hand for a handshake. "This is Jakob Mortensen and that's Ned Diaz."

"Adeline Coburn, nice to meet you."

"So, Adeline, where are you from?" Ned asked as he took a sip from his coffee mug. "And what brings you here?"

"I needed a change of pace from Seattle. I'm from Kentucky." She hoped her short answers wouldn't be interpreted as rudeness.

"What about you?"

"Born in Delaware. Moved here because the Chancellor was worried about flooding."

She tilted her head to the side and furrowed her brow. "What?"

"My family's had a certain ... talent for controlling rivers and preventing them from flooding going back several centuries. Back in 2003 or 2004, this area got an unusual amount of rain and there were concerns about nearby rivers flooding. My family volunteered me to come out here to try and mitigate any that might occur. By the time the Chancellor stopped worrying about floods, I'd already met my wife and wasn't planning to leave. So, here I am." He shrugged.

"Is there a name for that? Your talent? If it's not rude of me to ask." Vampires, werewolves and witches were normal to Adeline, and she knew vodyanoy who lived in rivers, but hadn't heard of anyone able to control the flow of water.

"My abuela said we'd been blessed by the river, but didn't give it a name. My dad thinks it was lost to time. One of my brothers just calls it river powers. Simple, but it fits."

"That it does." She turned to Rebecca. "What about you, Rebecca?"

"Human." Rebecca looked away and started to fidget with the tea bag in her mug. "I learned about this world after—"

"No, I-I meant where are you from?"

"Oh, I grew up in Nashville and went to the University of Kentucky."

The next few minutes consisted of awkward small talk among the trio. No one asked Adeline whether she was supernatural, possibly seeing the question as inappropriate or too personal. While Rebecca and Ned asked questions to get to know her and shared details about themselves, Jakob said nothing. He watched them talk, but made no attempt to join in. Instead, he sat at his desk, drinking his coffee and observing.

When his silence began to bother Adeline, she addressed him directly. "What about you? You gonna sit there like a bump on a log or what?"

Jakob opened his mouth to answer just as Steve strolled into the office, interrupting the conversation.

The older man cleared his throat. "Well, since the team's all here, we might as well get started. You've all met Adeline, I see, so there's no need for me to make introductions. She grew up in the area, but has been working out west in Washington as part of the Seattle — What did you call it again?"

"The Alliance of Supernatural Species."

"A. S. S?" Jakob said before letting out a snort of laughter. His voice was huskier than she'd expected and his accent was difficult to pinpoint. "Millions of words in the English language and that's the name they picked?"

"Seattle also had the South Lake Union Trolley, so it's not a one-off," Adeline replied, feeling vindicated by his reaction. She had laughed at the name the first time she heard it, to the annoyance of others in the Alliance. It had been a sign that Seattle wasn't the right place for her, but she'd been young then and didn't recognize the warning for what it was. "The person who named it didn't see an issue with the acronym. Anyway, my work for the Alliance sounds similar to what you all do here, from what Steve told me yesterday. I focused on making sure the secret supernatural world stays that way."

Steve gave her a nod and picked up the conversation. "Seattle's more rigid about things than we are, as I mentioned. No one around here cares too much about what their neighbors do until it affects them. It's a little easier for wolves, vampires, and the like to live without worrying about scrutiny, so we've got several communities out here. You probably saw more variety out west, but I'd wager we've got a different mix." He crossed his arms. "Our job's mostly mediating disputes between factions. Every now and then, something happens that's too strange or blatantly supernatural for ordinary humans to ignore. That's when we run interference to keep them from looking at things too closely. The rest of our work, and how it's done, you'll learn as you get settled."

"Great. Where am I starting?" She wasn't eager for the inevitable grunt work she'd get as the newest Guardian, but she could handle it.

"You're with Jakob. We don't have formal partnerships, but he'll show you the ropes for the time being." His gaze flicked over to Jakob. "Take Adeline with you on your visits. Show her how we handle the normal check-ins." He walked into his office, leaving the bullpen behind.

Jakob stood and grabbed his keys from his desk. He was only a few inches taller than Adeline's five feet, five inches. "All right, let's go. We've got multiple stops to make. I'll drive."

She drained her coffee cup and followed him out to his car, a large black SUV. Without a word, he waited for her to climb in, then turned the engine on and drove off.

***

The beginning of the drive was quiet. Adeline studied Jakob as he drove, but found she couldn't get a read on him. He maintained a neutral expression and relaxed posture, and he kept his eyes on the road.

As they crossed into Kentucky, she felt a surge of power, but the punch wasn't as strong as it had been the day before. She focused on the bright blue sky to steady herself. How had she lived so long in a city as overcast as Seattle?

She must have made a noise because Jakob looked over at her after a moment. She spoke before he could. "So, these visits Steve mentioned: what's the purpose of them?"

"Ninety to ninety-five percent of our job's staying in contact with the various supernatural coalitions. I drive out every other week to visit the larger one to make sure they're doing okay, getting along with each other, and not having issues with humans. Steve likes to get ahead of any problems rather than letting something fester and winding up with the Steward or Chancellor involving themselves."

"And you're the only one who does it? Visits each faction?"

"Steve's too busy. Ned will do it if he has to, and Rebecca did it a few times before I was here. Apparently something happened, but I don't know who the confrontation was with or what it was about. Only Ned or Steve did check-ins after that, until I arrived last year."

Adeline was intrigued, but tried to push the feeling down. Jakob claimed he didn't know what happened, and Rebecca might not want to talk about it. She wasn't entitled to hear the story either, for that matter. She cleared her throat and focused. "Okay, so we're doing outreach. Who are we meeting with?"

"Last night was the full moon, so the werewolves are our first stop. They live in southern Letcher County." She tried to hide her grimace. Letcher County was northeast of Harlan County. She'd be a little too close to her former home than she was ready for.

Jakob raised an eyebrow at her reaction. "You got a problem with wolves?"

"In general? No."

"A specific werewolf then. Let me guess. An ex-boyfriend?"

"My ex-partner was a wolf and a dick. He's a big reason why I left Washington," she said. "I don't want to get into that now. What do you think of this job, compared to your last one? And don't just say it's a lot different from being an Army Ranger. That's a given."

He started to slow the SUV and eyed her suspiciously.

"The coffee mug on your desk—the one you've got a bunch of pens in—says 'Army Ranger' on it and I can see the outline of your dog tags," she said with a shrug. "If your past's supposed to be a secret, you aren't hiding it well."

"I didn't realize you'd noticed that." He accelerated. "I don't hide my past, but I don't advertise it either. People find out I'm a veteran and all they want to talk about is my time in the military. And when they find out I was a Ranger, they start asking questions they really don't want to know the answers to."

"I don't care all that much about your service if I'm being honest, so you can relax. It doesn't matter what you were before. Everyone's got a past. I asked because I want to know what led you here. That's the thing I find the most interesting, especially when I meet someone like you."

"Someone like me?"

"Rebecca and Ned told me plenty about themselves; you didn't and that's intriguing. I love a good mystery. You're clearly a long way from wherever you're from."

"My story's not that exciting. I was in the Army; now I'm not." A haunted expression crossed his face as his hand gripped the wheel tightly, but it was gone a second later. "And I'm from Arkansas. There's not much else to say about me."

"Oh, I don't believe that."

Adeline was tempted to repeat her question about his impression of their job when Jakob turned onto a rural dirt road. She kept her eyes on the trees as they wound through the woods. After about twenty minutes of driving, he brought his vehicle to a stop in a clearing and got out of the car. Adeline followed after a beat. The air had the slight smell of tobacco and pine, yet the woods around them consisted of oak and cedar trees. To her right, something moved in the trees. Then, a man and a woman entered the glade.

The woman stopped about a yard away from the SUV. She was around forty and wore jeans with a faded red flannel shirt. Her dark hair was pulled into a messy bun. "Who's she?" She kept her eyes on Adeline.

"She works with me," Jakob said.

"Boss finally gave you a babysitter, huh?"

"Something like that. Adeline, this is Dylan Bartley, the leader of the local werewolf pack. Dylan, this is Adeline." He put his hands on his hips as he turned fully towards Dylan. "You know why we're here. Last night was a full moon."

"And yet, you're here this early," said the muscular man standing a foot behind Dylan. He squeezed his eyes shut and blinked a few times, trying to remain alert. When that failed, he rubbed his eyes. "Don't know why you can't even wait until the afternoon to come around."

"Randall, be quiet," Dylan said without turning to face the other werewolf. "You can ignore him. Nothing noteworthy happened. No run-ins with humans or lone wolves last night. We stuck to the woods the whole time. Everyone's accounted for."

"Great." Jakob pulled out a small notepad and began writing. "Anything of note I need to tell the others at the office? Like an issue with another faction?"

"No. I tell you during every visit that we keep to ourselves." She crossed her arms as she spoke. "We don't want trouble with anyone else."

"Well, if that changes, you know how to get in touch."

"If that changes, we'll handle it ourselves like we've always done." She turned towards Adeline and assessed her. Her eyes scanned Adeline's outfit, and Adeline had the fleeting thought that she wished she'd known she'd be spending her first day in the hills. "You're not from around here, are you? A transplant from somewhere like Baltimore, I'm guessing."

"I grew up just south of here, right over the county line, actually."

She tilted her head to the side as she took a step closer to Adeline. The scent of tobacco and pine grew stronger. "Interesting. I didn't know there were still folks like you in Harlan."

"Folks like me, huh?" Adeline asked. "I didn't know there were werewolves out here, and you didn't know there were people like me—whatever that means—there. So, I guess we're even."

"We don't tend to mingle much, so I suppose we are." Dylan waited a moment. "I didn't mean it as an insult. I want to make sure you know that."

"I didn't take it as one. I've been accused of worse than looking like I don't belong somewhere."

"Have you?" She broke eye contact with Adeline to look between her and Jakob. "Speaking of Harlan, we were near the county line last night, and something about it raised my hackles. That's not a metaphor, and I wasn't the only one. It slipped my mind earlier."

"And that's a new sensation? You haven't felt it other times you've been close?" Jakob asked.

"I don't remember the last time we got that close to the border, to be honest. None of us like being on the edge of our territory. It was like we were being drawn towards the county line last night, but the closer we got, the more apprehension we felt." She sighed. "Could be nothing."

"Probably is," Adeline said.

She regretted not visiting her brother last night; it hadn't been that late. Were the wolves sensing the same thing that had Elijah so worked up? She set aside that train of thought for the moment and turned to Jakob. "We've checked in with the werewolves. Now what?"

"We leave. We've got other stuff to do, and I'm sure the pack does too."

***

As Jakob drove them away from the werewolves' territory, he informed her that they only had two more stops to make.

"There are a few other factions you need to be introduced to, but I don't have the patience for all of them today so we'll deal with the last one sometime next week. It's too early to pay the vamps a visit, so they'll be our next stop. Meantime, we'll head to Harlan County, your old stomping grounds."

"Fantastic," she said flatly. She had hoped to wait a bit longer before her homecoming. "Why didn't we make any stops in Virginia? Isn't that part of our jurisdiction or whatever?"

"We're responsible for a good chunk of western Virginia, but the only supernatural beings in that area are a family of kitsunes in Lynchburg. We don't check in with them often because we don't need to. Most of their problems are among themselves, and no one wants to get dragged into someone else's family drama," he said. "The office might be in Virginia, but we wind up in Kentucky most of the time. For whatever reason, a lot of supernatural factions put down roots here."

"Of course they do," she muttered.

***

As Jakob's SUV crossed into Harlan County, magic crashed into Adeline like a freight train. If simply being nearby made her feel stronger earlier in the day, being back on Harlan soil made her feel nearly invincible, lighter. The sky seemed even bluer, the trees greener. It was as if she'd spent years looking at the world through a dull filter, and now the veil had been lifted.

A strange pain shot through her chest moments after the wonderfully invigorating sensation of being close to her birthplace. An unseen force pressed in on her, restricting her ribcage. Were the ancestors making known their displeasure at her absence? She struggled to breathe for a few moments. Jakob slammed on the brakes.

"What's wrong?"

"Nothing. I'm fine. Keep driving." She opened her eyes to see him staring at her. "I'm serious. Drive."

He put his foot on the gas and sped up. As Adeline recovered from the strange chest pain, she recognized the road. They were heading towards Evarts. For the first time in sixteen years, she would be back in her hometown.

She had assumed that not much in Evarts would have changed while she was gone; she was right. The hair salon had changed owners, or at least names, but it was still a hair salon. The Druther's on the edge of town was now a Dairy Queen. Some new stores had opened along Main Street. An abandoned house near the busy part of town, one that had been empty since Adeline was young, had fallen apart even more, with the roof rotted away in sections and a few more broken windows. It felt like she had been gone for both fifty years and only a few days.

They made their way through town, stopping at the Gas'N'Go for Jakob to top off the car. The sign at the pump said to pay inside, so he parked and walked into the gas station. Adeline followed, as she'd barely eaten anything all day and didn't know when they'd be heading back to the office. Snacks were definitely in order. The bell jingled over her head as she walked into the store.

"You've got some nerve," a male voice called out. She spotted a teenage boy sitting behind the register, but he seemed just as startled by the voice as she was. The voice spoke again to her left and slightly behind a shelving unit. "You've always had, and it's one of the things I've always liked about you, Miss Adeline."

Only one person ever called her that, especially with that inflection.

"Wyatt? Wyatt Dunn?" She turned towards the voice. He walked out from behind the chip display holding a six-pack of beer. "It's been a while."

"That it has. 1998 was a long time ago. You've spent almost half your life away from home. You missed your daddy's funeral."

"Elijah told me not to come. He said he had it handled and didn't want me to spend the money to fly out here for the service. We were never close, John and me." She studied him. He was starting to develop wrinkles around his dark eyes. His hair—that same ebony color—had begun to recede. He was no longer the eighteen-year-old troublemaker she remembered. "You look good."

"I look like shit. It's kind of you to pretend otherwise." He let out a laugh. "You're a different story. Quite the sight for sore eyes. Are you visiting Elijah?"

"No. I moved back. I figured it was time."

"I imagine he's delighted about that. I ought to get going, but it was nice to see you." He walked over to the clerk to pay while she retreated down one of the aisles.

She spent a few minutes browsing the snack options while eyeing the door, hoping to see him leave. Once she was sure that he had left, she grabbed a few random snack foods off the closest display and walked over to the register. The teenager behind the counter started to ring her up, eyeing her warily.

"Why do you keep staring at me?"

"Is it true what they say about you?" the boy asked. He had brown hair and a few spots of acne. He was trying, and failing, to hide the book he was reading underneath the counter. "You're Adeline Coburn, Elijah's sister, right?"

"That I am. As for the rest, it depends." She looked over her shoulder to see Jakob wandering around the store. He was a few aisles away, standing in front of a refrigerator. Too far to overhear the conversation or ask questions she might not want to answer. "What do they say about me?"

The teenager shifted his weight and refused to look at her. "That you killed your father, and that's why you left town all those years ago."

"No, he died five years after I was gone." She handed him a twenty-dollar bill. "But in a town this size, folks hear a rumor and run with it."

"Why would you ever come back here? You finally got away. Why not just stay gone?"

"Let me guess." She took a long look at him and saw something familiar in his gaze. "You're working here, hoping to earn enough money so you can leave and never come back?"

The boy nodded his head, and she gave him a sympathetic smile. "I had the same idea. It's normal to want to see the world rather than be stuck in the same place your whole life. Life's got a way of working out different than how you want, though. I came back because I'm needed here. When word gets around that I'm here and people start wondering why I'm back, do me a favor and tell them that's what I said, if they ask you."

"Is that why you came back?" He handed her the change she was owed.

"Maybe," she said with a smile. She put the change he'd just handed her into his tip jar. "For your escape fund."

She exited the gas station and climbed back into Jakob's car. A minute or two later, he walked out of the store and tossed a few things onto the driver's seat before he started to pump the gas he'd bought. As Adeline was settling down to wait with her snacks, another vehicle pulled into the lot. The driver got out to pay for his own gas, spotted her through the windshield, and did a double-take. He obviously debated coming over to say something, but Jakob got back in the car and started the engine. They were driving away before the other driver made up his mind and before Adeline could figure out who he was, but some hairs on the back of her neck stood up.

"You didn't say this was your hometown," Jakob muttered.

"I don't walk around introducing myself as Adeline Coburn from Evarts, Harlan County, Kentucky."

"That's fair. I heard that kid at the register mention your brother. Does he know you're back?"

"Not yet. I didn't tell him I was coming and I haven't had a chance to go see him." She watched the scenery from the window. "Are we just passing through Evarts?"

"More or less. Our next stop's up in the hills. The people we need to see refuse to live any closer to town." The drive continued in silence as they wound their way up into the mountains. The road was paved, but hadn't been maintained the further up they drove. He parked at a clearing a few miles past the edge of town and got out of the vehicle. "We're walking the rest of the way. Come on, let's go."

Adeline got out and stared at the peak. The route Jakob had taken was new to her, but the destination was familiar. In hindsight, Broden Mountain was the only place they could've headed to. Harlan County wasn't a hotbed of supernatural activity, aside from the witches who had called the mountain home for centuries. They had come to visit her mother's family.

Wyatt Dunn wasn't the only person Adeline would be reuniting with today.

CHAPTER 5

— • —

J akob and Adeline walked through the woods for about ten minutes before he came to an abrupt stop. They were surrounded by cedar and black walnut trees in every direction. A gust of crisp October air blew by, rustling the leaves.

Adeline took a deep breath and slowly released it. The smell of fallen foliage and soil filled her nose as warmth crept through her chest and the tension in her shoulders released. Like an animal settling down to sleep, the power that churned underneath her skin became calmer. It was a pleasant feeling, unlike the stabbing pain from earlier.

Her eyes began to water as relief washed over her. The ancestors were happily welcoming her home. For years, she'd been nervous about the reception she'd receive from them when she returned to Evarts. She'd left so suddenly and had stayed away for so long that she feared they'd punish her for leaving at all.

Jakob, meanwhile, focused his attention on two trees to his left. "Do we have to do this every time? I know you're there, and you know that I know that."

Two men stepped out from behind the trees. Adeline first looked at the man closest to her, and then glanced at the one who was a few feet further away. Both men appeared to be within five years of her age, wearing dirty jeans and faded tan jackets. Their hair was dark, and she couldn't see their eyes from her position. The far man had a hunting rifle sling over his shoulder.

In front of her, she watched Jakob's arm move, and saw one of his hands resting at his side under his jacket. She wasn't sure if he was reaching for a gun or knife, or simply adjusting his posture.

A weapon wouldn't help him, but she appreciated his attempt to be subtle.

"You usually come alone. Who's she?" the man closest to them demanded.

"She works with me. I'm showing her the ropes." Jakob answered as he turned towards Adeline, but he didn't take his attention off the two men. "This is David and that's—"

"Stay right here. Don't move," David ordered. He nodded to his companion and they moved a short distance away, far enough to be out of earshot but close enough to watch Jakob and Adeline as they talked.

Adeline watched them whisper to one another. As they argued, she tried to dig up some long-forgotten memory that would help her identify the two men. Her memory was fuzzy, worn down by time and distance, so she couldn't quite place either of their faces. If they lived on the mountain, she'd met them before. She didn't know the second man's name, so she had to rack her brain trying to recall who she knew, or knew of, named David. Maybe he'd gone by a nickname the last time she was here?

Then, the unnamed man made a face in response to something David said, and everything clicked for her. She recognized not only David, but his younger brother Caleb, too.

"The witches are a little paranoid," Jakob whispered, looking in the same direction she was. "They don't take kindly to strangers."

"Oh, they don't?" She raised one eyebrow. She hadn't mentioned being a witch that morning when they'd been talking in the office or on their way here. She needed to tell Jakob the truth, and that she was related to the two men arguing nearby. "Listen, you should know—"

David and Caleb finished their discussion and walked back over to where the Guardians stood. David waited a beat before clearing his throat. "We'll take you both up the rest of the way. But only because we knew you were coming today, and you're expected up there." He glanced at his brother, who pulled a bundle of fabric out of one of his pockets. "Since you brought a stranger and this is our mountain—"

As Adeline's heartrate picked up, the sky grew dark above them, and her skin began to tingle. "Caleb Atkins, you're out of your mind if you think you're gonna blindfold me," she said, addressing the man who was moving closer to her with the fabric. She nearly cringed at the twang in her voice, frustrated that her accent was so pronounced after years of trying to hide it. A rumble of thunder followed her declaration.

All three men froze and David fell silent. Caleb stopped in his tracks a foot from her. "How'd you know my name?"

"You don't recognize me at all, do you?" She rubbed her forehead and sighed. The sky began to clear. "I didn't think I'd been gone that long. I know your name for the same reason I know David used to go by Natey, because he liked his middle name better. You and I—"

"Adeline, what are you doing?" Jakob cut her off, eyes moving between her and the brothers.

"You're not Addy. Elijah made her leave and convinced her not to come back." Caleb shook his head. "She didn't even say goodbye. I don't know how you know her name, or mine, but she wouldn't have—"

"And yet here I am." She held her arms out. "If you don't believe me, let's go see your grandmama. Agnes'll recognize me and confirm I'm who I claim to be."

"Granny Agnes died four years ago," David said.

The news was a punch to the gut and her excitement at being here diminished slightly. "I'm sorry. I didn't know." Sorry felt too insignificant but she lacked better words.

"Of course you didn't, because you weren't here." He stood there for a moment, looking at the ground and working through something in his mind. He stepped to the side, out of her path. "If you're who you say you are, then you already know the way."

She walked past him to head up the mountain, not looking back. After a few seconds, she heard footsteps behind her as Jakob, David, and Caleb followed, their feet crunching on the fallen leaves. She allowed her intuition to guide her as she hiked. After about ten minutes, she reached another clearing.

Four buildings spread out before them—two cabins, a shed and a barn. Adeline knew she'd find other cabins if she went past the barn and up the footpath behind it.

"Believe me now?"

"Not quite," David nodded over at Jakob. "He's been here before. He could've told you the way. Stay here."

Two men walked out of one of the cabins. They didn't move closer, but Adeline could feel their eyes on her. She could also sense Jakob watching her, though when she turned towards him, he was facing away from her, eyeing the people who stopped their work to watch them. "What?" she asked, crossing her arms over her chest.

"How do you know them?"

"We're related. Second cousins, I think. Their granny, Agnes, was my grandmother's sister. I didn't recognize them at first. I haven't been up here in ages."

"That would've been nice to know before now. As would the fact that you're a witch."

"You didn't ask." She couldn't see much of his face, so she wasn't sure what to make of his sigh. "Witches are paranoid for a reason. We don't have a great track record when it comes to trusting strangers with too much information about ourselves. It's gotten too many of us killed."

"Nobody burns witches at the stake anymore."

"None of the women killed back then were witches. The witch trials ended, yet we're still dying. My aunt's murder from 1994 is unsolved. My cousin Noah still doesn't know who killed his mama, and she died because someone thought she killed a man down in Evarts with magic." She clenched a fist, angry that she felt the need to explain herself. "Look at me for a second." She waited for him to meet her eye. "It wasn't personal, me not telling you I'm a witch. I met you today, and it's not like you've opened up to me about anything other than being from Arkansas."

"Okay, that's fair," he said. "Can you—?"

"I've had enough of people asking me to do parlor tricks and not respecting my Gift." She refused to continue allowing the treatment she'd tolerated in Seattle. "So, if you're about to demand I prove it, you should reconsider doing that."

"Your little trick with the thunder earlier proved you're a witch. I have a question, if that's okay."

She eyed him skeptically. "You can ask. Depending on the question, I might answer."

David returned with a woman in her late fifties, cutting off their conversation. The woman had grey hair and wore jeans and a blue sweater that had been mended a few times. She walked up to Adeline and didn't speak for a few moments as she studied her. "I see Lilah in you. You have your mama's eyes." She turned to David. "This is definitely Adeline."

"Hi, Aunt Mary." Adeline did an awkward wave.

Mary's eyes scanned the area, taking stock of the onlookers. "Y'all can go back to what you were doing. Adeline didn't walk all the way up this mountain to be gawked at."

The observers started to disperse, and soon only David, Caleb and Jakob remained. Mary's attention was back on Adeline, who relaxed slightly now that she wasn't being scrutinized by so many people.

"You've been gone a long time. Let me take a good look at you." Mary moved closer as Adeline fought the urge to squirm under her gaze. The woman's sight went beyond the outward appearance and Adeline found the idea frightening now. "I'm surprised you're still standing. You look just about starved, deep within your soul. How'd you survive for so long, so far from home?"

"I forced myself to get used to the feeling." Adeline shuddered as she recalled the emptiness. The aching. The hunger deep within her soul that food couldn't satisfy. "After a while, I became accustomed to the absence everyone used to tell me about when they would try and scare me away from leaving. And I had this." She pulled a small vial out of her pocket that she'd held onto for years. Inside, there was some loose dirt. "I kept a piece of home with me."

"You shouldn't have had to, just like you shouldn't have left at all. Starving like you were, it ain't natural." Mary said, taking the vial from her. "Not that it matters, since you finally quit being stubborn and came home. My mama said you'd come back one day."

"She said that?"

"Yes. She claimed that your destiny lies here, and you could only run from it for so long."

"I've heard something like that somewhere before." Tatiana's words rang through her head, and Adeline turned and admired the view from the mountain. She had forgotten how stunning it was and how quiet the woods were. She was a world away from the busy, loud city she'd left behind. "I don't suppose she told you what that destiny is?"

"No. A person isn't meant to know too much about their own future, else they could cause a self-fulfilling prophecy. After you left home, all she'd say was she knew from the mountain and the trees that your destiny was here. If she knew something beyond that, she never told me a word." She looked at Jakob as if just noticing his presence. "Thanks for bringing her home—"

"He didn't." Adeline shifted her weight slightly. "I work with him."

"You're working for the Chancellor?" Her aunt's tone was mostly anger, with some confusion thrown in. "Why?"

"When I was living on the West Coast, working for the Chancellor of the Pacific seemed like my only option."

"It's not your only option now. You have family and a coven up here. You're free to choose your path. You have a place here, and you always will."

"I don't belong up here in the hills any more than I belonged in Seattle or down in Evarts."

"That's not true." Mary raised a finger for emphasis. "Now, I don't know what your father—"

Adeline clenched her jaw. "I don't want to talk about my parents or the past. Jakob and I came here because—" She glanced at the man in question. "Why are we up here?"

"I intended to introduce you to the witches in case you ever need to come up here to meet with them, but it seems there's no need," Jakob replied, looking out over the hills.

"Don't act so upset. It's not as if she's the only one with secrets," Mary said. "I'm sure you have quite a few of your own."

He tensed and straightened his spine, but said nothing. Mary turned back to Adeline. "I imagine you'll want to start heading back. Come back as soon as you can. I'd like to hear about where you've been."

"Thanks. I'll come back when I've got time." Adeline often wondered what having a real coven might feel like. It wasn't meant to be, but it was a nice dream to have.

"I hope you return soon." Mary's gaze flicked over to where Jakob stood and then back to Adeline. "I meant to tell you some things years ago, things that your mother should've told you, but it's best we talk without an outsider here. There's a lot about your Gift that you still don't know since you left the way you did."

Adeline had started to turn away, but paused as her curiosity got the best of her. "Does it have something to do with why my brother's been calling me almost daily for over a week? Or why he told me that I needed to come back home?"

"I wasn't aware that he'd called you. I haven't heard from him in a while, truth be told. What did he say his reason was?"

"I haven't talked to him about it yet." She shrugged. "But I figured if something was going on, something serious, you'd also know."

"I don't, so I imagine it's personal in nature."

"What about the pain I felt when I crossed over the county line?"

"Pain? What pain?"

"I couldn't breathe for a moment. It wasn't overwhelming, but it wasn't pleasant either. The feeling passed, but it was hard to ignore. At first, I thought it was the ancestors—"

"They wouldn't punish you for coming home. I've felt it too, the pain you describe. That's — It started about two weeks back. I don't know what it is yet, but I intend to find out." Mary turned to her son. "Caleb, take your cousin and her friend back down to their car."

"Yes, ma'am."

He started to walk, and Adeline followed. They had gone a few feet when she realized Jakob wasn't following. He hadn't moved from his spot and seemed to be staring at something in the distance, but she couldn't tell what it was he was looking at. "Jakob!"

It seemed like it took the man some effort to turn his attention back to her, but eventually his blue eyes met hers. "What? Are you done?"

"Yeah. Something wrong?"

"Nope."

"You didn't ask any questions."

With the werewolves, he'd asked how they were doing, or if they were having any problems, but he hadn't even tried to ask Mary anything.

"The witches are ... handled differently. Let's go."

She narrowed her eyes at him as he walked past her to follow Caleb.

"You should come back tomorrow night," Caleb said when they reached the clearing where the truck was parked. Jakob continued over to the vehicle.

"What's tomorrow night?" Adeline asked.

"Edith's birthday is in a few days, so we're having a party. Lots of people will want to see you. And if we're celebrating Edith, Mama won't try to pull you away to talk about things you're not ready to discuss yet."

"I'll think about it. I'm still getting settled and all."

"I hope you stop by," he said as she started to turn away. "I missed you."

She stopped and gave him a small smile before continuing on her way.

***

Adeline was still curious about Jakob's odd behavior by the time they were driving out of Evarts. "What was that up there? While we were leaving?"

"Nothing. I spaced out." He didn't look over at her. "I could ask you the same thing."

"Ask, then."

"What did she mean? About you starving or whatever?"

She took a deep breath. "Every member of my mother's family going back over two hundred years has lived, died, and been buried in the hills of Harlan County. Living or dead, most of them are on that mountain, especially the witches. Hell, you know that cabin to the left of where we were standing? Elijah and I were born in that house."

"And?"

"And that history has given my family a special connection to Harlan County and the souls of our ancestors. At least, ever since my many-times great-grandmother, Adeline Broden, and her coven settled down here, giving Broden Mountain its name. Witchcraft is mostly about channeling energy, and for my Gift that energy comes from the ancestors."

She braced herself for his response. Trying to explain her Gift to other people usually ended in her frustration. Some people didn't believe her when she told them. Some said it made her sound like a hippy. Others tried to convince her that she didn't understand her own Gift.

"That's a lot of words to say that you practice ancestral magic, and draw power from where they're buried. Shit, no wonder you nearly started hyperventilating when we crossed the county line. Explains a few things about my past interactions with your family too." He studied her. "Never thought I'd meet an ancestral witch."

She raised an eyebrow. "I know ancestral witches aren't the most common kind of witches, but I'm not that special."

"'Uncommon' isn't the word I'd use, but that's beside the point. After so long away, you must've been running on fumes before you got here."

"Yeah, something like that. Reconnecting with the source of my magic was an overwhelming feeling, and I wasn't expecting it."

"Someone should've warned you, like your brother. What was with the vial of dirt?"

"Elijah doesn't have the Gift. He wouldn't have known. And I didn't believe my mama when she warned me about it when I was younger. As for the dirt, it was a piece of home, like I said. Some genuine Evarts soil I stole from my backyard before leaving for college." She peeked over at him. "Was my Aunt Mary right? About you having secrets?"

"You said it yourself: everyone's got a past. And everyone's got secrets."

"Well, you know some of mine, yet I know none of yours. How did you wind up as a Guardian? Did someone else volunteer you for this?"

Sometimes factions volunteered individual members to become Guardians if the enclave leaders believed having a member working for the Chancellor would give them more power and influence with the Steward or Chancellor. She'd worked with one or two people who'd been in that spot, and they'd rarely been happy about the situation. She wondered if Jakob's story was similar. It would explain why he seemed reluctant to share anything about himself.

"Ask me in a week, and I'll tell you." He was quiet for a moment. "I'm not here because of anyone else."

He turned on the radio to fill the silence. Adeline reached over and turned it off after a few minutes. "You said you had a question. What was it? And remember, I won't answer if I don't feel like it."

"Could you kill someone with ancestral magic?" He asked before backtracking. "Never mind, don't answer that."

"Could I cast a spell and make you drop dead? No. When it comes to magic, nothing is free. Every spell has a cost, and the bill always comes due." She stared unfocused at the road ahead of her for a few seconds. "There's nothing I could give, no price I could pay, that equals the value of someone's life, not even another life. I don't know—and I don't want to find out—what would happen if I tried. Not to mention what my ancestors would do to me for trying." She paused as she considered how to explain the next bit. "But, if I used witchcraft to do something else, something not inherently fatal, such as light you on fire, that's a different story. You could survive that, or you could die from smoke inhalation, or infection, or something. Killing directly and raising the dead are the two hard limits."

"Everything else is fair game then?"

"Maybe not everything, but the other rules are more flexible." She glanced over at him. "Why was *that* your question? Are you trying to determine if I'm a threat?"

He let out a sigh. "No. The soldier in me was concerned about you being able to handle a threat."

"Well, everyone who's tried to kill me failed, so I think I can hold my own."

"Who tried to kill you?"

"I'm done sharing for the day." She smirked. "Ask me again in a week, and maybe I'll tell you."

"Guess I had that coming." He turned the radio back on.

***

The cracked and loose gravel country roads of Evarts gave way to smooth paved asphalt as Adeline and Jakob drove towards the suburbs of Somerset. As they passed the sign informing them they were leaving Harlan County, the now-familiar absence settled into her stomach. It wasn't the hollowed-out emptiness she'd forced herself to endure while she'd been in Seattle, but the sensation indicated that something had been taken from her.

Once they were in Somerset, Jakob turned up a long driveway, which led to a large mansion without any others nearby. The building was two, if not three, times the size of her childhood home. It was more secluded than other vampire nests she'd visited, a sign the enclave was either bigger than most or valued their privacy more.

The sun had finally set by the time Jakob came to a stop at the top of the driveway. A cluster of five men and four women of various physical ages and ethnicities waited outside the house. Nine vampires weren't a large nest, assuming the entire nest was waiting to greet them.

"Great. A welcoming committee," Jakob grumbled as he opened the door.

"Your SUV is rather loud. We heard you a mile away, and you woke up the whole nest." The vampire at the front of the crowd said. He had dark hair and eyes and wore an expensive suit. Physically, he resembled a man around thirty years old, but there was an ageless quality to him common in older vampires, which made Adeline assume he was the master of the nest. "And I see you have brought a friend."

"No, Alexei. He's brought us breakfast." A different vampire licked his lips as he looked Adeline up and down. He appeared to be around twenty and lacked the ageless feature that others possessed. Instead, he looked like a college student who'd woken up from an all-night bender, wearing only baggy sweatpants and no shirt. "How thoughtful."

In terms of appearance, the remaining vampires ran the gamut between Alexei and the vampire who'd spoken. Some wore workout gear, while others were dressed for a night out or a shift in an office.

"Try it. You won't like what happens," Adeline said.

"Oh, I like a challenge. There are—"

She swiped a loose branch from the driveway. Closing her eyes, she pictured the branch alight, and a few seconds later, the smell of a campfire filled the air. She opened her eyes to see it burning. "Like I said, try it."

"You aren't gonna kill her. And while she could, she's not gonna kill you. Not tonight, anyway. The next per — Never mind, it doesn't matter," Jakob said in a bored tone. There was something unsettled about his words and the way he cut himself off mid-sentence. "Adeline, this is Alexei. He's the leader of the vampires around here."

"A pleasure, my dear," Alexei said. She doused the fire and reached out for a handshake, but he kissed the back of her hand instead. His hand and mouth were both cold, causing her to flinch slightly at the sensation. "I must apologize for Tyler. He was only turned five years ago, and vampires are quite immature and reckless for their first few decades."

"I'm aware. I've heard some call it a second puberty."

A few of the vampires in the crowd laughed at the comment.

"I'm not the one with a body count. The soldier, sorry ex-soldier, has me beaten on that front." Tyler shot Jakob a glare. "Let me ask you something, Adriana—"

"It's Adeline."

"Whatever. Who's more deadly? A young vampire or a trained sniper?"

"The vampire," Alexei said, when Adeline's only answer was a blank look. "While I cannot claim to have met many snipers recently, I have known some in the past. They are capable of discipline and control, something you know little about. And if you cannot stop antagonizing our guests, you should return to the house." He then addressed the two Guardians. "What are you two here to discuss?"

Adeline watched the other vampires as Jakob asked Alexei the same list of questions he'd asked Dylan. The master vampire was incredibly verbose when answering, offering up more details than strictly necessary when discussing recent events. The crowd behind him grew bored, and the majority walked back into the mansion midway through Jakob's list of questions. Adeline tuned back into the discussion when Jakob cut Alexei off halfway through a long story about something that happened in 1978.

"Okay, so things are fine. You don't have any disputes with other coalitions currently, and you're not having any issues with humans." He continued to jot down notes as he spoke. "I'll tell the others at the office. That's all we needed to know." He put his notepad into his pocket and turned to leave.

"Adeline," Alexei said, stopping both Guardians in their tracks, "you would not happen to be the same Adeline who worked for Gabriel Reynolds in Seattle, would you? The one who killed that vampire in March?"

"And if I am?" She took a deep breath and changed her stance, getting into a more defensive position. She didn't try to use her magic yet, but she kept it simmering beneath the surface of her skin, ready to be harnessed at a moment's notice.

"I will not defend the actions of that vampire—Robert, I believe his name was. What he did was despicable. I warned my esteemed sister that she was taking a great risk by not giving more thought to whom she and her sirelings were turning into vampires, but she did not heed my advice. And she is too arrogant to admit that the consequences for her nest would have been far more dire and far-reaching than merely Robert's death if he was allowed to continue. They are lucky you acted as quickly as you did in response to his behavior."

"Estelle is your sister?" Alexei's calm, authoritative demeanor couldn't be more different from Estelle's brash and demanding personality.

"In a sense, given that we share a sire. I hope you will not hold that against me, or allow your dislike of her to taint how you may see me."

"Make sure your fledglings don't do what Robert did, and I won't," she warned. "And if that fails, and the past repeats itself, don't react the way your sister did to shift the blame."

"In nearly four hundred and fifty years, I have never appealed to the Steward, any Steward, over such a small matter. I have no intention of breaking that streak."

"I see she didn't tell you the whole story." Adeline crossed her arms. "Not surprising."

"She did not tell me anything. I learned of it from another. If you would care to enlighten me?"

"She claimed she was going to go all the way to the Moranaa Dessis in order to make sure justice was served for my actions."

Alexei let out a short laugh. "She has always been melodramatic. I apologize that you had to endure her ire."

He shot Jakob a look, but it passed over his face quickly.

"Have a safe drive."

Adeline heard herself and Jakob bid him goodbye, but she was too busy trying to decipher the meaning of the look Alexei and Jakob had shared to register if anything else was said. They knew something about Estelle that she didn't, though it wasn't clear what that something could be.

"What did he do?" Jakob asked after about ten minutes of silent driving. "The vampire you killed?"

"He was feeding on kids. One girl had already turned up dead. She was a fourteen-year-old runaway named Josie. They found her body before she'd even been reported missing. I figured out Robert was the vampire responsible and went to find him to remind him that feeding on kids wasn't allowed. Dead bodies, especially dead kids, attract the wrong kind of attention. When I found him, he was feeding on another teenage runaway, meaning what happened to Josie hadn't been an accident. I stopped him, since he wasn't going to stop himself. Estelle claimed it was her infraction to handle."

"She would've done that already, if she was gonna do anything at all, before you tracked him down. Seems like she threw a fit to cover her ass."

"That's exactly why, but she was the most powerful vampire in the city, and I was a witch without a coven. Popular opinion sided with her, and she got sympathy from other groups—factions that had had issues with the Alliance's way of handling problems. She claimed Robert was a young and inexperienced vampire who'd made a mistake, even though he was old enough to know not to feed on children. Anyway, she painted him as the victim of an overzealous Guardian, not a dangerous predator that needed to be stopped."

"You should've called her bluff. Forced her to either drop the matter, or follow through on her threat to involve the Moranaa Dessis," he mused. "She would've dropped it. No one ever takes a dispute that far, especially over a situation where one side is clearly in the right. And if it did get that far, they would've sided with you in a heartbeat."

"It wasn't my call to make, and my bosses weren't willing to take a chance on it."

"They didn't have your back?" He raised an eyebrow.

"Nope. Not after she mentioned the Moranaa Dessis. The Alliance was determined to avoid their notice."

"How'd you kill him? Did you set him on fire?"

"No, I waited and confronted him at dusk, when his hunger put us on a more even playing field." She looked out of the window. "Were you a sniper? Or was Tyler full of crap back there?"

"I was, a lifetime ago. Or that's how it feels anyway."

"Because you're ashamed of it, or because you miss it?" She had no idea who the man next to her was, or how dangerous he was. She didn't feel threatened, but one of his earlier comments put her on edge. "Actually, no. What I want to know is this: was it difficult?"

"For some. I knew plenty of guys who got through sniper school with no problem, but off base, out in the real world, they froze the first time they got the order to kill an enemy combatant." There was a twinge of something in his voice, though she couldn't tell if it was regret or resignation. "It's different when the figure on the other end of the scope is another person. A living, breathing guy. They couldn't pull the trigger."

She opened her mouth to ask a follow-up question.

"I think we've both shared too much about ourselves today. More than enough for the first day we've known each other." He turned the radio on.

She wondered what his answer would've been, and couldn't determine what he was trying to hide. Was he trying to seem tough, so he didn't want to answer "yes" and admit that he'd struggled to pull the trigger that first time? Or would his answer have been "no," and he didn't want her to think he was a sociopath who enjoyed killing? She made a mental note to ask him about it later, after they knew each other better.

They drove in silence back to Virginia. He dropped her off at her car and headed into the office, giving her a terse goodbye.

CHAPTER 6

— • —

Adeline arrived at the office the next day to find Rebecca and Ned seated at their desks. Jakob and Steve weren't in sight. Since it was only her second day, and she'd spent her first day out of the office, she wasn't sure what to do. In Seattle, her job was exclusive to tracking down supernatural individuals who the Alliance wanted to speak with. Steve said this office worked differently, but yesterday didn't reveal much about what else the Guardians here did.

"So, other than paying folks a visit like yesterday, what do we do?" Adeline asked the pair after saying hello.

"It's pretty much visits and helping the community out when we're needed." Ned took a sip from his mug. "There's also writing up reports about what we do for whichever Steward needs it. They never read past the first page before handing it over to the Chancellor who doesn't even open it."

"The Chancellor doesn't, but someone in that office does," Rebecca added. "I've gotten calls about a few of my reports. This building's also neutral ground. The werewolves might use it as a meeting place to sit down with an out-of-town pack. The vampires use it sometimes for mediation, if Alexei's concerned about something. There's a rotation for which one of us acts as a witness for those kinds of meetings."

"Sounds thrilling," Adeline remarked with a pause. "That wasn't supposed to come out as snarky as it sounded. It means some days will be slower than others."

"Is Seattle that busy?"

"I was. My whole job was tracking down people who might've broken the Alliance's rules. I didn't get to do anything else because of all the bureaucracy. Hell, sometimes I didn't even know why they wanted someone brought in." Not knowing why someone needed to be found was annoying, but it wasn't nearly as frustrating as not knowing what happened to the person in question after they'd met with the Alliance.

"The Alliance's rules? Not the Arcane Codex? I thought the Codex laws were the only ones."

Steve walked into the office at that moment. "Morning, everyone. I'm not sure if any of you alre—" He looked around. "Where's Jakob?"

"He's late, which is strange. He's normally here before I am," Rebecca answered.

"Maybe he decided to follow through on his threat to quit," Ned said.

"You're the one who keeps threatening that, not him."

The room went quiet. Steve seemed unwilling to make whatever announcement he needed to make without Jakob present. Rebecca sat down at her desk and started reading over some papers. Ned pulled out his phone. Adeline decided to get herself a cup of coffee in order to have something to do.

"Where could he be?" Steve asked after they had been waiting for ten minutes.

"Where's who?" Jakob asked, walking into the building.

"You. You're not usually this late. Actually, you're never late."

He let out a sigh as he sat down at his desk. "A situation came up that I needed to deal with."

"And that situation was...?"

"I had to help one of my sisters with something."

"You have sisters? Plural?" Ned asked.

"Considering I've got more than one, yes. Don't get any ideas about meeting them. They would eat you alive."

"First, I'm happily married. Second, you're talking about metaphorically, right?" Ned paled when Jakob didn't reply. "Right?"

"Yes, I was being figurative." He grinned, which made him look years younger. "That's what you might call a hyperbole."

"Considering the work we do, you can't say shit like that and laugh at a man for thinking you might be completely serious."

"I don't know. Seems funny from where I'm sitting. None of my sisters is a werewolf or vampire." He waited a beat. "They're worse, way worse."

Ned opened his mouth to reply, but he was cut off.

"Since we're now all here, Ned, you're on visitor duty," Steve nodded towards the door. "Adeline, Rebecca, Jakob, come on. We need to talk in my office."

Intrigued, Adeline followed after him. Jakob closed the door to Steve's office behind him as they entered.

Steve waited for everyone to sit. "The Harlan County Sheriff called. They found a woman's body this morning not far from the outskirts of Evarts, and asked that I send some people over there to take a look at the scene."

"Why did the sheriff call you? And not the state police?" Adeline asked.

"Because her death could be supernatural."

"I still don't understand."

"Because he's been told we're cult specialists. Whenever there's a bloody or odd death, something that might be supernatural, the local LEOs call us. As far as they know, we're consultants who specialize in crimes with cult-like elements. It keeps them away from supernatural threats and allows us access to crime scenes with less scrutiny," Rebecca explained. "I take it that supernatural deaths in Seattle were handled differently."

"It's too hard to cover up blatantly supernatural deaths in a city of that size. We got what we could from sources inside the department and handled it ourselves."

She hadn't been involved in that part of the process, only in tracking down the culprit for someone else to handle. Supernatural deaths were pretty rare there to begin with.

"I want the three of you to go and take a look at the scene," Steve said. "Determine if the locals can handle it or if it's more our wheelhouse."

"Does it happen a lot? Suspicious, possibly supernatural deaths?" Adeline couldn't remember hearing about any strange deaths growing up. John was drinking buddies with a few deputies, so he would've heard about them and wouldn't have been able to keep something like that to himself.

"It's not uncommon. Appalachia's home to a lot of supernatural groups," Jakob said. "Normally, it's bullshit. It's been, what, nine months since the last time it was a real case?"

"Closer to ten," Rebecca corrected with a frown. "Do we know who the victim is? Did the sheriff give you a name?"

"Her name's Sandra Russett, according to the call I got," Steve replied. "Does that name mean anything to you, Adeline? If I'm not mistaken, you're from around there."

"Evarts only has about a thousand people living there. Even if I didn't know her, I probably know someone related to her." She leaned back and searched her memory. "I don't remember meeting anyone named Sandra Russett, but I think my brother Elijah knew a Jeff Russett, years ago."

"Knew him how?" Steve steepled his hands under his chin.

"From work, maybe? He mentioned the name once or twice. At least I think his name was Russett."

She realized that Jakob, Rebecca, and Steve were all studying her, each with different expressions. She didn't like being analyzed and assessed. It made her want to fidget, especially since she had no idea what they were looking for. Were they expecting her to have a certain reaction to the news? She may have known the victim, but it was equally possible that she didn't.

"You said you wanted us to head over there," she reminded Steve, hoping to divert attention from herself. "Who do you want to take the lead?"

Steve shifted in his seat and her colleagues finally looked in his direction. "Let me think. Let's have Rebecca do documentation, Jakob handle the locals and LEOs, and Adeline puzzle out the supernatural elements."

The three Guardians filed out to Steve's office, and Adeline stopped at her desk long enough to grab her bag before heading towards the exit. "I'll meet you both there."

She'd drive herself; she needed solitude to think.

First, Elijah was leaving her peculiar voicemails. Then, Adeline felt like she was having a heart attack when she crossed into Harlan County and Mary said something felt off in the last few weeks. Now, a woman was dead.

She had no confirmation, but the connection was clear to her. Something sinister was happening in the holler and it was getting worse.

***

As soon as her car crossed over into Harlan County, Adeline felt the achingly familiar rush of power crash into her. When the sensation passed, the chest pains from the day before hit her again noticeably worse this time. An intense pressure constricted her chest, and she had to remind herself to breathe. After the feeling passed, a tangle of emotions overtook her, though she couldn't discern if the feelings were her own.

Her hands became clammy, and she forced herself to keep her eyes on the road. A pit opened in her stomach.

Was Sandra's death the reason for her chest pains? Had the ancestors been trying to warn her yesterday? Or was the dread entirely in her own mind, the result of being forced to return to her home, a place she loved and loathed in equal measure, just in time for an untimely death?

More than dread, an immense sense of melancholy filled her. Her shoulders slumped and she had to blink a few times to prevent herself from crying.

Wishing to collect herself a bit, she turned off the road that led directly to the crime scene. It would send her on a slightly longer route than necessary but it wasn't a long detour, and her delay shouldn't raise any suspicions. Once she had calmed down, she continued to the scene.

She parked outside Sandra Russett's house a few yards from the spot where someone had put up police tape, and next to Rebecca's car. She and Jakob had beaten her to the scene, as she hoped. The small house was on a big lot with the neighbor's house barely visible over the hill.

Exiting her vehicle, she caught the tail end of the conversation her colleagues were having with the sheriff's deputy who was standing next to the crime scene tape, tasked with keeping onlookers away.

"—neighbor was heading to work and saw the door open. He went inside to check on her and found the body. I bet y'all see weird shit all the time, but I ain't ever seen a sight like that." His fair complexion grew paler at the memory. "The amount of blood — Well, you'll see."

"Has the coroner come yet?" Adeline asked as she joined them.

"No, not yet. The sheriff said to wait until you folks showed up and had a chance to look at the scene, because if it's a cult case, he wants the body sent to a different morgue." The deputy turned to look at her. "Adeline? What are you doing here?"

"My job."

"You investigate cults? I'll admit, that comes as a bit of a surprise. Elijah nev—"

"I'm not surprised he didn't mention it. I've never shared much about my job with him, especially the stranger aspects of it." She turned to Jakob and Rebecca. "You two go ahead. I'll be right there."

She watched them walk into the house before turning her attention to the deputy. He was taller than her, around five feet, ten-inches, if she had to guess. He had blond hair, a beard, and brown eyes. He looked familiar, but his face wasn't distinct enough for her to instantly recognize him from when they were younger. "Forgive me for asking, but who are you? I've been gone too long, and I'm struggling to match a name to your face."

"Well, that smarts a bit. It's Paul Lee." He shifted his weight from one foot to the other. "You know, from high school?"

"Yes, of course. Sorry, I recognize you now. I think the beard threw me off." She pointed to his chin. "You didn't have one the last time we saw each other."

"I was too young to properly grow one back then. Elijah didn't tell me that you'd moved back."

"I didn't move back to Evarts, but I'm pretty close." She couldn't figure out why Paul expected Elijah, someone he'd barely interacted with in school, to have mentioned she was back in the area. "Why would—?"

"*Adeline*," Rebecca called from inside the house.

"I should go. Call the coroner, please. And tell your family I send my best." She ducked under the caution tape and walked into the house. A spike of panic overtook her, but she pushed through the feeling and ignored the creeping sensation of goosebumps on her arms. Her colleagues were waiting a few feet inside the doorway.

"Did he think of something else be needed to tell us?" Rebecca asked once she was inside. She was all business, a trait Adeline appreciated in the moment.

"No, he wanted to catch up."

"You know him?" Jakob asked.

"It's a small town, and we went to high school together. His name's Paul. I didn't expect to run into him here, of all places." Word of her return and what her job entailed would start spreading before the day was over. She didn't want to imagine how the truth would get twisted through gossip. "Shall we go see why they called us here?"

She walked further into the house. The building's layout felt familiar, and the pit in her stomach deepened as she moved from room to room until she finally reached the kitchen where the body was. The house had the same layout as her childhood friend Jeanette's home. As the kitchen door swung behind her, she was transported back over two decades. She had countless fond memories in a kitchen nearly identical to this one. The resemblance between the room before her and the one she remembered unsettled her further.

"Sheriff wasn't exaggerating about the blood," Jakob said, looking around.

Blood pooled on the floor and splashed across two of the walls. It dripped from the ceiling. Sandra's body lay in the middle of the large pool of blood on the floor, face down. Her limbs splayed, like she'd fallen and had yet to push herself back to her feet. She didn't seem to have any wounds, defensive or otherwise, despite the carnage around her. A blackish powder of some kind mounded in a far corner of the room, on one of the few linoleum floor tiles that wasn't covered in blood.

Adeline knew that she should want to look away. A normal person would lose their breakfast at the sight. Yet, her time in Seattle, seeing the aftermath of brawls between warring werewolf packs, feuding vampires, and worse, had desensitized her to bloody crime scenes. She was grateful for that experience today, but still took a deep breath to steady her nerves.

"Would've been nice if Paul had warned us about the weird smell too," Adeline grimaced. The stench of something rotting wasn't overpowering, but it was too strong to ignore.

"I don't smell anything besides blood and a corpse." Jakob seemed unaffected by the gore.

"Go see a doctor, then. This whole scene smells ... Have you ever had bread start to mold? Or fruit that should've been thrown out? That sort of smell," she said. "It can't be from the body, and I couldn't smell it from the hall, but it's strong in here."

Rebecca took a few moments to collect herself before speaking. "I think we can rule out a vampire. Or a werewolf. The body's too intact."

"We can also rule out any wandering wraiths, ghouls, zombies, and vetalas," Jakob added.

"I have a degree in folklore, and I've never heard of some of the things you just said. How do you know about them, and why can we rule them out?" Adeline looked over at him.

"I read a lot." He continued looking around. "Why'd you get a degree in folklore if you were raised in the supernatural world?"

"I wasn't; I grew up around witches. When I left home I realized there was a lot more to this world than I thought, and I wanted to learn. One society's silly folk story is another's deeply significant and respected history."

"Wish I'd thought to do that, instead of trying to—"

"This isn't the time or the place for you two to be chatting about this," Rebecca interjected in a tight voice. "Why can we rule out the people you listed, Jakob?"

"Each of them feeds on humans. The intact condition of the body means it wasn't them." He walked across the room to look at the corpse from a different angle. "My money's on magic of some kind."

"We can't rule it out," Adeline said. She put her hands on her hips as she studied the room. "There's no way this blood is all hers. Does a person even have this much blood in their body?"

"It could be hers." Rebecca looked around. "I don't know about all of it, but some of it has to be."

"It's hers. All of it," Jakob said.

"How do you know that? It could be anyone's. It could be pig's blood." Adeline was getting tired of his unsupported pronouncements.

"How it got everywhere is another story and I can't say for sure." He started writing something down in the notebook he pulled out of his pocket.

"This is one of our cases then. I'll go call Steve." Rebecca moved to step outside but stopped in front of the open kitchen door. "Adeline, come look at this."

Turning, Adeline saw a sigil painted in black on the side of the door that would be visible from inside the kitchen when the door was closed.

Adeline racked her brain as she crossed to stand by Rebecca. "I don't know what that is. It doesn't look like any runes I'm familiar with."

The image was of three mountains, with one positioned in front of the other two. The front mountain had an arrow shot into what looked like a sideways eye, with blood dripping down from the wound. She pulled out her phone and snapped a photo.

"Can you think of any resources that we could dive into to identify it?"

"Off the top of my head? No, but let me think about it."

"Thanks," Rebecca said as she exited the room.

"You said you loved a good mystery. Still feel that way?" Jakob asked Adeline.

"Not this kind. Not in the slightest." She surveyed the room again. Everything about the scene was wrong It wasn't just the body or the blood or the moldy stench, but it felt unnatural on a more primal level. The goosebumps she'd gotten earlier were now too extreme to be ignored, and something deep within was screaming at her to run.

The coroner and an assistant walked in a few moments later. "Deputy Lee said you're the specialists the sheriff called in." He was a white man in his mid-fifties with greying hair. "What exactly are y'all experts in?"

"Unusual deaths, mostly. He thought we'd be able to provide some unique insight on the case, given the state of the victim" Jakob said. "The body needs to be taken to a morgue in Somerset for the autopsy."

"Our morgue's not good enough?"

"I'm just passing along what I was told by my boss." He raised a hand in surrender. "I didn't decide anything."

With a grunt, the coroner pushed past him to inspect the body. After taking in the blood on the floor, walls, and ceiling, he cleared his throat. "I think the body ought to go to Somerset. They've got some equipment we don't have yet, and more staff. It's better for the examination to be done there."

Jakob smiled for a moment before his face relaxed into a more neutral expression. Adeline was impressed by how deftly he had handled the situation and convinced the other man to concede.

"This some kinda weird cult shit or something?" the coroner's assistant asked. He was in his mid-twenties with a buzz cut and a slight five o'clock shadow.

"Possibly. You hear about any cults 'round here?" Adeline asked, exaggerating her accent slightly. He might let some information slip if he thought he was talking to a local and not an outsider.

"Just those freaks up in the mountains. You know, the hill people who live at the edge of town. I hear they kill anyone who goes on their land, offer them up as sacrifices to some pagan god."

Jakob's head snapped up at the comment. Adeline felt his eyes on her, waiting to see what she would do. She simply raised an eyebrow at the statement. Being accused of paganism was a new insult. She'd grown up hearing about witches being Satanists. She spent years hearing tall tales about her relatives up in the hills and their supposed backwards ways. She'd grown so accustomed to being talked about that way that she hadn't blinked the first time someone out west heard she was from Kentucky and asked her if she'd grown up with indoor plumbing.

"Kyle, stop running your mouth and help me lift the body," the coroner said.

When they turned Sandra's body over, Kyle almost threw up, and the coroner's face turned a little green. While Sandra's back was unmarked, something had torn a gaping hole in her chest, and some of her organs were falling out. The two worked quickly to collect Sandra into a body bag before zipping it, then wheeling it out on a stretcher. Adeline and Jakob were left alone in the bloody kitchen.

"That organ that was dangling out of her torso, did you see what it was?" Adeline asked. The sight was disturbing, and while she hadn't almost lost her breakfast, she understood Kyle's reaction.

"No, it was too bloody to tell for sure."

A team of CSIs arrived and yelled at Adeline and Jakob for wearing only gloves and booties and no other protective gear. They were ushered out of the room and told to stay out of the way to avoid further contaminating the crime scene. Since she now had an excuse, Adeline left the house altogether after a glance at the photographs and art. A framed picture of a family of three hung near the door.

As soon as she was outside in the open air, she felt like she could breathe freely again. The house hadn't felt stuffy when she walked in, yet breathing had been difficult due to the rancid smell in the kitchen.

"Are you okay?" Jakob asked from behind her.

"I'm fine. Just needed some air. The last case like this you had, the one ten months ago, tell me about it. It might give us a head-start."

"It won't. It was a werewolf issue. Some guy was adopted as a baby and didn't know he was a wolf; he killed two campers out in a national park. He wasn't hard for us to find. Dylan's been helping him get adjusted." Jakob scratched the back of his head. "The scene in there? We haven't seen anything like that since I've been here."

"I was scared that would be your answer."

Rebecca walked over to join the pair. "I filled Steve in. He wants us back at the office to tell him about the scene. He's got questions and doesn't want the CSIs or coroner to possibly overhear."

Adeline nodded and walked back over to her car. She was so focused on her own thoughts that she didn't notice Jakob following her. He didn't say anything as he slid into the passenger seat. The crunch of tire on gravel told her Rebecca had just driven off alone, so she had no choice but to let him ride with her.

As she got further from Sandra's house, the intense feelings she experienced before returned. Her heart was pounding. She was struggling to focus on the road in front of her. She realized she was clenching her jaw. At the same time, she felt hollow, as if a vast emptiness had awakened inside of her. Despair and anger threatened to consume her.

She cleared her throat and tried to let the sensation wash over her. The hills were angry, but giving in to that anger wouldn't help her find Sandra's killer. She needed to focus on what mattered. She had never seen such a gruesome scene nor had she felt the utter despair that she was experiencing right now, not even when her mother or Aunt Eve had died.

Sandra's death seemed supernatural, though she hoped it wasn't, as unlikely as that hope might be. Her intuition told her this murder was only the beginning, and she dreaded what that meant. She wanted her instincts to be wrong for once.

Jakob said nothing as she drove, which she was thankful for. She doubted she'd be able to keep up a conversation if she tried.

***

As soon as Rebecca, Jakob, and Adeline returned to Virginia, Steve called them into his office for a debrief. Rebecca had told him the basic facts over the phone, but she hadn't given him as much detail as he wanted. Jakob and Rebecca conveyed how bloody the scene was and how odd certain things were, such as the victim not having any defensive wounds. Steve's expression grew more troubled as he listened.

"Adeline, you seem distracted over there. Maybe that's not the right word, but something is off. Anything you want to add?" Steve asked, drawing attention to the fact that Adeline hadn't said a word.

"No, Rebecca and Jakob covered everything pretty well," she said.

"What did you think of the scene? I'm getting the sense that you noticed something they didn't."

"My magic's tied to the land in Harlan, and someone just died there. I sense a lot of things no one else would. Something's been not quite right since I've come back, and I'm not the only one who noticed it either. When I crossed over the state line, I was overcome with this feeling of dread. Dread and sadness. Harlan is ... grieving Sandra Russett."

"I didn't know it did that, or that you could feel it," Jakob commented.

She was afraid to admit that she hadn't either and didn't know what that meant for the future. "I saw a picture on the wall as I was leaving—a family photo of Sandra and her parents. I've met Jeff Russett, years ago, because he knew Elijah. Sandra was the last of her family, as far as I can tell. Just like that, generations of family history are gone." She snapped her fingers for emphasis.

"It's sad, certainly." Steve shook his head. "Anything else?"

"The smell was terrible."

"You were standing over a dead body."

"The body was too fresh to be the cause, and it didn't smell like a rotting corpse. It smelled like mold or decaying food. I couldn't smell it from outside the room, so it wasn't naturally that strong. There was a symbol painted on the back of one of the doors; Rebecca found it. It was a sigil of some kind. I didn't recognize it, but it's been a while since I went through all my grimoires. I'll see if I can find it in one of them."

"If it's not in one of yours, let me know," Jakob said. "I've got some books I can lend you that might have answers."

Steve observed his three subordinates. "Do any of you have a theory worth looking into at this stage? Or should we wait for the autopsy?"

"Jakob suggested witchcraft at the scene. Adeline said it was possible." Rebecca informed him.

"I said 'magic' not 'witchcraft.'" Jakob clarified. "Adeline mentioned yesterday that witchcraft can't be used to kill someone."

"I said *my* witchcraft can't. I don't know everything there is to know about all branches of witchcraft," Adeline responded. "Could Sandra have been killed by witchcraft? It's possible. I'd want to know the cause of death before I'd say it's the only explanation, but we can't rule it out."

"And I don't suppose there's a spell or something you could do? To point us in the right direction?" Steve asked.

"You'd need a witch with the Sight for any kind of divination, which I don't have. The last witch in my family who had the Sight, my great-aunt Agnes," Adeline paused and took a moment to collect herself as memories of Agnes ran unbidden through her mind, "she died a couple years ago."

"Guess we're waiting on the autopsy, then," he concluded with a sigh. "Focus on your other work for now, and Adeline, maybe you can start digging into your spell books. It'll be a few days before the autopsy's done. The sheriff said he'd pass along any crime scene reports he gets, but who knows how much of a priority he thinks they are, or when we'll get them."

Jakob began to grab books from a shelf behind his desk while Rebecca filled Ned in on what had been found at the crime scene. Adeline grabbed her jacket and headed towards the parking lot.

"Where are you going?" Ned asked.

"Somewhere I can get clarity on a few things," she called over her shoulder.

She'd made a mistake, putting off visiting Elijah for so long.

CHAPTER 7

— • —

Adeline stopped at her house to leave some extra food for her cat and change into jeans and a hoodie before driving to Harlan County to see Elijah.

For two days, she had been close enough to visit her brother. Now she couldn't help but wonder if Sandra would be alive if she hadn't procrastinated seeing him. Nothing connected Sandra's death to Elijah's insistence that she come back to Kentucky, but her instincts told her it wasn't coincidental.

He'd been adamant about her leaving years ago and went out of his way to make sure she stayed away from their hometown. That all changed with his calls during her last week in Seattle. Suddenly, he claimed she was needed here, days before a woman had been gruesomely murdered.

As she drove through Evarts, she began to notice the less obvious changes around town, things she'd been too distracted to see earlier. Lou's Diner had gotten a new sign. A few houses had been repainted. The school had been renovated. A passerby or two stopped to watch her car as she drove down Main Street. Before she knew it, she was turning into the driveway of her childhood home.

Elijah's truck was parked in front of the two-story farmhouse. It desperately needed a new coat of paint, but about half of the windows seemed new. It looked smaller than she remembered. Her stomach churned at the idea of going inside. She half-expected her father to be passed out on the sofa.

She got out of the car, but couldn't bring herself to walk up the porch steps. She wasn't sure what to say to Elijah, How would he react when he saw her after so many years? Would he be angry? Relieved? Happy?

She needed to talk to him, but wasn't ready yet. She hadn't figured out what to tell him. She turned away, wanting extra time to collect her thoughts and to see how the land had changed.

Her view of the horizon to the west was blocked by a line of trees about fifteen yards from where she stood. She could see the faint outline of the neighbors' house between the branches. Had the Beckett house always been that far down the road?

A door slammed open behind her. "I don't know who you think you are, but around here you don't just come onto someone's land without invitation."

"Well, that's one hell of a way to greet your sister after all these years," she said before turning around. "Hey, Eli."

Tears burned in her eyes as she looked him over, and the urge to run towards him and wrap him tightly in a hug nearly overcame her. Two days ago, she'd returned to Kentucky, and yesterday, she'd come back to Harlan County, but now she was finally, fully home. Phone calls and emails weren't the same as having her twin in front of her.

He was standing on the highest porch step, wearing jeans and a faded t-shirt with a red flannel shirt thrown over it. His hazel eyes widened when he saw her.

"You're here." His voice was barely above a whisper.

The hard part, breaking the ice, was done. She walked up the stairs and stopped right next to her brother. It was unfair that she was older, but he was six inches taller. He seemed dumbstruck.

"Addy, I—," his voice cracked.

She gave him a hug, cutting him off. "Can we talk inside?"

He collected himself. "Yes, I'm sorry. Come on in."

He held the door, and she made her way through the house to the kitchen. The fridge was new, but the wooden cabinets on the wall hadn't changed. Neither had the paint, the table, nor anything else in this room. It was like she'd walked right into her memories, as unpleasant as some were.

"I don't know if it's a good or bad thing that you didn't sell this place after John died."

"Mama paid for this house. It was hers more than it was ever his," he said from behind her. He was standing with his hands in his pockets. After a beat of silence, he walked over to his coffee pot. "You want some coffee? I don't know how hot it is, but I can—"

"I've got it."

Heating liquid with her Gift wasn't a difficult task and she needed to get used to harnessing it again. She rubbed her hands together before she placed a hand on each side of the carafe. The cold liquid within started to warm beneath her fingertips, and a peaceful, mellow feeling overcame her as she made the coffee hot enough to drink.

Before she could pull her hand away, however, all the coffee vaporized, and the glass shattered in her grasp.

Elijah froze, his own cup of coffee halfway to his mouth.

"I'm sorry, I'll buy you a new pot." She stared at the shattered glass all over the counter. "I was just trying to heat it up. I-I guess I forgot how finnicky that spell is."

"I've never seen you do something like that before," he said, eyeing her. "Don't worry about replacing it. I bought a newer one, for real cheap, at a yard sale a year or so back. It's around here somewhere. That old dinosaur," he nodded to the broken pot, "was on its last legs anyway."

"I feel better about shattering it then. Where's your broom? Cleaning up the glass is the least I can do. And I'll spare you having to awkwardly ask why I'm here. I want to talk about the messages you left me," she said as he handed her the broom. His messages were an easier starting point for a conversation than Sandra's murder.

"You didn't have to come all the way here from Seattle. All you had to do was answer my calls."

"I'm not here to visit. I live here now, so coming to see you sounded like a better idea." She dumped the broken glass into the trashcan. "It's easier for me to gauge if you're hiding something when we're face-to-face."

"You've moved back to Evarts? When?" he asked, crossing his arms. "And why didn't you tell me?"

"I'm over the state line, but it's close enough. And I've only been back for a few days." She studied the scowl on his face and the slight worry in his eyes. "I thought you'd be happy to see me, at least a little bit."

"It's not that I'm not happy, but ... Remember the conversation we had right before you left?" He uncrossed his arms and tapped his fingers against the countertop in front of him. "About why you had to leave?"

"Yeah, I remember." It was a conversation she'd never forget, and there were times that worrying whether she'd chosen correctly kept her up at night.

"Small towns don't forget. People still whisper about Mama. And you. Hell, they still talk about Aunt Eve, and she's been dead nearly twenty years. After you missed John's funeral, people had a lot to say."

"Well, as I told Wyatt Dunn—"

His expression darkened. "You went to see Wyatt before you visited me?"

"Not intentionally. I ran into him at the Gas'N'Go. I was heading in as he was walking out and – You know what? It doesn't matter how I bumped into him. As I told him, you said not to come back for it. And what would I've done if I came anyway? Mama always said it wasn't polite to speak ill of the dead."

"Some folks said that your absence was proof that you'd gone and sold your soul to the devil."

"Nothing I haven't heard before. The Gift's plenty of things, but evil isn't one of them. I didn't care what folks thought when I was young, and I'm too old to start caring now."

Adeline gazed out the window over the sink, taking in the view of the hills. She'd taken it for granted when she was younger—being able to look out any window and see the world, see natural beauty and not cold, lifeless buildings. "You don't get views like this out west. They had mountains, but they didn't look right; it wasn't the same. They were missing something."

"Why are you back? It wasn't because you missed it here, or you would've come home years ago."

"It's a long story. Short version is that I lost my job over some bullshit, and then I got your message and was offered a similar job around here. It seemed like fate or something." She crossed her arms. "You left me a voicemail, saying I needed to come back and something wasn't right, and now you don't seem to want me here. Why the sudden change? What's going on?"

He let out a sigh. "Lately, I've been getting these strange feelings, and inexplicable things have been happening."

"Strange in what sense?" She leaned back against the counter. "Does it feel like your chest is being pressed down on by something? Like you can't remember how to breathe for a second?"

"No. Have you been feeling that?"

"Only when I enter Harlan County. The feeling you're getting, describe it."

"It's this ominous feeling, like something terrible is about to happen. And the hills keep trying to tell me something."

"The hills are trying to tell you something?" She tried and failed to keep the incredulity from her voice. "Like they did during the cave-in? That sounds—"

"Crazy? Says the witch who offered to hex my ex-wife."

"She would've deserved it."

"You met her *once*."

"Once was enough." Adeline had only met Sheila a few days before the wedding in Dallas eight years ago and hadn't thought about the woman once since she divorced Elijah a year or so afterwards.

"The divorce wasn't her fault, you know." He ran his tongue over his teeth. "Since we're on the topic, there's something I've been needing to tell you. I should've told you a while ago, really, but I wanted to do it in person. The reason Sheila and I split was—"

"Quit trying to change the subject. We can talk about your divorce later. Explain what you mean about the hills."

"It's rude to interrupt people, you know." He gave her an annoyed look. "They talk to me. It's only happened a handful of times. Four, maybe five. And when I say they talk, I mean that I hear a voice in my head."

"How long has that been going on?" she asked. "And why didn't you tell me?"

"It first happened the day of the cave-in, right before you left. I told you I heard a voice, but I convinced myself it was Mama's ghost that day."

"No, I remember that. You didn't tell me there were other times they spoke to you." Adeline hadn't fully believed that Elijah heard a voice the day of the cave-in. Her twin had been in shock and trying to make sense of what happened. Imagining a voice as a coping mechanism wouldn't have been the strangest reaction. She wished he'd told her that wasn't the only incident.

"I heard the same voice again, a couple of years later. A few more times since then."

"What's different this time?"

"She—the voice is always a woman's voice—she seems worried, but I don't know why." He began to fidget and wouldn't meet her eyes. "And that's got me all twisted up inside. I can't stop myself from worrying when Harlan herself told me you're needed here."

"That was the message? Harlan was telling you that I needed to come back?"

He nodded, but still wouldn't look at her. "I heard the voice last night too. Except, she wasn't saying you need to come back. She was crying about her child being torn away from her. I don't—what does that even mean?"

"It means Harlan felt Sandra Russett die," she said, and Elijah finally locked eyes with her. "She died early this morning and it wasn't of natural causes." She shuddered at the images of the crime scene that passed through her mind. "I don't want to talk about it."

"No, you need to explain how you know she's dead."

"My job's to keep the supernatural community secret from everyone else. Part of that means that when a death's caused by something supernatural, we investigate it." She hadn't lied when she told the sheriff's deputy that she never told Elijah details about her job. "The sheriff thinks we're cult experts, so he called my boss to have someone look at the crime scene. I saw her body myself this morning. That's how I know." She cleared her throat. "You said impossible things were happening. What kind of things?"

"I said 'inexplicable,' and what I really mean is that witchcraft's the only thing that explains them." Elijah took a deep breath. "I heard a couple of farmers talking, and a good chunk of their crops went bad, but only in the last few weeks. To hear them tell it: one day the crop was fine, and the next it was moldy at best and dead at worst. Marcus Jackson, down the road, lost his whole corn crop to some unknown blight."

"Maybe it's just a bad harvest season, and they missed the signs the crop was starting to turn."

"How do you explain what's happened to Shawn Brown's livestock then? Two of his pigs and one of his cows were killed by something. Torn apart, but it didn't look like a wolf or coyote had done it, and they all died on different nights. Hasn't happened to anyone else. Yet, anyway."

"They were torn apart?" Adeline asked, as her stomach dropped. Sandra's body had been torn open, rather than torn apart, but Elijah's story about the livestock had some alarming parallels.

"Was Sandra torn apart? Actually, forget I asked that. I don't want to know." He shook his head. The room fell silent. After several seconds, he glanced at the clock. "Shit, I need to get to work."

"You still working at the hardware store?"

"Yeah. Max's been talking about selling it to me recently. Says he's not as young as he used to be, and it's time for him to slow down."

"Hard to imagine the store without him," she said with a fond smile.

"I know." He started to gather his things. "I suppose you want to start heading back to Virginia."

"Not quite yet. I was hoping to look through some of Mama's belongings down in the basement. I told myself I'd do it when I came back. Today seems like a good day for that." She had her mother's spell book, but didn't know if others were gathering dust somewhere in the house, books that might have answers about the sigil from Sandra's kitchen. "If that's all right with you."

"You're only looking in the basement?"

"Unless some of it's in the attic, yes." She stepped away from the counter and spotted the conflicted look on his face, which stopped her in her tracks. "If you want me to come back later, I can."

"No, just— if I'm not here when you leave, lock up after yourself." He headed towards the door. "Addy, I'm happy you're back. I just – You're the only family I've got left. I don't want anything to happen to you."

Elijah walked out of the house and closed the door behind him. She watched him drive away before heading into the basement.

It was split into two rooms: a small laundry room and a large storage room. She entered the storage room, where she and Elijah had stacked the boxes they'd filled with Lilah Coburn's belongings after her death.

Adeline went to the far side of the space and searched until she saw a box with "Mama – books" written on the side in her own handwriting. She opened the box and started to dig through it.

Over the next few hours, Adeline found plenty of her mother's clothing and random knick-knacks as she searched through the boxes, but nothing magical. She made slow progress, as each rediscovered item caused her to stop and reminisce.

Adeline only pulled herself away from her task when she looked at her phone and saw how late it was. The sun would be setting soon. Her cousin Caleb's invitation to Edith's birthday celebration echoed through her head, along with his comment about people wanting to reconnect with her.

She didn't see the harm in attending a party, even if not everyone was happy to see her. It would distract her from the morning's events, if nothing else.

CHAPTER 8

— • —

The only noises Adeline could hear were the cicadas' song and the crunch of leaves beneath her feet as she wound her way up the mountain path to Mary's home. The sun was setting, which bathed the forest around her in a golden hue.

She was a few yards away from the clearing where Mary's house stood when the first sounds of a party reached her. She let herself smile and then braced herself as she took the final steps away from the tree line.

People were talking, laughing, and dancing with one another. Four or five tables ringed the edges of the clearing, some covered in food and others cleared for people to sit and eat at. Glass jars, each holding a candle, hung among the trees to illuminate the area after sunset.

Adeline stood and observed for about a minute before someone spotted her. The volume of conversation died down as more people noticed her presence. Caleb's voice broke through the building tension before the party became completely silent.

"Addy! You decided to come," he called out, pushing past a few people to approach her. He then spoke to the crowd. "Addy came. Isn't that great?"

"It's better than great!" someone shouted back, though Adeline couldn't see who had spoken. The woman sounded earnest and spoke without a hint of anger or cynicism.

"Yeah, I couldn't miss Edith's party, could I?" she said with a tight smile. "Hi, everyone." She waved before running a sweaty hand down the leg of her jeans before looking at Caleb. "Where is she? I want to wish her a happy birthday before I forget."

"Last I saw her, she was over by the barn." He motioned towards the building in question.

The crowd didn't part as she walked forward, but a few people stepped out of her path and soon, she was face-to-face with Edith. She stopped short, taking in the woman in front of her.

Edith's hair, which had been greying the last time Adeline saw her, was now completely white. Her face was wrinkled, and she seemed fragile. She looked so much older than the stern, formidable witch Adeline remembered from her childhood. Edith's eyes began to water when she saw her.

"Oh, thank the ancestors." Edith glanced up at the darkening sky for a moment before turning her attention to Adeline. "You finally came back to us."

"I did." She nodded.

"Well, don't stand there nigh as a pea and not hug me. Come over here."

Adeline walked over to the older woman and engulfed her in a hug. As they broke apart, she struggled to find the right thing to say. "I don't — I'm so — Happy birthday," she choked out. She blinked a few times as tears started to run down her face. "I'm sorry. I don't know why I'm crying."

"Because you're home, and that's something to be happy about." The elderly woman gave her a sad smile. "Let's get you a plate. You're much too skinny." Taking Adeline's arm with one of her shaking hands, Edith slowly walked over to one of the buffet tables.

Adeline's stomach rumbled as she took in the platters of brisket and pulled pork. Good barbecue—real barbecue—was something she hadn't had in a very long time. Large dishes of potato salad, homemade coleslaw, macaroni and cheese, collard greens, and succotash rounded out the spread, along with so many other foods she's forgotten she loved. She piled as much as she could onto her plate as she moved around the table, then found an empty seat and sat down to dig in.

After about thirty seconds, she heard a laugh from her left and looked up to see a woman about ten years older than her. Her dark hair only had a few scattered greys.

"Can't tell if she came back to see us or because she missed the food." The woman smiled as she spoke to the man across from her. She then turned to Adeline. "I'm Bethany, I don't know if you remember me. This is my husband, Hal." Hal was bald and looked a few years older than his wife.

Adeline had a few memories of Bethany from when she was younger. She was Edith's niece and had lived on the other side of the mountain her whole life. She'd been too old to be Adeline's friend as a kid, but too young for her to be an authority figure. Hal had also been around when Adeline was young, but she hadn't interacted with him often.

She swallowed slowly, considering what to say. "Can't it be a bit of both? I wanted to see everyone, but I couldn't pass up a chance for some home cooking. I tried and I failed to find food this good when I was out west," she said. "And yes, I remember you."

"Of course it's not as good." Mary scoffed from a few seats down. "Folks out there don't know how to make things with love. And they always leave out the butter, so everything's bland."

"Or they take shortcuts, and then their green bean casserole looks like a crime scene," Adeline laughed. She considered some of the things she ate at "barbecues" after she moved west and grimaced. "They almost made me hate mac and cheese."

"How the hell do you ruin mac and cheese? It's the easiest thing to make." Bethany's tone was incredulous.

"One time, someone made boxed mac and cheese, and threw it in the oven after making it on the stovetop. Another time, they used some kind of fancy noodle that was supposed to cook faster, which turned into mush. No one's willing to take time to layer the flavors properly." She shuddered. "Hell isn't fire, screaming, and torture—it's being stuck at a barbecue on the outskirts of Seattle, hearing folks talk about how much better they made a dish by cutting corners."

"You're a stronger woman than I am." Bethany shook her head. "I would've come running home screaming if I heard someone even mention trying to 'improve' a food that's already perfect."

"Is that where you were? Seattle?" Hal asked.

"For the last twelve years. Before that, I was in college down in Tennessee." She heard a few gasps and peered around. She saw Edith and Mary share a meaningful look with another grey-haired woman at the table. She recognized the third woman as Norma, another witch from the coven.

"What?"

"We didn't know you'd been that close when you first left," Edith said.

Adeline turned towards Mary. "When I left, Elijah promised he'd come tell you and Agnes about my decision to leave. I didn't want anyone to worry about me, thinking I'd gotten into some kind of trouble. Did he not do that?"

"He came and told us that you had left. It must've slipped his mind to tell us where you'd gone." Her voice had an odd inflection, as if she found the idea hard to believe.

"What was Seattle like?" Bethany asked after several seconds of silence.

"Rainy, mostly. It gets warm there, but never hot," Adeline said. "It was a big city—lots of people, and a lot going on all the time. Being able to see the sunset over the water was pretty, but it was the only nice view I had. I saw the mountains every day as I went about my life, but I'd have to drive for over an hour to be near them."

"Did you have a coven there?" Norma asked. "In a big city, there had to be plenty of witches."

"There were a few dozen witches, and they were all in one coven. A friend was a member, but I didn't join it. Our Gifts were too different. When they would cast spells, it felt ... sterile and cold. And the air always smelled like a hospital room afterwards. It wasn't like the cozy, welcoming feeling that fills me every time I draw power from the ancestors." She shook her head. "The Seattle witches and I didn't have compatible Gifts, and I didn't like most of them anyway."

"So, you were all alone out there?" Her voice was thick as she asked the question. "That's a damn shame."

"I survived it. And I'm here now, anyway." Warmth filled her chest. Coming to this party had been the right call.

Adeline picked up her fork and continued to eat. Conversations started up around her, and the dancing resumed. She stopped being the center of attention.

After she finished her food, she stood up to stretch her legs and walk around. She made her way over to David, who was sitting on a tree stump near the edge of the clearing, looking up at the stars. He kept his gaze on the sky when she silently settled on the stump beside him.

"Want some?" he asked, holding out a clear mason jar and finally looking her way. "It's from my newest batch."

"Sure." She took the jar from him and held it up to her lips, taking a sip. The moonshine burned as it ran down her throat. She handed the jar back to him as she let out a cough and blinked a few times as her eyes watered.

"I think you've been gone a little too long," he said with a laugh.

"Yeah, just a bit," she told her cousin. "Are you avoiding me?"

"Maybe a little. I'm still mad at you."

She looked at him with a raised eyebrow. "For leaving? I—"

"I was with Granny Agnes when she died. Mama, Caleb, and I took turns sitting with her, not wanting her to be alone when she finally passed." He sighed. "It wasn't pleasant to watch."

"I'm sorry you had to see that."

"I'm not. She was my granny, and while I wish she didn't have to suffer like she did, I wouldn't trade those days for the world. But at the very end she kept asking where you were. It pissed me off because you should've been here too, but you weren't. You were somewhere else, and you missed her final days. She didn't get to say goodbye to you."

Adeline swallowed as she tried not to picture the scene David was describing. She'd never met her own grandmother, but Agnes filled that role in her life. The woman was tough, but had a loving side. What the tiny white-haired woman lacked in stature, she'd made up for in sheer determination. She felt her eyes start to water.

"When you told me she died, it was the first time I regretted not coming back sooner. I wish I'd had the chance to say goodbye to her." Her eyes went to the ground. "I never got to thank her for everything she did for me."

Silence fell between them. She looked up at the stars, awe-struck to see how bright and clear the view could be. "I've missed looking up at night and being able to see all this."

"They didn't have stars out where you were?" David passed her the moonshine again.

"Not this many. Too much of the sky was blocked by clouds or dimmed because of the city lights." She sighed before taking another sip.

A loud burst of laughter behind her caused her to glance back to see what everyone was laughing at, but all she saw were a few people dancing and a few others talking. It wasn't until now that she realized how small the group was. There were only about three dozen people standing in the clearing.

"Where are the others?" she asked David.

"What others?"

"The rest of the people living on the mountain. There aren't that many people here."

"Addy, this is everyone," he answered. "You were gone a long time. You can't expect everything to be exactly the same as when you left."

"There's at least five people I remember from the last time I was here who aren't here. For example, Noah. Where's he?" She hadn't seen her cousin since he was five, and wondered how he was doing.

"Noah's in the county jail for another few months. He got into some trouble. Some asshole made a comment about Eve's death, and he didn't take the remarks about his mama lightly."

"What about Jefferson? Sue? Where's—"

"Got a job on an oil rig five years ago. Died. I don't know what other names you were gonna say, but most of the people you're wondering about are dead. A few moved away, but they didn't have the Gift."

She furrowed her brow. "What's that have to do with anything?"

"Mama should be the one to explain it." He shrugged. He held the jar of moonshine up again. "Another?"

"Not a good idea." She shook her head. "What have you been up to since I left?"

"Growing food. Raising chickens and pigs. Hunting. All the normal stuff that needs to be done around here." He stretched out a little. "Living off the land ain't easy, but we make do."

"Do you think it was a mistake for me to leave like I did?"

He waited several seconds before speaking. "I wouldn't have, but—"

"Are the two of you gonna sit in the corner the whole night?" Edith called from behind them. "This is a party! Come socialize. Don't make me drag you over here."

"We should go. She's gotten older, but she'll still try to do it," he said, standing up and holding out a hand to help her do the same.

***

Adeline lost track of time as she caught up with the people who had gathered to celebrate Edith's birthday. Before she knew it, the party was winding down and people were heading back to their homes in the dense darkness.

She had stayed longer than she planned to. She turned to leave, but Mary's voice stopped her. "Where do you think you're going?"

"Down to my car to drive home." She gestured down the hill in confusion.

"I'm not sure you want to try walking down to your car this late. You know this mountain well, but do you know it well enough to try and hike down it in the pitch black?"

"I have work in the morning, and I don't have anywhere else to sleep," she countered. "I don't expect anyone here to have extra space."

"I have an extra bed," Norma cut in. "You can stay with me and leave at first light, if you want."

"I don't want to impose," she said awkwardly.

"You're not. I'm offering you the extra bed."

"Fine. That's very nice of you. I'd appreciate it." She relaxed a little bit.

Adeline followed Norma up the footpath that led to her small house, which consisted of a great room with a little kitchen in the corner, two small bedrooms, and a bathroom.

"The door on the left leads to the guest room. Let me grab you some sheets."

After making the bed, Adeline thanked Norma and tried to fall asleep, but it didn't come easily. When she wasn't picturing Sandra's home in her mind, her brain drifted back to the image of Lucy Radassi sprawled out on the pavement. The two scenes, the two deaths, couldn't have been any different, yet Adeline couldn't think of one without picturing the other.

***

Adeline woke up as dawn was breaking and quietly stripped the bed. She left the folded sheets laying in a stack on the end of the mattress before leaving.

As she passed another cabin and the barn, she thought about the party the night before. Everyone had seemed so happy to see her. It had been a welcome distraction from the troubling questions she had about Sandra's death.

"I see you're sneaking away again."

Adeline jumped at the sound and found Mary behind her. She was standing a few yards away behind her, drinking something from a steaming mug.

"I'm not sneaking away. I have to get to work."

"You have to go to work. Because you have a job as a ... preserver or whatever it's called." She shook her head. "It ain't right, a witch like you working for them, and believing it's your only choice. Breaks my heart a little, you feeling like you don't belong among us."

"I wouldn't, though. It's not like I'd be of any use around here."

"Being useful ain't what matters, and never has been. Keep that in mind. But I don't want to argue with you. You have your opinion and I've got mine." Mary sighed. "I'm happy you came last night. It was good to see you. You made Edith's week."

"I'm glad I came too. I ... had a nice time."

"Why'd you say it like that? Like you're surprised you enjoyed yourself?" Mary tilted her head to the side.

"I wasn't expecting everyone to be happy to see me. I didn't say goodbye to anyone here."

"And some of us were mad about that. Your brother wouldn't say where you'd gone. My mama could only tell that you were safe. We were mad you left. We were worried that we'd lost – Now, we're relieved you came back to us. Not everyone who leaves makes it back."

"David mentioned a few people moved away while I was gone," Adeline recalled. "He also said them leaving was okay, because they didn't have the Gift. I don't see what that's got to do with anything."

"It has everything to do with it. Your Gift is why we were so angry when you left, and why we're all so relieved that you've come home. When you're ready to learn the things I need to share with you, we'll talk about it."

"Why don't we talk about it now, if it's so important?"

"It's not the right time. And you need to head to work." She took a sip from her mug. "You look like you want to ask me something else."

"Last time I saw you, I mentioned feeling chest pains. You said you'd felt them too."

"And I still do. They're a little worse than two days ago. In fact, they were so bad night before last that they woke me up."

The night Sandra died.

"Do you think it's a sign?" Adeline asked. Her chest pains had gotten worse. The hills were talking to Elijah. Crops were failing. People were dying. "Like the ancestors are trying to warn us about something?"

"Possibly, though I shudder to think what they're warning us about, if this is how they're doing it," Mary said. "I suppose we'll know when it's time for us to."

CHAPTER 9

— • —

"Any luck on your search yesterday? Ours was a bust," Jakob said as he stopped in front of Adeline's desk.

She raised an eyebrow and was about to ask him what on earth he was talking about when she remembered running out of the building to see Elijah with the excuse that she wanted to find clarity on something. "Some, but not like I hoped," she answered. "I wound up with even more questions, if I'm being honest."

"At least you have something. None of us found anything on that sigil. What'd you learn?"

"Something has been brewing in Evarts for a few weeks. They've had failing crops and a few animal deaths. Subtle enough to overlook in the moment, but menacing in hindsight." She tapped her fingers against the desk. "Dylan mentioned things felt off on the full moon, and that was before the murder. I wonder if other supernatural factions in the area would tell a similar story. I'm betting they've sensed something wrong, too."

Jakob drained his coffee mug and set it down at his desk. "Let's go ask them that, then."

"We aren't needed here? The investigation—"

"Has barely started. We don't have any leads, so what do you suppose we should do instead? Spend another day poring over books, searching for that symbol from the crime scene? Sit around and wait for the autopsy report to come in? It'll take a few days at least." He dug his keys out of his pocket. "We might as well test your theory. And we need to visit the vily anyway, since we didn't a couple days ago."

"Vily?"

"Forest nymphs."

"Yes, I know what they are. I just didn't know there were any in the area." Every vila she'd heard about lived deep within forests, as far from humans as possible. Eastern Kentucky was rural, but she hadn't thought it was remote enough for the vily to settle there.

"There's a small group who live deep in the woods out in Wolfe County." He stepped away from his desk. "I'll let Steve know where we're going."

***

Jakob followed the signs towards Wolfe County but turned off the main road to drive towards the forest before he got too close to Red River Gorge.

They passed through a gate and continued down a long, winding road that terminated near a cluster of abandoned buildings a few yards from the edge of the dense forest. He parked next to a building with a rotting sign advertising firewood and climbed out of the SUV.

"Hopefully, they're not far," he said.

"You don't know how to find the vily?" Adeline asked.

"Letting them find us is easier than wandering through their forest looking for them. Follow my lead. Vily can be temperamental around strangers."

They walked roughly a hundred yards into the woods, stopping every few minutes. Adeline looked back over her shoulder and could no longer see Jakob's SUV from where they stood. When she turned back towards the forest, a woman had materialized a few feet in front of her. The air around them began to smell of spruce and black currant.

The vila had piercing green eyes and honey-colored hair that cascaded down to the middle of her back, and wore a simple white linen dress. She was around Adeline's height but appeared ageless. As she turned slightly towards Jakob, the sunlight dappling through the forest canopy gave her a golden aura.

"Yakov, we were wondering when you would appear," the vila said before looking over at Adeline. She had a slight Russian accent. "I do not know you."

"Katerina, this is Adeline. She—"

"Is a *sestra* of the Baba Yaga. I can feel it." She didn't look in Jakob's direction when she cut him off. "You're a witch, yes?"

"Yes, I am," Adeline said, refusing to look away. "Is that a problem?"

"No, not a problem, but it is interesting that you are here with Yakov. Very ... unexpected." She turned her attention to Jakob. "I know why you've come."

"You do?" Jakob asked.

"It's been more than a lunar cycle since you last visited. You wish to question me about our activities, and determine if we have violated the law. I will confess, a handful of humans encroached on our territory since your last visit. They left disoriented but unharmed, and unaware of our existence. Their presence wasn't a provocation, so there was no need to act. Our dislike of most humans doesn't mean we will violate the decrees of the Arcane Codex."

"I know. I also know you'll get as close to the line as you can justify."

"If humans weren't as destructive to our home as they are, if they weren't intent on causing further devastation to this world, then my sisters and I would be more welcoming of their presence. Those who respect the forest are permitted to come and go without issue."

"That's actually not why we're here." Adeline's curiosity was piqued, but she stayed focused. "Well, it's not the main reason. Have you noticed anything strange recently?"

"Your question is frustratingly vague, as I find many things strange. Could you be more specific?"

"The feeling that something is wrong. Like something unnatural is happening. The sensation that something dark or evil is nearby."

"I have not, no. Though Anya felt something unusual a few days ago. She was south of here when she began to feel a darkness coming from the earth. She claims it was as if vitality was being leached out of the land itself." She tilted her head to the side. "Why do you ask?"

"A woman was gruesomely murdered in Harlan County early yesterday morning," Jakob said. "Her death couldn't have been caused by humans, which means something from the supernatural world killed her."

Katerina laughed. "And you believe us responsible? We're not rusalki; we have no need to leave our home if we wish to harm a human." She noticed Adeline flinch. "You have encountered the rusalki in the past, I take it?"

"Once. It ended tragically," Adeline said.

"As such events often do." She turned her attention back to Jakob. "I know nothing of this untimely death. I can send for Anya if you would like to question her. Or any of the others, if you wish to speak to them."

"I don't think that's necessary. I didn't think you'd drive three hours to kill someone, and it seemed like a targeted attack, but we had to ask," he said. "If you, Anya, or anyone else feels that sensation again, we ask that you contact us as soon as possible."

"If the incident occurs again and I deem it necessary, I will find you myself. As with many other human inventions, I'm not fond of those mobile phones they seem obsessed with."

"I guess that's the best I can hope for."

"It is the most I'm willing to promise to you," Katerina declared before looking at Adeline. "You are welcome to return, should you wish to. You are not vila, yet your connection to this land is strong. I find myself curious about it."

The open and honest curiosity on Katerina's face warmed something in Adeline's chest. She bent down and picked up a fallen stick. Focusing her attention on it, she slowly wrapped her Gift around it and willed buds to form on the end of the branches. Once the buds appeared, she pushed her Gift a little further until leaves burst out of them. The vibrant green leaves stood in stark contrast to the red and orange leaves on the ground surrounding them, typical for October.

"It's strong because my family's connection to this area goes back a long time." She held the branch out to Katerina.

"Fascinating. Now is the season for change, to prepare for death and rebirth, yet you are able to create life, on a small scale." She took the branch from her. "Your magic, it is quite beautiful. I thank you for this gift."

"We should probably go," Jakob motioned back the way they came. "There are others we need to see. Thank you for your time."

"Farewell." Katerina turned and took a few steps before vanishing among the trees.

Jakob turned and walked back towards his truck, with Adeline following a few strides behind. "I wasn't expecting Katerina to know anything concrete about the murders, but your theory seems to be holding up."

"If you weren't expecting helpful answers, why were the vily our first stop?"

"I wanted to ease into it, since they'd be the nicest to deal with, and we had to check in with them anyway." He shrugged. "You didn't seem to be complaining."

"She seemed excited that I was a witch. That's rare for me," Adeline said as they got into the SUV. "It was nice to be met with curiosity and not suspicion for once." She smiled. "Why did Katerina keep calling you Yakov?"

"Because it's 'Jakob' in Russian and I never corrected her on it. It's still my name, so I don't care. It's not like she's calling me 'Kevin'."

Adeline said nothing and continued to watch the scenery go by.

"I didn't explain the politics of all the factions to you, did I?" he asked after a few minutes of the radio being the only sound in the truck. "It's been a long few days, so I can't remember if I did that or not."

"No, you didn't. You told me witches were paranoid and that was it."

"Well, I guess I should now." He turned the radio down and settled his hand on the parking brake. "The wolves, vampires, and vily are the three big factions around here. The wolves get along fine with the vily now, but they've been at odds plenty of times in the past. No one knows how the last feud started or what ended it. It was one-sided, with the vily hating the werewolves and the werewolves not caring. When I brought it up to Dylan, she said she had actual problems to worry about and didn't give a shit what happened over ten years ago."

"Okay. What else? Who do the vily have problems with?"

"The vampires, but everyone hates the vampires because they're dead." He tilted his head to the side and let out a short laugh. "No one likes being reminded that they're gonna die, like ignoring the inevitable accomplishes anything."

"Well, you're not using their logic. Sure, billions of people have died over the course of history, but that doesn't mean it'll happen to me. If I don't acknowledge it, it can't happen."

"I'm so glad you came to this office," he said with a smirk. "The beauty of my sarcasm is lost on some people around here."

"It feels good for my wit to finally be appreciated. Few people out in Seattle saw its value. Everyone hates the vampires. What else do I need to know?"

"That's pretty much it. Everyone else keeps to themselves. The other groups are either too small to have conflict with anyone, or they're too isolated to ever come across others."

"Which category do witches fall into? Are we too small or too isolated?"

"Neither; y'all are too terrifying."

"Are you saying people think I'm scary? What, am I the boogeyman that werewolves tell their children about at night to get them to behave?"

"Maybe not the boogeyman, but from the outside the idea of witches is scary. Vampires might drink blood, and a werewolf could kill a person on a full moon, but witches aren't limited in that way. You can curse people and turn them into frogs or whatever. You said yourself that, short of outright killing someone, there's very little you *can't* do to someone who pisses you off."

"I could, but why would I want to hurt someone like that?" She looked over at him. "Wait, are you scared of me?"

"No. Turn me into a newt; it'll solve most of my problems."

"I just might, but not today. Transmutation's more fun when you don't know it's coming."

"Sentences like that, out of context, is why folks are scared of pissing off a witch." He turned his attention back to the road to pass a tractor trailer. "Not me, though. I'm hard to kill." He grinned. "Like a cockroach."

As he smiled, Adeline noticed his dimples and couldn't help but think about how wrong he was. With his dry demeanor and the boyish charm he wielded when he wanted to, he didn't remind her of a bug at all.

"She was right, you know," he said a few minutes later. "Katerina."

"Right about what?"

"The magic you did with that branch was pretty impressive. Don't get me wrong, your whole 'you couldn't kill me if you tried' demonstration at Alexei's was imposing, but it didn't seem as complicated as what you showed her."

"Thanks." As nice as the compliment was, Jakob didn't know what he was talking about. Her mother's ability to use her Gift had been amazing, as had Agnes's. Adeline's own talent paled in comparison to theirs and she felt arrogant for letting him assume she was anything to be impressed by.

They lapsed into silence for a few minutes.

"Speaking of Alexei, if we were to head to Somerset now," Adeline said as an idea struck her, "when would we reach his house?"

"Two-thirty, maybe three, in the afternoon. Alexei might be awake, but the rest of his nest wouldn't be."

"Good. He's the one I'm hoping to talk to." An idea occurred to her, and given what she, Mary, and Elijah were experiencing, she wanted to investigate it as soon as possible. "I doubt he killed her, but he could be a useful source of information."

***

The door to Alexei's mansion was unlocked, so they walked inside without knocking. As they proceeded through the main hall, Adeline was struck by exactly how quiet and still everything was. The steady clip of Jakob's and her footsteps rang through the house like gunshots; it was disconcerting.

She sensed something behind her and reacted instinctively, aiming a brief burst of her magic towards whatever had moved.

"Well, this is simply unfair," Alexei said, causing both her and Jakob to jump. They turned and saw that he was standing right behind them. "Would you mind releasing me?"

"Releasing you from what?" Jakob asked.

"Your lovely companion seems to have cast some kind of spell on me, leaving me unable to move anything below my neck." His gaze moved over to Adeline. "It is quite impressive, but there's no need to restrain me in such a manner."

Adeline closed her eyes and took a deep breath. A moment later, Alexei fell sideways, his shoulder knocking into the wall. "Sorry. I sensed movement and just kind of reacted."

Alexei straightened himself up. "An understandable response, and a smart one to have. May I ask why you are trespassing in my home?"

"We need to ask you a few questions, and waiting until nightfall wasn't an option."

"Very well. Let us speak in my office." He turned and walked away, leaving the pair to follow. He led them to the other side of the house and walked into a windowless room lined with bookshelves. He sat behind the dark wooden desk that occupied the center of the space. "Now, am I correct in assuming your visit is related to the murder in Harlan County early yesterday morning?"

"How do you know about that?" Jakob asked.

"There are these wonderful inventions called newspapers," he replied. "And Lucinda works at the morgue where the victim was sent for autopsy. She told me about the state of the body, but nothing about the coroner's findings." He then addressed Adeline. "She was among the people who greeted you during your last visit. I must apologize, as I neglected to make proper introductions."

"Was she one of the blonde ones? Or the Latina woman in the blue dress with long hair? Or the woman with braids?" she asked, "I'd like to be able to match a name to a face."

"Lucinda was the woman wearing blue." He looked back at Jakob. "Am I correct? Are you here because of the murder?"

"Yes, that's why we're here," he said. "Do you have any information?"

"I do not."

"Is it possible someone else around here might know something about it?"

"From what Lucinda told me and what the article said, the scene was quite gruesome. We no longer need to kill to feed, so no vampire would leave such a messy scene behind. And no one from the nest has traveled out towards Harlan County in some time, aside from myself. There has been no need, and traveling there entails risks that we cannot currently justify. A trip to Lexington allows us to easily meet our needs. Though, you expected that to be my answer."

Jakob leaned forward. "What makes you say that? Last I checked, mind-reading isn't among the list of vampire powers."

"It is not. But if you had a strong suspicion, you and your partner would not be my only guests. You would have brought others, because you would want to be prepared. Instead, you only brought Adeline. Though, having now seen two demonstrations of her abilities, I believe she could kill me entirely on her own. Back to my point, she certainly would not have released me from her spell simply because I requested it, if I were a suspect. No, if you truly thought I knew something, that any vampire in this house did, you would have handled your arrival much differently. Or at the very least, you would have loaded your gun with different bullets."

"How—?"

"Lead smells decidedly different from wood." He looked at the open door and motioned to the hallway. "But if you wish to question the others, say the word. I will wake them up."

"You're very open about this," Adeline cut in. "You don't seem upset or insulted at the idea that you might be under suspicion for murder."

"I have no reason not to be. We have nothing to hide." He paused. "I am a vampire, and an old one at that. A few generations ago, I had to kill to feed. Finding myself accused of killing someone is a consequence of being what I am. This is not the first time I have been a suspect, and it is unlikely to be the last." He turned his attention to Jakob. "Do you have any other questions you need to ask? Information you would like to know?"

"No. That's all we came—"

"We think dark magic played a role in the victim's death," Adeline interrupted. "There were details about the crime scene that indicate its involvement, and a few of those details gave me the idea to come speak with you." Assuming the killer was acting alone, finding the spell might be easier than finding the specific witch.

"And what might those details be?" Alexei asked, one eyebrow lifted.

"There was a sigil scrawled on the wall that we haven't been able to identify." She unlocked her phone and began swiping through her pictures, stopping when she landed on the photo she'd taken. "We haven't found it in our books, but I recall you saying you were over four hundred years old. Maybe we didn't find any answers about the symbol because the dark magic in question is very old. Old enough that it's already been forgotten." She showed him the photo. "Does this look familiar to you?"

Alexei took the phone from her and studied the symbol intently for several moments. "It does not. However, I have only ever had a passing interest in witchcraft since my first death. It compelled me at first, but I soon found myself invested in mundane history rather than magic, and other pursuits drew my attention."

"You said 'however' like you were gonna follow it up with something useful," Jakob grumbled.

"And I was, but you interrupted before I could finish my thought." He clasped his hands in front of him. "Some of my siblings are more knowledgeable than I am on this subject. They have taken it upon themselves to preserve what they can and prevent any knowledge from being lost to the sands of time. I would be happy to contact them, on your behalf, to inquire if they know anything of this sigil. Or of a spell capable of causing the wounds Lucinda told me of."

"Can you do it without mentioning us or the murder?"

"I would need to be delicate in my approach, but it is possible," he said. "If the murder was caused by dark magic, certain ... urges I recently felt begin to make sense."

"Urges?" Adeline asked. "What urges?"

"I was in Bell County a few weeks ago to fulfill an obligation for a friend. It was two, perhaps three, weeks if I recall correctly." Bell County bordered Harlan County to the west. "An unusually strong desire to find a human, any human, and tear their throat out came over me. I did not indulge the urge, as I have strict control over my hunger, and I am far too old to lose control in such a manner. A witch I knew centuries ago once told me that certain spells can impact the impulses of my kind. Logic suggests a spell that could kill would also be able to influence vampires."

"Why didn't you say anything when we were here two days ago?" Adeline pressed.

"I could not identify its cause, and as such was unsure if it was relevant or not." He brushed invisible lint from his jacket. "Please know that if I had any indication, I would have."

"I know you would've." Jakob sighed. "I think that's all we came here to ask, right?"

"I asked the questions I wanted answers to, for now." Adeline eyed the vampire warily.

"It seems your interactions with my sister tainted your view of my kind," Alexei said.

"And I'm sure your past interactions with witches have impacted how you see me. Our pasts shape who we are."

"Indeed, they do. I hope to someday earn your trust, my dear. Let me show you out." He stood and walked them towards the front door, but stopped where the hallway intersected with the entryway. "I am afraid the sun prevents me from going any further. Please close the door on the way out."

"Thank you for your time," Jakob said, walking over to the door.

"If there is any way I can be of assistance, please let me know. Incidents like this death put the entire community at risk."

Adeline understood it for the token offer it was but made no comment as they walked out of the mansion, closing the door behind them before climbing back in the car.

"How do you know it was dark magic?" Jakob asked as they merged onto the highway. "We don't have the autopsy report yet."

"Remember that smell I mentioned at the crime scene? Of mold and rotten food? I'm starting to think that the reason I could smell it and you couldn't was because I'm a witch and you're not," she explained. "Magic and its effects can leave behind a sensory impression. Sometimes when I use my Gift I'll smell a dish my mama used to make or feel the wind blowing through my hair when there is none. When I was around witches who drew their power from the stars, their spell casting felt different than my own." Ancestral magic was warm and comforting. Cosmic magic felt lukewarm and a little bland. Following that logic, harmful magic would smell and feel unpleasant. "The sensory thing doesn't happen every time, but it fits with what we saw and the little amount that we do know."

"I won't say I completely understand your reasoning, but I can't think of a better explanation." He shrugged. "I guess we'll see what the crime scene reports say."

***

When Jakob and Adeline arrived back at the office, everyone else had left for the day. Steve left a note taped to the door of his office, asking them to make sure the exterior door was locked, and saying he'd get their report in the morning.

"How are we explaining asking Alexei to look into long-lost dark magic for us? We don't have a cause of death yet or proof it was dark magic." Adeline's instincts told her that she was on the right track, but she had nothing but a feeling to back up her theory.

"I wasn't going to. Neither of us outright asked him to do that; he offered to contact his siblings," Jakob answered. "I'll lock up. Have a good night."

She drove home, where Whiskey met her at the door and meowed in greeting before endeavoring to be underfoot as much as possible as she cooked and ate.

"You've gotten very friendly since we got here." She cooed as she scratched Whiskey's chin. "Do you forgive me for cat-napping you from Seattle now? Is this your way of telling me you like your new home?" The cat began to purr as she continued to pet her. "Well, I'm gonna take this as a sign that I'm forgiven."

CHAPTER 10

— · —

F our days after Sandra Russett's death, Adeline's nose was buried in yet another musty book when someone called her name. She held up a finger and went back to reading. Aside from the day she and Jakob had visited Katerina and Alexei, she'd spent all her working hours searching through books, hoping to find answers. She had yet to find out anything about the sigil they had found on Sandra's wall, and Alexei hadn't been in touch with any updates.

"Adeline?"

"Just a second, Jakob. I want to finish this section."

A calloused hand reached into view and pulled the book out of her grasp. She looked up to find Jakob looking down at her.

"What?" she asked with a frown. "What's so important?"

"We've been trying to get your attention for five minutes. Steve called us all into his office." He turned the book over to see what she'd been reading. "You're on page 217." He closed the book and set it down.

Rebecca and Ned weren't at their desks. Steve was standing in the doorway of his office, looking annoyed. She stood up and walked past Jakob into the room. She took the remaining chair and cleared her throat. "Sorry, I was—"

"Too engrossed in that book to hear me say that we have the autopsy and some crime scene reports back from Sandra Russett's house," Steve remarked. "I can understand that."

"I'm sorry, y'all, that everyone had to wait for me." She refused to look at anyone.

"We weren't waiting for long," Ned said sympathetically.

"The ME found no drugs in Sandra Russett's system. He also found no defensive marks and no knife, gunshot, or puncture wounds on her. That also means no vampire bite." Steve read out the report to the Guardians in his office. "Time of death was somewhere between one and three in the morning."

"Her chest was torn open. What explanation did he have for that?" Adeline asked.

"He didn't have one, at least not one that made sense. The injury was too neat to be some kind of wild animal, but he couldn't identify what tool caused the damage. She had almost no blood left in her body, but he couldn't say how so much of it was drained, or why it wound up all over the place." He gripped the page tighter as a look of disgust crossed his face. "All the blood at the scene was her own."

Adeline turned to Jakob. "You said at the scene it was her blood."

"I know. I remember saying it."

"How did you know it was hers?"

"Lucky guess, I suppose." He leaned back in his chair and ignored the curious looks being sent his way. "Did she die from bleeding out?"

"No, she died from shock," Steve said before steeling himself and turning the page, "caused by the back-alley surgery the killer performed."

"What?" Rebecca asked.

"Her lungs were missing." He looked ready to vomit. "Her rib cage was torn open, and her lungs had been removed. It wasn't a clean removal, but they're gone. From what the ME observed, she — Oh, shit."

"'Oh, shit,' what?" Ned looked between the three other Guardians.

"If she died from shock, it means she was alive, and possibly awake, when the killer cut them out." Jakob stared at the wall as he spoke. "Or at least when they started."

"How do you cut a person up while they're awake and not have them try and fight you off? No one would just lie there and let someone do that to them. They'd fight back on instinct." Ned sounded incredulous.

"There could be two killers," Rebecca posited. "One to ... remove the lungs, and one to keep her immobilized."

"Or the killer used witchcraft to subdue her. There are spells that can paralyze someone. I've heard stories. And plenty of other rumors are floating around about spells that can make a person impossibly strong, strong enough to tear a person's rib cage open," Adeline admitted. "But it would have to be some very dark magic. Nothing like what I can do."

"So, it's witchcraft, but not your kind of witchcraft. Is that what you're saying?" Steve asked. "You couldn't do it, but some other witch could. We should start looking into all of the nearby witches."

The witches living on Brodens Mountain were the only ones Adeline was aware of and Mary wouldn't stand for anyone living there to mess with something so dark. It had to be a witch who was new to the area or one who'd flown under her family's radar until now. "No witch worth talking to would touch something like this. Most witches draw their power from something in nature, whether the earth itself or the stars, and nature-based magic can't be used to kill someone. At least, not in the way Sandra was killed. There are always — You know what, let's not get into the ways I could skirt the rules. Sandra wasn't killed with normal, benign magic. The witchcraft we're talking about is dark, evil stuff. The kind of magic that requires you to sell your soul or drown a puppy or kill someone you love to use it. Witches who tap into that stuff cross a line they can't come back from, assuming they survive it in the first place."

"I want you to look into this kind of witchcraft and find out what you can, however you can. As a witch, you'll understand it better than the rest of us. Maybe something about it will make the killer easy to find," Steve said, before turning to Jakob, Rebecca and Ned. "Dark magic aside, the spouse or ex-spouse is the most likely suspect in killings like this. Have we verified where her ex-husband was the night of the murder?"

"We haven't found an alibi, but Scott Johnston moved to Alaska in 2007," Rebecca read off her notes.

"So, chances are slim that he's the culprit. I want y'all to figure out who'd want Sandra Russett dead. If we take the supernatural part out of it, what happened to her seems personal; she might've known the killer."

Everyone else went back to their desks, but Adeline stayed put. "What's gonna happen to the body?"

"What?" Steve asked.

"Sandra's body. Do you know when the coroner is planning to release it?"

"He didn't mention it. Why?"

"She needs a funeral. She needs to be put to rest."

He sighed. "I'm sure her family—"

"Her parents are gone. She was an only child. She was divorced and didn't have kids, but she had people who cared about her. People who'll miss her and want to say goodbye." She looked away for a few moments to prevent herself from getting agitated. "She needs to be buried. She deserves that much."

"I don't disagree."

"Then, what's the problem?"

"There's no problem with what you've said. The issue lies in what I think you're gonna say next. Which is that you'll pay for the funeral if no one else will. Am I right?"

"Maybe." She crossed her arms.

"And that offer, on its own, isn't an issue. But I need you here, using your knowledge of witchcraft to help find her killer. News of this is gonna spread. It might cause a panic. When people panic, the politicians get involved and muck everything up," he said. "Her funeral will need to wait."

"I don't know what the symbol we found painted on the wall is, and I know my own book collection. Nothing I own contains dark magic or sheds any light on practicing such dark magic. I won't find the answers I need here."

"What does that have to do with a funeral?"

"I know other witches in Harlan County, ones who might know about dark magic, or at least might be able to give me some insight on the matter." The coven didn't use dark magic, but Mary might still know something about it. "They know things I don't and have gone through things I've never experienced. A funeral gives me a good reason to return to Evarts. And wouldn't it be a wonderful stroke of luck if I happen to run into some witches I know while I'm there? No one would find a chance encounter suspicious." She paused. "Also, there's a chance her killer will come to her funeral."

"Why on earth would they do that?"

"Maybe to get some sick satisfaction from it. Maybe they'd attend because it's what's expected. When someone dies, you go pay your respects. Evarts is a small town, so when someone misses a funeral, people take notice. Anyone who doesn't come will look like they're hiding something."

He leaned back in his chair. "All right. Have the funeral. Let me know when it is. I'll send someone with you, to get a second pair of eyes on other mourners."

Adeline walked out of his office and spent the rest of the day planning a funeral for a woman she barely knew.

***

The following day, Adeline headed to Evarts as soon as she was awake enough to drive. She skipped checking in at the office, seeing no point in going into work only to immediately leave to head to Kentucky.

The chest pain that struck as she drove over the county line was so intense that she had to pull over or risk losing control of her car. It took her a few seconds to recover from the sensation before merging back into the flow of traffic along the state route.

Dressed down in jeans and a comfortable jacket, she visited the funeral home to finalize plans for Sandra's service first. Then, after plenty of people had seen her around town, she drove towards the mountains via a different route than she'd taken for her last visit. Finally, she parked at a convenient look-out spot before hiking the rest of the way into the hills to where her Aunt Mary and cousins lived.

"We knew you'd be back," David said as he looked up from the fence post he was repairing. "I don't think anyone expected you back so soon, though."

"I didn't think I'd be back already, but I need to talk to your mama about a few things. Where can I find her?"

"The house hasn't moved." He looked over his shoulder to the small cabin Mary had lived in for the last forty years before returning to his chores.

Adeline knocked on the door and waited for Mary to yell that the door was open before walking in. The interior of the cabin hadn't changed since she was a child. The door opened into a sitting room, with a small kitchen and a hallway leading to bedrooms further into the house. The older woman walked out of one of the bedrooms as Adeline closed the front door.

"I didn't think you'd be back already. I thought you'd need more time."

"And I do. I'm not here for me."

"That makes more sense. Go on and sit down." She glanced at a sofa in the middle of the room. "I've got the feeling we're about to have a long conversation. I have some sweet tea, if you're interested."

"Thank you." Adeline sat down and accepted the tea her aunt offered her. "There was a death on the edge of town four days ago. A murder. The victim was only a few years older than me. And her death was ... odd. Odd enough that witchcraft must be involved."

"The only witch that's come or gone from this mountain in the last week is you. So, if you're here looking for a suspect, you'd be the only plausible one."

"I'm not accusing you, or anyone here, of anything."

"It's only a matter of time before someone does. We get blamed sooner or later any time someone around here dies, if they're young or they weren't sick. It's been that way for years." She sighed. "You're here because of how she died then?"

"Yes. Sandra's—the victim's—death was definitely supernatural. If witchcraft killed her, which looks pretty damn likely, it would have to be dark magic. I'm wondering what you can tell me about it, what you know."

Mary pursed her lips and her eyes narrowed. She then closed her eyes and let out a deep breath, and when she opened them, her expression became neutral. "I'd feel less insulted if you'd come here to accuse me of killing that girl. Are you accusing me of practicing dark magic? Of tainting my Gift in such a manner?"

"I wasn't – I don't – I know you wouldn't touch dark magic, or associate with anyone who practiced it. I remember the warnings my mama gave me. But you must've heard things about it. There has to be something you can tell me, things I don't already know." She took a deep breath. When that didn't calm her nerves, she took a sip of the tea. "I want to find the person who killed that woman. I want to get justice for her. And I want to stop feeling this pervasive sadness that's consuming me right now because the land itself is mourning her death."

Mary's brow furrowed. "You can feel the sadness of the land?"

"Yes. I felt it when we found her body and again today when I drove into town. There's this ache inside of me that isn't mine." She knew the emotions weren't her own, but knowing that didn't make experiencing Harlan's sadness any easier.

"We'll have a lot to talk about, regarding your own craft, when you're ready. Since that's not why you're here today, I'll refrain from inundating you with questions. Turning back to the woman who died, why do you assume dark magic was involved?"

"She was killed in her kitchen, which was covered in blood. She had no defensive wounds, and her chest was torn open while she was still alive, according to the medical examiner. It didn't appear to have been an animal. Her lungs were missing; some form of black magic is the most likely explanation. We found a weird symbol drawn at the crime scene, too. It looked like a sigil of some kind, but I haven't been able to find it in any of the books I own."

"What did the sigil look like?" When Adeline showed Mary the photo she'd taken, the older woman took the phone from her to get a better look at it. She handed back her phone shortly and commented, "I don't recognize this symbol either. I'm afraid I don't know much about the darker branches of witchcraft."

"Please, tell me what you can, no matter how little it is. It's better than nothing." The more answers Mary could provide, the less indebted Adeline would be to Alexei later. "I have to find whoever did this, and the symbol's the best lead I have."

"You've described the aftermath of dark magic. The blood and viscera you saw make that clear. The practice goes against nature itself, and the price a person must pay for using dark magic is steeper than using any other kind of magic. It's also addictive, which is what makes it so dangerous."

"And the symbol?"

"I don't know. It might have something to do with dark magic, or it could be a distraction. Something to unsettle or unnerve the person who found the body."

Adeline was quiet for a minute. It wasn't the answer she'd hoped for, but it was better than stumbling around learning how inadequate her own knowledge of dark magic was. Another thought dawned on her. "When I was younger, my mama said she could feel it whenever I used my magic. She died before I was old enough to learn if she was making that up—"

"She wasn't. Since your magic stems from the same source as hers, she could feel the push and pull of it at work. If she'd lived longer, she would've taught you to do it."

She leaned forward. "What about you? Can you feel it?"

"Yes, it's how I know you did two spells a few days ago. You were too far away for me to know what they were, but I felt you harness the ancestral power. One felt like a nature spell, and the other I couldn't pin down at all. If you were within a mile or two of here when you did it, I would've been able to tell you the exact spells."

"Then you wouldn't have felt anyone using dark magic a few days ago to kill Sandra." She slumped back into the couch cushion.

"No, I'm afraid I couldn't sense that. You know that ancestral magic cannot be used to commit such an atrocity. Neither of us could sense dark magic being performed unless we witnessed it. I'm sorry."

"It's not your fault. Things like this aren't supposed to happen here." She stood to leave but paused at the sink after setting down her empty glass. "The chest pains you and I've been getting—I've noticed they've gotten worse. And I didn't tell you when I was here for Edith's party, but Sandra died the night you said the intensity of the pain woke you up."

"You knew that night that there'd been a murder, suspected it had been caused by dark magic, and didn't tell me? Why not?"

"I wanted to reconnect with my family and not ruin the party. And part of me still hoped I was wrong, and it wasn't dark magic." She responded, raising her arms in a placating manner. "I'll tell you next time, but that's not why I mentioned it. When did you say the pain started?"

"A few weeks before you returned." Mary tapped her fingers against her knee. "Which supports your theory about the pain being a warning. If your killer was practicing on stray animals before testing their power on a human, the darkness would start to taint the land and the ancestors would want to warn us. There's a body count now, which means more darkness and more danger. And it would become more necessary for someone to act."

"Except they didn't practice on strays."

"What?"

"Elijah was calling me repeatedly during my last few weeks in Seattle. He said it was because something felt off and that I was needed here. A few weeks ago, crops down in town started going bad. Then, suspicious livestock deaths began. Pigs and a cow got ripped apart by something, just like Sandra." She took a deep breath. "And right when that started, you started getting chest pains."

"That's telling."

"It certainly is." She nodded, lost in thought. "The information you want to tell me about my Gift, could any of it be used to find who killed Sandra?"

"Unfortunately, no. Given how magically different ancestral magic and dark magic are, it would be like asking a botanist how to perform brain surgery."

***

Adeline spotted a vehicle parked next to her car as she made her way down the mountain. When she got closer, she saw that it was Jakob's, and he was leaning against it with his arms crossed.

"What are you doing here?" she asked him.

"I was supposed to go with you to visit your aunt so you could ask her about dark magic, but it seems you beat me to it. Steve's annoyed you came here without backup. Don't be surprised if you get a lecture next time you're in the office."

"I didn't need backup; they're my family. Besides, you've gone up to see them on your own." She had nothing to fear from Mary or anyone else up in the hills. The thought of needing to bring reinforcements was laughable.

"Twice. I've gone up there twice on my own. Before that, they took me somewhere else, on a lower part of the mountain, to talk." He looked up at the path she'd been walking down. "Did she tell you anything you didn't already know?"

"I described the crime scene to her, and she agreed it was dark magic then confirmed the murderer had to pay a steep price to kill her in that way. She didn't have much insight to share beyond that. At least, none relevant to the murders." At the look of confusion he gave her, she continued. "We talked briefly about my Gift, too."

"How hard did you press her for answers?"

"As much as I could without her getting pissed off and telling me to leave. When I showed up asking about a murder, it put her on edge. When I mentioned dark magic, she felt insulted. I had to tread lightly."

"Maybe I should give it a shot." He turned and took a step towards the woods.

"If you go up there, you might not make it back down the mountain."

"I'd make it back. Like I said, I'm not easy to kill." He glanced over at her.

"You're an outsider. They're not gonna share much with you, no matter how you ask."

"They haven't had a problem talking to me before."

"Yes, but I'm one of them, and you're not." She fought the urge to cringe. "How important were the conversations you had with them anyway? Because there's a world of difference between you asking basic questions about how the community's doing, and you asking anything to do with witchcraft. You've said yourself that witches are pretty paranoid. I guarantee that if you go up there, as soon as you ask about witchcraft, they'll say that they'll only talk to me about it."

He stood there for a moment and tapped his fingers against his hipbone a few times before speaking. "As you said, you're one of them. You know them better than I do. If you believe Mary told you everything she knew, I won't argue otherwise."

"Great. Let's go then. There's no need to stay here." She started her car and drove off, not waiting to make sure that he followed.

About halfway to the office, Adeline pulled over at a roadside diner. Jakob parked alongside and was a few steps behind her as she walked into the restaurant and sat down at a booth.

"What are we doing here?" he asked as he slid into the seat across from her.

"Eating. I'm hungry, and it's close to lunchtime." She pulled a menu out from behind the napkin dispenser and started looking it over. "You can go back to the office if you want. I'll head straight there once I'm done."

"No, I'll stay. I'm not exactly eager to get back to the office and drown in files." He grabbed his own menu.

A waitress came by, and Adeline got a burger and fries while Jakob ordered pork chops and eggs.

"You realize I'm your partner, right?" Jakob asked, breaking the strained silence that had built after the waitress walked off. "Steve's not formal enough to put it in writing, but we're partners."

"I know."

"That means you're supposed to trust me."

"Why should I? You don't trust me, and that door swings both ways." She leaned forward. "You know plenty about me. I don't know anything about you, and every time I ask, you dodge the question. Am I that intimidating? Or do you have something to hide?"

"Ask me a question, then. But for every question you ask me, I get to ask you one. Just to keep it fair. And we each get a veto." He leaned forward so he could look into her eyes. "But only one."

"Fine by me. I'm an open book." She didn't break their eye contact. "How'd you wind up working for Steve?"

"I needed a job after I got discharged from the army. The Chancellor's office was the only place to give me a shot."

"Why were they—?"

"Nope, it's my turn. Why'd you leave Seattle?"

"My ex-partner decided to screw me over one last time, so I couldn't stay working for the Alliance, and I didn't have anything keeping me there after that." She paused. "It's odd that this job was the only one you could get. A lot of government agencies would kill to hire someone like you."

"That's not a question."

"I'm getting there. The only reason I can think of why the government would pass you over for another candidate is if you'd done something questionable. Something that couldn't be ignored." She leaned in even more, before pulling back slightly when she realized how close their faces were. "Did you get discharged for doing something you shouldn't have?"

"No, it was a medical discharge." He broke eye contact and slumped his shoulders, leaning back in his seat. "How did your old partner screw you over?"

"Nothing was ever his fault. Any mistakes were because of me, or that's what Dominic told everyone. I'm not perfect by any means, but I didn't mess things up nearly as often as he did. Anyway, he had this delusion that I was holding him back. He once told someone that if he wanted to, he'd be the Steward of Washington. Even though he's younger than both of us, ignorant of a lot of things, and extremely unlikable. He was that cocky about how smart and special he is."

Jakob snorted. "Yeah, I know the type. Guys who think they're some big badass when that couldn't be further from the truth."

"Oh really? Tell me about yours."

"Finish your story first and maybe I will." He smirked. "Dominic had an ego, but that doesn't answer my question about how he screwed you over."

"I was hoping you wouldn't realize that." She wrapped her arms around her stomach. "Our last assignment, things didn't go according to plan and someone died. He pinned the blame on me again, even though he was the one who escalated the situation while I tried to calm things down. A woman fell to her death, and her body wasn't even cold before he went running to Gabriel, our boss's boss, to demand a new partner."

"Every time you talk about the Alliance, it seems like you don't like anyone involved. Why work for them?"

"I kind of stumbled into it. A druid friend of mine, a girl I went to college with, asked for help with a ritual. Word of me got around to some higher-ups within the Alliance, and they offered me a job. I didn't think I had other options given what I am."

"Meaning?"

"Do you know how the Arcane Codex defines a witch? A person born with the innate ability to harness magic drawn from the cosmos. That's the only option: your magic has to come from the stars. The fact that I don't fit that definition made some high-ranking people within the Alliance antsy. If I'm not a witch as defined by the Codex, am I still subject to those laws? No one ever said it outright, but my choices were to work for the Alliance or leave Seattle. I didn't have anywhere else to go except back here, and I wasn't ready for that yet."

"So, they took advantage of you being on your own and swooped in to offer you a job as a way of controlling you. And you were too young to realize it."

"Sums it up pretty well," she said. "Kind of shitty of them in hindsight and stupid of me not to notice. I want to smack my twenty-two-year-old self in the head sometimes."

"I know the feeling." He gave her a sympathetic smile. "Uncle Sam got the entirety of my twenties because I signed them away at eighteen for some nebulous opportunity that becoming a soldier was supposed to give me."

"And look at you now." The waitress returned with their food, and Adeline picked up her burger once they were alone again. "You asked three questions."

"You still answered them. Now I owe you three, so fire away."

"Are you psychic? Because I don't buy your explanation that it was a lucky guess that you knew about the blood."

"No, I'm not psychic. The blood was either hers or the killer brought it, and bringing the blood didn't make any sense. It didn't fit the rest of the scene. Next question."

"I don't have anything else I want to ask right now, and I don't want to ask basic things, like your favorite color or author."

"Green and J.R.R. Tolkien. Don't worry, I still owe you two." He cut into his food. "Why did you head up into the hills on your own?"

"I needed to talk to Mary, and I needed to make sure she'd tell me what I wanted to know."

He ate a bite of food before responding. "You think she would've lied if I'd been there."

"I don't know if she would've outright lied. She sees the Gift as a family matter, or at least she did when I was younger. Meaning the only people who should concern themselves with it or ask questions about it are people within the family. It's like I said before: you're an outsider, and I'm not. There was a chance she would've brushed us both off if you'd been there, and I was asking the kinds of questions we needed answers to."

"She could've pulled you away if what she needed to share was some great secret that I'm not allowed to know. Neither of us would've realized what she was doing," he said. "What did she have to say?"

Adeline peeked over her shoulder to verify the waitress was at the far end of the diner before turning back to Jakob. "No witch she knows does dark magic. She couldn't sense it being performed, which isn't what I hoped, but does make sense. She didn't recognize the symbol we spotted at the crime scene, either."

"So, the visit was a bust."

"Not exactly. Remember how I reacted that first time we drove into Harlan County?"

"Yeah. Being close to your ancestors made you start hyperventilating."

"That's not quite all that happened. Being home after so long away was over-whelming—that's true—but I've also been getting chest pains that get worse every time I cross over the county line," she said. "It was uncomfortable but manageable that first day. On the way here today it felt like someone was trying to rip my heart out. Mary feels it, too, and said it got worse the night Sandra died. We think her chest pains started when the killer began using dark magic; they would've had to practice on something to hone their skills, which explains the crop failures and animal deaths I told you about. The dark magic's been harming the land for weeks, but now that there's been a murder the magic's a bigger problem."

"Can that help us find the killer? This sensation or knowing it's impacting the land?"

"I don't know yet. Maybe I'll find out at Sandra's funeral if and when I run into her killer." She shrugged.

"Steve better send someone else to that with you, and not me," he said.

"You don't like funerals?"

"I've never seen the point, if I'm being honest. Funerals are for the living. The dead don't care if they're given one or not."

"Let's agree to disagree on that one."

His expression softened a little bit. He studied her for a moment before leaning forward. "Do you still – How is Harlan feeling today? Still sad?"

"No, not sad. Anxious. The feeling that I'm being watched keeps coming and going, but I know I'm not the one feeling it, if that makes sense."

"What do you think it means?"

"I have no idea."

Was the killer close by? Was she being watched? Would there be another killing? The anticipation felt almost as awful as seeing Sandra's body.

They finished their meal, paid, and left. Once Adeline was in Virginia she still felt uneasy, but the sensation wasn't as overwhelming. On her way back into Big Stone Gap, she stopped at home to throw some of her spell books into a box.

Walking into the office, she set the box down on her desk before clearing her throat to get everyone's attention. "I have good news, bad news, and worse news. Good news: Sandra definitely was killed by dark magic, so we know where to focus our attention."

"What's the bad news and the worse news?" Ned asked.

"Bad news: none of the Harlan witches practice dark magic, so they weren't able to tell me anything ground-breaking about it. Worse news: because dark magic is unnatural and violates the normal rules of witchcraft, it's tainting the land itself. My chest pains will likely continue to worsen due to my connection to the land until we catch the killer."

"You didn't say anything about chest pains before now," Steve said in alarm.

"They aren't constant, and I didn't know what was causing them until today."

"I need to go make some calls." He ran an agitated hand through his hair. "Keep me updated." He walked into his office and closed the door.

"What are those?" Ned asked, eyeing the stack of old books Adeline had taken out of the box on her desk.

"Some of the spell books I've acquired over the years. I bought some of them, and others were given to me."

The only grimoire she'd left at home was the one she'd inherited from her mother. It was too valuable to her to risk anything damaging it, and it was so specific to ancestral magic that only another ancestral witch could decipher it. She'd look through it in private later.

"I dug through them looking for that sigil we found on the wall of Sandra's house, but came up short. Now, I'm looking for the spell that could've killed her, which means taking another look at each one."

Adeline spent the afternoon looking through the collection. Occasionally, she would find a spell that called for blood or some kind of animal sacrifice, but the books didn't contain any spell that explained what had happened to Sandra.

CHAPTER 11

— • —

Three days later, Adeline stood in Elijah's house as mourners arrived for Sandra's wake. The coroner had released her body the day before, and the funeral service had occurred earlier at a small church twenty minutes outside of Evarts. The burial that immediately followed had been a short, quiet affair.

Ned had attended the funeral to be an extra set of eyes, but she convinced him to go home afterward. He was an outsider, and Adeline needed everyone at the reception to feel comfortable enough to let their guards down if she was going to get the answers she wanted.

"Remind me why we're doing this again," Elijah said as he spotted the first car drive up towards the house. "And why we're doing it here."

"Sandra didn't have a lot of people in her life, so I offered to organize a reception for her, and you agreed to let me use the house rather than have to rent a space." She wrapped her black sweater around her midsection. "I need to see who comes, who doesn't, and who's acting weird."

"People will think she and I were involved," he scoffed, looking uncomfortable at the thought. He fiddled with his tie for a moment. "Which isn't something I'm too keen about."

"I told anyone who asked that I was an old friend and wanted to do this for Sandra. A few people might think I'm covering for you, but most won't think about it twice. Everyone wins."

"Except Sandra, who shouldn't be dead."

"That goes without saying. By hosting the wake, you might help me find her killer and get justice for her."

Wyatt Dunn and his sister-in-law, Joan, were the first to arrive, walking in and giving the siblings a subdued greeting. Before much time had passed a crowd had gathered both inside the house and out on the front lawn. Adeline stuck by her brother at first, but then he got called away.

Adeline and Joan were reminiscing about the latter's late husband, who had died six months earlier, when Adeline overheard her own name.

"Adeline came back for Sandra's funeral, but not her daddy's," Dolores Beckett commented to her friend, Kimberly Ransom, loudly enough for the whole room to hear. The old bat had lived down the road from the Coburns for as long as Adeline could remember, and had never been fond of her.

"There's something wrong with kids these days."

Adeline felt several sets of eyes on her. She turned slightly to face the women who were talking. "Yes, I missed my father's funeral. Today isn't about John or me. This event is supposed to be about celebrating Sandra's life."

"Today is about Sandra, yes," Dolores conceded. "It doesn't make what you did any less wrong. He was your father, and you couldn't be bothered to come lay him to rest."

"I wasn't here, but Elijah was. He made sure our daddy got the send-off he deserved. Maybe missing the funeral was a mistake; maybe it wasn't. Either way, it's about eleven years too late for me to do anything about that," she retorted. "I wasn't here then, but I'm here now."

"Well, two days after you came back, someone turned up dead."

Her heartbeat spiked, and she forced herself to take a few deep breaths to calm herself before she did something inappropriate, like scream at the woman or place a hex on her. "Mrs. Beckett, if I didn't know better, I'd think you were accusing me of something. I know you'd never be intentionally hurtful, especially in my family home. You're welcome to leave if my presence makes you uncomfortable."

She turned to Joan and ignored Mrs. Beckett's sputtering at her comment. "I'm gonna get some air. I'll have to catch up with you later."

Adeline walked onto the porch, but even after she'd stepped outside, she felt like too many people were watching her. She moved around to the side of the house and stood there for a few minutes trying to calm herself before she returned to hosting.

She was turning the corner toward the backyard and the kitchen door when she bumped into someone. "Sorry."

"No need to apologize. It was my fault," the man she'd run into said. "Wow, Adeline, I can't believe it's you."

"Do I know you?" She looked him over. He was taller than her at around six feet and muscular. His dirty-blond hair fell in neat waves and his blue eyes stood out against tanned skin.

"It's Dale. Dale Blevins."

"That's not possible. The kid I knew was – Well, you've certainly grown since I last saw you." She couldn't quite reconcile the man in front of her with her memory of the boy she used to babysit.

"Last time you saw me, I was in kindergarten. I hope I don't look the same." He scratched his chin sheepishly.

"You don't. How have you been?"

"Good. I've been good. I can't believe you're back."

"I'm not back in Evarts specifically, but I'm not far from here." She heard Elijah call for her. "I should go see what my brother needs. It's good to see you."

She continued on her way but stopped when she realized everyone else was in the front yard or inside. When she turned around to ask Dale why he'd been in the backyard alone, he was nowhere in sight.

She wanted to let the incident go, ignore that Dale had been somewhere no one was supposed to be, but the investigator in her refused to head inside until she had an answer.

"It's only paranoia if it's unfounded. If it's not unfounded, it's being smart and having good survival instincts," she reminded herself as she began to search the area.

A yard from the backdoor, she saw the familiar brown of a cigarette butt lying in the grass. With a sigh, she picked it up to throw away and walked into the house.

***

Adeline couldn't see Elijah when she entered the kitchen. She did a circuit of the ground floor to ask a few people if they'd seen him, but no one had. She wandered back into the kitchen, in case he'd gone in there while she was looking for him. It was the only room on the ground floor that was empty. Rather than continue to look for him, she decided to let him find her. She leaned against the counter and pulled out her phone.

"So, you study cults now," someone said from the doorway, causing her to jump. Wyatt Dunn was standing there. "Sorry, I didn't mean to startle you."

"Wyatt, stop sneaking up on me! That's the second time you've done that."

"It wasn't my intention." He stayed in the doorway. "As I was saying, you investigate cults, which I wasn't expecting. I was surprised when Paul Lee told me about seeing you at the crime scene. Weren't you always going on and on about how you were gonna become a big hotshot lawyer?"

"That was the plan. Then I got to college and realized I didn't like my pre-law classes all that much. They were about as engaging as watching ice melt. Sociology fascinated me, and that led to me studying topics from folklore to new religious movements. No one calls them cults anymore, by the way. The term has a bloody, tragic history."

"They can change the name all they want; it doesn't change what they are. Calling a horse a duck don't make it one." He paused. "You think Sandra was killed by a cult?"

"I don't know. The sheriff thinks it's a possibility, or else he wouldn't have asked my firm to get involved."

"Your firm. It sounds so fancy. You talk like you ain't from around here anymore." He took a step towards her. His dark eyes met hers, and she found herself unable to break eye contact with him. "I know you, Adeline Coburn, better than you think, and more than you want to admit. You're just as much of a hillbilly as everyone else here. Running away can't change that. No matter how deep you try to bury your roots, they can't stay hidden for long. You might've forgotten where you come from, but the rest of us remember."

"I didn't forget, and I'm not trying to hide shit about my past or myself. I just know where I'm from doesn't define my whole life. Some folks don't understand, though, and I guess you're one of them. You done trying to goad me into an argument, or are we gonna have a problem?"

She scoffed when he didn't reply. "People wonder why I stayed away for so long. Behavior like yours is one of my many reasons for not coming back sooner."

"It was a really shitty thing you did, leaving like that. We weren't friends, and I wasn't hurt by it, but you can't fault people for being mad at you for it. Did anyone get a goodbye?"

"Elijah did. I wasn't expecting anyone else would miss me that much. It took Johnny a few days to realize I'd left. If my own father didn't even miss me, why would anyone else? And, for a man who claims he doesn't care about the past, you seem determined to make me rehash my choices."

"That's not what I'm getting at. It makes no difference to me what you did or why. I just want you to understand why some people here might not be too happy about your return."

He walked off, letting the door close behind him. Adeline stood there for a moment, wondering why he'd felt the need to say that. She'd already had a few people make snide comments about her absence or her coming back. He'd told her something she already knew. She was about to walk out of the kitchen when she heard someone talking in hushed tones on the other side of the door.

"I'm not accusing her of anything, but she has always been odd," a woman's voice remarked.

"Maybe she learned it from her mother. Lilah was a bit odd too," a man responded.

"She's been dead a long time. She should've outgrown her mother's ... quirks by now."

"You remember what they always said about Lilah, Eve, hell, that whole family."

Their voices faded to a murmur as Adeline focused on staying composed. It would be easy for her to lose control right now. She could ignore comments about herself, but comments about her deceased mother were unfair. She noticed her fists were clenched. She uncurled her fingers as she tried to calm herself.

"I really don't understand how the two of them turned out so differently." The man sighed. "Elijah so normal, and his sister so—"

"Have either of you seen Addy?" Elijah's voice cut in.

"I can't say that I have." There was a pause. "Oh, let me get out of your way."

She heard footsteps, and then the door to the kitchen swung open as Elijah walked in. He took two steps into the room and stopped when he saw his sister.

"Why are you holed up in here?"

"I'm not exactly welcome out there." She removed a plate from the drying rack next to the sink and put it in one of the cabinets, turning her back to him. "I wasn't expecting – I knew some folks were – The hostility caught me by surprise."

"Hostility?"

"Before you cut in, whoever was standing right outside the door had plenty to say about Mama and I, and about how abnormal we are." She grabbed another two plates and put them away.

"I told you that people still talked about you and Mama."

She spun to face him. "Hearing 'I told you so' isn't very helpful right now." She gave up on putting dishes away and started to pick up some discarded wrappers on the counter. "I thought you meant only a few people."

"It's not everyone. It's just because you're back and no one knows why, so they're speculating. It'll die down. Who gives a shit what Mrs. Beckett or Lou Winter think anyway?"

"That was Lou? The man who was talking right outside the door? Lou, my old boss at the diner?" The wrapper Adeline was holding caught fire. "Crap." She dropped it into the sink and turned the faucet on.

"Addy, did you mean to do that?"

She didn't say anything for several moments. "It doesn't matter. Let's just get through the next few hours. People will start to head home soon." Adeline pasted a smile on her face and walked out of the kitchen.

"Adeline Coburn, I always wondered what happened to you," a man called from the doorway of the dining room.

Adeline's gaze, and the gazes of several others, turned towards the voice. A blonde man roughly her age stood in the doorway. With a few steps, he crossed the room to approach her.

She recognized him as Troy Perkins. He'd been the star quarterback in high school and the boy everyone in Evarts was rooting for to find big success somewhere after graduating. She, along with most of the girls in town, had had a crush on him when she was younger.

"Hi, Troy." She took him in. His hair was cut short. He'd lost some of his boyish good looks. He wasn't as muscular as she remembered him being, but he had clearly been taking care of himself or his job kept him in shape.

"Good, you remember me. I was hoping you would." His confident demeanor turned awkward. "Can we talk?"

"Sure." She walked out onto the porch, not looking back to see if he followed. She took a seat in one of the chairs and waited. "So, how have you been?"

"Good. I've been good. What about you? I heard you moved to Seattle?" He fidgeted as he talked.

"I did. After college I moved out there for work."

"You went to college? What was that like?" Troy said, taking a seat.

"Wouldn't you know?" She raised an eyebrow. "Your mama told everyone she saw about your scholarship to University of Kentucky for a whole month after you got accepted."

"I dropped out during my first year. Football was going fine, but I couldn't – There were too many other things I had to juggle, and I couldn't do it," he admitted. "Been working for my father ever since."

"I'm sorry to hear that. But being an electrician's a pretty good job."

"It's not what I wanted, though. I was gonna be a doctor." A dark look crossed his face. "But enough about me. When did you move back?"

"About a week ago."

"Why? And why after so long? I remember a lot of people didn't think you'd ever come back."

"I was offered a job, so I took it." She shrugged. "I missed Kentucky. I missed Elijah. I ... It was time for me to come back."

"And did you move here by yourself?" His tone had the forced feeling of someone trying to sound casual. She raised an eyebrow. "Not with a boyfriend or a husband, I mean."

"Nope. I'm single."

"Will you have dinner with me?"

Adeline was stunned for a second. It took a moment for her to wrap her head around the words that had just left his mouth. "Troy Perkins, I know you're not hitting on me at a funeral."

"Should I take that as a no?"

"Yes, it's a no. If you want to ask someone on a date, don't do it at a funeral. It's not the right time or place for that."

"You're right. It's not. I just ... I had such a crush on you in school. And I spent all these years wondering—"

"Now's also not the time to tell me any of this," she interrupted. "Can you please wait and tell me this on a different day?"

"I suppose that's for the best." He relented, jumping to his feet. "I don't want to embarrass myself any further. I'll – I should go." He walked down the porch steps and got into his truck.

***

While not many people would talk to her, almost everyone would forget Adeline was there if she didn't draw attention to herself. Doing so gave her ample opportunity to eavesdrop and observe how people were acting.

She sorted the attendees into different groups. The easiest to identify, and sadly the smallest group, consisted of true mourners. A handful of people, mainly women about five years older than Adeline, appeared to be truly distraught over Sandra's death. Their eyes were red, and they often had to wipe or blow their noses. They reminisced amongst themselves, gathered in one corner of the sitting room.

The second group were people who were there because they were nosy. They claimed they wanted to celebrate Sandra's life, but their behavior didn't line up with those statements.

"I can't believe Sandra's gone," Ian Beckett, a former classmate of Adeline's, said.

"I know. It's such a tragedy." Debra Hawkins, the daughter of the sheriff and another former classmate, shook her head. "I can't believe Adeline's back after this long."

"I heard she was gone so long 'cause she was in prison."

"I heard that, too, and asked my daddy about it, and he said there was no record of her ever being arrested or serving time. Anywhere." She sighed. "It's a damn shame Elijah's the only one who knows where she's been or why she's back."

"All he'd tell me was she moved back for work. But if that's the case, why now?"

The other conversations Adeline overheard from this particular group were in the same vein. People would say the right things, comment about how sad Sandra's death was, but soon enough they'd devolve into gossiping about some neighbor's affair or rumors about someone's son being on drugs. Or, of course, Adeline's return.

The third and final group were the people Adeline didn't know how to categorize. They weren't truly distraught by Sandra's death, but they weren't focused on gossip either. Some seemed antsy, others tired. A few were a little too interested in talking about Sandra's death.

"I heard Sandra's house looked like something out of a horror movie," a young man, around eighteen or nineteen, said to his friend. "Sounds kinda awesome. Wish I could've seen it."

"I know. Sad she died and all, but it's about time something finally happened around here."

"Celebrating someone's death is an awfully shitty thing to do," another man said, cutting into their conversation. He was a few years older than Adeline.

"Folks hear you talking like that, they might think you have something to do with it."

"We were just talking, is all."

"Find something else to talk about, before someone overhears you and mentions what you've been saying to your mamas. I don't think either of 'em would be happy."

"I'm an adult," said the boy who started the conversation, puffing out his chest.

"That don't mean shit. She's still your mama," the older man said. "Or should I go pull her away from the conversation she and Joan Dunn are having so you can tell her that since you're an adult now, you can say what you want and don't have to listen to her?"

The two younger men walked away, muttering under their breath. Their mamas wouldn't care if they were eighteen or eighty; they'd drag them out by the ear for talking like that.

"And the Blackburn family's self-righteousness strikes again," a bald man from across the room said. "You don't have to be such a dick, Ryan."

"Someone's dead," Ryan replied. "Saying the scene of her death sounded cool, or being happy something 'interesting' happened around here is a shitty thing to say."

"Never said it wasn't." The bald man turned back to the conversation he'd been having.

"It wasn't a death. It was a murder," another man said. He looked to be twenty-five, with black hair.

"Murder? What are you talking about, Chad?" Dale Blevins asked. "Thought she was killed by a wild animal."

"There's no way an animal did that to her," Chad said, looking out the window. His hand was shaking around his cup.

Adeline was seated on the couch in Elijah's living room, messing with her phone to appear busy, about four feet from where the two men were talking. Chad's comment made her pause. For him to say that, he had to have seen Sandra's body. She glanced over at him. His posture was guarded. He didn't shirk from the looks being sent his way, but his back was slightly hunched over, as if ashamed of something.

"That's right. You're the one who found her," Dale said. "I can't imagine what it must've been like, seeing that. Has the sheriff brought you in for questioning yet?"

"I was questioned, and he said I'm not a suspect." He met Dale's eyes. He was still tense and his body language indicated he was hiding something. Maybe he didn't kill Sandra, but someone's skeleton was hiding in his closet.

"That's good, I suppose. Unless he lied to you." Dale walked out of the house without another word. Adeline couldn't help but think he looked slightly pleased with himself just for a moment, despite the unsettling topic of conversation.

***

Eventually, people began to filter out, until the last people left were Zachary Lennox, his wife Charlotte, and their son Thomas, the clerk from the gas station. The teenager slumped in a living room chair, and his eyes were bloodshot.

"I'm sure you three want to head on home. We won't keep you any longer," Adeline said as sweetly as she could. She didn't want to be rude, but she was exhausted and wished they would leave already.

"Oh, but we didn't get a chance to catch up," Charlotte frowned.

"I don't live too far from here. We'll have to do it another time."

"Yeah, Addy's less than an hour away," Elijah said. He looked at his sister and picked up on what she was trying to do. "And it's been a long day."

"It certainly has. A long, sad day." Zachary turned to his wife. "We should go, Char. We've both got work in the morning." He turned back to the twins. "Good night."

The family left. Elijah waited to see their car drive off before turning his sister. "You should be careful around Charlotte Lennox."

"Why? She seems fine. Our talk was pleasant enough."

"She's been giving you strange looks all day. They're not angry, per se, but not friendly either."

"Why would she be doing that?" She had some memories of Charlotte from high school, but nothing stood out. As far as she remembered, the two of them had gotten along just fine when they were growing up, but hadn't been friends.

"I don't know. I'm just telling you what I saw. And what I remember from when you left." She frowned and said nothing, so he elaborated. "Charlotte was one of the folks who spread rumors about you after you were gone."

"It's been over fifteen years. Whatever her issue with me might've been, I'm sure she's forgotten it by now." She shrugged and went back into the house, with her brother following after her. "Have the hills had anything to say today?"

"Nothing new. They seem sad. They seem anxious. I wake up and I'm filled with this dread. I – Never mind." He refused to look at her.

"No, don't tell me 'never mind.'" She reached for his arm. "What is it?"

"I have this strange, sinking feeling that Sandra's death is only the beginning. Can't say why I feel that way, but that's what my gut is telling me."

"I hope your gut's wrong." She had the same feeling, and she was desperate for both of them to be overreacting. She looked around the messy kitchen, wanting something to distract herself. "I'll wash the dishes if you'll dry and take the trash out."

"Don't worry about it. You can head on out."

"No, I should help you clean up. This wake was my idea."

"And I'm saying that you don't have to. Go home." He started to fill the sink. "I'm sure your cat's wondering where you are."

"She'll be fine for a little bit longer."

"Addy, I'll handle it. I kinda – I want to be alone for a bit."

"Well, if you're sure. I don't want to overstay my welcome." She paused. "Call me tomorrow."

He gave her a thumbs up and turned his attention back to the washing up.

Once Adeline had returned home and greeted Whiskey, she wrote down everything she'd observed at the wake. Quite a few people had behaved suspiciously, and she wanted to keep a close eye on them over the next few days. Perhaps she'd ask Elijah to do the same.

CHAPTER 12

— · —

A deline was reading over Sandra Russett's file for what felt like the tenth time when her phone rang.

She was tempted to ignore it, but answering the call would give her an excuse to put down the report that identified the strange black powder they'd collected from the scene. It was a mixture of salt, coal dust, and a third, currently unspecified substance. Salt and coal dust weren't difficult to source in eastern Kentucky, so the powder was an unofficial dead-end until they learned what the third substance was. She hadn't found anything new in it yet, but she had reviewed it again in the hopes some detail would stand out to her this time.

She answered the phone after seeing who was calling. "Hey, Elijah, what's going on?"

"You don't hear her, do you? How can you not hear her? She's been screaming all morning." Elijah sounded out of breath and let out a groan of pain as he finished his sentence. "I can't get her to stop."

"Whose yelling do you hear? Harlan's?"

"Of course it's Harlan's, Addy! She's mad. She's real mad, and sad too. So, so sad. She ain't ever sounded like this before, not as long as she's been talking to me. You don't hear her?"

"No, I've never heard the voice you're talking about—"

"Adeline, Jakob, Rebecca," Steve called from the doorway of his office. He had a troubled look on his face. "I need to talk to you. Now."

"I have to go. I'll call you back later. I want to know what she's saying," Adeline promised before ending the call and heading into Steve's office.

Steve didn't even wait for Adeline to sit down before he started talking. "The Harlan County sheriff's office found another body this morning, and the scene's similar to Sandra Russett's. This time, the victim was a man named Derek Green."

"Do you have a picture?" Adeline asked.

He handed her a printout of a driver's license photo. "The sheriff sent one. You know him?"

She studied the image. Derek Green was an average-looking man. The only distinct thing about him, from what Adeline recalled, was a birthmark under his left eye. The birthmark wasn't as visible in his license photo, but she still spotted it.

"Sort of. Better than I knew Sandra Russett, anyway." Derek had worked at the Rock Ridge mine when Elijah dug coal there, years ago. "We've met."

***

Adeline was overcome with an avalanche of emotions as she made the drive to Evarts. It was becoming uncomfortably routine. The sadness returned, causing tears to form in her eyes. Her heart pounded, and she gripped the steering wheel harder. Her breathing turned shallow as she adjusted to the whirlwind of feelings overtaking her.

Then, the chest pains hit her. She slammed on her brakes and shifted into park in the middle of the state highway, thanking the ancestors no one else was heading this direction. She clutched at her chest, trying to alleviate the feeling of an invisible fist squeezing her heart. Not only was the pain worse than before, but it seemed to be lasting longer. Reminding herself to take slow, deep breaths, she waited for it to subside.

A sound, one that had been teasing at the edge of her senses for several seconds, became clear. It was a voice, and the voice was calling her name.

"Adeline! Are you okay?" Rebecca asked from the passenger seat.

"I'm fine," she said, shaking off the experience. "Well, I'm not but I'll live." She put the car into gear and began driving. The only way to stop the pain permanently was to find the killer; there had been enough delays already.

Unlike after Sandra's death, Adeline couldn't put a name to the emotions she felt separate from Harlan's evident grief. Someone she knew—not simply knew of—had been murdered. She and Derek Green weren't friends, nor were he and Elijah, but she had spent a good deal of time with him. They'd been more than just passing acquaintances.

"Hmmm ..." Rebecca clearly was skeptical regarding Adeline's physical state, but instead of pressing further, she cast a long look Adeline's way before changing the subject "How well did you know the victim? And how did you know him?

"He worked in the same mine my brother did. They hung out outside of work sometimes, and he and his wife had us over for dinner a few times. I wouldn't call us friends; I didn't know him well enough for that, but I knew him. Why?"

"I wanted to be sure that you're not too close to this. If he was a relative or an ex-boyfriend, or even a lifelong friend, then I was going to say Jakob and I will handle the scene," she said. "But that's not the case, so it's a moot point."

"Is it too late to change my answer?"

An excuse, any excuse, to avoid the scene waiting for them was one she'd gladly take. The land was upset and lashing out, the crime scenes were too chaotic to make any sense of, and every instinct she had was telling her to run while she had the chance. Everything about this case rubbed her the wrong way.

"Yes, it's too late. Besides, you're the only witch in our office. Even if Steve officially took you off this case we'd still need your input on the witchcraft side of things."

She didn't have anything further to say, and Adeline wasn't in the mood to talk, so the rest of the drive was quiet. That left Adeline with plenty of time to consider the thoughts racing through her head.

It was hard to keep any of it straight, much less make sense of it. Given what Elijah said about Harlan begging for her to come home, would Sandra and

Derek still be alive if she'd left Seattle earlier? And why was Elijah the one the hills were talking to when he didn't have the Gift?

When they reached the Green residence, the same sheriff's deputy, Paul Lee, was waiting outside for them. He looked just as ready to be sick as he had last time.

"You can go ahead inside. He's in the front room." He pointed to the door without meeting anyone's eyes. "I'll call the coroner."

"Who found the body?" Rebecca asked.

"His wife Nina. She worked third shift last night and got home around eight this morning. She was distraught when we got here, so another deputy took her to get medical attention."

Jakob's SUV pulled up and parked beside Adeline's car a moment later. As he made his way towards the house, something about him seemed off. Even stranger, he stopped a few times to look off into the distance. Adeline wondered what he was looking for and hoped he wasn't expecting the killer to be lurking among the trees. They weren't that lucky.

The crime scene in the Greens' sitting room resembled the one at Sandra Russett's house enough for it to be clear that the two deaths were connected. Blood covered everything, from the furniture to the walls to the ceiling. Adeline thought there might've been even more blood at this scene than at the last one.

The only notable difference was the position of the body. Sandra had been found face down on the floor, with no obvious wounds. Derek Green was lying on his back, staring up at the ceiling. His chest gaped open, which distracted from the state of the rest of his body. It was a bloody, gory mess.

Adeline felt bile rise in her throat at the sight, to her own frustration. These scenes shouldn't affect her. She was supposed to be desensitized to blood and gore by now.

Rebecca hovered on the threshold and immediately started making notes. Adeline moved further into the room, careful to avoid the blood, and tried not to look at the victim's face too often. It was easier to pretend he was a stranger that way.

The same strange mountain symbol they'd seen at Sandra's house was painted on one of the walls, and there was another pile of dust on the floor. The pile looked just as out of place here as it had at the other crime scene. The same smell of rot and mold, stronger this time, lingered in the air.

"Did you find anything on what spell or ritual could do something like this?" Jakob asked Adeline as he took in the amount of blood and carnage in front of them.

"You know that I haven't. The blood?"

"I'd say it's all his." With that, Jakob turned and walked out of the house.

"What the hell was that about?" Adeline asked Rebecca, who shrugged and kept writing notes.

She rolled her eyes, made a comment about not wanting to be in the way when the coroner arrived, and left the house. Jakob was outside leaning against his truck, staring out in front of him.

"Are you good?"

"Fine." He clenched and relaxed his hands a few times as he spoke.

"The scene in there was—"

He looked past her, towards the road leading up to the house. "I've seen worse. A lot worse."

She crossed her arms. "If you've seen worse, how come you were in such a hurry to leave the house?"

"You don't want to know. Trust me." His eyes seemed far too old for a man who wasn't much older than thirty.

"If I didn't want to know, I wouldn't have asked." She would've ignored his comment and odd behavior if they weren't standing outside of a murder scene. The surroundings made everything feel that much more ominous. Perhaps she was giving in to paranoia, but something wasn't adding up with him. "What don't I want to know?"

"You wouldn't understand. Forget I said anything." Jakob yanked open the driver's side door of his truck so hard that Adeline was surprised he didn't damage it, then got into the vehicle. "See you back at the office."

"Where are you going?"

He didn't answer as he closed the door and drove off. The coroner arrived with the crime scene technicians as she watched him drive away.

Rebecca came out of the house when the CSIs arrived and approached Adeline. "Jakob left already?"

"Yeah. Said he'd see us back at the office," she responded. "Was he acting weird? Or was it just me?"

"He didn't seem weird to me."

With nothing else to do at the crime scene, they decided to return to the office, too. About half an hour into the drive, the quiet became too much for Adeline. She needed to think about something other than the bloody crime scene they'd just left.

"I never really asked you what your story is, which was rude of me. How did you wind up knowing about all this?"

"A vampire tried to kill my sister," Rebecca answered. "It's hard to say the supernatural is all myths and stories after you walk in on something that shouldn't exist feeding on someone you know. Once I learned the truth, I couldn't unlearn it. I started to track him down—the vampire who attacked her, which others noticed. It ruffled some feathers, and after the dust settled, I wound up being offered a job as a Guardian."

"Did you report the attack? Leaving out the vampire part, the human police—"

"I knew they wouldn't believe me." There was a hardness in her voice. "They would've written me off, thinking I was trying to cause trouble. I had to search for him on my own."

"Did you find him? Is your sister okay?" she asked. Rebecca didn't answer and wouldn't look at her. Her sister appeared to be an off-limits topic, so she moved on. "What about Jakob? What's his story?"

"I don't know. I haven't asked. I think Steve has, but I don't know if he got a real answer." She pursed her lips. "Jakob seems to know more about the supernatural world than anyone else I've met. I don't know if he's human or not, and part of me wonders if it even really matters as long as his quirks don't cause a problem. Was Derek Green at Sandra's funeral?"

"I didn't see him there, but he might've attended. I'll ask Elijah if he saw him at some point." She had quite a bit to talk about with her brother already.

***

A vein in Steve's forehead threatened to bulge as Adeline, Jakob, and Rebecca told him about Derek Green's crime scene. The volume of blood and a few other elements, such as the strange mountain sigil and weird dust pile, enabled them to connect the murder with Sandra's.

"I know that no one's been sitting around twiddling their thumbs on this, but we need to solve it sooner rather than later," Steve said, crossing and uncrossing his arms. "Before the Steward of Kentucky or the Chancellor try to get involved. I respect them—hell, I voted for them both—but their involvement will muck things up."

"What would they even do? Other than tell us to find the killer, which we're already trying to do?" Jakob frowned. His anger seemed to have abated somewhat, and his posture was much more relaxed. "It's not as if politicians are qualified to investigate murders. Were either of them Guardians before taking office?"

"No, but they'll find an angle. We're lucky it's not an election year, or they'd already be breathing down our necks." He cleared his throat. "Was the victim missing his lungs, like Sandra was?"

"It was too bloody to tell one way or the other, but his chest was torn open and something had been done to his organs," Rebecca reported. "His death was definitely messier than Sandra's."

Steve turned his attention to Adeline. "Derek Green and Sandra Russett were both human?"

"As far as I know. They lived in Harlan County, as opposed to somewhere in Letcher County by the wolves or out in Somerset near the vampires. And they weren't witches or descended from witches." While it wasn't written in stone, supernatural beings nearly always lived with, or at least near, others of their kind, unless they were outcasts from their community. Adeline figured it was a survival method passed down from earlier, bloodier points in history.

"Can you think of any connection between the two of them?"

"No. Sandra was a year or two older than me, and Derek was a good decade older. They probably knew of each other, but didn't know each other. Other than being killed by the same person, I'm not sure what links them."

Steve leaned back in his chair and rubbed his chin a few times. "Rebecca, I want you to find out what you can about Derek Green; get Ned's help if you need it. Jakob and Adeline, I need you to go talk to Bartley and the werewolves."

"This wasn't them," Jakob said, his better mood evaporated.

"It wasn't a full moon last night, or the night Sandra was killed," Adeline said at the same time.

"I know." Steve's face became a neutral mask.

"Why are you sending us to talk to them, then?" Jakob pressed.

"So I can tell anyone who asks that we explored a possible connection and ruled it out. You're doing it so I can check a box saying you did it. Otherwise, the werewolves are gonna be the prime suspects if and when someone higher-up than me becomes part of this, because of how the bodies were found. Hopefully, Dylan understands, and if not, we'll smooth it over with her after we find the killer."

"Fine." Jakob clenched his jaw and glared at the wall for a few moments before turning to Adeline. "Let me know when you're ready to leave."

"I'm ready now. We might as well get the unpleasantness over with."

***

The pair made the drive from Virginia to the werewolves' territory in Letcher County in complete silence. They didn't even bother turning the radio on for background noise. Jakob's bad mood had permeated the air, and Adeline saw no purpose in trying to talk to him. She understood his anger at both what he was being asked to do and the flimsy reason why; she felt the same.

The werewolves were being questioned solely because they were wolves. Steve could call it being proactive all he wanted, but it didn't make this step in the investigation any less discriminatory.

They drove into the hills and stopped at the clearing where they'd met Dylan and Randall days earlier. This time, the wolves weren't waiting for them, so they sat in the truck until the werewolf leader appeared in the clearing, followed by a few other wolves.

"Hey, what brings you out here?" Dylan asked when she entered the clearing. She took in the expression on Jakob's face and her friendly smile dropped. "What is it? What happened?"

Jakob placed one hand on his hip and let out a sigh. "I need to ask you some questions. I'm not happy about it."

"Someone's dead, aren't they?"

"Two people. One last night, and the other about a week before that." Adeline said. "We don't think it was a werewolf and we know it wasn't a full moon, but—"

Dylan scoffed. "Funny how that never matters after a suspicious death." She crossed her arms. "Ask your questions."

"Do you recognize the names Sandra Russett or Derek Green?" Jakob asked.

"No. I've never heard of either of them. I'll ask around, but like I've told you, we keep to ourselves."

"Does anyone in the pack have witch ancestry of any kind?"

"No. You can't be a witch and a wolf. If you suspect witchcraft, why are you here?" She looked over Adeline. "Shouldn't you be questioning them?"

"We have, and we are." She tried to keep her voice level. Dylan's anger was understandable. Adeline wanted to go off on a tangent, to share her thoughts about this situation, but now wasn't the time or place. "No one with a brain thinks werewolves killed the victims, but if the Steward or the Chancellor involve themselves—"

"You just said no one thinks we're responsible," Randall said.

"I said no one with a brain, but they're politicians," she clarified, turning her attention back to Dylan. "We're asking because we want to rule you and your pack out as suspects."

Dylan stood there for a moment, saying nothing. Adeline wasn't sure if the other woman was searching for the right words, trying to control her emotions, or considering what they had said.

"Other factions love claiming that they're just as ostracized as we are. That they face the same struggles, the same prejudice, but it's a lie. Sure, humans would hate us all the same, and some would kill us just for existing, but I know you didn't go and ask anyone else if they know anything about what happened. Just like I know that this conversation won't mean anything if you don't find the killer soon." She bit out. "It hasn't mattered before. It won't matter now."

"I know you'll think I'm full of shit, but I'm angry that I was ordered to come here and ask." Jakob was about to say more, but stopped himself. "We'll be going now."

"I hope you find the killer you're looking for." The werewolves turned and walked off into the woods without further comment.

Jakob and Adeline got back into the truck and drove off. "That was a waste of time," he muttered.

"I agree, but I don't know what else we could've done," she replied. "If anyone outside the office got involved, the first group they'd ask about is the werewolves."

"It's bullshit that they're suspects when the victims were clearly killed by witchcraft. She's pissed, and she should be. And all the trust I've built up with Dylan and her pack over the last eleven months is gone now."

"You'll earn it back," she said. Looking out the window, she noticed he wasn't heading back the way they had come. "Where are you going?"

"Dylan had a point. Why are we only asking the wolves about what's happened? Any other supernatural being around is as likely to be behind the killings. So, let's go ask them about it."

"Fine." It wasn't fair to single out the werewolves. She didn't see the problem in asking the vily, vampires, or anyone else a few questions. "After all, if they've got nothing to hide, they won't have an issue answering our questions."

"Exactly."

***

Somerset was Jakob and Adeline's final stop to question supernatural creatures about the killings. While the werewolves had been shocked and angry about being questioned, the vily they spoke with had seemed mostly amused by the inquiry, citing how contradictory the murder was to their true nature. Alexei wouldn't take issue with their questions, but Adeline suspected other vampires would react similarly to the wolves.

It was mid-afternoon, so they let themselves into the house again, knowing most of the nest would be asleep. While the mansion was quiet, it wasn't as silently still as on their previous visit. Jakob led the way towards Alexei's office, and two voices became barely audible as they neared the closed door.

Suddenly, the office door was torn open and a blur ran into the hallway, coming to a stop about a yard in front of Adeline. Using her Gift, she created a flame in her palm, but didn't attempt to use it as a weapon yet. It was Tyler, the young vampire she'd met weeks ago, and he seemed agitated.

"What are you doing here?" He asked, eyeing the pair of Guardians.

"Selling cookies. What does it look like?" Jakob replied.

"I could kill you in the blink of an eye."

"You could certainly try." Jakob moved a few steps closer to Tyler. "It wouldn't end well for you, fledgling."

"Are you two done? Or do I have to use this to get you both to knock it off?" Adeline asked, waving around the hand that still held a flame. "Immolation's not gonna be as much fun as it sounds."

"While perhaps not entirely undeserved, the carpet is rather expensive and I would hate for your flames to damage it." Alexei stepped into the hallway.

"Tyler, you and I will finish our conversation later. You should try to get some rest." He then turned his attention to Jakob and Adeline. "Shall we?"

Tyler rushed off as Adeline doused the flame in her hand. She walked into Alexei's office a moment later and took a seat. "Should I ask what that was about?"

"Tyler's deathday is nearing and, given how young he is, this is a difficult time for him. He thought you overheard the rather private discussion he and I were having," Alexei explained. "I will not divulge more than that, other than to say he poses no threat and the entire nest is watching him closely." He leaned back in his chair. "An ancestral witch with the Sight. You are quite the curiosity, Adeline."

"What are you talking about?" Adeline didn't have the Sight. She couldn't see the future or perceive things others couldn't. "I don't have the Sight or any – I'm not psychic."

"It is happenstance, then, that you two came here of your own accord to speak with me within an hour of me deciding I should make contact with you."

"It's not happenstance." Jakob cut in. "We're here because there was another murder last night. The crime scene was worse than the first one. Your siblings, what did they say? What do they know?"

"The first two I spoke with knew very little, as they study magic but have not studied dark magic. They find it less compelling than more traditional magic," he said. "The next one I spoke with admitted to studying dark magic from a purely academic perspective. Then, my endeavor became somewhat more complicated. Many of my siblings are distrustful of technology and contacting them via a medium that prevents—"

"Get to the point," Adeline said. The longer Alexei had talked without saying anything of value, the more annoyed she became Her patience was nearing its end. "So far, you've said a lot of words, but nothing useful. And my home is under attack. People are dying, and we don't have time for this." She felt as if her inability to counteract the dark magic that killed Sandra had cost Derek his life; she couldn't let another person die.

"My apologies. I recognize I can be rather loquacious. I was attempting to give a thorough answer, not talking in circles. Many of my siblings make it intentionally difficult to contact them. I have only spoken to three of them. One of my sisters, Rosanna, informed me of a website, a ... black-market of sorts, on what she called 'the dark web' where dangerous spells are bought and sold without oversight. I would suggest looking into that while I continue my efforts."

Alexei passed along the information Rosanna had shared with him, and the Guardians left.

"We've got time for a stop in Evarts, right?" Adeline asked before Jakob had driven them off the property.

"It's on the way back, so we could make a stop. Why? Do you have more questions for your aunt? Did the crime scene make you think of something? Or talking to Alexei?"

"No. There's someone else I need to see."

Jakob nodded and drove towards Evarts. They pulled up outside the Coburn house two hours later to find Elijah's truck parked in front. She got out of the car as soon as it came to a stop.

"Why are we here? Whose house is this?" Jakob asked, following her up the porch.

"This is my childhood home. I need to talk to my brother."

"You said your brother's not a witch. He probably knows nothing about dark magic. Why are we here if he can't help us?"

"He doesn't have the Gift, but he can help. Maybe." She knocked on the door. "Eli! It's me. Open up."

There was movement inside the house and a few moments later, Elijah opened the door. He saw Adeline, smiled, and then noticed Jakob and scowled. "Who's he? Why did you bring him here?"

"His name is Jakob Mortensen. He works with me. There's been another death," Adeline said, stepping into the house and walking towards the sitting room. She sensed Jakob and her brother following her. "Our phone call got interrupted before we could really talk."

"You could've called me back."

"Seeing you in person seemed smarter." She sat down on the sofa. "I want to hear what Harlan's been telling you. You said it was distraught and kept trying to tell you something. What was it?"

"He talks to Harlan?" Jakob asked. "As in, the land?"

"Mostly, Harlan talks to me," Elijah said. "And lately, she's had a lot to say."

CHAPTER 13

— · —

Adeline let out a short laugh at the utter confusion on Jakob's face. Her own reaction a week earlier hadn't been any better, but it was nice not being the only one baffled by the news.

"Jakob, sit down for a second." She pointed to a chair. "We encounter werewolves, vampires, and the like regularly. Harlan talking to my brother isn't that weird if you think about it."

"No, it's still strange." Jakob shook his head. "Still, it'd be a weird thing to lie about. And you don't strike me as the type to joke around when people are dying, so the only explanation is that y'all are serious. I've got questions, but I'll ask later." He looked at Elijah. "You talk to Harlan, or Harlan talks to you. What's it been saying?"

Elijah hadn't sat down when the others did. He shifted his weight and sent his sister a pleading look. "Do I have to talk to you about this with him here?"

"Why not? John's been dead for eleven years. I think it's time we stop tiptoeing around things, forcing ourselves to live our lives based on his expectations," she answered. "He's not gonna come through the door looking for a problem just because someone thinks I'm weird. I need to know what you've been hearing to find the person who's murdered not one, but two people. Jakob wants to find the killer as badly as I do. Besides, he might think of a question that slips my mind, since he's less accustomed to our family's eccentricities."

Elijah finally sat down and took a deep breath. "Fine. Who's the second victim?"

"A man named Derek Green," Jakob said. "Adeline said you know him, or knew him at some point."

"That's a name I haven't heard in years. I knew him, years ago. We dug coal together, but fell out of touch after I left the mine," he recalled. "I woke up around two o'clock this morning—screaming woke me. It was an anguished, guttural cry, the kind that rattles you down to the bone. There was no one around; it was entirely in my head. When the screaming stopped, I heard a woman's voice, Harlan's voice. She was talking, yelling about what had happened. Then, I called Addy."

"What was she saying?" Adeline asked, ignoring the look on Jakob's face. She supposed it was odd that she was calling Harlan "she" and not "it," but that was how Elijah had referred to the land and now wasn't the time to argue over semantics. He claimed Harlan sounded like their mother, so it was fitting.

"She was torn up, essentially inconsolable that 'one of her sons' was dead. Screaming, crying, and carrying on. Angry not only that he'd died, but about how painful and unnatural his death was."

"How did she know Derek's death was painful? Could she feel him die?" Jakob leaned forward.

"I don't know. Harlan talks to me, I ain't got a way to talk back or ask questions of her." He looked at his sister. "Harlan normally doesn't talk to me when something like this happens. I mean, when someone dies, even when it's an ugly death. Do you know why it's happening now? And why I felt the hills' sadness before I knew someone was dead?"

"Not a clue." She shook her head. "When I drove over the county line after Sandra's death and Derek's I was consumed with this feeling of dread. Dread and sadness. I wonder if that's connected to what you're feeling."

"I'd say so."

"Don't forget about the chest pains," Jakob added.

"Chest pains? What chest pains?" Elijah asked.

"Ever since I came back to Kentucky, I get this pain in my chest when I cross into Harlan County. It subsides, but it's there. Since Sandra died it's gotten substantially worse." Adeline pursed her lips. "Mary and I figure the killer's using dark magic to commit the murders, and that it's having an effect on the land." She cleared her throat. "Back to this morning. Did anything feel off or strange yesterday? You said Harlan's grief woke you up, but did Harlan have anything to say during the rest of the day?"

"No. I told you that I had a feeling Sandra's death was only the beginning. I've had that feeling since I found out she died. Yesterday, Harlan didn't seem any stronger or more emotional than the days before that."

"Did you ever mention Harlan talking to you to Aunt Mary?"

"I haven't seen her since the year you left, so no."

"Why not? Did something happen?"

"You could say that. She—"

"Your family drama's not important right now," Jakob cut in. "What do Sandra Russett and Derek Green have in common? Is there anything?"

"Other than living here, I don't think so. She was divorced; he'd been married for over twenty years. They weren't related. She worked up in Pikeville at the black lung clinic."

"Black lung?"

"It's a disease coal miners get from inhaling coal dust."

"Derek dug coal, and Sandra worked at a clinic to help coal miners. So, they're connected because of coal mining."

"That's not the smoking gun you think it is." Adeline gave him a sad smile. "This is coal country. More than half of the men in this county have worked in coal mines at one point or another. Even if we just talk to men who worked for the same coal company as Derek, it'll take us too long to get any real answers."

"There might be a better, more relevant connection." Elijah looked out the window and then back at his sister. "Let me think about it."

Adeline didn't have any more questions for her brother, and Jakob didn't seem to have any either. As they were leaving, Adeline stopped in the doorway.

"Give me a few minutes," she told Jakob. "There's something I need to do."

He studied her for a moment before nodding and heading out to his truck. When he was out of earshot, she turned to Elijah. "I need a candle, a match, some salt, and yarrow, if you have it."

"For what?"

"To cast a protection spell. Folks are getting attacked in their homes. What kind of older sister would I be—?"

"You're not even five minutes older."

"I'm still your big sister." When he laughed, she glared at him. "Yes, I'm short. That's not the point. I want to protect you. Let me cast a protection spell over the house."

"You think I'm in danger?" His face paled.

"I hope you're not, but it will give me some peace of mind."

Elijah led her to the kitchen and withdrew all the materials she needed from various drawers.

"I call upon the strength of my ancestors and ask them to grant me this boon. Protect this house and those who inhabit it." As she lit the candle, she pictured her magic bursting out of her in a wave of light and creating a barrier around the house. She encircled the candle in salt and yarrow as she repeated the words two more times. "The candle needs to burn until sunset. Do not blow it out before then or the spell won't work."

Once the casting was complete, she hugged Elijah and left the house. Jakob was leaning against the door of his truck, looking at something on his phone. His head shot up when the bottom step of the porch creaked under her foot. "Ready to go?"

"Now that I've given my brother some extra protection, yes," she said, getting into the passenger seat.

"Kind of unfair to use your witchcraft to protect him, but not anyone else."

"I'm not anyone else's older sister. Wouldn't you do the same if you were in my shoes? If there was a chance something might happen to one of your sisters?"

"They wouldn't need it." He started the engine. "Do you think it means something? Sandra working at a clinic for patients with lung problems, and the killer taking her lungs?"

"Maybe. Regardless, though, the only reason for the killer to take the lungs is if they have a plan for them. That thought leads me down a road I'd rather not travel." She turned the radio on in the hope he'd let the conversation end there.

Thankfully, he let the music fill the silence.

***

When they arrived back at the office, Steve was the only person still there. He was on the phone in his office when they walked in, and he waved them both into the room when he spotted them. He signaled for them to sit down as he took notes on what the person on the other end of the line was saying.

"Yes, let me know as soon as you can. I need to go now." Steve hung up the phone and looked at the pair. "Where the hell have you two been?"

"I don't know what you mean," Jakob said, feigning innocence.

"You've been gone for several hours. I told you to go talk to the wolves. That doesn't take five hours."

"And we did. Then we decided to talk to the other factions, show some initiative by going above and beyond. Now, if asked, we can say we've talked to every supernatural group in the area."

"It did seem like the smart thing to do," Adeline added.

"Well, it's too late to undo it, but you might've just kicked a hornet's nest." Steve's expression indicated he wasn't impressed by their reasoning. "Do you know what you've done by going around to each faction asking if they know anything about the murders? It could cause discord between the different groups. It might lead to a conflict between this faction and that one. That's the last thing we need with people dying, and no leads on the killer. But what's done is done." He let out a sigh. "I also got a call from the ME. He didn't have much to share."

"Of course the ME's got nothing. He's not done with the autopsy yet."

"No, but he called to give me his initial findings. You recall that Sandra Russett's lungs were missing?"

"It's hard to forget a detail like that. Were Derek Green's taken as well?"

"No, but his liver was."

"The killer left his lungs, but took his liver?" Jakob turned to Adeline. "Is that indicative of something?"

"The only spells that mention human organs center around doomed attempts to raise the dead. Most other dark spells I've found call for copious amounts of blood or animal deaths, at most."

"This case keeps getting weirder," Steve scoffed. "Well, until we get the final report there's not much to do, so I sent the others home. You two should head out as well. It should be a fairly quiet night. It'd better be, anyway."

Adeline walked over to her desk to grab her things and was surprised when Jakob followed her over. He stood there as she dug through a drawer, then he cleared his throat and ran a hand through his light brown hair. For a moment he looked a few years younger.

"I don't know about you, but I could use a drink right about now. Especially after what we just heard."

"A drink sounds nice," she admitted. "Just one, though."

They found a dive bar outside of town. There were two or three other patrons inside. They ordered and waited for the bartender to wander off before speaking to each other.

"Who's John?" Jakob asked.

"What?"

"Your brother didn't want to talk with me around. You said John wasn't gonna storm in and overreact if he answered your questions. Who's John?"

"Our father. He was a real piece of work. I think he loved the idea of our mama more than he loved her as a person. Just like he liked the idea of children, but couldn't stand the ones he brought into this world. Elijah wasn't the star athlete he wanted, and he had no clue what to make of me. So, he resented us both."

"He didn't like that you were," he scanned the bar to make sure no one was eavesdropping, "a witch?"

"He didn't know about that. Mama never told him she was one, and he thought the rumors about her family were all nonsense. Elijah and I were both scared of what he'd do, what he'd try to make *me* do, if he found out, so I kept it from him. All he knew was that others thought I was strange. He didn't like that, not one bit."

"I grew up in a small town too. No one wants to be the town outcast." He nodded sympathetically. "You weren't like everyone else, and he held it against you."

"The feeling was mutual." She tapped her fingers lightly against the bar. "He hated me for my strangeness, and I hated him for being alive when my mama wasn't. When Elijah called and told me he was dead, I felt relief. But everyone in town thinks I'm a terrible daughter for skipping his funeral. They think I owed him that much."

"I don't. I know my opinion doesn't matter much, but at least you didn't show up and make a scene. Not everyone would've been that nice. I wouldn't've. Then again, my view on fathers is heavily skewed."

"Skewed how?" The bartender returned with Jakob's beer and Adeline's bourbon before wandering off to stare at her phone at the other end of the bar.

"My dad was a piece of shit. I enlisted because if I stayed any longer I'd've killed him. Or he would've tried to kill me. Either way, I had to go." He took a pull from his beer. "That sack of shit put me through eighteen years of hell, then had the nerve to drop dead while I was at basic training."

"But you went to his funeral?"

"There wasn't one." He let out a bitter laugh. "No one would've shown up or cared. He was a miserable bastard with no friends. Hell, I don't even know if anyone claimed the body."

"One of your sisters—"

"What are—? No, they didn't do anything for him." His brow furrowed for a moment before his face became neutral once again. "He wasn't their father."

"What about your mother? You lose her too?" Adeline sipped her bourbon.

"Nope. She's out there somewhere." He started to peel the label off his beer from where the glue had become loose. "Left of her own accord."

"Are you sure? When was the last time you saw her?"

"Trust me, she's still around." He took a sip of his beer. "You done trying to psychoanalyze me?"

"You started it, asking about John. Turnabout's fair play, as the saying goes."

"Sure." It was quiet for a few minutes. "You wonder what being normal would feel like? To not have this job, and live entirely in the human world?"

"All the time. When I first left home, I had this crazy idea that if I ran far enough, I could pretend I was normal. That the distance would let me forget all about it. I wanted to act like everything I knew, the lessons my mama taught me, were stories paired with an overactive imagination." She took another sip of her drink. "It didn't work for long. My Gift wouldn't let me forget it was there."

"What's it feel like?"

"What's what feel like?"

"Don't act stupid, I know you're not." He leaned closer. "When you use your Gift, what does it feel like?"

"I feel it even when I'm not using it. No matter where I went or how long I was away from home, it always pulsed inside me to some extent. It's there, under my skin, buried deep down in my bones, wrapped around every part of me. It's too ingrained in everything I am for even the world's best surgeon to be able to cut it out." She paused. "Using it feels … freeing. I feel more alive than ever. It's also heavy, like I have a legacy and a responsibility to live up to. Imagine feeling like you're on top of the world, while also having the eyes of everyone you've ever cared about on you, depending on you to do what needs to be done, and you don't know what that is." She looked down at the bar top. "It's a great and terrible burden, as my mama once told me."

"Is that why you've been running from it for so long?"

Her head snapped up to look him in the eye. She narrowed her eyes. "Why don't we talk about you, and what you're running from, for a second?"

"I'm not running from anything."

"Let me let you in on a little secret." She leaned in closer to him, as if she had information no one else could overhear. "Anyone who winds up in a place like this, doing our job, is running from something. The only question is what, and if they realize it."

"That's two questions. And I see I hit a sore spot." He took another drink from his beer. "I guess we should stick to talking about work then."

"Absolutely not, given the case we're working on. Unless you have a new theory on who did it, how, and why, so we can put it all behind us." She took a sip of her drink. "Dark magic's the only explanation, but that's all I know. Or do you think I'm wrong?"

"I'm an asshole, but I'm not enough of an asshole to claim I know more about witchcraft than you do."

She watched him for a moment. "Speaking of, you haven't told me how you know as much as you do."

"I told you, I read a lot."

"Plenty of people read a lot. Reading doesn't explain how you found out that magic, vampires, any of it, is real in the first place."

"My mother told me about it before she left. Not a lot, since I was a kid, but enough to make me want to know more. I spent a lot of time at the library learning about myths and legends. It gave me somewhere to spend my time, somewhere that wasn't home. I started collecting rare books once I'd read through the volumes that were easy to get."

"But how did your mother know? Was she—?" She watched a flash of annoyance cross his face. "You know what? Never mind. I guess it doesn't matter all that much."

"I don't believe you're satisfied with not knowing."

"Oh, I'm not. But I don't want you to get up and storm out, so I'll drop it. For now," she said. "One day, you'll trust me enough to tell me."

"Assuming you don't head back to the West Coast before then. Or somewhere else."

"Who said I was going somewhere?" She leaned in closer, but pulled back when she realized how close their faces were.

"We're all running from something, aren't we? You're running from your past. Your past's here." Jakob put a few bills on the bar top and stood up. "I'm heading home. I'll see you tomorrow." He walked out of the bar without looking back.

"That's a shame," the bartender commented, wiping a glass with the rag in her hands. She placed the glass down and picked up the cash Jakob had left. "Thought you two were a cute couple."

"We're not together." Adeline shot her a blank look.

"Keep telling yourself that. You two were about three seconds away from making out," she said. "And he paid for both drinks."

Adeline didn't reply as she left the bar.

***

Adeline arrived at work at the same time as Ned the next morning, so they struck up a conversation as they entered the building. Ned wanted to know how the investigation was going, and she reluctantly told him about their lack of leads.

"How come you didn't go to the crime scenes with us?" Adeline asked. "If anyone was going to be stuck on visitor duty, I was expecting it to be the newbie. Or for there to be some kind of rotation."

"I-I don't do well with blood. I can deal with detailed reports or even photos without an issue, but for some reason, if I see blood in person, I get all queasy. It's better for everyone if I stay behind, which is why Steve 'needed' me to handle any visitors." He looked away from her.

As she got settled, she observed the room. Rebecca was talking to Steve in his office. Jakob was on the phone with someone and writing notes on a legal pad. Adeline had some paperwork to fill out, but nothing pressing to do. She grabbed a pen from her desk and started writing.

Jakob hung up his phone just as Rebecca walked out of Steve's office. She stopped in the middle of the room and looked between Jakob, Ned, and Adeline. "I'm headed to Lexington."

"Pass." Jakob didn't look up as he spoke.

"Too long of a drive?"

"No." He went back to his notes, ignoring the looks Ned and Rebecca were sending him. Ned seemed perplexed, while Rebecca's frown and furrowed brow indicated her annoyance.

"I guess I'll go with you," Adeline offered.

"Great." Rebecca smoothed out her jacket and picked up her keys. "We should head out."

***

The first few minutes of the drive were quiet as Rebecca headed towards the interstate. After five minutes had passed with no explanation of why they were heading to Lexington, Adeline cleared her throat.

"What's in Lexington?" she asked.

"Oh, right. So much has happened in the last few weeks that I forget how new some of this is for you," Rebecca replied. "Sorry for leaving you in the dark. It's not what's in Lexington; it's who."

"I thought you didn't do check-ins. Jakob mentioned you focus on other types of assignments."

"I don't, usually." Rebecca's hand grip on the steering wheel tightened for a moment. "Because of what happened to my sister, I—"

"You don't have to explain," Adeline said. "Whomever it is, you must feel safe with them."

"I do. Siobhan and Astrid are – One's a banshee, and the other is the daughter of a Norn. I'm hoping they can help us with solving the murders, or at least point us in the right direction."

"Okay. Why didn't we visit them after the first murder?"

"Lexington's a long drive, so we don't ask Astrid or Siobhan for help very often."

"And Sandra's death could've been a one-off, rather than the start of something. Now that we've got a second victim we might figure out a pattern," Adeline added as she thought through the timing. "Is there anything I need to know before we get there? Topics to avoid, words I shouldn't use, things I shouldn't do, anything like that?"

"Astrid's eyes are two different colors, so don't stare. Other than that, they're both incredibly laid-back. Don't worry about formalities."

"That's a nice change." She saw Rebecca's raised eyebrow. "When I first moved to Seattle, I referred to a clairvoyant as a psychic. She didn't even hear me say it, but I got reprimanded for it."

"The more I hear about your time out west, the less I understand why you stayed there for so long and didn't just move back."

"I wasn't happy, but it was routine, if nothing else. Better the devil you know and all that." She shrugged. "And I wasn't ready to come back then. I've got—"

"Complicated feelings about Kentucky; I picked up on that." Rebecca interrupted. "Mind if I turn the radio on?"

She shook her head. They spent the remainder of the drive listening to music.

***

Rebecca drove through downtown Lexington as Adeline tried to figure out where they were headed. She'd been to the city a few times years ago, and some spots looked familiar. They turned down one side street, then another, close to the center of the city, but not in the busiest part of town.

The apartment building Rebecca parked in front of had once been something else, probably a factory, before being turned into apartments. It wasn't rundown, nor was it overly extravagant. It was designed for residents looking for a decent apartment, but nothing too fancy or expensive.

Adeline followed Rebecca to the fourth floor and down a hallway, where they stopped in front of Apartment #407 and knocked.

"Who lives here?" Adeline asked as they waited for someone to open the door. Footsteps could be heard on the other side of the door. "Astrid or Siobhan?"

"Both."

"We're ... roommates." The woman who opened the door was tall, with light brown skin and dark brown eyes. She had a heart-shaped face, curly black hair, and a straight nose. Her ripped jeans had paint stains on them, and she'd rolled up the sleeves of a long-sleeved blue shirt. She looked at Adeline. "Hey, I'm Siobhan."

"Adeline."

"Nice to meet you." She held up her paint-spattered hands with a wry smile. "I think it's best if we don't shake hands."

"We'd like to talk to you, and Astrid if she's here," Rebecca said. "It shouldn't take very long, and it's important."

"Of course." She cleared her throat and then called over her shoulder. "Astrid! Wake up!" She then stepped out of the doorway to let the two Guardians into the apartment. "Follow me."

There was a bump, followed by a crash deeper into the apartment as Rebecca and Adeline followed Siobhan to the living room area. She invited them to sit on one of the navy-blue couches along the wall, as she grabbed a rag and started to wipe her hands off. A moment later, a blonde woman with cream skin stumbled into the room wearing gym shorts and an old t-shirt. Her hair was tangled. A blue eye looked around sleepily while she rubbed the other.

"Why are you wailing at such an ungodly hour?" the blonde grumbled.

"A banshee wailing. How original. And it's afternoon." Siobhan rolled her eyes. "We have visitors."

Astrid tore her eyes away from her and noticed the two other women in the room. "Give me just a minute." She walked back into the room she'd come out of.

"Sorry about her." Siobhan gave them a polite smile. "She tried to drink an entire fraternity under the table last night." The living room lapsed into silence.

"I didn't try. I succeeded," Astrid quipped as she walked back into the room. She'd pulled her hair back into a ponytail and had swapped her sleepwear for yoga pants and a band tee. With her hair up, the difference between her eyes was stark. While her right eye was blue, her left eye had a cloudiness over the iris. "I had to make my Viking ancestors proud." She took a seat beside Siobhan. "So, what brings you here Rebecca?" She noticed Adeline. "And who are you? Have we met?"

"No, we haven't. My name's Adeline. We're here because of some recent murders a few hours east. The victims were human, but the deaths are the result of dark magic."

"If the deaths are the result of dark magic, shouldn't you be talking to your own people?" She turned her head to face Adeline more head-on. "You're a witch, are you not?"

"I am, and we did. It wasn't as helpful as I'd hoped. Rebecca thought one of you might have more information, either about the murders that have happened, or future victims."

"Well, I'm sorry you came all this way, but we're not going to be any more helpful." Siobhan shook her head. "I haven't wailed for a human in months, and Astrid—"

"Hasn't seen anything of the deaths that already happened. And, despite having an eye that only sees potential futures, hasn't been shown much of what will come to pass." Astrid pointed to her cloudy eye. "Something's blocking me."

Rebecca's eyes widened, and her jaw dropped. Adeline's brow furrowed in confusion. She didn't have extensive knowledge of the Norns, but the Norse seers, heralded to be goddess of fate, were said to see the past, present, and all possible futures.

Siobhan grabbed Astrid's hand and gave her a look of concern, ignoring the others. "Blocked? You didn't tell me that. Why didn't you say anything? How long has this been going on?"

"It started at the beginning of the month. My sight's not blocked entirely. It's more like there's a growing blind spot hiding things from me. Another event, an inevitable consequence of fate, will soon come to pass, and it eclipses everything else, limiting what I can see beyond when it happens. I can see threads of futures, possible outcomes of events, but this incident—this calamity—is interfering with everything."

"Do you know what it is? This terrible thing that's coming?" Adeline asked.

"I can't see the full picture, only glimpses. My mother claims that's normal for a significant event, but wouldn't admit if she's having the same problem." Astrid's gaze became unfocused as she stared at the far wall. "It's an image here, a sound there. Blood splattered across a concrete floor. The sound of a gunshot.

A hand clutching at a wound, trying to stem the flow of blood. Silence." She shook herself. "I don't know what the event is, only that it's happening soon."

"How soon?"

"Within the next six months, but as for the exact date, I don't know for sure." She cleared her throat. "I'm sorry I haven't seen anything about your murders. I can't help you."

She looked shaken to admit that her abilities were currently unreliable, and Siobhan seemed even more unsettled.

"Don't apologize. I knew there was a chance you wouldn't be able to help," Rebecca said, standing up. "We're sorry we – We'll leave now."

Adeline and Rebecca walked towards the door, with Siobhan and Astrid a few steps behind them. A few feet from the door, Adeline came to an abrupt stop when Rebecca turned around. "If either of you think of—"

Siobhan bumped into Adeline and grabbed the witch's shoulder, steadying herself. Then, she let out an ear-splitting scream. "Two lives have been ended; two souls remain. Beware the silent wood, for there you shall meet the land's bane," she spoke in a flat tone.

"What does tha—Am I gonna die?" Adeline asked. "A banshee's wail foretells death, doesn't it? Or was someone messing with me when they told me that?" Today was the first time she'd ever met a banshee, and her knowledge of them was limited.

"Yes, the wail foretells death," Astrid answered.

"That wail wasn't for you," Siobhan said, refusing to meet Adeline's eyes. "Have a safe drive."

"If either of you needs to get in touch, if you see or sense something that might be helpful, you have my number." Rebecca nudged Adeline towards the door. "Even if it turns out not to be related, still let me know."

***

Adeline was in a daze until she and Rebecca were back on the road and exiting the city. The fog around her subsided and her brain began to process what had happened in the apartment.

"I don't believe her." Adeline drummed her fingers on her knee.

"What?"

"Siobhan said her wail wasn't for me, but I think she lied. She wailed after she bumped into me. I don't think that's a coincidence."

"She said it wasn't."

"She wouldn't look at me when she said that."

"I've known Siobhan for years. She wouldn't lie about something like that," Rebecca said confidently. "I don't know what it means—her wailing right when she collided with you—but if she foresaw your death, she'd tell you. She thinks anyone destined to die prematurely deserves to know."

Adeline spent the rest of the drive trying not to think about Siobhan's cryptic words or the strange visions Astrid described. It felt like the drive back to the office took half as long as the drive to Lexington. Everyone was still there when they returned.

"Is she okay?" Ned asked Rebecca while inspecting Adeline. "Adeline, are you okay?"

"Not really."

"Y'all's trip to the seer and the banshee didn't go well, I see," Jakob drawled as he ate a potato chip from the bag on his desk. "What happened?"

"They weren't able to give us any answers," Rebecca answered. "Neither Sandra's murder nor Derek's triggered anything on their radars."

"Siobhan bumped into me as we were leaving and immediately let out a wail before giving some cryptic, poetic warning." Adeline looked between her coworkers. "Then, she told me her wail wasn't for me."

"The first and only time I met them, they both said they saw death in my future." Jakob smirked.

"You will die someday. Everyone does."

"Making their prediction about as useful as telling me the sun will rise." He ate another chip. When he saw his attitude wasn't helping, he leaned towards

Adeline. "Hey, a banshee wailing means that someone will die, but it doesn't mean that someone is you." He met her eyes. "There are stories of men on the battlefield thinking they're marked for death, only to discover the wail was for their opponent. Maybe you'll kill our murderer."

"That's not any better." She had caused so much death already. Her inaction in Seattle killed Lucy Radassi. Her inability to combat dark magic in Evarts resulted in two deaths. "I don't want to kill anyone."

"Not even in self-defense? The point I'm trying to make is this: Siobhan isn't infallible. She could be wrong. We don't know what will happen. If you keep stressing out about it, you'll drive yourself crazy."

"What was the message?" Ned cut in.

"Huh?" Adeline asked.

"You said Siobhan wailed and then gave you a cryptic warning. What was the message?"

"Something about avoiding the silent woods. Except the woods are never silent between the insects and all the critters living there. I don't know what the message's supposed to even mean. Her warning made about as much sense as the crap I kept hearing from Tatiana."

"Tatiana?"

"This clairvoyant woman I knew in Seattle. She kept telling me that I needed to move back east, but would only give me a vague reason involving destiny to explain why." She waved a hand. "My point is that the message doesn't make sense."

"Yet another reason why you should ignore it and go about your life." Jakob leaned back in his chair. "What about Astrid? Did she also have some vague warning to share?"

"No, her gift of foresight is being blocked by something, according to her," Rebecca said. "Something big is happening sometime in the next six months, and that event is preventing her from seeing much of the future."

"And she has no clue what it is?" He shook his head. "See? This is why I didn't come to Lexington. Because when you talk to people who can see the future or foretell deaths, everything they say gets inside your head, and you start thinking the end of the world is around the corner."

CHAPTER 14

— · —

Two days after Derek Green's death, Steve called the Guardians into his office to go over the medical examiner's report.

"Similar to the first victim, Derek Green had no knife wounds and no puncture marks on his body. No drugs in his system that would've stopped him from fighting off his attacker, and no defensive wounds. Unlike Sandra, he died of blood loss," Steve read off the report. "I guess losing your liver doesn't kill you as quickly as someone stealing your lungs. All the blood at the scene was his. Time of death was between one and three in the morning."

"Anything else?" Rebecca asked. "Any crime scene reports?"

He flipped to a different page. "The powder y'all found is a mixture of coal dust, salt and an unknown third substance. It matches what you found at the first murder, but they still don't know what it is." He skimmed a few more pages. "The black paint used on the sigil is common house paint, making it a dead end."

"Not the best phrase to use right now," Adeline said, crossing her arms.

"Right. Poor choice of words. That's all I've got. Everyone, get back to work."

Adeline went back to her desk and opened the thick tome she'd been reading, ignoring the looks some of her colleagues were sending her way.

"I'm not the type to apologize for other people, but Steve really didn't intend to sound so callous," Jakob said, taking a seat at his own desk.

"Oh, it's not about him. It's not even entirely about Derek or Sandra." She turned the page of her book.

"Who or what is about, then?" He leaned back in his chair and studied her.

She closed the book. "I've been a witch my entire life. I performed my first spell before I could read. Magic's in my bones, it's part of my DNA, and I've spent my whole life learning as much as I can about it. Figuring out this dark magic spell and how to stop it is the one thing I'm supposed to be good at, and I'm failing miserably." The windows began to rattle as she spoke. "I failed to find Sandra's killer, and now Derek's dead. How many others are gonna die horrifically because I keep failing?"

Ned cleared his throat. "It's not all on you. It's all of our jobs to—"

"This ain't about work." She got to her feet and grabbed her jacket. "I need to – I can't be here right now."

***

Three days after the team reviewed the autopsy, Adeline found herself standing beside Elijah in Larry Wagner's house. Since Derek Green's home was a crime scene, his in-laws were hosting the wake and funeral on his widow's behalf. Nina had disappeared into the house as soon as other mourners began to show up.

"It really is quite a shame," Wyatt Dunn said to them, glancing around the room. "Derek and I weren't friends, but he watched my back down in the mine."

"He watched everyone's. That's the code." Elijah gripped his cup tighter. "It's a tragedy all the same. I saw him a week, maybe a week and a half, before he died. He was talking about leaving the mine, finding other work."

"Yeah, he didn't think his body could take it anymore."

"What do you mean?" Adeline asked, her brow furrowed.

"I ran into him at the free clinic not too long ago. The one up in Pikeville. He was starting to have trouble breathing. His daddy died of black lung, his granddaddy too. He didn't want to go the same way." Wyatt shrugged. "Same story we hear every day around here. It's a shame he didn't get a chance to move on from the mine. Though his condition meant he didn't have many good years left anyway. I should go pay my respects to Nina, if I can find her." He wandered off, leaving Elijah and Adeline alone.

People kept glancing over at the corner where the Coburn siblings stood. Adeline couldn't hear what they were saying, but the murmurs and looks being sent their way made it clear one or both of the twins was the topic of discussion.

"I need another drink," Elijah said stiffly. "You want anything?"

"No, I'm fine."

After he walked away, she scanned the room, trying to spot anyone who had attended Sandra's wake. Derek was well-respected in town, so quite a few people had gone to the service. There was bound to be some crossover between the two memorials.

"I feel really bad for Beatrice," Charlotte Lennox said from Adeline's left.

Adeline jumped at the voice. With her attention on the people milling about Larry's sitting room, she hadn't noticed the woman approach her. "Sorry, I was lost in my own world."

"I didn't mean to startle you. I was saying that I feel bad for Beatrice. Can you imagine having to plan the funeral of your late brother-in-law? She wasn't too fond of Derek. I'm sure Larry's less than thrilled about the celebration of his life being held here, too. He didn't exactly hide his disdain for Derek's ... indiscretions."

"Indiscretions?"

"I'm not the type to speak ill of the dead. Derek wasn't the best husband to Nina, and let me leave it at that. Larry didn't appreciate the way Derek acted towards his sister. It can't be easy for Larry or Beatrice, holding the reception here, given how strained their relationship was."

"It would've been an uncomfortable conversation, I'm sure." She observed Charlotte from her periphery. Charlotte had slight bags under her eyes, which were red from crying. Adeline didn't want to overstep or be rude by saying she looked tired. "Did you know Derek well?"

"Not very well, if I'm being truthful, but he was a big help to my mama before she passed, doing chores and things around her house. I don't feel like I ever properly thanked him for that, wrapped up in my own problems as I was. What about you?"

"Not really. I'd met him a few times, but didn't know him all that well."

The two women fell silent until Charlotte spoke again. "Where did you go when you left all those years ago? I've always wondered."

"Here and there. First, down to Tennessee for school, and then I moved out to the West Coast for work. I wish I'd known, before I came back, how little Elijah shared with people about where I'd gone."

"Maybe he did, but I wouldn't know seeing as I was so angry at you back then."

"Why? I don't ... From what I remember, we barely spoke to one another in school. If I did something to upset you, I can't remember what it was."

"Oh, no. It was nothing like that. Nothing you did. I was angry at a lot of people back then."

"Why? If you don't mind me asking."

Thomas Lennox walked into the room and made a beeline for the spot where Charlotte and Adeline stood, jostling a few people out of his path. The teenager's eyes were bloodshot, but unlike his mother he didn't look like he'd been crying. He seemed antsy as well. "Dad sent me to find you. He's got an early shift tomorrow, so we need to go." He didn't look in Adeline's direction or acknowledge her presence at all.

"Tell him I'll be right there," Charlotte instructed her son. Then she turned to Adeline. "We should meet for lunch or something. It'll give us a chance to catch up somewhere other than a funeral."

"We should," Adeline agreed, but Charlotte walked away before they could exchange phone numbers. "Or not."

Adeline's stomach grumbled, so she headed into the dining room where the table was covered with platters and casseroles. She filled a plate and then wandered around, looking for a spot to sit and eat. She received only a few stares as she made her way through the house. Some people were still avoiding her, but they didn't give her quite as wide of a berth as they had at Sandra's funeral.

She spotted a seat at a table outside, so she walked out to claim it and began to listen to conversations as she ate. She wasn't the type to eavesdrop, but with two people dead and no leads, she made an exception. Everyone agreed on two things: that Derek's death was unexpected and how tragic it was that Nina was the one to find him. The rest was the same small talk and gossip she'd heard at Sandra's wake. Didn't anyone get tired of having the same conversations, day in and day out?

Adeline had finished about half of her food when someone sat down across from her. She looked up to see Dale Blevins, and his appearance was startling.

His clothing was disheveled like his attire was an afterthought. His hair hadn't been washed in a few days. Bags were starting to show under his eyes, and his skin was paler than the last time she'd seen him.

"I hope it's all right if I sit here."

"It's fine. Go right ahead." She gestured with the plastic fork in her hand before taking another bite of food.

"I didn't get much of a chance to talk to you last time when I ran into you at Sandra's wake."

"It wasn't the right situation for us to try and catch up, not that today's any better. Last time I saw you, before last week, you were a rambunctious five-year-old who wanted to be a cowboy when he grew up." She paused, struck by how many years had passed since then. "What are you doing now?"

"Right after I finished school I started working at a garage over in Corbin. I also sometimes help my neighbor with things at his place from time to time."

"What kind of things?" she asked. "You still living at home, or did you move out after you got out of school?"

"Still living at Mama's. The property line ends right where the Morris's farm starts. That's where I help out, repairing their equipment or butchering livestock. They ain't supposed to, but they'll sell their meat to folks around here for a decent price."

"I'll keep that in mind. Didn't something happen to someone's livestock recently?" While she hadn't forgotten about the livestock deaths Elijah mentioned, this was her first opportunity to talk to anyone with information about it. The affected farmer had gone to Sandra's wake, but Adeline hadn't spoken to him then. Even if she'd had the opportunity, she didn't have a way of approaching the topic without raising suspicion. "I think Elijah mentioned that someone's pigs got torn apart or something. At least, that's what I think he said."

"Yeah, the Browns lost a pig. Coyote got past the electric fence." He shrugged before taking a few bites of his food. "Seeing you a week ago had me wondering a few things."

"Wondering about what?" She stopped speaking when he began to have a coughing fit. "Are you okay? Should I get you some water?"

"I'm fine. Something just went down the wrong pipe." His coughing subsided. "And I was curious about what you've been up to since you left. You were here one day and gone the next. Did you wind up going to college? Where did you go, and what do you do for work? Are you married? Do you have kids? All that." He let out a nervous laugh. "Okay, most of those questions are things my mama wanted to know when I said I'd run into you. She couldn't make it today, otherwise she'd be asking you herself."

"I went to college. I work in consulting. And no to those last two. No husband, no kids," she answered. "It's sweet of your mama to ask about me."

"I'll pass it along. I—"

"Hey, Addy," Troy Perkins said as he slid into the seat next to Dale. He wasn't as athletic as he'd once been, but he was a pretty large man so Dale had to move over for him to have room. "I was hoping I'd run into you."

She grimaced at both the nickname—she only let her family call her Addy—and his interruption. "Derek's funeral ain't the right place for—"

"I want to apologize for what happened at Sandra's wake," he said. "It wasn't polite of me to act that way or put you in that kind of position. I'm sorry. Please forgive me." When she didn't immediately respond, he began to beg. "You have to forgive me for doing that. I need you to tell me that you forgive me."

Dale stood up and walked away in the middle of Troy's pleas, glaring at the back of his head for a few seconds before wandering off to talk to someone else.

Adeline sighed and looked away to collect her thoughts. She didn't want to cause a scene, but she could feel her anger rising and clenched her hand under the table. "It's fine."

"No, it's not." His expression was frantic, and he had a crazed look in his eyes. "It's not okay at all. We were having a pleasant conversation, and then I ruined it. I need to make it right with you." He leaned forward, unwilling or unable to take his eyes off her. "Please. I want to make this right. I have to—"

"I'm fine. You apologized, I've acknowledged it, and now we can move past it."

"Great. I'm glad you forgive me."

Adeline was a bit too startled by his behavior to point out that she hadn't said she forgave him, only that she acknowledged his apology. She was concerned for him, based on his behavior. "Are you—?"

"There you are," Elijah interrupted, walking across the backyard. He stopped next to his sister and tried to help her up from her seat. "We should probably get going before it gets to be too late."

Adeline looked at her phone and saw the time. "It's not that late."

"You've been gone too long. It'll be getting dark before you know it," he said. "You don't want to be driving on those twisty, turny roads on the way back to your place in the dark."

There was a strange stiffness in his voice. His eyes were moving back and forth, and he seemed on edge. He shot her a pleading look, so she stood up. "You're right. We should go."

She turned to Troy. "We'll have to catch up another time. Give your family my best when you see them."

Elijah led her away from the house and over to where her car and his truck were parked. He stopped to peer over his shoulder every few feet, as if he expected someone to be following them.

"You mind telling me what that was about?" she asked.

"I had a feeling that we needed to go."

"What kind of feeling? Are the hills trying to tell you something?"

A few people exited the house and began to head in their direction.

"We should both head home. I'll call you tomorrow."

She made it home and spent the rest of the evening watching television on the couch. Whiskey sat by one of the windows, staring outside and periodically hissing at something only she could see. The first few times, Adeline walked over to the window to see what had her so transfixed, but after the third time she ignored it. She hadn't spotted anything except a cluster of normal-looking trees when she stared into the darkness.

CHAPTER 15

— · —

The next morning, Adeline called Elijah to ask him why he insisted they leave the memorial as quickly as they did. She caught him as he was heading to work, though, and he claimed he didn't have time to explain the strange feeling beyond reiterating that he'd been overcome with dread and the urge to leave.

Adeline considered his words for a moment, concerned with the side effects Harlan talking to Elijah might be having on his mind, before setting it all aside as she got ready for a morning run. Her frustration about the lack of answers had grown over the last few days, and she hoped a run before work would dispel enough energy so she wasn't on edge and ready to snap all day.

Jakob was the only person at the office when she arrived, and he was absorbed in something on his computer.

"How was the funeral?" he asked, not looking away from the screen.

"It sucked. Most people were there hoping to learn something juicy and scandalous about Derek rather than pay their respects. Or trading theories about why whatever killed Sandra would go after Derek, given how different the two were," she said as she sat down. "That's not even touching on the folks who wouldn't stop staring at me or Elijah. I'm so sick of people whispering about us when they think I'm not paying attention."

"What were they saying?"

"I don't know, as I couldn't hear them. It wasn't too bad last night, not like at Sandra's funeral, but every so often, a room would go quiet as I passed by."

"Come on. You're pretty observant; you must have some idea." He leaned back in his seat with a smirk. "Maybe not what they were saying verbatim, but you've got to have some inkling about why they'd be whispering about you."

"Other than me leaving for sixteen years and coming back with no explanation?"

"Yes, other than that. By now, people know you were in Seattle. It's not some earth-shattering revelation; there's no dramatic potential in that information. So, what else could it be?"

"You'd be surprised how many people think Elijah and I are lying about that, trying to cover up 'what I did,' whatever that means. As for others, the important detail is that I moved back to the area on the 9th."

"And?"

"Sandra died on the 10th. No one's come out and said it, aside from our batty, bitchy old neighbor, but some people might find that kind of timing suspicious. I certainly would, in their shoes. Some folks think I've got something to do with the killings."

"Maybe you do." He turned and faced her. "At face value, like you said, the timing is a weird coincidence. The first murder happened the day after you came back. Witchcraft's involved; you're a witch. It's not a big leap for people to make, especially the ones who only know the public information about the killings. To a random person, you could very well be the killer. And, from where I'm sitting, it feels an awful lot like the killer was waiting for you to move back to Kentucky before they started their killing spree."

"That's a good theory, but there's only one problem. No one except my family in the hills and the people working in this office knew I was back until after Sandra's death. Not even my brother knew I was here."

"Some people did, remember? There was that kid working at the gas station and that other guy. What was his name? The one with the beady eyes and receding hairline? William? No. Wilbur? No, that wasn't it."

"The name you're looking for is Wyatt. Fine. So, two people knew I was back before Sandra died. But Tommy, the gas station clerk, didn't know who I was until Wyatt confronted me, and Wyatt—" she cut herself off.

A puzzle piece fell into place as she remembered a comment Elijah had made the day she left and put it together with Wyatt's strange comments at both Derek's and Sandra's funerals.

"What about him? You just realized something; it's clear on your face. What was it?"

"One of the reasons I left was because people around town had started making comments about me possibly being a witch. One or two people even asked my brother about it. Elijah was scared for me, worried I'd die under suspicious circumstances like Aunt Eve did after she was accused of being a witch. There's always been rumors about the women in my family practicing witchcraft."

"Are they rumors if they're true?"

"That's not the point." She shot him a glare. "Wyatt knew I was back in town before everyone else. Sixteen years ago, Elijah told me that Wyatt had made a comment to him about me being a witch." She took a deep breath. "He brushed Wyatt off, but maybe Wyatt decided to try and find out for himself, which could have led him to dark magic. He also said something weird to me at one of the funerals. I ignored it at the time."

"Let me play devil's advocate for a bit before we waste time and energy chasing down a loose end. After all, saying something strange to you is hardly a murder confession. Especially if he didn't mention witches or magic or anything." He spun his chair to face her fully. "Why would he turn to dark magic? What would he gain?"

"I don't know yet, but I've looked further into dark magic by now than I ever wanted to. We're not just dealing with magic but also organ harvesting. The only reason for that combination would be some kind of sacrifice. Or resurrection."

"The second one seems unlikely, given how God-fearing people out here seem to be."

"Unlikely doesn't mean it's impossible."

"Let's say the culprit killed them as some kind of sacrifice. It doesn't point to this Wyatt guy being our killer. Other than a comment made sixteen years ago, a comment a few days ago, and living in the area, does anything connect Wyatt to Derek Green or Sandra Russett? A reason to want them dead? Or a reason he'd want to sacrifice anyone?"

"For Sandra, I don't know. Then again, I didn't think to look for a connection. A thousand people live in Evarts. I haven't had time to investigate every single resident. Maybe Rebecca or Ned has looked into him; I'll ask them. As for Derek, he was starting to get black lung, and Wyatt knew that. If he was already determined to sacrifice someone, wouldn't a victim who's already sick be ideal? Or easier to justify?"

"Ok. If we say he might be our killer, he would need to be a witch to perform witchcraft. Are there any witches in his family?"

"Not that I know if, but that doesn't mean he isn't one." She grabbed her jacket. "Are you coming or what?"

He stood up from his desk. "Where are we going?"

"To ask my brother about Wyatt and talk to my aunt again. My family keeps extensive records not only of witches from our own family but also of any we've encountered. If there are witches in Wyatt's family history, she'd know."

They walked out of the building as Rebecca, Ned, and Steve were arriving. "Where are you two going?" Steve asked.

"I have a theory, but I need to confirm some information first. I don't want to waste time chasing down a bad lead," she said. "Can one of you see if there's a connection between the victims and a man named Wyatt Dunn? Particularly between him and Sandra Russett. His last name is spelled D-U-N-N. Let us know what you find out."

"Do you think he's the killer?" Rebecca asked.

"I don't know for sure, but I suspect he's involved somehow," she called over her shoulder as she and Jakob got into her car and drove off.

***

When Adeline reached Harlan County, the blinding, excruciating chest pain that was far too familiar struck again. She pulled over by the side of the road until she recovered from the sensation. Each second felt like an eternity, though when she looked at the time she saw the attack had lasted only a few minutes.

"You didn't react so strongly the last time we were here," Jakob remarked.

"The pain gets worse with every visit; it's a side effect of the murders going unsolved," she said through clenched teeth. "It started out feeling like heartburn, but now it feels like someone's trying to tear my heart out."

"Should you be driving?"

"It's manageable, but safety-wise, you should probably be driving until we find the killer."

They switched seats so Jakob could drive. "Does anything help?" He pulled back onto the road.

"Finding our killer will."

The hardware store appeared to be empty when they arrived. After entering, Jakob walked down one aisle and up the next, scoping the store out and making sure no one was lurking in the back.

"Looks like it's just us," he said when he returned to the front of the store where Adeline was waiting next to the register her brother manned. "No need to worry about eavesdropping."

"Addy, what's going on?" Elijah asked, flicking his eyes over to Jakob before turning his attention to his sister.

"I was thinking about Derek's wake and some other events and realized I need to ask you a few things." Adeline rested her arms on the counter to close the distance between herself and her bother. "Yesterday, you demanded we leave the wake but wouldn't say why. And this morning, you didn't have time to talk about it."

"I said I'd gotten a weird feeling. I can't explain it better than that. The hills wanted both of us to leave Beatrice's house. I've learned to listen to that feeling."

"I know, but that made me start considering why the hills would try to warn you and why they'd warn you at that moment. Simplest explanation says it's because the person responsible for Derek's and Sandra's deaths was there."

"Wasn't that the reason you planned a funeral for Sandra and insisted on attending Derek's?" He raised an eyebrow.

"Yes, back when I thought the killer wasn't someone I knew, and I was looking for unfamiliar faces. Now, the answer might be closer than I thought." She placed her hands on the counter and leaned forward. "Someone close, like Wyatt Dunn."

Elijah let out a snort. "Wyatt's not the killer you're looking for."

"How do you know? He knew Derek well enough to know he was sick. He asked you about witchcraft in the past, or so you claimed, and dark magic killed Derek."

"I can't imagine him doing something like that, killing someone." He shook his head. "No one in town has enough evil in them to do what's been done to Derek or Sandra."

"Someone new to town, then?"

He frowned and gave his sister a withering look. "No one moves here. They only ever move away. You know that."

"So, Wyatt could be our killer," Adeline said.

"We're not saying he definitely killed Sandra or Derek," Jakob said when it looked like Elijah was going to argue. "Only that it's possible. Your sister wanted to come out here and ask you some questions about what your buddy's been up to while she was gone."

"He's not my buddy," he said with a clenched jaw. "And never has been." He looked down at the counter. "He quit mining a few months after I did and joined the Marines, only to get kicked out after about a year. He bounced around from job to job after that, and he's been working at Joan's restaurant for the last few months."

"And Joan is who?"

"His sister-in-law," Adeline said. "Her husband Clay died this past spring." A thought occurred to her. "Eli, when exactly did Clay die?"

"Mid-April."

"So, he's been dead about six months."

"Yes, I suppose. Does it really matter? He died in a car wreck."

"It might," she answered. "How well did Wyatt know Sandra? Did he know her from one of his old jobs or something?"

"Yeah, you could say he knew her. A lot of people blame him for Sandra and Scott splitting."

"Why? What happened?"

"I don't know." He shrugged. "We weren't friends and I didn't want to pry. It wasn't any of my business. Some people said Sandra cheated on Scott with Wyatt. Others said that Wyatt introduced Scott to the woman he cheated with. All I know is that they were at odds, but they settled their differences and things were fine between them recently."

"Well, Sandra's dead. Fine doesn't seem like a very apt description."

"Just because they were at odds at some point doesn't mean he killed her. It definitely doesn't explain why he'd kill Derek. How do you explain what happened to him?"

"I don't know. Like Jakob said, we're just exploring the possibility." Adeline spotted a car pulling into the lot next to the building. "You've got customers, so we should go. Let me know if you think of something else that might be useful."

Adeline didn't want to draw extra attention to herself, so she didn't look over to see who was walking up to the store as they headed to where Jakob had parked. The last thing she wanted was to seem paranoid or tip a random passerby off that they had questioned Elijah. She and Jakob could have countless innocent reasons to go to the hardware store in the middle of the day.

***

"Did you pick up on that tidbit about Clay Dunn's death?" Adeline asked as they drove towards the outskirts of town to visit Mary.

"If you're talking about the 'tidbit' that Clay Dunn's been dead around six months, then yes. You said a resurrection is one of the two explanations for killing someone and taking their organs. I do pay attention."

"I'm still getting used to having a partner who listens to me."

"Resurrections have worked a few times in recorded history, but never on someone who was dead for longer than a year," Jakob mused

They arrived at the mountain road and exited the car. Adeline started to walk towards the woods. "I didn't know any resurrections had been recorded as successful. The Arcane Codex—"

"Forbids it. That's why nearly every person to accomplish it has been executed, along with whoever they resurrected."

"That's not true. Yv– Never mind." She waved him off before she said too much.

"No, I want to hear more."

"And I'm telling you to forget it." Two years ago, Adeline had met a woman who'd accidentally resurrected a friend who'd been dead for a few hours. Adeline didn't report the incident to the Alliance. If the woman, Yvette, had been caught, she would've heard about it. "Nearly everyone isn't everyone. Someone could've done it, not gotten caught or not been executed, and lived to pass along that spell to our killer."

"It's more likely they were still executed, but it wasn't recorded." He focused ahead of them. "Welcoming committee's here."

David stepped out from behind one of the trees a moment later. "You here to ask more questions? Or to—"

"I have one question." Adeline interrupted. "People are dying and the land's suffering. That takes priority over everything else."

He put his hands on his hips and let out a groan. "She won't like that."

"I'm not thrilled about the situation either."

"Yet, here you are. Let's go." He went to head up the trail.

She clenched her fists as she felt her anger rise. "I wish this was a social visit because I'd love it if people stopped dying. I'd love to be here to hear all about the things my mama wasn't able to tell me." Around the trio, the wind picked up and began to swirl fallen leaves around them. She let out a deep breath. The wind died down. "But we don't always get what we want, do we?"

David said nothing. They walked in silence until they arrived at the clearing. The only person in sight was Mary. She gave Jakob a polite smile before turning to Adeline. "I assume you came to ask more questions about dark magic and not your Gift."

"Yes, I'm here about dark magic." She took a deep breath to collect herself. Her priorities and Mary's differed, and arguing about them wouldn't get either of them anywhere. "I'll tell you when I'm here about my Gift."

She glanced around. Usually, people milled about at this time of day, doing chores or passing by on the way to or from their own houses. No one was outside now, though, nor could she spot anyone peeking out of the windows, curious about the raised voices. "Where is everyone?"

"Around. I told them to make themselves scarce if you stopped by, since the things I need to tell you aren't meant for them to hear. Some things, only a handful of us need to know," Mary said. "But, as you said, you came to talk about dark magic so you can find and stop this killer you're after. And the sooner the deaths stop, the better for everyone. What do you want to know?"

"Our family are witches. I know which other families up here have witch blood in their veins. I don't know anything about other witches—ones who don't live on this mountain. Growing up, it never occurred to me that there might be others, much less to ask if some folks down in town could have the Gift. Is anyone down in Evarts descended from a witch line?"

"Some families had the Gift, once upon a time, but lost the connection to the land and their ancestors for one reason or another. Others never had a touch of it at all."

"Which category would the Dunn and Harris families fall into?" Harris was Wyatt's mother's maiden name.

"The second one. Those family lines bred a few so-called witch hunters but no witches." Adeline felt her face fall, and her aunt picked up on it. "Why do you ask?"

"I had a strong suspect in mind, for the murders, but he's not descended from witches."

Mary didn't speak for a moment and instead stood there studying Adeline. "Your mother died when you were far too young. There's so much she didn't get a chance to teach you. It was unfortunate then, and it's more unfortunate now."

"I told you that I don't want to discuss that now."

"I know, but it's relevant to your theory. Dark magic breaks the rules by its very nature. Including the most obvious one."

"Which means what?" Jakob asked. "Dancing around the subject isn't getting us anywhere."

"Witchcraft can only be performed by witches. Witchcraft is magic. Dark magic is magic, but it's not necessarily witchcraft. One does not need to be a witch to harness those forces. Humans can perform dark magic, but only at a great cost to themselves." She focused on Adeline. "I assumed you knew that when we last spoke, or I would've said so earlier."

"Well, I didn't. And nothing I read about the subject mentioned non-witches being able to use it." Adeline could feel her face getting red and her pulse skyrocketing. She took a deep breath. "But now I know. When you say it's possible for a regular human to use dark magic, but it would cost them, what would that entail?"

"It would kill them, eventually. After it makes them sick and eventually drives them mad."

"How come Mama never told me that? I was thirteen when she died. I knew plenty of dangerous spells then. I was old enough to know."

"You were in junior high, and teenagers are idiots who think they're smarter than they are. If you'd known about dark magic as a teenager, you might've been tempted to try it. Or one of your friends might've tried it, wanting to be a witch too. And you can't unring that bell. It's one of many things I need to tell you."

"I'll come back, and you can tell me anything and everything you've been waiting years to share with me, after I know the killings have stopped. I have to prioritize this threat. Aren't you tired of feeling how anguished the ancestors are about what's happening?"

"Of course I am. I've also spent sixteen years waiting for you to return." Mary placed her hands on her hips. "I'll hold you to that promise of yours."

"I know you will." She turned and started to walk back towards the car without looking behind her to see if Jakob was following. Evidently he was, since he joined her at the car a few seconds after she opened her door.

"I don't get it. Mary seems like a nice lady. But any time she brings up the past or your magic, you start acting weird," he said as they drove off. "What were you running from all those years ago?"

"Other than the rumors about my family, the memory of my mama, my neglectful father, the lack of opportunities out here, and the increasing tension between my brother and me because I have magic and he doesn't?" She counted each item off on a finger. "Gee, I can't think of why I'd be eager to leave. And now I'm back, and people keep dying."

"None of those explain why you're running away from your aunt now."

"That's not any of your business."

"Unless the reason you ran, and keep running, has something to do with why two people are dead."

"It doesn't." The shame that she felt for leaving Elijah behind, abandoning her extended family, and not being there when Agnes died burned within her. People were so happy she was back, but that happiness couldn't and wouldn't last forever. She wasn't ready to face the judgment and anger that would follow. "And if you keep pushing me about it, I'll kick you out of this car."

He snorted as he brought the car to a stop. "I'd like to see you try."

She turned in her seat to look at him. "You sure you want to go poking at me right now?"

"I'm not poking, but yes."

"Fine." She flicked her finger like she was shooing away an insect and released an iota of power. A gust of wind moved through the car, and the driver-side door flung open. "My blood runs through this place, and my family's been here for a long, long time. You've no idea what I can do." She muttered something and Jakob's door slammed closed. "Piece of advice: next time you want to taunt me, wait until we're over the county line. Then, you'll have more of a chance."

"Noted. It doesn't make anything I said wrong, but you've made your point. I wasn't trying to be a dick, by the way."

"Yet, you decide to annoy me when I'm already pretty on edge."

"Yes, because you needed to let some of your frustration out, and I knew you wouldn't kill me."

The rest of the drive was quiet. Adeline tried to wrap her mind around just how much power she'd felt coursing through her veins when she tapped into her Gift. She didn't even have a good sense for how much she'd shown Jakob, after the accidental bursts of magic she'd experienced over the last few weeks. She was only half convinced that she hadn't caused the gust of wind that picked up when she was arguing with David.

She needed to figure out how strong her magic was now. She didn't remember having this much power before she left back in 1998.

***

Papers covered the conference room table, anchored by stacks of books and half-empty coffee mugs when Adeline and Jakob returned to the office. Rebecca, Ned, and Steve were studying the papers intensely and didn't react when Jakob and Adeline joined them.

"Did we miss something?" Jakob asked.

Steve let out a sigh. "Got a call about ten minutes after you left."

"Before you get to that, we have updates to share," Adeline said. "Wyatt Dunn and Sandra Russett were known to butt heads, and he was involved in her divorce, but I don't have the full story. He was friends with Derek Green, who was starting to get sick. Also, Wyatt's brother died about six months ago. A resurrection explains the organ theft and—"

"Do you have proof? Anything that links Wyatt Dunn to the murders?" Steve cut her off.

"Not yet. We only—" She noticed Ned and Rebecca, who shared a grave expression. "What is it?"

"The call I got was from Frank Werner," Steve's expression was grim.

"I don't know who that is. Should I?"

"The Steward of Kentucky," Jakob told her, before looking back at Steve. "He called you himself?"

"Yes. Murmurings about the murders made their way to him, and he claims folks are concerned. We have a few days to find the person responsible, or he's sending people here to take over the investigation. Said he had to talk the Chancellor out of sending someone today."

"How many days is 'a few days'?" Adeline asked. "Does he want it solved by Halloween?" That only gave them three days.

"He didn't specify."

"Of course he didn't." She crossed her arms.

"What's the rush? The humans think it's cult activity, and no supernatural beings have been harmed." Jakob furrowed his brow.

"No, but the former Steward's making noise about it and hinting at running again in the next election."

"Of course that's what matters to them!" Adeline threw her hands in the air. "People are being massacred; the land itself is crying out. I feel like my heart's being torn out with a rusty spoon every other day, but what matters to him? His damn job!" A column of air gusted around her, which blew some papers across the table. Her skin began to prickle with heat. "He doesn't care that people are dying. He just doesn't want to look bad. And what help could he give, anyway?" The wind picked up and several files flew into the bullpen area. Something deep inside Adeline's chest begged for her to finally unleash the anger she'd pushed down for so long. "He's sitting in some office, hundreds of miles from here, threatening that if we don't work harder he'll step in. Step in and do what? You know, shit like this is the reason why—"

"Adeline, can you—" Jakob tried to intervene. "It's shitty that the Steward cares more about his polls than the deaths. We all agree on that."

"Don't try to placate me." She glared at him. "My community's the one in the killer's sights and I'm physically experiencing the land's reaction to what's happening. I don't have the capacity to pretend to care about some politician's ego right now. And the implication that we're not doing enough is something I'm taking personally."

"I'm not trying to placate you. I'm reminding you that we're on your side. No one's happy about this."

"I'm livid about it." Steve's frown deepened. "Werner was clear: we need a perpetrator as soon as possible. Not *the* perpetrator, mind you. I don't like that one bit."

"Does he want the killer found? Or the murders to stop? Because one will happen faster than the other given the kind of magic we're talking about." Adeline seethed.

"What do you mean?" Rebecca asked.

"Dark magic's dangerous. It's addictive, and the more a person uses dark magic, the faster it corrupts and kills them. The killer's probably already feeling the effects: getting sick or going crazy. It's entirely possible that it will kill them before too long."

"So, the problem might take care of itself?"

"Maybe, but I don't know how soon we should count on that happening. Oh, and our killer probably isn't even a witch."

"What?" Steve asked.

"All witchcraft is magic, but not all magic is witchcraft. You don't have to be a witch to use dark magic. A human could learn to cast dark spells if they found the right materials."

"Why didn't you say so before now? Isn't that something you already knew?" Ned asked as Jakob flinched. "You know what, never mind. I retract the question."

"A wise choice, considering the situation," she replied. "What are y'all looking at?"

"All the reports we have, the photos from the crime scene, witness statements from the sheriff's department: all of it," he said. "We've been pouring over it, looking for something that we might've missed on the first ten go-rounds."

"What do you want us to do, Steve?" Jakob asked, beckoning between himself and Adeline. "Lend a hand pouring over the files? Or head back to Kentucky and keep an eye on the only suspect we have?"

"He's not even really a suspect, more of a person of interest at this point." Steve waved the idea off. "Stay here for now."

"You said the killer's probably already feeling the effects of the dark magic." Rebecca tapped her pen against the file in front of her. "Did anyone seem unwell or off at either funeral?"

"It's hard to say. How can I tell if someone's on edge because of dark magic-induced madness as opposed to worrying about two murders as opposed to dealing with a drug problem? Does someone look pale because they're ill or because they're tired? If someone makes a weird comment, was it an accidental slip or did they say it because they don't know what else to say? It's not easy to discern what's suspicious behavior and what isn't, and we don't have the manpower to track down false leads."

For the next few hours, the team sat around the conference table, looking over the evidence that they had. Adeline felt like the reports were all starting to blur together and couldn't help but wonder how the others could look at the photos and not want to be sick. Maybe it was easier for them because the victims were strangers to them.

"Adeline, take a look at this." Rebecca held out a photo. "At the pile in the corner."

Adeline looked up from the report she was re-reading. The other woman's finger was pointing to a pile of dust and debris in the corner of Sandra Russett's kitchen. "Yeah, the mysterious dust. What about it?"

"We got a report back right before the Steward called. I don't know if anyone's looked over it yet." Ned started to rifle through one of the stacks of papers in front of him. "It's here somewhere. Let me find it."

"There's no blood around it. Its placement is intentional," Rebecca said as she started flipping through the other photos. "And it's the same in the photo from the second crime scene." She pulled out a photo from Derek Green's sitting room.

There was another pile of dust visible in the photo. It looked like it had been put there deliberately, and it was in an area free of blood.

"It's blood," Ned said. "They finally figured out the third substance was human blood that didn't belong to either victim."

"The report said the pile was salt, coal dust, and blood?" Adeline paled.

"Yes."

"Did they find anything else? Any other substances mixed in?"

Ned scanned the report again. "No. Salt, coal dust, and dried human blood not belonging to either victim. Nothing else present in either sample. Why?"

"It's a dark trinity," Adeline said in disbelief.

"What?" Steve asked.

"Non-ancestral magic utilizes something jokingly called "the holy trinity." Certain spells, powerful ones, will call for a binding agent that's usually salt, something from the earth to ground it, and a sacrifice from nature to power it. Ancestral witches don't use it because we don't need to." She glanced around the table. "Anyway, the dark trinity swaps out one or two of those ingredients with something harmful, blood in this case, to allow magic to be used with malicious intent."

"Whose blood does it have to be?"

"Probably the killer's, but I'm not completely sure. Dark trinities aren't mentioned often in books, and nothing I read said anything definitive about whose blood it had to be."

"I guess it was too much to hope for more detail." He turned his attention back down to the report he was reading. "What about the symbols? Does knowing the dust's a dark trinity knock anything loose?"

She pulled out the photos of the sigils that had been painted on the walls of both crime scenes. "I'm sorry, but I've got nothing. Mountains with an arrow shot into the eye. It's not one I've seen before."

"Is it an eye?" Ned asked, tilting his head to the side. "It doesn't quite look like one from this angle."

They worked their way through the files for another hour before Steve sent them home to get some rest.

Adeline went home and curled up with her cat. Whiskey was still acting oddly and was even more clingy than normal. That night, she was plagued with nightmares about the unsolved murders and other people she hadn't been able to save, like Lucy Radassi and Josie, the Seattle runway killed by vampires. In another dream, something chased her through the woods. She woke up covered in sweat and out of breath, with an urge to call Elijah, but saw it was 1:30 in the morning and decided to wait until dawn.

CHAPTER 16

— · —

Adeline was the last person to arrive at the office the next day. The first time she tried to leave the house Whiskey followed her. Once she'd corralled the cat back inside, she started howling every time Adeline went near the front door. No amount of soothing kept her from starting up again each time Adeline tried to leave, so she finally gave up and left despite the wails coming through the front door.

When she walked into the building, Ned and Rebecca poured over case files in the conference room and Steve was on the phone in his office. Jakob was nowhere in sight, but his jacket sagged over the back of a chair. Adeline sat down next to Ned and grabbed a file, diving back into a report she'd already read a few dozen times. She was halfway through re-reading it when Steve entered the room.

"We're no longer working under a strict deadline to find our suspect. At least, not the 'few days' timeline the Steward gave yesterday." Steve said without preamble.

"He changed his mind?" Ned asked.

"No, this came from over his head."

"I thought the Chancellor—"

"The decree came from above the Chancellor as well."

"There's no—Are you suggesting the Moranaa Dessis stepped in? I thought they didn't do that," Rebecca said, eyes wide in surprise.

"Because they don't. Werner wasn't happy about it, and I'd wager Chancellor Finley isn't either, but they don't have a choice. The Codex is clear that the buck stops with the Moranaa Dessis, and they've declared there will be no intervention by the Steward or Chancellor in this case. According to the call I got from Werner, the decision comes 'sua sponte' which is fancy wording for—"

"'Of their own accord,'" Jakob cut in, walking back into the room. Everyone looked at him in surprise. "What? Sound carries in here."

"I think we're all just surprised to learn you speak Latin," Rebecca said.

"I don't. I was an Army Ranger; 'sua sponte' is the motto of the 75th Ranger Regiment." He shrugged as he sat down. "What announcement did I interrupt?"

"The Moranaa Dessis have decreed, for reasons unknown, that no one at the state or regional level is to interfere with our current investigation until they say otherwise," Steve repeated. "We're on our own for now."

Jakob snorted. "How much of a conniption did Werner throw when he heard that?"

"Something about them stepping in rubs me the wrong way," Adeline admitted. To her knowledge, the Moranaa Dessis weren't concerned with murder investigations and hadn't intervened like this in decades, if not centuries. "But I'm glad we're not under as much of a time crunch now."

"I'm not. I'm scared shitless—pardon my language—if I'm being honest." Steve picked up a file and opened it. "The last time they interfered on an issue unprompted like this was August 1939. Germany was about to invade Poland, and the Moranaa Dessis urged everyone to get out of Europe before the war started." He closed the file and threw it onto the table. "An estimated eighty-five million people died during that war. Given that context, I don't like what their intervention suggests about this case or what might come next. They only get involved when an issue has broad implications for the supernatural world. Let's solve these murders before we have to find out what those might be."

For thirty minutes, the five of them sat in silence and read over the files. Then, Steve's cellphone rang.

"This is Steve Kresler," he said, answering the call. "There was? When? Okay, I'll send some people over." He ended the call. "That was the Harlan County sheriff."

"There was another murder." Jakob sat up in his seat.

"Yes, right outside Evarts. And the victim was Wyatt Dunn." His gaze turned to Adeline, whose mouth was slightly agape. "Our only suspect is dead."

He then looked at the others. "Don't just sit there. We've got more time but no leads. Go to the crime scene and take a look at what's there."

"All of us?" Ned asked nervously. "Blood and I don't—"

"Yes, that includes you. Don't look at the blood unless you have to; try to get the local LEOs talking, search the yard, I don't care how you handle it, Ned, but y'all need to go. Now."

They were on the road within minutes.

***

Jakob insisted on driving himself and Adeline to Evarts. He reasoned that, given the physical toll entering Harlan County was taking on her body, it wasn't safe for her to drive.

Adeline's pulse skyrocketed as soon as she crossed into Kentucky. Her mind was torn between overwhelming fear and unbearable sadness. At the same time, the burning, clawing pain overtook her as she felt invisible fingers wrap around her heart and start to tug on it. This was the first time she felt both the physical pain and emotional rawness strike her at the same time.

"Pull over," she bit out as she clutched her chest.

Jakob slammed on the brakes and ignored the honks coming from the car behind him. "Maybe you should've stayed at the office. I don't—Did you ever explain to Steve how bad the pain has gotten?"

"No, because I can push through it." The pain was slowly starting to subside, but the pressure remained. "Keep driving. I feel better. I'm fine."

"You don't seem fine at all. Are you sure?"

"The land's distraught and wants what's happening to finally be over." She could focus on the task at hand and suppress the whirlwind of emotions and accompanying pain that threatened to consume her. She had to. "I can handle it. I'll be fine. We don't have time for me to fall apart anyway."

A different deputy waited when they pulled up outside Wyatt Dunn's house. Rebecca and Ned arrived a moment later. The deputy waved to them but didn't say anything as they approached.

"Do you know who found the body?" Rebecca asked as they walked past.

"His brother's widow. She came to drop something off and found him like that. She's at the station if you need to talk to her."

"I'm not sure that's necessary," she replied. "Where's the body?"

"Inside to the left."

The Guardians walked inside but Ned didn't move further than the entryway. "I'll stay out here."

"Don't think of it as blood. Think of it as ... paint. Dark red paint with a strange consistency," Adeline suggested.

"I've tried that tactic. It doesn't work because I know I'm lying to myself." He shook his head. "I'll talk to the deputy some more, find out when Wyatt was last seen alive." He wandered off.

Adeline was about to call out to him when Rebecca stopped her.

"Let him go. He'll be fine and we need to get this over with."

Rebecca, Jakob, and Adeline walked into the room where the body was. Wyatt was laid out in his living room, facedown on the ground. The scene was just as bloody as the previous two had been, but Wyatt's body had been torn open along his back, unlike Derek and Sandra. His ribcage appeared intact from what little they could see, but his organs were on full display. Blood had seeped into the area rug under his body and the overpowering scent of decay hung in the air. Adeline's stomach became queasy.

Yet another pile of dust littered the ground, once again away from all the blood. The heap of black powder served as a silent reminder of Adeline's continued failure. A black sigil spread across the wall, just like at the last two scenes.

"It's a shame," Adeline said, looking down at the body of a man she'd known since daycare. "He was a pretty decent guy."

"Yesterday you thought he was a murderer," Jakob reminded her.

"Because the information we had suggested he was connected to the murders. Now that he's dead, I feel bad for suspecting him. I've known him almost my whole life."

"Let's get what we need and get out of here." Rebecca glanced around at the walls, then froze. "Is it just me or does that sigil look different from the others?"

"It looks a little different," Adeline agreed.

"It's clearer." Jakob studied the drawing. "On the other two, you couldn't really tell what the arrow was stabbed through. We assumed it was an eye, but I'm not sure anymore."

"If it's not an eye, what is it?" Rebecca wondered as she stepped closer to take a photograph.

"Do I seem like the kind of guy that's real good when it comes to symbolism? Maybe it's an eye, maybe it's a heart, or maybe it's just a blob to throw us off."

An odd sense of relief overcame Adeline as soon as Jakob said the word "heart." The pressure constricting her chest eased slightly. She didn't know what the sigil meant, symbolically or for the spell at play, but some deep intuition of hers whispered that Jakob's guess was right.

"It's a heart," she said, smiling for a brief second at the reprieve. "I can't explain it, other than just a gut feeling, and I ain't sure how it ties into everything, but I've survived this long by listening to my instincts. It's a heart."

The medical examiner arrived without his assistant about five minutes later. "I'm getting tired of seeing y'all's faces."

"I wish I'd stop seeing you too." Adeline gave him a tight smile. "Hopefully, this is the last time,"

"It better be. Is Wyatt here missing anything?" Jakob gestured to the body.

"'Missing'? What do you mean 'missing'?" the coroner asked.

"Well, his body's been torn open. It looks like his insides have been ripped apart. I'm just wondering if any of his parts are missing."

The coroner didn't look amused as he bent down to examine the body. With a gloved hand, he reached into Wyatt's wound on the left side.

"Shit!" He moved his hand to the other side of the cavity before looking up at the group. "Both of his kidneys are missing. How did you—?"

"It fits in with the other murders." Jakob exchanged glances with Rebecca and Adeline. They now had the information they needed from the crime scene. "We'll, uh, leave you to it."

Ned, who was lingering in the hallway just in sight, looked relieved. Rebecca moved to follow Jakob out of the room. Adeline, meanwhile, was looking at the floor when the coroner moved the body slightly.

"Wait, what is that?" she asked, pointing to a spot underneath the body. A section of flooring just beyond the rug under Wyatt's right shoulder seemed relatively blood-free.

"What's what?"

"There's something on the floor near the body. Lift him up again. Please."

The coroner called for his assistant. Kyle came rushing in, and together they lifted the body onto a gurney. "I'll be damned. He carved something into the floor."

"The killer or the victim?" Ned called from the hallway.

"The victim." He lifted one of Wyatt's hands. "He has bits of wood under his fingernails."

Adeline offered her phone to the coroner's assistant. "Kyle, do you mind taking a photo of that mark for me?"

He hesitated to take the device. "The crime scene guys will—"

"They'll get a better picture, I know. But if we have a photo of it now, we don't have to wait until we have the pictures to start trying to figure out what it means."

He looked between Rebecca, Jakob, and the coroner. When none of them objected, he removed his gloves, took Adeline's phone, snapped a photo of the scratch on the floor, and handed it back to her.

"Now we'll get out of your way." Adeline left the room and followed her colleagues out of the house.

As soon as they were past the police tape, Jakob and Rebecca asked to see the photo. She passed them the phone and let them study it. The mark was a straight line, with part of another curved line attached to it.

"It looks like a letter, but I can't tell what letter," Rebecca said, tiling her head to the side. "A capital 'B' maybe? Or a 'D'?"

"It could also be a 'P' or an 'R,'" Jakob added. "Assuming it's a letter at all." He looked at Adeline. "Smart as it was for him to try and leave a clue for whoever found his body, his attempt doesn't tell us much."

"Wyatt always was smarter than people gave him credit for, me included," she said fondly. "It tells us more than you realize. He was laid out on the floor long enough to carve the mark into it. He carved it, so he could use his hands, and he had enough awareness of what was happening to try."

"That also means he died slowly and painfully, since he was able to do that," Jakob added.

She knew that, logically, but her mind hadn't wanted to acknowledge it, much less accept it. Wyatt, the boy she and Elijah met on the first day of pre-school, wasn't only dead but had died a horrible death. Her gorge rose at the idea, but she shoved the feeling down.

"It's a bittersweet discovery. I'll give you that," she said once the urge to vomit subsided. "Ned, what did the deputy say?"

"In addition to finding the body, Joan Dunn was the last person to see Wyatt alive. According to what she told the deputy, he worked his normal shift last night and returned home around one this morning. She stopped by a little after eight to drop off his schedule for next week."

"The other two victims were killed between one and three in the morning," Jakob reminded everyone.

"At one-thirty this morning, something woke me up out of a dead sleep," Adeline admitted. "It didn't happen with the other murders, and I don't know what it means, but it means something. It has to."

"A warning of some kind from your ancestors?"

"Between being woken up, my instinct about the symbol, and the chest pains, I'd say so."

***

Steve called everyone into his office as soon as they stepped through the door. He was still visibly on edge, but he seemed less agitated than he had been an hour earlier.

"You're in a better mood," Jakob remarked.

"We're probably not staring down the barrel of a catastrophic loss of life. At least, that's the impression Chancellor Finley has of the Moranaa Dessis' order."

"Why are you relying on the impression the Chancellor got? Doesn't the order say why they intervened?" Rebecca asked.

"The order says there's to be no intervention by the state Steward or regional Chancellor due to the nature of the magics involved in these murders."

"That's it?"

"They don't have to explain beyond that." Jakob shook his head. "The wording in that order meets the bare minimum."

"We'll find out eventually, or we won't," Steve said with a shrug. "Either way, we've still got a killer to find. What did you find at the crime scene?"

Rebecca did most of the talking, explaining the state of Wyatt's house as well as the damage to his body. Steve was just as surprised as the coroner had been when he heard about Wyatt's missing kidneys.

"We have a victim missing her lungs, another missing his liver, and now a third with no kidneys. What the hell do kidneys, a liver, and lungs have in common?"

"You can't live without them," Jakob said almost absentmindedly from where he sat.

"I don't claim to know much about anatomy, but I'm pretty sure you need all of your organs to stay alive," Steve quipped.

"You can live without a gallbladder or a pancreas, though. Having them's better, but losing either won't kill you. Only five organs are important enough to be called vital organs: kidneys, liver, lungs, heart and brain. If any of them start having major issues, you'll be dead in hours. Our killer's only collecting those."

"All he needs now is a heart and a brain. Is that what you're saying?" Adeline's mind whirred as she drew the natural conclusion.

"It seems so. Meaning—"

"Resurrection's still our main theory, right?" Ned asked after working through something in his mind. "If you were going to bring someone back to life, wouldn't you use their brain? So they've got the same personality as before? That means one more victim."

Adeline's heart began to race. "I need to go back to Evarts. I—" She needed to get out of here. She had to make sure Elijah was safe. "Keep me up to date on everything. I've got my phone with me."

She was up from her chair and out of Steve's office before anyone could stop her. She heard someone yell her name as she left the building, but she didn't stop or turn to see who it was or what they wanted.

***

Adeline went home, packed a bag of essentials, and put Whiskey in her cat carrier before driving to Evarts.

She had to get to her brother as quickly as possible. It wasn't rational. She couldn't explain how she knew she needed to see Elijah or why, but the thought wouldn't leave her alone. Something deep inside her, more visceral than a simple gut feeling, told her that she had to stay nearby until they found the killer.

She pulled over to wait out the wrenching pain of crossing the county line, then drove on. Once she reached the Coburn house she knocked on the door and called Elijah's name until he answered. His eyes were red and his voice was thick. "Addy, what are you doing here?"

"I'm here to check on you. I thought it'd be a good idea if I stuck around for a few days, given everything that's going on." She paused. "I take it you've already heard the news about Wyatt."

"Yeah, I heard. Everyone in town has heard." He stepped out of the doorway to let her into the house. "Word spreads fast around here when it wants to. Coffee?"

"Sure." She put her bag down, released Whiskey from her carrier, and followed him into the kitchen to lean against the counter as he grabbed a mug. His hands shook as he poured coffee from the pot, and he sniffed a few times. He was losing the battle to keep his tears at bay.

"I got the impression that you and Wyatt weren't that close, but you seem awfully torn up about his passing. More upset than I expected you to be, given how you talked about him yesterday."

"I'm not sad because he's dead. Well, yes, I am. Anybody dying's sad. What happened to him was a tragedy, but I – Now I'm the only one left."

Adeline's arm froze midway through lifting the coffee cup to her mouth. "What do you mean? Only one left of what?"

He walked out of the room and returned holding a framed but faded photograph. "My second week at the mine was Derek's fifth or sixth year working there. Nina told him to get a photo of him with the guys he worked with to celebrate the day. There was this one guy who worked on a different crew, and he was always taking pictures on his breaks or after the shift was done. He took a photo of our group and gave everyone a copy after he got the film developed."

He handed her the photo. In it, seven men stood in a line and smiled through the coal dust and dirt covering them. Elijah stood at the end of the line next to Wyatt with an arm thrown over his shoulder. Next to Wyatt was another young man around the same age as them but still with some baby fat on his face. Next to him stood two men in their late twenties. One was laughing at something the other said. Derek was on the men's other side trying to look serious, but he'd cracked a smile. At the very end of the line stood an older man she didn't recognize, with a neutral expression, who gave off the aura of being important.

"It's a nice picture."

"I'm the only one in it that's still alive."

Adeline's blood chilled at his words. The smiles, frozen in that moment forever, seemed haunting rather than joyful. Six of these men, young and so full of possibility, were dead now.

"Wyatt's dead. Derek's dead. Pete, Jeremiah, and Freddie died years ago—" He pointed to each man in turn.

"How'd they die?"

"The mine collapse back in '98, on the last shift I worked," he said. "I should've listened to you and not gone into work that day. You tried to warn me; told me the mountain had had enough. I thought I knew better, thought you were just being paranoid. A few hours in, the world started shaking around me. There was all this shouting, everyone yelling as we tried to get out of the shaft. Wyatt and I were the last ones to make it out. Pete, Jerry, and Fred weren't so lucky." He paused. "Their families were hoping they'd find them alive. The shaft wasn't too deep, so it wouldn't take more than a few days to dig them out. It wasn't to be."

Adeline's mind flooded with memories as he spoke. She could never forget that day, but the finer details had blurred over the years, worn down by time and buried beneath newer memories. She thought she'd told Elijah not to go into the mine a few days before the cave-in, not the morning it happened. She didn't remember telling him that the mountain had had enough, but his words drew everything she'd buried back to the surface.

"What about him?" She tapped the photo below the last man's face, the only one Elijah hadn't said anything about. The man was middle-aged at least. Something about him seemed familiar, but she couldn't place his face.

"That's Jeff Russett. He died three Christmases ago. Heart attack, I think," he said. "He died, those three died. These two were murdered. Like I said, I'm the last one left."

Adeline's eyes went from her brother's grim expression to the smiling face of a younger Elijah, looking up at her from the photo. With her old memories resurfacing, she remembered something else that had happened on that fateful day sixteen years ago. Elijah had burst into her room while she'd been in the middle of casting a spell to protect him. Had she finished the spell and offered up something in exchange for Elijah's safety? Witchcraft always came at a cost. What had she offered? And who had paid?

Elijah was the only person in that photo still alive, and too much had happened for her to believe that was a coincidence. She downed the rest of her coffee and put the mug in the sink. "I need to go."

"What?"

"I have to go, I—don't leave the house. Don't let anyone in. No one, no matter how much you might trust them. Stay here. Look after Whiskey."

"Whiskey?"

"My cat. She's probably hiding under a bed somewhere." She threw her jacket on and walked out of the house.

She stopped on the porch to collect herself. Had she done what she thought she'd done? Her heart was pounding. She could hear her own shallow, rapid breathing. She couldn't drive like this, but she needed answers.

As her breathing evened out, Jakob's truck came up the driveway. He stopped and rolled the window down. "You ran out of the office like a bat out of hell. You want to explain—"

"I had to check on my brother," she said, getting into the passenger seat. "I need to talk to my aunt. Can you drive me?"

"Why?" When she didn't answer, he cut the engine and took his key from the ignition. "I'm not moving until you give me a good reason to take you there. I'll wait all day if I have to."

"It's relevant to the killings."

"You can't just give me that."

"I think the murders have to do with something that happened sixteen years ago, a mining tragedy that killed three people. And it might be my fault."

"That's a pretty good reason," he conceded, starting the engine. "Let's go."

CHAPTER 17

— • —

Adeline didn't speak as Jakob drove them towards Brodens Mountain. Every few minutes, she felt his gaze on her, waiting for her to say something.

Despite his clear curiosity he asked her no questions, and she offered no further explanation. She wouldn't have known how to answer whatever questions he had if he'd attempted to ask them.

She spent the driving trying to keep her breathing under control. This wasn't the time to pass out from hyperventilation.

Upon arriving at the base of the mountain, they walked in silence up the hill until they reached the clearing where Mary and her family lived. A few of the people working nearby saw her and smiled, only for their faces to harden when they saw Adeline's expression. No one walked over to the pair. A young boy—Adeline guessed he was Bethany's son—ran over to Mary's house, knocked on the door, and said something to the person who answered.

Mary and Caleb came out of the house moments later. Mary was leaning slightly on her son as she walked. The normally calm and collected woman looked startled by Adeline and Jakob's presence. "I wasn't expecting you back so soon."

"Neither was I," Adeline said, looking around. "Is there somewhere we can talk where we won't be overheard? I need to ask you about something … personal. A few things, actually."

Mary beckoned Adeline to follow her into the house. When Jakob stepped forward to go with her, Caleb blocked his way. Adeline stopped and glanced behind her.

"You stay here," Caleb said.

"That's not happening. Right now, I go where Adeline goes," Jakob said before meeting Adeline's eye. "You told me something pretty damning so I'd drive you here. I didn't push you to explain. I didn't ask you questions because I trust you. But if you think I'll wait out here and not hear whatever it is you two need to discuss, you're sorely mistaken. Not after what you told me outside Elijah's house."

"The knowledge of witches is only meant to be shared amongst witches." Mary's tone was firm. "You don't interfere with our affairs. Regardless of who you are or what you've been tasked to do, you have no authority here."

"He needs to hear this," Adeline countered. "My boss might not trust my version of events when I explain this mess to him,"

"Why wouldn't he believe you? You're not a liar. If your word isn't enough, then it proves you shouldn't be working for him. You've done nothing wrong and to act as if you're untrustworthy is—"

"Whether I've done something wrong is up for debate." She let out an exasperated sigh. "I need to talk to you, Jakob needs to hear our discussion, and we don't have time to argue about it. Can we go inside and talk now?"

With an annoyed huff, Mary led Jakob and Adeline into the house. Adeline and her aunt sat down at opposite ends of the sofa. Jakob remained standing, but moved across the room to lean against the wall next to one of the windows.

"Well, what is it?" Mary asked.

"Sixteen years ago, right before I left, there was an accident at the mine where Elijah worked. Rock Ridge. Do you remember?"

"I remember finding out about it. The mine shaft caved in during the middle of a shift. Three men never made it out alive."

"Elijah begged me to leave that same night. No one knew what happened, what went wrong. He said people were gonna want to blame someone for it, and he didn't want attention to fall on me. He was worried some of the guys he dug coal with had heard stories about Mama being a witch or the rumors about Eve, so they'd start thinking I'm one and would say I caused it."

"Elijah's very smart, but he can be an idiot sometimes. If someone was gonna blame you, it wouldn't matter if you were here or not. It's one of the reasons I told him that he was a fool for convincing you to leave. You could've stayed. No; you should've stayed. If anything, leaving made you look more guilty, like you were running from what you'd done." She paused. "What's done is done; why are you wanting to talk about it now?"

"He was scheduled to work the day it happened. I had this feeling that something wasn't right, that something bad was inevitable. I tried to stop him from going into the mine that day, but I didn't try hard enough. He wouldn't listen, and he went anyway. He was down in the mine when the cave-in started."

"And you were proven right. Is that why you left? Because you felt guilty over it? You shouldn't. You had an intuition and you tried to follow it; that doesn't mean you're the one to blame. Not when—"

"This ain't about the feeling I had that morning. It's about what I'd done earlier that day." She took a deep breath. "Mining's safer than it used to be, but it's not a safe job. I didn't want my brother to die, but I couldn't stop him from going and I couldn't get him a better job. All I could do was try to protect him. Which I did. Every day Elijah worked, I cast a spell on him: it was meant to protect him, stop anything from happening to him while he was working."

"How does that connect to the murders?" Jakob was no longer leaning against the wall, and his expression was perplexed as he tried to connect her story to what she'd said outside Elijah's house.

"I'm getting there." She turned back to her aunt. "The morning of the cave-in, I was casting my usual spell, and he interrupted me, wondering what I was doing. He was worried about John seeing me using my Gift, even though he was passed out and – How I got interrupted doesn't matter. Elijah stormed in, and I can't remember if I finished the spell. I think I might've, but I'm not completely sure. I might've gotten distracted before I could offer something in exchange to keep Elijah safe." Witchcraft depended on balance. For a spell to work, the witch had to offer something up in exchange. Usually, it was the energy it took to cast the spell, but some spells required more.

"What are you asking me?" Mary asked. "I'm not sure what question you want answered from that story."

"Seven men were working down in the part of the mine that collapsed. Four made it out. Now, almost all of them are dead. Is what's happening, the deaths of everyone, because of me? Are people dying because my protection spell might've been only half-cast, and my plea to the ancestors and to the mountain to keep Elijah safe backfired? Did I cause the cave-in?" Her pulse skyrocketed and she felt her breathing start to pick up. "Am I the one to blame?"

"I need you to take a breath before you work yourself up." Mary waited until Adeline had calmed down slightly before she spoke again. Once Adeline was calm, she let out a slight laugh. "You really don't know much about your own power, do you?"

"I know what Mama taught me, the bits and pieces she was able to pass down to me before she died. I taught myself some more using her grimoire and learned the rest from other witches during the time I was gone as I needed to. Why does that matter right now?"

"None of them were ancestral witches, that's why. There aren't any ancestral witches out west, so you learned the bulk of your craft from the wrong kind of witches. You're like a cat that was raised by wolves. Those witches, no matter how powerful they were or how much they knew, couldn't teach you as well as one of your own. Ancestral magic's different. It's intricate and specific in ways other witches, ones who draw from the stars, don't and can't understand. Stronger in a lot of ways, but more restricted in others and with different rules. Your spotty education when it comes to your Gift is apparent in times like these."

"I know it's different and I know there's plenty I don't know." She clenched her jaw. "I didn't come up here to have you say I shouldn't have left the holler, that I should've come up here and stayed with you after my mama died." Thunder rumbled, though the sky looked clear from the window. Unlike the day before, Adeline knew the thunder was her doing. "I'm here because three people are dead and I think it's my fault!"

"I'm not trying to rile you up, Adeline. The gaps in your education are relevant, as I was trying to explain." She paused and spent a few moments collecting her thoughts. "If you'd learned from me, you would've known that you didn't need to protect Elijah when he was down in the mines. He doesn't have your Gift, but he's connected to the land. The holler protects its own. Even if it didn't, your mama's buried not far from that mine. She'd protect her son from harm coming his way while he was underground. Whether you finished the spell or not doesn't matter all that much."

"But did she cause the cave-in?" Jakob asked.

Both women gaped at him.

"You said she didn't need a spell to protect her brother from a mining accident, but you didn't answer her question about her causing the cave-in."

"Could she cause a mine to collapse? Yes, it's possible. Did she cause the incident that happened sixteen years ago because of a half-done spell? No." Mary turned her attention back to Adeline. "What's the first thing your mama taught you about witchcraft?"

Adeline closed her eyes and let out a humorless laugh. "You get out of a spell what you put into it." Her pulse slowed to a normal rhythm. She hadn't caused the cave-in; she didn't have to answer for the deaths of three people.

"Exactly. Protection spells don't require much effort. There was no way you were channeling enough energy to cause a large enough backlash to collapse that mine. We'll probably never know why that tragedy happened. It could've been a genuine act of God, something no one caused or could've predicted. Or it might've been the result of a shady and greedy mining company cutting corners, wanting to dig further down into the dark of the mountain, tearing the heart out of it for the sake of profit."

"The heart of the mountain," Adeline said absentmindedly. "I told Elijah that the mountain had had enough, that she couldn't take it anymore and – I should've tried harder."

The sigil on Wyatt's wall hadn't been a complicated metaphor to unravel. An arrow shot into the heart of the mountain. It was so simple, yet she'd missed the significance of the image in light of the bloody crime scene and gory wounds.

"At this point, the cause of the mine collapse is irrelevant. The men who died down in that mine all those years ago were put to rest, and their kin have moved on." She leaned forward and took her niece's hand. "Adeline, agonizing over what you could've done differently sixteen years ago does nothing. You'll just torture yourself with questions that'll never be answered."

"I'd believe that, except two of the three victims of dark magic over the last few weeks were two survivors of the mining accident."

"I thought there were two murder victims."

"We found the third one this morning," Jakob said.

"That's a shame. How many of the survivors of the accident are left?"

"Elijah's the only one. Of the three other survivors, two have been killed by dark magic. The third one passed awa—Shit." Adeline's eyes widened in realization. "Sandra threw me off. She was the first victim, and I couldn't see a pattern between her and Derek. Because her murder wasn't about *her*."

"What pattern? What did you just figure out?" Jakob asked, looking between Adeline and Mary. "I need someone to clue me in here."

"You were right, for one thing. I said the murders weren't connected to coal mining, when it's the source of all of this," Adeline said. "Do you remember, the day we went to the first crime scene, when Steve asked me if I knew Sandra Russett?"

"Yeah, you said her name didn't ring a bell, but you thought your brother knew someone named Jeff Russett."

"Jeff Russett was Elijah's supervisor at the mine. He was also Sandra's father. He died about three years ago." The answer had been staring her in the face for weeks. "Sandra was murdered because her father was already dead. The killer's targeting the survivors of the mining collapse, or the closest living relative of the survivors, in Sandra's case."

"Seems a bit extreme to kill three people over an accident."

"Grief does funny and inexplicable things to people," Mary said. "Some people would do anything, give anything, for the chance to see a loved one just one more time, to be able to say goodbye. Feeling like you've been wronged will also make people act uncharacteristically. Some people will stop at nothing to get vengeance, even if it means waiting years."

"Sandra Russett had no family. Derek Green was married, but had no kids, and Wyatt Dunn's only family is his sister-in-law from what we know," Jakob said gravely. "Are we supposed to believe that's a coincidence?"

"It might be important, or it might not be." Adeline started to pick at her cuticles. "Powerful spells tend to require specific ingredients, like bones from a goat born during an equinox, or leaves from a rare plant. Or blood from a firstborn. The killer's been stealing organs from each victim; maybe whatever spell they need them for requires the victims be the last of their bloodline."

"Or it doesn't matter at all." Mary's voice was calm, but the worry was evident in her expression. "People die, they become estranged or move away. Maybe the victim having no family matters, or maybe the killer doesn't care who dies, as long as they're a survivor or close relative of a survivor."

"If that's the case, things don't bode well for you, your sons, Adeline, or Elijah," Jakob said before looking over at Adeline. "I probably should've kept that comment to myself. Sorry."

"You didn't say anything I wasn't already thinking about. We should leave now." She stood up and turned to her aunt as Jakob walked out of the cabin. "Thanks for your help, Aunt Mary, but I need to go."

"You want to make sure Elijah's safe. I understand."

"I don't want the killer coming after anyone up here."

"No one gets far up the mountain without us knowing, and when people come up here looking for trouble it doesn't end well for them. We'll be fine. We always are. Don't worry over me and mine."

"It's hard not to. I'll be back when this mess is over."

"Adeline wait just a moment," Mary said getting to her feet. "From the way you describe the murders, and unless my imagination's gotten the best of me—and I like to think it hasn't—this killer you're after is powerful. The thing is, they're borrowing it. It's stolen strength, bought using the deaths of others and fueled by rage and pain. Your Gift's not borrowed; it belongs to you. It's been passed down through generations and it's amplified by your connection to this mountain. The reason I've never left Harlan County, the reason your mother never went further than Lexington, the reason everyone was so angry when you up and left is because we're at our strongest here."

"If you're trying to make a point, please hurry up and make it. I'm running out of time." The sooner she left, the sooner she could make sure Elijah was safe and reinforce the protection spell she'd cast over his house. "I need to find the person doing this before they come after me, Elijah, or anyone else."

"Until you find your killer or the dark magic kills them, don't leave the area. You need to stay where you're strongest. Generation after generation of our family and other witches' families have lived and died here. We buried our ancestors here so their power could return to the land and so later generations could call upon that power. Nowhere outside of Harlan is safe for you or Elijah right now."

"Oh, I don't plan on going anywhere until these murders stop."

"Good. There aren't many of us left. We can't afford to lose you."

Adeline didn't fully process what Mary had said until she was out of the building, but knew she didn't have time to seek clarity about herself when Elijah was so clearly in danger. She resolved to ask about it later, when she came back to learn about her Gift after the killer was caught.

"Back to your brother's?" Jakob asked as they reached the spot where his truck was parked.

"Yes. We've got work to do." Now that she had a theory about the killer's motives, figuring out who it was hopefully wouldn't be that hard. There were only so many people who'd lost a loved one the day of the mining disaster that Elijah had barely survived.

"This isn't your fault."

"It certainly feels like it is."

"I think we should blame the guy running around tearing out people's organs, but that's just me." He looked over and saw that she wasn't going to respond. "Why not stay up in the hills with your aunt? Fewer people know where Mary lives than where Elijah does."

"I'd be endangering everyone living there if the killer shows up looking for me. I can't ask them to take that kind of risk."

"You'd also be surrounded by other witches. There's strength in numbers."

"Not everyone up there is a witch." Mary's parting words about how the coven couldn't afford to lose Adeline struck a chord within her. She wondered just how much their number had dwindled while she was gone. "More witches don't mean better odds of surviving."

"If it were me, I'd opt for some backup. That's all I'm saying. You've seen what the killer has done to people. The blood, the gore. The pain. Do you think you can handle that all on your own?"

Adeline could understand the point Jakob was tiptoeing around. Part of her recognized he was trying to be helpful, but a larger part of her was sick and tired of people questioning her abilities. She knew her strength, her power, her limits. She was tired of being treated as a liability. "Pull over for a second."

"Why?"

"I want to show you something. Anywhere is good." There were no other cars in sight. "It will only take a few seconds."

He pulled over on the side of the road and parked before raising one eyebrow at her. She took a deep breath before opening the door and climbing out. She bent down and grabbed a handful of dirt, letting it slowly slip through her fingers. Turning away from the vehicle, she focused her attention on a nearby tree and hoped the demonstration she was about to give would be effective in proving her point. She didn't perform spells like the one she had in mind very often.

She took another calming breath as she heard Jakob's footsteps approach from around the front of the car. She raised one hand. Out of the clear blue sky, a bolt of lightning appeared and split the tree, then a massive branch broke off and fell to the ground. A moment later, she wiggled her fingers and the remainder of the tree burst into flames. Despite being on fire, neither the trunk nor the branches looked charred. She waved her hand again. The fire stopped and the fallen branch grew back onto the tree. It showed no sign of damage, either.

"I think I'll be able to hold my own just fine if I need to. I don't think I need witchy support," she said before walking back over to the car.

Jakob stared at the tree, seemingly in awe of what she'd just done. "Point taken." He snapped out of his stupor and got back into the truck. "I wasn't trying to be a dick."

"I know."

After driving in silence for several minutes, Jakob spoke again. "How long would it have lasted?"

"Huh?"

"The fire that was burning but not damaging the tree. If you hadn't stopped the spell, how long would it have burned for?"

"I don't know. I usually set things on fire for a purpose, not just to see how long they'll burn. So, it could burn out in a few minutes or ... longer."

"That was a weighty pause."

"You hear rumors all the time about magical fires that only die when the witch who cast the spell dies. There are so many urban legends and folktales about it that it would take me an hour to list them all. Every time there's a wildfire and it's hard to contain, someone suggests that a witch with a grudge might be behind it. I've never put stock in those kinds of stories."

"But, in theory, you could set a fire that goes on for hours."

"I mean, someone would notice before then. No one's that oblivious. Unless I was deep in the forest, but I wouldn't even do it there." She paused. "You never know what else might be living in the woods, like the Leshy or a huldra. I don't want to mess with either of them."

"Or Mothman."

"Like I said, you never know."

CHAPTER 18

—•—

When Adeline and Jakob arrived back at the Coburn house, Elijah was sitting on the front porch with a shotgun across his lap. He set the weapon to the side as Adeline slammed the truck door behind her.

"What the hell are you doing?" she asked as she walked up the porch stairs.

"You ran off with no explanation like you were on fire. You didn't tell me what was going on or nothing. I figured it'd be smart for me to sit out here and keep an eye on things in case any trouble was coming."

"A shotgun ain't gonna be that useful against dark magic, Eli."

"Well, my choices were to sit out here and wait for you to come back, or sit inside and wait for you to get back. Out here, I could at least pretend I was useful." He got to his feet. "Now, you owe me answers. What the hell is going on?"

She let out a sigh, put her hands on her hips and looked at the mountains in the distance for a few moments. "Let's go inside and I'll explain."

"Is your shadow staying or going?" He nodded towards Jakob, who stood a few feet behind Adeline at the bottom of the porch steps.

Adeline hadn't noticed Jakob leaving his truck to follow her. "He should stick around. I'll need his help after you hear what I learned from Mary."

Elijah said nothing as they walked into the house. As soon as the door closed, a gray blur came rushing towards them. Elijah and Adeline both jumped, but the latter relaxed when she saw it was Whiskey.

The cat rubbed against Adeline's leg before moving over to inspect Jakob. After a moment or two, she rubbed against his leg and he crouched to pet her.

"Well, aren't you a beautiful girl?" He looked up at Adeline, who was staring at him in shock. "Boy? Which is it?"

"She's a girl."

"Why are you looking at me like that, then?"

"She's not usually so friendly with strangers. Normally she runs and hides." Whiskey hid from Elijah and Adeline's close friends in Seattle, but she was cozying up to Jakob.

"What can I say? I've got a way with animals." He smirked. "Or she smells my cat and it's made her curious." He scratched under Whiskey's chin. "I'll be in big trouble when she smells you on me." He looked at Adeline. "What's her name?"

"Whiskey."

"You're shitting me." He shot her a look of disbelief. "I named my cat Gin."

"Gin and Whiskey. Sounds like a great combination." She smiled.

"Yes, it's all very cute. It's like you two were fated to meet or something," Elijah said, reminding them they weren't alone. "I hate to rush a tender moment, or whatever this is, but there's a killer at large. And you're acting like I'm next."

"I haven't forgotten." Adeline's smile disappeared. "We have a lot to talk about."

With the cat-bonding moment over, she snagged her duffel bag from where she'd left it by the door, then led the men into the dining room and made Elijah sit down. Then she explained everything she and Mary had discussed earlier, sparing only the details connected to the gruesomeness of the crime scenes she'd been to. Her twin's eyes grew wider, and his expression became increasingly serious the longer she talked.

"So, I'm not the only one in danger. You're a possible target too because we're related."

"Yes, but not for long; we're gonna find the killer before Halloween and put an end to this. Thirty-four is too young for me to die, and if you die, I'll kill you." She reached for the duffel bag and started digging through it.

"How are we gonna do that? I work in a hardware store, and the two of you," he motioned between Adeline and Jakob, "might be investigating these murders, but you're not real detectives."

"No, but we've investigated supernatural deaths before. Or I have, anyway," Jakob said. "The point is we have some experience, which is better than nothing. Especially given that this is way beyond the county sheriff's abilities."

"And we've got an ace in the hole." Adeline handed Elijah a notepad and a pen. "You. Fred Blevins, Peter Blackburn, and Jeremiah Lee: they're the men who died in the mine collapse, right?"

"Yes."

"I want you to write down the names of any of their relatives you can think of. Anyone who'd want to avenge their deaths. You survived the accident when their father or brother or whoever didn't make it, and now someone wants revenge."

"You think that's why this is happening? Because of the collapse?" He uncapped the pen and began writing.

"She said she thinks the murders are because of the cave-in. You could've at least paid attention to what she was saying," Jakob grumbled.

"After I heard Addy was a target, I forgot about that. Because my sister's life matters more to me than the reason why folks are dying." He shot Jakob a dirty look.

"Stop it, both of you," Adeline said in a firm tone. "Elijah, you said it yourself. You're the only man in that old photo you showed me who's still alive. One death is an incident. Two deaths could be a coincidence. Three deaths, and it's a pattern. Sandra's death initially threw me off since she didn't work in the mine, but with Jeff Russett dead, killing her was the only way to get revenge for his survival."

"Why now? It's been sixteen years. Even if they were waiting for Walter to be the last Dunn, Clay died half a year ago."

"I don't know, Elijah. I've told you everything I know and what my theories are. I don't know why the killer waited this long."

"I guess I'll be the asshole and say it," Jakob said after several moments of silence. "Assuming you're right, and the murders started because of the accident, this is happening now because you came back."

Elijah's face started to turn red. Jakob cleared his throat and continued. "You're not to blame for this, Adeline, but you basically said it yourself. Every victim we've had so far didn't have any living relatives, at least no immediate family. If that's not an unfortunate coincidence, and if Elijah's the final target—"

"Then the killer was waiting for me to come back because they want me dead too," she completed the statement. "When I was twenty-five hundred miles away, they couldn't get to me. When I came back to Kentucky, I did the killer a favor."

Her hands began to shake as the implication hit her. Sandra, Derek, and Wyatt had died because she came home. Their blood was on her hands. Tears burned in her eyes. "This is all my fault after all."

"I just said that you weren't to blame, but it's cause and effect. After you left Kentucky, whoever the killer is didn't know where you were. You can't kill someone you can't find."

His spine straightened, and he turned slightly so he had a better view of the closed front door. "Someone's coming."

"How do you know that?" Elijah asked.

"A car just drove up, based on the sound of loose gravel shifting. Also, a shadow passed by the window."

"So, all that training you got from Uncle Sam's finally paying off." Adeline tried to keep the tremor out of her voice. The joke fell flat, but no one commented. "The protection spell I cast a few days ago should still be in effect. We're protected as long as we stay in the house."

"Okay, let's wait for them to leave." Elijah seemed to be speaking more to himself than anyone else.

"Or, we can see who it is first, and then decide," Jakob proposed.

Everyone stayed perfectly still. After a few moments there was a firm, but polite, knock on the door, and another followed after a few more seconds. None of them could see who it was through the three small windows at the top of the door; the angle wasn't right from where they were sitting.

"I'll get it," Adeline said a moment before there was another knock. She got to her feet. "They're clearly not gonna leave."

"No, I've got it." Jakob grabbed her arm to stop her.

"This ain't your house. If it's a random neighbor and you answer the door, they'll have too many questions about who you are and what you're doing here." She fought the urge to cringe at how thick her accent had become from stress and spending so much time in the area. "Elijah can't answer it, in case the person has bad intentions. That leaves me, or have you forgotten that little display with the tree? If you want to stand out of sight so you can jump in if something happens, be my guest, but I've got to answer it."

She took a deep breath before pulling the door open and immediately let out a sigh of relief when she saw Rebecca standing there with an annoyed expression.

"Why haven't you been answering your phones?" Rebecca asked. "I've called you and Jakob twice at least. Each"

"Cell reception's pretty spotty out here." Adeline quickly unlocked the storm door and let the other woman inside. "What are you doing here?"

"Steve sent me. You ran off with no explanation, other than saying you needed to check on your brother. He sent Jakob after you to find out what realization made you run off, and then we didn't hear anything from him. After my second call to Jakob went unanswered, he sent me." She looked to the left where Jakob stood. "You can stand down now."

Jakob moved his hand off the holster at his hip and relaxed his shoulders. "Shit's gotten complicated. Our killer's next—and final—victim is Adeline's brother. And he or she possibly wants to kill Adeline as well."

Rebecca spun to face Adeline. "Why? The killer – If he or she is after your brother, why kill you too?"

"It would take too long for me to explain all of it, but the killer's after revenge for something that happened almost twenty years ago. The victims not having any living family might be intentional. If that's the case, in order to fully get revenge, both Elijah and I have to die."

"I need to tell Steve about this." She pulled out her phone. "He needs to know there's a chance the killer wants to murder you and take your brother's heart, or vice versa."

"What's this about me losing my heart? I assume that ain't a metaphor," Elijah said, coming into the entryway where he spotted Rebecca. "I don't believe we've met. Elijah Coburn." He held out a hand.

"Rebecca Cooper, I work with your sister."

"I figured as much. Addy, what's this about my heart getting stolen?"

"Don't worry about it, because it's not gonna happen." When she told Elijah everything she knew about the murders she had omitted the goriest details, including the fact that the killer had taken Sandra's, Derek's, and Wyatt's organs. She hadn't wanted to worry him, and once he knew about the bodies being mutilated in such a manner he couldn't unlearn that information. "It's not something you really want to know."

Rebecca let out a sigh of frustration when her attempts to make a phone call failed. "You were right about the spotty cell reception."

"You'll get a better signal towards the back of the house. It's not great, but it's something." She pointed to the kitchen before turning her attention to Elijah. "Did you finish it?"

"Yeah, here's the list." He handed her a folded-up piece of paper.

"What's happening? What list?" Rebecca asked.

"We can't say for certain, but if you don't believe in coincidences—"

"I don't."

"I figured something out earlier: the killings are all connected to a mine collapse back in '98 where three miners died. Elijah survived it, and so did Derek Green, Wyatt Dunn, and Jeff Russett. Jeff had a heart attack a few years ago, which is why Sandra was killed," Adeline said. "One of the dead miners' relatives wants revenge. I asked Elijah to make a list of the surviving relatives of all three men."

"It could take days to go through everyone."

"It's not a long list," Elijah said.

Adeline unfolded the piece of paper he'd handed her and scanned the names. "Some of these names shouldn't be on here."

"Yes, they should."

"Dale Blevins was five when the cave-in happened."

"It still killed his father. You told me to list out every relative, so that's what I did."

"Charlotte Lennox isn't related to anyone who died that day."

"She was nearly Charlotte Blackburn. She and Pete were dating until he died and he was about to propose. Or that's what everybody said anyway," Elijah told her. "And before you question the next name on the list, Troy Perkins is Pete's cousin on his mama's side."

"Oh, I'm happy he's on this list. There's something not quite right about him. He thought asking me on a date at Sandra's wake was a good idea."

"He did what?" he asked in disbelief.

"You heard what I said. Then, at Derek's, he tried to apologize, but got all weird about it, and you interrupted before I could find a way to get away from him."

"Put him at the top of the list then. I don't like that."

"Neither did I, which is why I yelled at him for it."

Jakob moved closer to Adeline and started to read the list over her shoulder. "What were the names of the miners who died?"

"Fred Blevins, Peter Blackburn, and Jeremiah Lee."

"The sheriff's deputy, Paul Lee – He any relation to Jeremiah Lee?" he asked. "He's not on the list."

"He's not a direct relation." Elijah shifted his weight from one foot to the other a few times. "Jeremiah was a second cousin or something along those lines."

"He's as related to him as some of the other names on this list are to other miners who died that day. And he's a sheriff's deputy. Wasn't half of the point of Sandra's funeral to see if the killer would show up?"

"He didn't come to her funeral, or Derek's." Elijah looked at his sister. "Addy, can I talk to you for a second?"

"He wasn't at the funerals, but he was at two of the crime scenes," Jakob reminded everyone, "which makes him a suspect, at the very least."

"This wasn't Paul. He-he didn't kill anyone."

"If he has nothing to do with it, then it shouldn't be too hard to clear his name." Adeline noticed that her brother was getting defensive of Paul, more defensive than she'd expected. He was more adamant about Paul's innocence than he'd been about Wyatt's, and Elijah hadn't even been friendly with him when they were younger. "He's a suspect, but we'll try to rule him out first. Do you have a computer?"

"I brought one," Rebecca said.

"I'll go grab mine out of the truck," Jakob said, walking out the door. He crossed over to his truck, grabbed it, and walked back towards the house. He stopped next to the porch steps. "Are you expecting a package?"

"No. Why?" Elijah called back.

"Someone left a box on the porch. It wasn't here when Rebecca arrived."

"Don't bring it into the house!" Adeline rushed outside. She saw a nondescript cardboard box sitting on the bottom porch step. "Call me paranoid if you want, but—"

"It's not paranoia if there's a genuine threat," he said, moving the package onto the loose gravel of the driveway. He then raised his foot and kicked the lid off the box.

As soon as the box was open, the unbearable stench of rot and decay filled the air. It smelled like rancid meat left out to decompose in the hot summer sun for weeks. Adeline stopped midway down the steps and vomited over the side of the railing into a hydrangea bush.

"What's going on?" Elijah asked as he and Rebecca came outside.

Adeline finished emptying her stomach and continued down the steps.

"Are you okay?" Jakob asked, low enough not to be overheard.

"No." She sidestepped him to look into the box.

Inside, rested an animal skull. Dried-out flowers and herbs had been affixed to the bone with wire and there were strange symbols drawn onto the skull in blood or something resembling it. A pit opened in her stomach the second she laid eyes on it. The smell wasn't rot or decay; it was evil. Pure, unfiltered malice and death. Her palms became clammy at the thought of someone possessing so much hate within them.

"Close the box!" She waited until Jakob put the lid back on the box before speaking again. "I don't know what poor animal lost its life to make that thing—"

"Looked like a rabbit's skull," Elijah said.

"That bunny deserved better. There's darkness and evil wafting off that thing from whatever spell is on it." Adeline considered their options. The spell on it wasn't just harmful, it was malicious. She could try and unravel it, possibly learn something about its construction, but the risk wasn't worth the potential reward. "It has to be destroyed."

"How do you expect to destroy *that*?"

Everything she'd read had said a dark idol was best destroyed using fire. "Eli, do you still have that metal tub Mama used to use for washing her nice clothes?"

"Yeah, it's in the shed." He gestured to the weather-worn wooden shed on the other side of the driveway.

"I'll get it." She looked at her brother. "I need something flammable too, like paint thinner or lighter fluid. Hell, gasoline's fine."

"I've got some in the basement." He walked inside.

Adeline walked over to the shed and found the metal wash basin. She carried it to the yard where Elijah, Jakob, and Rebecca waited. Elijah was gripping a container of lighter fluid like a lifeline. Adeline dropped the basin onto the driveway and Jakob placed the cardboard box into it.

Elijah doused the box in lighter fluid and handed the bottle to Adeline, who emptied the rest into the tub. She took a step back and snapped her fingers, and the liquid caught fire. The group stood in silence and watched the contents of the basin burn.

After about five minutes, Adeline walked over to the tub and found the cardboard had completely burned away, as had the dried herbs and flowers. The bloody symbols had vanished. The skull itself was charred but intact and she didn't sense any malice emanating from it. She doused the flames with her Gift.

"The spell feels broken," she told the others.

"What about the skull?" Elijah asked.

With a gloved hand, Jakob lifted the skull out of the tub and placed it onto the ground. He lifted one leg and then stomped down on the skull, shattering it into multiple pieces. One at a time, he picked up each piece and threw it as far as he could in different directions away from the house.

"That was evidence," Rebecca said.

"It was also a weapon. We don't know what it was supposed to do, only that it was malicious. Breaking it into pieces and separating them was the only viable option. I'll take the fall for any trouble we get into over destroying it." He waved her off. "What now?"

"We need to get back to what we were doing," Adeline said, purposefully avoiding everyone's eyes. As her panic subsided, Adeline could finally process what that cursed skull meant: someone was after her and Elijah. Someone truly wanted them dead. She forced herself to remain calm. She could panic later, in private, once they had some kind of lead. "Figuring out who our list of suspects is."

"Who around here has access to animal bones?" Rebecca asked. "That will probably narrow things down."

"Almost everyone," Elijah admitted. "Rabbits ain't exactly hard to find."

"Let's start going through your list, then," she said.

Adeline moved to walk up the stairs, but Jakob stopped her. "Here." He held out a bottle of water. "To get the taste out."

"Thanks." She opened it and took a sip. "The curse on that thing—"

"Must've been pretty nasty to make you react that way." He waved towards the house. "We should head back inside."

Using Jakob's and Rebecca's laptops, they began to research the people on the list, eventually ruling out some names easily. Jeremiah Lee's mother was over eighty and wouldn't have the strength to perform black magic. Peter Blackburn's younger brother was in prison in Oklahoma. Fred Blevins' niece was living in Austin. Excluding everyone who had an alibi or lacked the means to be the killer left them with six names.

Paul Lee was one of them. They couldn't rule him out as a suspect just yet, but Adeline moved him to the bottom of the list at Elijah's urging. He was adamant that Paul was innocent, but refused to offer up any more than that. She trusted her brother but wouldn't consider Paul innocent until she had proof or an explanation of how Elijah knew he couldn't be the killer.

CHAPTER 19

— • —

A deline listened as Rebecca called Steve to relay what they had learned and what was happening.

"I don't fully understand the reason behind the killings, if I'm being honest," Rebecca said in response to a question Steve had asked that Adeline couldn't hear. "I'll let Adeline explain."

Adeline took the phone from Rebecca and brought it to her ear. "Hey, Steve. How's your day going?"

"It keeps getting better and better. First, our only suspect is dead, and now I'm hearing that you're directly connected to what's happening," he said. "Now, what in the hell is going on? Rebecca said you figured out why the killings started, but didn't share how you'd worked it out or what that means."

"The murders are all connected to a mining disaster that happened about sixteen years ago." Eyeing her brother, she stood up and walked into the kitchen. Rebecca followed her, but Adeline had to at least try to keep the nastier parts of the truth from Elijah. "It was a mine collapse. Three men were killed, four survived. Three of the four survivors are dead as of this morning."

"Our killer's the fourth survivor then."

"No, the fourth survivor's my brother, and he's the only potential victim left for our killer to target. Someone wants revenge against the survivors of the accident." She paused, debating the best way to tell him the other pattern she'd figured out that morning. "And, since the killer waited for each victim to be the last living member of their family, I'm also a target."

"Don't you have other family in the area? I could've sworn you mentioned a cousin or something."

"They're distant cousins. I've warned them too, but they might be too far removed for the killer to bother with. I'm definitely not." Adeline kept her eyes focused on one of the trees outside the kitchen window as she spoke. She'd identify the killer, one way or another. It was the only way to keep Elijah alive.

"So, to summarize, this morning our biggest problem was that our only suspect was dead. Now, we have to protect you and your brother from a crazy, powerful, and unscrupulous killer on a revenge mission. A killer who we don't know anything of substance about."

"Yes, that sums it up nicely."

Steve sighed on the other end of the line. "I'll make some calls. A buddy of mine works up near Philly. He owes me a favor and should be able to spare a few Guardians for the time being."

"You don't need to protect me. I'll be fine."

"Uh-huh. And the rabbit skull you found on the porch was, what? Some kind of local 'welcome home' gift you didn't think to explain to Rebecca or Jakob? Rebecca certainly thought it was worth mentioning."

"It was a threat, or an attempt to curse someone in the house, but it was for Elijah since no one knows I'm at his house. We cleansed the skull of the dark magic and disposed of it," she said casually. "Don't fret over protecting me. I can keep myself safe. Elijah's a different matter. And we've got leads. The killer's related to someone who died in the cave-in. Those three men didn't have a ton of family, and we've narrowed down our list to six."

"What are the names? I want to look into these people as well, find out what we're dealing with, and formulate a plan for how to handle each one."

"Charlotte Lennox, Troy Perkins, Paul Lee, Dale Blevins, Ryan Blackburn, and Helen Blackburn."

"Do any of those six seem more likely to be a killer than the others?"

"No. There are one or two I don't like on a personal level, but that doesn't make them murderers."

"Okay; can you give the phone back to Rebecca?"

Adeline passed along the phone and then walked back into the dining room where Elijah and Jakob were waiting.

"We could hear everything you said on the phone. You know that right?" Elijah asked when she returned.

"Let me live with the illusion, okay?" She grabbed her duffel bag. "I'm gonna take my crap upstairs."

"Upstairs hasn't changed that much. You'll know where everything is."

She went to the second floor and found that Elijah had done quite a bit of remodeling upstairs. The wallpaper in the hallway was new, as were some of the light fixtures. The bathroom had received an upgrade. She didn't want to go snooping around in his room, but the changes elsewhere were obvious.

Her previous concern that Elijah was living in a house inhabited mostly by ghosts waned a bit. He was taking steps to turn it into his home and not their parents' house.

She dropped her bag on the bed in what had been her room and unzipped it before looking around. The walls had been painted a pale green color. The furniture from her childhood, except for the bed, had been swapped out for different pieces. A larger dresser stood where her old one had been, and a bookcase from the foyer now occupied one corner.

"How does it feel the same but look so different?" she muttered to herself. "It's unnatural."

***

After getting settled, Adeline walked downstairs to find Rebecca and Jakob in the middle of a discussion. Elijah was nowhere in sight but based on the sounds coming from the kitchen he was making himself something to eat.

"—stop in and feed her. She might hide while you're there, but if you leave the food out she'll eat it. There's a key under the mat by the back-door," Jakob said, counting off on his fingers. "Yeah, that's all I need you to do."

"All right. I'll stop on my way home. I'll let you know in the morning if I'm heading straight here or if I stop by the office first." Rebecca gathered her belongings as she spoke.

"Sounds like a plan."

"What's going on?" Adeline asked as she walked into the dining room.

"Steve wants one of us to stay here to keep an eye on you and Elijah until we find the killer or have reason to believe the situation's resolved. Jakob's staying tonight since I can't do an overnight assignment like this on such short notice."

"I don't need a bodyguard." She crossed her arms. "If I wanted to, I could—"

"This isn't about your power; it's about your life. Someone's trying to kill you and your brother," Jakob interrupted firmly. "Don't think of me as being a bodyguard. Think of me as a support element." Adeline opened her mouth to argue, but Jakob quickly followed up with, "And Elijah invited us to stay if that's what we need to do to keep you safe."

"Of course he did. I've got witchcraft and he doesn't, but he's worried about me."

"He wants to protect you just like you want to protect him. Isn't that a good thing?"

"I'm not mad about the sentiment. I'm furious this is happening, and that you two have gotten pulled in." The last thing she wanted was for anyone to be hurt or killed trying to protect her. She already had enough blood on her hands. "Steve's overreacting about this whole situation."

"Well, he's the boss," Rebecca said as she walked towards the front door. "I'll see you tomorrow."

Adeline walked over to the window to watch as Rebecca got into her car. Jakob moved to join her, and the two watched their colleague drive away. Once Rebecca was out of sight, she cleared her throat.

"You don't have to stay. I won't snitch on you if you decide to head home." When she turned to face him, she realized that he was standing closer to her than she'd thought. "If you want to, you know."

"I think I should stay. Two Guardians are better than one, right? You might need me."

"I'm a powerful ancestral witch. We're standing on land that my family's been tied to for generations, and the kitchen holds a stockpile of spell ingredients that I can use in case my natural Gift isn't enough for me to cast whatever spell I want." She raised an eyebrow. "What can you do that I can't?"

"Well, if the killer shows up, I can always shoot him in the head while he's distracted by what you're doing."

Adeline frowned. "You want to use me as bait?"

"No, not as bait." His gaze moved across her face. "But you are very distracting."

"If that's supposed to be a joke, it didn't land. And if you're serious—"

"I am." He took a step closer to her and kept his eyes locked with hers.

"You picked a terrible time to start flirting, then." Jakob was attractive with his blue eyes, chiseled jaw, and defined muscles that didn't make him appear too brawny. Adeline would have to be blind not to notice that.

She didn't know him well, though, and attraction didn't mean anything beyond that would happen.

"Addy," Elijah called from the kitchen.

"Let's talk about this after we find and stop the killer." She turned away.

"Looking forward to it," he said over his shoulder as she went.

Adeline walked into the kitchen to find Elijah stirring something in a pot. "The only thing I've got is leftover chili. Help yourself to what's in the fridge, by the way. Are both of your coworkers staying?"

"Just Jakob. Rebecca will be back in the morning. I'm sorry they're imposing on you like this." She took a seat. "I can kick him out if you want. It's your house."

"If you kick him out, he'll just spend the night camped out in his truck watching the house. He seems the type to do that. And your boss wanted someone to stay."

"How do you know Steve said that?"

"I heard Rebecca tell Jakob that those were his exact words. Seems like he knows you pretty well."

"I was kind of hoping he didn't know me that well yet. It would've made things a little easier. Regardless of what my boss ordered, I'm sorry for cramping your style like this."

"What do you mean?"

"Just that I'm sure you'd rather be spending time with your mystery woman than with me." She walked over to the fridge and grabbed a beer without looking at the label.

Elijah stopped stirring and watched her with a guarded expression. His whole body was tense, and his voice was tight.

"What mystery woman?"

"When we talked a few months back, you said you'd started seeing someone." She opened the bottle and took a drink. "Is that not the case? Did you two split?"

"No, we didn't split." He eyed her cautiously before looking away. "I, uh, with everything going on, we haven't talked in a little bit. Or spent much time together."

She put her beer down. "You're acting weird. Is there something you're not telling me?"

"Someone wants to kill both of us with magic because I survived something that killed other people. I think I'm allowed to act a little off, given the circumstances."

"Okay, you have a point."

Elijah wouldn't look at her. He'd always done that when he was trying to hide something. Now wasn't the time to push him on it, but she'd get answers from him later. She groped around for another topic, settling on the smells coming from Elijah's chili. It wasn't the recipe their mother used to make. "Chili smells good. Whose recipe?"

"My own. I took Mama's and made some adjustments." He went back to stirring. Jakob walked into the kitchen and Elijah looked over at him. "So, how are you gonna find the killer?"

"It depends on what we find out about the six names you gave us," Jakob said. "If we have to, we'll go visit each one to try and suss out if they're hiding something while you stay here."

"You, Steve, Ned, and Rebecca won't make much headway doing that."
Adeline frowned. "Like I said when I went to talk to Aunt Mary alone,
some people won't talk freely with outsiders around. That's particularly
true when the questions you'll be asking will make you seem like cops."

"You're part of the 'we' I was talking about." He looked at Elijah. "You're
not."

"I figured. I'm not torn up about being left out of hunting down the
killer," Elijah said. "I hope you find them soon; I can't afford to be cooped
up in here for days on end and lose my job."

"You won't," Adeline insisted. "I'll make sure of it. And if Max fires you,
I can always hex him or turn him into something unpleasant."

"Why do you threaten to hex or transform anyone who causes me problems?"

"It's my way of being a supportive sibling. I offered it once, and it stuck.
Kind of like you offering to beat up that boy who made me cry in first
grade." She shrugged. "Is the chili ready?"

"Just about. Do you mind grabbing some bowls and spoons?"

Adeline pulled three bowls out of one of the cabinets and placed them
on the counter next to the stove for Elijah to fill. Jakob looked like he was
planning to refuse the meal.

"Eat the damn chili. It'll make both of us feel better about you being
forced to stay here." Elijah handed him the bowl.

The three ate in silence. No one was in the mood to try and maintain
a conversation over dinner. Once they were done eating, Jakob mentioned
checking the perimeter and wandered out of the house, leaving the Coburn
twins in the kitchen.

"Be honest with me, Addy. When is this gonna be over?" Elijah asked as
he gathered the dishes. "I can't spend weeks, or even days, looking over my
shoulder or wondering if the person I'm talking to wants to kill me."

"I don't know. It will be over soon, but I don't know how soon. What
have the hills been saying lately? Do they seem worried?"

"The entire time you were out visiting Mary they were in my head, talking to me. But what they said doesn't make much sense, not when it's all said at once. Lots of contradictions."

"What did they say? Word for word, including the contradictions. I want to know."

"A lot of it—most of it—was about you. You needed to come back. You shouldn't have come back. You were fated to come back. On repeat. Then, 'a river only flows one way, but tides may come in or out.'" He paused. "Also, something about an olive tree."

"So, talking to Harlan is like talking to a psychic now. Nothing makes sense except in hindsight." She put her hands on her hips. "I don't know what I was expecting."

"I wish it made sense. Normally, the message is clear. She told me to run when the mine shaft was caving in. She warned me when a bad storm was coming a few years ago. She said danger was on the horizon, and only a week or so later, Sandra died. This is the first time Harlan's been cryptic with me."

They finished their clean-up. Jakob returned from scoping out the rest of the property and declared that everything looked to be in order.

With nothing else to do, Elijah went into the den and turned on the TV, flipping through the channels until he stopped on an action-comedy. Adeline let herself be drawn into the movie, though she spent the first commercial break trying to decipher the message Elijah said he was getting from the hills.

During the second commercial break, headlights appeared, coming up the driveway. The sun had set an hour or so earlier, so the lights were impossible to miss. Jakob nudged Adeline and turned his attention toward the door.

"We've got company."

"The killer didn't walk up to the front door and knock," she said with an eye roll.

"We don't know how they got in, only that there was no forced entry." He stood and put a hand on his holstered weapon.

"Hey, Elijah!" a man called from the driveway. "It's me! You got a second?"

"What in the – Stay here but keep an eye outside. I might need back-up for this." She stormed outside, letting the screen door slam behind her. "Now ain't a good time."

Troy Perkins froze before he scratched the back of his head sheepishly and looked down at the ground. "Adeline, I ... What are you doing here?"

"I could ask you the same thing. I came over to have dinner with my brother, if you must know." She crossed her arms. "Your turn. Why are you here?"

"Came to talk to Elijah about something." He shifted his weight from one foot to the other and started to wring his hands together. He wouldn't meet her eyes. "It's – I really need to talk to him."

"Well, like I said, now's not a good time. Come back tomorrow when the sun's up."

"I've got work for most of the day."

"This weekend, then."

"Look, I came to talk to Elijah, but since I'm here, could we—"

"Do I look like I'm in the mood for this?" she asked with a glare. "You show up after dark, uninvited and hollerin' for Elijah. Now, you want to ask me to talk. Whatever it is can wait, I promise you that."

"I should go home, shouldn't I? I'm making an even bigger ass of myself than I already did." He took a few steps back, towards his truck. "Sorry to bother you."

Adeline said nothing as she watched him drive away. Once his headlights had disappeared, she let out a sigh of relief and unclenched her fists. Marks from her nails dug into her skin. She took a deep breath and walked back into the house.

"I don't think you should've done that." Elijah's eyes widened in fear. "You might've just pissed off a murderer."

"You saying that because he's on the list or because you didn't think to add him?" Jakob asked.

"That was Troy Perkins. He's already on the list," Adeline said as she sat down.

"Tell me about him. As a matter of fact, let's go through all six names again. Maybe something will stand out now that didn't before," Jakob said, pulling out his trusty notepad. "But start with Troy."

"He's a cousin of the late Peter Blackburn. He's the same age as Elijah and me, and he was a football star back in high school. Got a scholarship and everything, but flunked out of college," she answered. "Now, he's an electrician."

"And why would he come here this late?" He turned to Elijah. "He do that often?"

"No. Other than Sandra's funeral, I don't know if he's ever stepped foot in this house," Elijah replied with a shrug. "Addy?"

"Me neither."

"Okay. What about Charlotte Lennox?" Jakob scribbled down a note. "She's connected through Peter Blackburn too, right?"

"Yeah, they were – Pete was planning how to propose when the accident happened. They found the ring in his locker when they cleared it out after he died." Elijah seemed a world away, but shook himself after a moment. "I didn't know until a few days after the funeral. She works at the elementary school."

"She should be at the bottom of the list," Adeline said. "I can't see her doing this. Not when she's got her son to worry about."

"Thomas is out of school."

"He's still just a teenager."

"Helen Blackburn?" Jakob asked. "What about her?"

"Helen's a waitress and was Pete's niece. Don't know her that well. She keeps to herself. She had a baby that she gave up about seven years back and some folks had strong opinions about that," Elijah said. "Can't say much about her beyond that."

"Ryan Blackburn?"

"Pete's older brother. Works for the county. He's a pretty okay guy."

"He almost got into it with someone at Sandra's wake," Adeline said. "These two boys were eighteen, maybe nineteen. One of them mentioned how cool the crime scene sounded, and the other mentioned wanting to see it. Ryan got angry and told them to shut up. I didn't think much of it at the time, but that could be something."

"Remorse, perhaps." Jakob made another note. "Dale Blevins?"

"Lost his father, Fred. I babysat him a few times before the cave-in, but, until Sandra's funeral, I hadn't seen him since he was five. He's a mechanic."

"All right. Last but not least, Paul Lee?"

"Works for the sheriff's department. Nothing about him stands out, but as a deputy sheriff he had access to the crime scenes and could've disposed of evidence that links him to the murders," Adeline said, and she held up a hand before Elijah could object. "I'm not saying he did; I'm saying he could have."

"At the funerals, were any of them acting weird? Did any of them seem sick or ... not-all-there mentally?"

"Aside from Ryan's confrontation with those two boys at Sandra's wake, he seemed fine. I don't remember seeing him at Derek's, though. Charlotte seemed tired and stressed at Derek's memorial, but otherwise fine. Helen, too," Adeline recalled. "Troy's behavior was a bit off at Sandra's funeral, like when he asked me out, and he was a little manic at Derek's. Something has been off with him since I came back. He also has crazy eyes. Dale said something weird to someone else at Sandra's funeral; I don't remember what it was about. At Derek's he didn't do or say anything too strange but was noticeably paler than before and had developed a pretty bad cough."

"Okay, any of them have medical or veterinary experience?" Jakob looked between the twins. "I feel like it got lost in the flood with the dark magic and other details of this case, but the killer has to have some familiarity with anatomy for the bodies to wind up in the condition they were in."

"Ryan's a paramedic," Elijah said. "Would that – Is that relevant?"

"It could be."

"Troy told me that he wanted to be a doctor when he was lamenting about dropping out of college. He didn't say what kind. I don't remember if he said when he dropped out either." Then, Adeline scoffed. "And Dale sometimes helps his neighbor butcher his livestock."

"Is his neighbor Shawn Brown by any chance?"

"No, Dale lives out near the Morris's farm."

"How does this Shawn guy factor into this?" Jakob asked. "His name hasn't come up until now."

"You remember how I told everyone at the office that some livestock died before Sandra's death? They all belonged to Shawn Brown," Adeline explained. "Some pigs and a cow."

"So, Ryan's a paramedic with familiarity with the human body, Troy wanted to be a doctor and might've taken some anatomy classes, and Dale knows how to butcher animals," Jakob summarized. "And each of them seemed off when you last saw them."

"I guess we know which half of the list to focus on first."

"This is why I wanted to go through the names again. I figured a break would shake something loose."

"I think I'm gonna head to bed now." Elijah stood up and stretched. "Today has been rough, and I'm tired." He walked upstairs without another word.

"Why's your brother so dead-set on Paul Lee not being involved in this?" Jakob asked Adeline once Elijah was out of earshot.

"Not a clue." She shrugged. "Guess they're friends now or something."

Adeline turned the TV back on and tried to tune out the rest of the world. Around eleven at night, she turned to Jakob. "Wake me up in four hours."

"Why?"

"So I can relieve you on the night watch. We might as well take shifts since we're both here. That way, you get some sleep tonight."

He studied her for a moment. "Yeah, four hours sounds good."

Adeline went upstairs with Whiskey following on her heels. The events of the last few days were catching up to her, and she fell asleep as soon as her head hit the pillow.

CHAPTER 20

— • —

When Adeline jolted awake, she wasn't sure how long she'd been asleep. Outside, the darkness showed no sign of an encroaching dawn. The bedside clock displayed 2:13 in the morning. She stared at the ceiling for a few minutes and willed herself to fall back to sleep, but as she drifted off, something large and heavy slammed into the side of the house. Whiskey remained fast asleep at the foot of the bed.

She rushed downstairs. The front door remained closed and deadbolted, and none of the windows were broken. Jakob was wide awake, standing in front of one of the large windows in the sitting room.

She cleared her throat, not wanting to startle him as she approached. He glanced over at her, acknowledging her presence, and then turned his gaze outside. The night was silent and a strange stillness hung in the air.

"Do you know what that noise was?" Jakob asked.

A loud crash a few feet from the front door startled them before she could answer. Moving closer to the window, she scanned the view outside, searching for something that would explain the noise. The weak lightbulb on the porch only illuminated a few feet of space beyond the steps, but no rain fell, and the trees shook only slightly from a light wind. As she stared out into the night, a flash of light preceded yet another crash.

"All that noise for a thunderstorm?"

"The weather didn't call for storms," Adeline said. "And it didn't wake Whiskey."

"So?"

"So, it means she didn't hear it. Neither did Elijah, or he'd have come rushing down here. You and I heard it, though. So, it's only audible to people attuned to the supernatural like we are."

"If I didn't know better, I'd think we were under attack."

"We are. By magic." There was another crash and flash of light. "But we didn't bring in that cursed rabbit skull, so my protection spell's holding."

"You cast it on Elijah."

"I cast it on the house and anyone inside it. As long as it holds, whatever harmful magic being sent this way can't get through."

"Only one person would send Elijah a cursed skull and try to attack using malicious magic at two in the morning: the killer we've been after." He pulled his handgun from his hip holster and checked the weapon. "I'll sneak out through the backdoor and circle around to the front through the trees. I might be able to take them by surprise. Stay here."

"Don't do that." She grabbed his arm. "You just said there's probably a murderer out there."

"Killer's not after me."

"They could still kill you for getting in the way."

"Adeline, I'll be fine." He gently extracted himself from her grip. "I told you before: I'm not that easy to kill."

"Famous last words if I've ever heard any," she scoffed. She didn't want to remember Jakob in the same way she'd remember Sandra Russett, Derek Green, Wyatt Dunn, or Lucy Radassi—as someone who'd died because of her.

"I've been in more dangerous situations for stupider reasons. Besides, I'm great at sneaking around," he said with a lazy smile.

He walked towards the backdoor and slowly opened it. It let out a quiet creak, but another crash came moments later, masking the sound. He closed it behind him and disappeared from sight.

She turned her attention back to the front window. The crashing sound stopped, as did the flashes of light. She looked into the darkness with only her pounding heart and the sounds of her breathing to accompany her. She wasn't prone to panicking, but as seconds passed she grew more convinced that Jakob had gone to his death moments ago.

Eventually, something moved in the darkness. A shape came walking out of the tree line and drew closer to the house. Several tense moments later, the figure was close enough for the weak light coming from the porch to light up their face. It was Jakob, or someone identical to Jakob anyway. He walked up the steps and stopped in front of the door.

Adeline unlocked the door and took a few steps back, waiting. After several more seconds, the door opened and Jakob stepped inside.

"Is there a reason why you couldn't just open it for me?" he asked as he closed the door behind him.

"My protection spell keeps out anyone with bad intentions. I had to be sure you were really you, and not some illusion created using dark magic. If I'd opened the door for you, it would've negated the protection spell, since opening a door is an invitation inside, regardless of intentions. It's why there's no welcome mat outside. I guess Mama wanted to keep vampires out."

"Smart. I didn't cross paths with anyone out there. The killer must've run off after their attack didn't work. I found their hiding spot, though."

"Lead the way then." She started to put on her discarded shoes.

"Absolutely not. You said it's safe in the house. I'm not taking you outside in the middle of the night, right after we were attacked by magic. We'll look in the morning. You should go back to sleep."

"There's no point. Now that I know the killer's been here, I won't be able to sleep." She took a seat on the sofa. "It's almost my shift anyway."

Jakob sat down in the chair he'd claimed earlier. Neither of them slept, and they watched the sunrise a few hours later.

Adeline finally looked away from the window after she heard the floorboards creak overhead. She listened as Elijah moved from his bedroom to the bathroom and back again before coming downstairs.

He was dressed in jeans and a faded t-shirt, rubbing his eyes as he reached the bottom of the stairs. He locked eyes with his sister and sighed at the exhaustion on her face. "Don't tell me that you sat up all night."

"Only most of the night. The same can't be said for him," she nodded towards Jakob, "who didn't sleep at all."

"I couldn't, not after the adrenaline rush we experienced at two in the morning." Jakob said, tearing his eyes away from the window. "Something magical attacked in the middle of the night."

"*You weren't supposed to tell him that.*" She looked at Elijah. "Ignore him, and don't worry about it."

"Why not? Lying to him about what's going on won't keep him alive."

"What good does it do, telling him we were attacked in the middle of the night? The protection spell stopped it. It's not as if he could've done anything about it."

"Can you stop talking about me like I'm not here?" Elijah asked. "My life's in danger just as much as yours is, Addy. You don't get to decide what I should or shouldn't know. I know that I'm useless when it comes to stopping this killer, but still."

"You're not useless. You're just—"

Human. Elijah was just human and he couldn't help them any more than he already had. As soon as she had the thought about Elijah only being human, she knew she had to stop talking. The situation was already fraught, and arguing with or alienating her brother wouldn't help.

"I'm gonna make some coffee," he muttered, walking into the kitchen.

"Well, now I feel like a bitch."

"I'm not proud of my part either, if that helps," Jakob said.

"Ever since I found out I had the Gift, I've tried to keep Elijah away from all the supernatural crap, because the more he knew, the more danger he was in."

"He's a grown man. Let him decide how much danger he wants to put himself in. Murder method aside, this killer targeting him has nothing to do with the supernatural world or anything you've done."

"He's an adult, but he's also my younger brother and I don't want him to die trying to protect me or something." She took a deep breath. She hated thinking about this. "I'll go change. Then we'll head outside, like we discussed."

"What?"

"You refused to show me where the killer was hiding earlier, because it was dark out. Now, we have daylight. I want to see it." She walked towards the stairs. "I'll be back in a few minutes."

***

Upstairs, Whiskey was curled up on the bed without a care in the world. She woke up to acknowledge Adeline's presence before going back to sleep.

Adeline unzipped her bag and started rifling through it, looking for something to wear. In her rush to get to Elijah yesterday she hadn't paid attention when packing and now she couldn't remember what she'd thrown into her duffel. As she pulled clothing out, she found only jeans, t-shirts and sweatpants. Nothing like the clothes she'd wear to work.

She tugged on a pair of jeans and grabbed a shirt at random from the pile, throwing it over her head. Deciding she needed another layer to protect against the cool October air, she grabbed the leather jacket at the bottom of her bag. She pulled her hair back into a ponytail and caught a glimpse of herself in the mirror as she opened the door.

For the first time in a long time, the face staring back at her felt familiar. She was at home in her skin, and finally recognized the woman in the reflection. For years, she'd needed to dress nicely to be taken seriously, for others to ignore her accent. Looking at herself now, she saw how big of a facade it was.

Shaking her head, she walked away and headed downstairs.

While she was gone, Jakob had changed as well. He'd swapped the gray button-down shirt for a dark blue one and one pair of black jeans for another. He was relacing his boots when she reached the sitting room.

"Ready to go?" she asked him.

"Yeah," he said, looking her over. "You look – Nice jacket."

"Thanks?" She yawned and turned towards the kitchen. "Actually, I'm gonna need coffee before we go." She needed to be fully awake or she'd miss something when they searched the killer's hiding spot. The smallest detail could be important.

Coffee was brewing in Elijah's new machine, and he was standing with his back to the door, watching the toaster. When she stepped on one of the creaky floorboards, he turned around. "I see you've stopped pretending."

"Stopped pretending what?" she asked, pulling a mug from the cabinet and pouring herself some coffee.

"Like you're someone else from somewhere else. Aside from the funerals, where everyone's wearing all black, every time I saw you since you came back you didn't look like yourself." He shrugged. "And you never seemed comfortable."

"I was dressed like that because I was working. I had to look professional."

"Our office doesn't have a dress code," Jakob said from the doorway. "I wear jeans ninety-nine percent of the time. As long as you're decent, Steve doesn't care."

"If that's true, how come Rebecca—?" The other woman always dressed in pantsuits and looked as professional as possible.

"She dresses like she's headed to a board meeting because she's an over-achiever. And she thinks she has to look and be the best to make up for being human, forgetting that Steve's human too, and everyone still respects him."

"I doubt being human's the only reason Rebecca might feel like she has to do more to prove herself. Steve's an old white guy." She refrained from outright saying that Rebecca was none of those things.

"You might as well start dressing for comfort and convenience, and not like you've got something to prove."

"He's got a point, Addy," Elijah said. "I might not know Rebecca, but I know you. You never felt the need to prove yourself to anyone when we were younger, why do you think you have to prove yourself to people now?"

"It's too early for this," she said, taking a sip of her coffee. She wasn't in the mood to explain how she'd put on a front for years to earn respect from others. "It doesn't matter anyway, since I don't need to prove myself anymore."

"You never did."

Adeline drank her coffee as the room fell silent. Once she had finished the cup, she rinsed it off in the sink and turned to her partner. "Okay, let's go." She then looked at her brother. "Jakob thinks he found where the killer was hiding last night. We're gonna go take a look at it, see if anything was left behind."

"What if the killer's still out there?" His eyes went wide.

"They were gone when I tried to flank them last night," Jakob said. "They likely wouldn't have come back."

"And if they have, I'm gonna turn them into a bug and squish them for waking me up at two in the morning," Adeline said.

Since Elijah's question had some merit, she and Jakob exited the house through the backdoor and circled around to the front of the house. They didn't run into anyone as they moved through the tree line.

Jakob guided her to what he'd found the night before. There was a noticeable depression in the earth, large enough for a person to hide in, a few feet behind where the tree line started. The trees blocked Adeline's view of the house, but a person lying on the ground would've had an unobstructed line of sight.

"I don't see any footprints leading away from here." Jakob surveyed the area.

"It wouldn't matter. Through these trees, we're about twenty yards from the main road," she explained. "At best, following footprints would lead us to where they parked."

She walked forward, pushed through the copse, and gasped. Her protection spell had held, but the dark magic had ricocheted off the barrier. All that energy needed to go somewhere. A tree at the far end of the driveway had split in half, scorch marks marred the lawn, and some patches of grass had completely burned away.

"There weren't even flames last night." She stared at the ground, at the flower beds her mother had put so much work into when she was a child and Elijah had maintained as best as he could. "All this damage, and I didn't see it."

"It's grass, some asphalt, and bushes. Nothing that can't be replaced."

"It was supposed to be me and Elijah. It almost was." She looked over at him and then away. "All day yesterday, I was worried about my brother dying. It didn't hit me until now that I could die—that there's a good chance I will—before we find the killer."

"No, you won't. Look at me." Jakob waited until she met his eyes. "You're not gonna die. Your brother's not gonna die. You're both surviving this."

"Don't lie to make me feel better. I don't need platitudes. I need a plan, I need answers."

"I'm not."

"How do you know we're not gonna die then?"

"I can't say why; I just do." He turned towards the house. "Let's go inside."

She walked across the lawn, but stopped a foot before the porch steps. She bent down and touched one of the scorched patches of earth before looking over her shoulder at Jakob. "I'll be right in. I need to do something first."

"Go ahead," he said, leaning against the porch post. "I'll wait."

She let out a breath and touched the ground in front of her once more. She closed her eyes and took a few deep, calming breaths before she spoke. "I call upon the strength of my ancestors and hope they hear my request. My mother rests here."

She felt her Gift buzzing at the tips of her fingers and focused it into the soil, pushing some of her power into the ground. "A dark and evil force has done damage to her final resting place. Remove the scars of last night's attack from this land. Allow growth and new life to prosper here in time."

When she felt warmth spreading up her hand, she let go and opened her eyes. The gravel driveway still showed signs of damage from the ricocheted magic, but the grass and surrounding shrubbery looked as if nothing had happened. The tree trunk had even fused back together.

"The ancestors don't like it when one of their resting places is disturbed by dark magic; that's good to know."

She walked into the house, passing a slack-jawed Jakob on her way up the steps.

CHAPTER 21

— : —

"What did you do on the lawn?" Elijah asked when Adeline walked into the house. He was drinking a cup of coffee in front of one of the large picture windows in the sitting room.

"Dark magic spells will damage everyone and everything in their path. I fixed what I could in the yard. The plants look the way they did before. There wasn't any damage to the house itself, but the driveway looks like someone tried to start a bonfire. I can't fix that right now."

"Don't worry about it. It's asphalt and rocks. I think you broke your friend, though." Using his mug for emphasis, he gestured to Jakob who hadn't moved from his spot in the yard. From the twins' perspective, he was staring blankly at the ground. "Has he never seen magic before or something?"

"He's seen me use my Gift a few times. I don't know about other witches." She opened the door and whistled to get Jakob's attention. "Are you coming inside? Or is the driveway that fascinating?"

Jakob shook his head and his gaze focused on her as he came back to reality. He walked into the house. "Sorry; I've seen spells cast before, but not something like that. Your witchcraft is something I'm still getting used to."

"I figured that part out." She took a seat on the sofa and leaned back into the cushions to get comfortable. He viewed her Gift with such awe, and his appreciation was refreshing even if she struggled to understand it. "Any word from the office? What's our next step?"

"No, but now that you mention it, I should give Steve a call. They need to know about our early morning surprise, and I need to pass along some of what you remembered last night about Ryan Blackburn, Troy Perkins, and Dale Blevins." He dug his phone out of his pocket and walked to the back of the house.

"Seems like you *bewitched* him," Elijah said with a laugh as he took a seat next to Adeline. "He looked real *spellbound* by your abilities."

"You're too young for jokes that corny. And what I did wasn't that impressive. Hell, I was probably only able to fix as much as I did because Mama's buried not five yards from where I was standing, and the ancestors don't want that kind of darkness lingering too close to her resting place. Jakob's probably seen bigger, better feats of magic performed than my little botany trick, just not by an ancestral witch."

With Jakob's extensive knowledge of the supernatural, she had no doubt that he'd seen truly impressive spellwork. The only thing that made Adeline's magic special was that her power came from her ancestors.

"I doubt that's it. You've never thought your Gift was impressive, but I've yet to meet someone who agrees with your opinion. Mama thought it was extraordinary when we were kids. So did Aunt Mary and Granny Agnes, and that was back when you barely knew how to use it or what your limits were. Hell, Harlan itself seems to think your abilities are stronger than most, and that you've got more power than you believe you do."

"Of course the hills think that. They're just happy that I fixed the grass and plants that were burnt or destroyed. It's not like mountains understand how witchcraft works, or what makes a strong witch."

"That's not what they said, or why they said it. Now's not the time to argue about it, though." Elijah drained his mug and set it down on the end table beside him. "What now?"

"Huh?"

"What happens now? The killer tried to attack us using dark magic, but it didn't work. We're not lucky enough that they'll just give up. I'm in over my head with all this, but you've clearly been here before. What comes next?"

"I haven't been here before, but I've been close enough." She sighed. "The attack last night makes one thing clear: the killer's eager to finish what they've started. There were a few days of quiet between killings before now, but that's stopped." There had been a week-long lull between Sandra's death and Derek's, and almost an entire week between Derek's death and Wyatt's. "We're still not safe."

"I know. What are we gonna do about it?"

"Well, we could—"

"The two of you aren't gonna do anything," Jakob said, walking back into the room. "You're staying here while the rest of the office tracks down leads."

"Witchcraft is the best defense against dark magic, as last night proved. If I sit this one out, one of you might die."

"Last night also proved that this house is the safest place for you and your brother to be right now. You're still a target. You don't need to be with us while we're tracking down and talking to people around here, or verifying some of the things we talked about last night."

"I told you that no one's gonna talk to any of you. That hasn't changed."

"That was before we got attacked at two in the morning. I was expecting a lull between Wyatt's death and the killer's next attempt, and I know you were too. That didn't happen, so Steve's on high alert. When I told him about the attack this morning, he said there's no way you're going anywhere."

"Did you also tell him that the attack failed solely because of my Gift?" She put her hands on her hips.

"I did, because it's relevant, but a week-old protection spell holding proves exactly why you should stay here for the time being and not be out wandering Evarts, searching for the person who wants you dead. We still need your help with all this and no one's saying otherwise, but no one wants to put you in mortal danger to do so if there's another option."

"Isn't that something I should get a say in? If I want to put myself in danger, let me."

"Addy, can you please just stop?" Elijah asked, sounding exhausted. "I know you hate being told what to do, but for once can you not turn everything into an argument? I'm not thrilled about this either."

"Fine. Only because you asked." She looked over to Jakob. "When this is over, you and I are having a chat. Steve too. I recommend you buy some ear protection. Good ear protection."

"Fine by me. When this is over and you're no longer being targeted by a murderer," he said, picking up his jacket. "Rebecca's on her way. She was about to leave the office when I talked to her. Ned found out a few things about Troy Perkins that are suspicious, but might not be relevant to the murders. She wants to go over what he found and get both your opinions on it."

"And where are you going?"

"Letcher County. I need to clear a few things up with the wolves. Dylan's pissed, rightly so, that we accused her and the whole werewolf pack of being behind the murders. They weren't, as last night proved, and I don't want to let any animosity linger. I'm dealing with that now."

"Great." It would take Rebecca around an hour to reach the house, and Jakob was leaving. Once he left, Adeline would have a solid chunk of time to talk to a few people. All six of the remaining suspects lived close by, and she intended to take advantage of that. Three people were dead, and she wasn't going to sit around while her colleagues dug into the meat of the investigation. At the very least, she could cross a name or two off the list—

"Oh, and to make sure that you stay here, I've hidden your keys."

"What?"

"I'm not stupid. I saw the way you got a little excited when I said I was leaving. I need to go. Rebecca's not here yet. If I just leave, you'll wait a few minutes and then head out on your own."

"And what's to stop me from walking to where I need to go?" she asked.

"Nothing, but you'd be easy to find on foot." He stepped closer to her. "I know you got fucked over by your old partner, but please trust us. We've got your back. Let us handle this."

"I promise nothing."

He gave a long suffering sigh and walked out of the house. Elijah and Adeline watched him get into his truck and driveaway. She stood there for a few moments after he'd left.

"Okay, let's go," she said to her brother. "I'm not gonna just sit around, waiting for something to happen. And I don't answer to Jakob."

"You do answer to Steve, though."

"Steve's not here, and he didn't tell me to stay put. He told other people not to let me leave, but he never said the words 'Adeline, don't leave Elijah's house' to me. So, technically, I'm not going behind his back."

"What was it that Mama used to say? 'If you have to rely on technicalities, you've already lost the argument, and you know it'?"

"She did say that. She also said to take advantage of any edge you had when you saw the right moment. Asking for forgiveness is better than asking for permission, anyway."

"But the killer—" he argued.

"Has only ever struck at night. They're not gonna attack in the middle of the day, and even if they were, wouldn't it be smarter not to be where they expect us to be?"

"That doesn't – What does that even mean?"

"We're safe in the house, but in the house is where they'd expect to find us. And if push comes to shove, they could always set the house on fire to force us to leave anyway."

"You think they'd go to the trouble of trying to smoke us out?"

"They went to the trouble of learning dark magic, killing three people, and mutilating their bodies. A little arson is child's play compared to that." She grabbed her phone and wallet. "Let's go. I'll drive."

"He took your keys."

She reached into the pocket of her jacket and pulled out a key ring, jingling it. "But he didn't take yours. Call it a hunch, call it a sixth sense, but I felt the urge to grab your keys just in case when I saw them laying on the counter next to the coffee maker." She turned towards the door, but stopped when Elijah didn't follow her. "Are you coming or what?"

"Give me a minute," he said, walking over to a closet and grabbing his coat. "I'm only coming because you're leaving whether I agree or not."

"Stop acting like we're headed off to war. We're just gonna have a chat with some neighbors, people we've known for nearly our whole lives. I understand the sentiment, the intention behind my coworkers wanting us to stay here, but I'm not some fragile little flower who needs to be protected. Neither are you."

Elijah let out a resigned sigh. "Let's go then. But we're making a stop first."

"Where? The store? I'm sure Max will be fine on his own for today."

"No, we're gonna see Joan Dunn."

***

Joan Dunn answered her door in a sweater and baggy gray sweatpants. She didn't say anything for a few moments.

"Good morning," Adeline said.

"Morning. I – Sorry, I wasn't expecting visitors." Joan wrapped her sweater tighter around her body before opening the door to let them inside. She had bags under her eyes and her hair was pulled up in a haphazard bun.

"Sorry to show up like this. We wanted to stop by and see how you were faring," Elijah said.

"Honestly? Not well. Clay's death feels so fresh, and now Wyatt's gone too. And the funeral home wants to know what Wyatt wanted for his service, but I don't know what to say and there's nobody else to ask. Folks stopped by yesterday to give condolences, but I-I can't do this again. It all just ... Why would anyone want to kill Wyatt?" She wiped her eyes with a tissue. "Oh, look at me. I forgot my manners. Do either of you want a cup of coffee or something?"

"No, we're fine," Adeline said softly.

"I thought you might be overwhelmed, so I wanted to offer my help if you need it," Elijah said. "I don't know what you need, but whatever it might be, don't hesitate to give me a call."

"I'll keep that in mind. I just– It doesn't make any sense. I know folks have been dying lately, but I didn't think he'd be one of them. I don't think I'll ever be able to get the image out of my head, how he looked when I found him."

Adeline began to fidget and found she couldn't look at Joan for more than a few moments. Nothing about the situation felt right, but Joan finding Wyatt's body was one of the worst parts.

"Well, we don't want to intrude on your day any more than we already have," Elijah said. "Call me if you need anything. Even if it's just someone to talk to."

"Okay."

Adeline bid farewell to Joan and followed her brother outside. She got into the driver's seat of his truck, but didn't turn it on. "Why?"

"Why what?"

"Why did you insist that we come out here? You could've easily given her a call; you didn't have to visit in person. And we didn't need to call or come today. You brought me here for a reason. What is it?"

"I didn't want you to lose sight of what actually matters here. This ain't about saving me or you. And we shouldn't make it about us either. What matters is getting justice for Sandra, Derek, and Wyatt. You've got to remember why you're doing what you're doing. Otherwise, what's the point in doing anything? And I wanted to remind you why we should've stayed home."

"I haven't lost sight of anything," she insisted. She put the key in the ignition and drove off. "But, maybe, you've got a point about this not being about me."

In her determination to prove she didn't need protection, in her desire to hurry this investigation along, she may have made a mistake by not telling anyone where they were headed.

They made it a quarter mile from Joan's house before Adeline's phone started ringing. She glanced at it, expecting the call to be from one of her colleagues. Soon enough either Rebecca or Jakob would be calling, angry and wanting to know where the Coburns had disappeared to. Instead, the phone number was unknown with a Washington state area code.

She pulled the truck over. "I need to take this. Then, we'll head back to the house."

"That's the smartest thing you've said in two days."

She shot him a look but didn't respond as she unlocked her phone. "Hello, this is Adeline."

"Adeline Coburn?" a man asked. His voice didn't sound familiar.

"Yes, this is Adeline Coburn."

"My name is Shane Kline. I work for the Seattle Alliance of—"

"What can I do for you, Mr. Kline?" she asked, tightening her grip on the phone. It wasn't polite to interrupt him, but manners and whatever the Alliance needed weren't her priorities right now.

"Shane is fine. Mr. Kline is my father." His attempt at humor fell flat. "Gabriel asked me to call you regarding the accidental death of Lori Risida a few weeks ago. We're very concerned about what occurred."

"Her name was Lucy Radassi, actually." She took a deep breath to stop herself from yelling. The Alliance claimed to be concerned over Lucy's death and the events that led to it, yet they couldn't get her name right.

"Yes, you're correct. I do show that was her name." His tone was bored, and it was evident how little he cared about getting a dead girl's name wrong. "Anyway, you left Seattle shortly after her death and before anyone could speak to you about what happened."

"And?"

"And we'd like to hear your version of events so we can learn as much as possible about what led to her death and identify how such a tragedy can be avoided in the future. I'm sure you'd agree it was a mistake everyone can learn from." The sound of papers rustling came across the phone line. "Now, Gabriel asked me to schedule you for an in-person interview."

"Shane Kline. The name doesn't ring a bell. Do you work for him directly? Or just for the Alliance?"

"I'm his personal aide."

"That's nice." Adeline dialed up the 'southern charm' a few notches for effect. "I'm sure you're aware, then, that I don't work for him or the Alliance anymore. You'll have my statement when I'm ready to give it. And I'm certainly not flying all the way to Seattle when a phone call would suffice. Have a nice day."

"I'm aware of your ... unique position, but we have to conduct a face-to-face interview. And it has to be done by—"

"Why's it so important for my interview to be in-person? Why does it need to be done by a certain time? Is there something going on I'm unaware of?" It seemed Gabriel and the Alliance wanted the matter closed as soon as possible, which she found strange. She wondered if Lucy's family was causing an uproar and pressuring them for answers. She hoped so; they deserved the truth.

"I – There's – I'm not sure I'm permitted to disclose that to you," Shane sputtered.

"Oh, so something is going on." Adeline dropped her polite tone. "Funny that Gabriel wants information from me, but won't tell me what's happening or why it's so urgent."

"As I said, at this time I don't have permission to inform you of anything except that we need your statement."

"Well, in that case, my answer's the same as before. I've got my own responsibilities, which take priority over your inquiry. You'll get my statement when you get it, and I'm not flying west to give it," she said. "Now, if Gabriel wants it sooner he's gonna need to cut the shit and tell me what's going on or get off his ass for once and fly to Kentucky, where I am, to get my statement. Please tell him that, verbatim. Goodbye."

"I'll call your supervisor then. I'm sure your responsibilities in Kentucky aren't so important that he can't spare you for a few days." The slimy smile was almost audible in his voice.

"You won't get anywhere with that." Adeline took a moment, weighed her options, and then bit the bullet, sharing the one detail that would stop Gabriel's ploy immediately and keep the Alliance off her back for at least a month. "I'm currently working on an investigation the Moranaa Dessis have become involved in, and that's all I can share at this time. The Alliance will need to contact them if the interview cannot wait until I complete my current assignment." The Alliance was scared of the Moranaa Dessis for reasons Adeline didn't know, so she knew they wouldn't be pushing this issue. "Goodbye." She hung up.

"Who are the Moranaa Dessis?" Elijah asked.

"The mysterious, and possibly lethal, supreme leaders of the supernatural world. No one I've met knows who they are, how they're chosen, or why they're the supernatural equivalent to the President, Supreme Court, and Illuminati rolled into one," she explained. "And my old boss is terrified of them."

"Is what you said true? About them being involved in the murder investigation?"

"They're 'involved' to the extent of letting me do my job without others trying to interfere for political reasons."

They came to a stop at a light, but instead of going straight when it turned green, she turned right. "I thought we were going home."

"And we are, but not yet. We might as well make this trek of ours count," she said. "Let's cross one name off the list."

"Who?"

"Charlotte Lennox. Her house is close by anyway."

The last thing she wanted right now was to spend the rest of the day bored out of her mind and having to think about not only the three murders she hadn't stopped, but also Lucy Radassi's death and how she hadn't prevented it.

CHAPTER 22

— • —

Adeline parked the truck in front of Charlotte Lennox's house, shut the engine off, and was about to step out of the car when Jakob called her. She closed the door and stared at her phone for a few seconds before accepting the call. "Hey."

"Where are you right now?"

"Elijah's. Where else would I be?"

"No, you're not. I know that because Rebecca just arrived and found Elijah's truck gone and no one around to answer the door. So, she called me wondering where you two are."

"Fine, you caught me." She rolled her eyes. "Did you honestly think hiding my keys would've been enough to stop me from leaving?"

"I didn't think you had a death wish. I thought you'd be reasonable about the situation. My mistake."

"I'm being reasonable. Running an errand in the middle of the day, when every victim was killed at night, seemed perfectly safe and thus reasonable."

"Steve's gonna have our asses if you get yourself killed."

"You tried to stop me from going anywhere, and Rebecca wasn't around when we left. What were either of you supposed to do? Tie me to a chair? If Steve gets pissed at anyone, it'll be me. I'm the one who did something. And after last night, I didn't think staying at Elijah's was the best idea."

"You don't know him that well. He'll have enough anger to go around. And how's the house not safe? Your protection spell seemed strong enough to me."

"It's strong, but that's not the problem. The issue is that it's the safest place for us to be, which makes it the obvious place to hide until this mess is over. It's the first place anyone would think to look. Why would I make us easier to find?"

"You can leave Sun Tzu out of this. You're not waging war. You and your brother are trying not to become murder victims four and five."

"Nothing's gonna happen."

"You don't even know who wants you dead. You can't say nothing will happen."

Adeline let out a sigh. "Look, there's something I need to take care of. Once it's handled, Elijah and I'll head back to his house. No search party needed." She looked at Elijah, who didn't seem amused. Instead, he was sending her a pleading look. "I'll call you when we're on our way back."

"No, tell me where you are. I'll have Rebecca meet you there."

"She's not familiar with the area, and I suck at giving directions. She'd get turned around."

"Fine. Stay where you are, "Jakob said. "I'm about five minutes from Dylan's, and my meeting with her shouldn't take long. Once I'm done, I'll come meet you."

"I'm not gonna sit around waiting for you so I can have a ten, maybe fifteen, minute conversation with someone. It's better if we talk alone anyway." Jakob's presence would put Charlotte on edge, and Adeline didn't want the other woman to get her guard up too high. "I'll explain later. Goodbye." She ended the call before he could reply.

Adeline unlocked the door and opened it, stepping out. Elijah stayed in the passenger seat. "Are you coming or what?"

"Maybe he has a point, about waiting for back-up or whatever."

"If you and I go and talk to her, we can explain it as old classmates wanting to reconnect. We can't do that with him around. If I knock on her door with someone she's never met, she's gonna get suspicious. She'll know it's not a casual visit. It's better that we do this just you and me."

"Someone wants to kill us. They tried to kill us this morning, and I'll be useless if we get into trouble."

"You're not useless, and I doubt Charlotte Lennox, who works at a damn preschool, is the bloodthirsty killer I've been chasing for nearly a month. She's easy to rule out as a suspect, so let's go talk to her. Unless ... Are you scared of a woman who's a foot shorter than you, and seventy-five pounds lighter?"

"You're only taunting me because there's a chance I'm right." He studied her for a moment. "What was that call after we left Joan Dunn's house about?"

"Nothing important." She shrugged and looked away. "My old job needs some information about an old case, but it's not a big deal." She crossed her arms, then immediately uncrossed them to hang at her sides. "It has nothing to do with what we're talking about. Why?"

"It wasn't nothing. You got that call and now you're acting weird and reckless, like you don't care what happens."

Adeline released a breath through her nose before looking back at Elijah. "Stay in the truck if you want. I'll talk to scary-Charlotte by myself." She slammed the door closed and walked up the gravel path, allowing herself a tiny smile when she heard Elijah's footsteps following her. A moment later, he was beside her as she knocked on the door.

"Never said I was scared to talk to her or didn't want to, but your behavior's fishy."

"Whatever."

Charlotte's son Thomas responded to her knock, the bags under his eyes making him look half-asleep as he stood in the doorway. It took him a minute to recognize them, and when he did, he jumped back, eyeing them with suspicion.

"Tommy, who's at the door?" Charlotte called from inside the house.

"Mr. Coburn and his sister," the teenager replied, ignoring Elijah's wince at being called Mr. Coburn.

The sound of a chair sliding across a tile floor echoed through the house moments before Charlotte came into view. Unlike the last few times Adeline saw her, Charlotte looked well-rested and happy. "Well, don't be rude. Invite them inside."

"Come in, I guess." He opened the door wider and walked away, heading upstairs as soon as they entered the house.

"Sorry about him," Charlotte said, looking in the direction her son had gone. "Teenagers, you know?" She then faced her guests. "I wasn't expecting visitors."

"We're sorry to drop by uninvited," Elijah began, "but you see, we—"

"I wanted to talk to you about something, and Elijah gave me a ride over since my car's in the shop. Do you have time to talk?" Adeline asked.

"Sure. Why don't we go into the kitchen?" She led them down the hall to a small, cozy kitchen.

A table and four chairs stood tucked into the wall by the doorway. The refrigerator and stove were along one wall with a counter between them. The opposite wall held a row of blue cabinets and a pantry. A door to another room was on the far side of the space between the fridge and pantry.

"You want some sweet tea or coffee?" Charlotte asked. The twins declined her offer as they sat. She took the seat opposite Adeline, with her back to the door on the far side of the room. "So, um, what did you want to talk about?"

Adeline's phone rang again. An unknown Kentucky number was calling. She silenced the ringer and put it back in her jacket pocket. "I wanted to clear the air about a thing or two."

"Is this about what I said at Derek's funeral? About me being mad at you when you left all those years ago?"

"Partly. I don't remember knowing you all that well growing up, so I was a bit taken aback when you said that. I can't think of why you would've been angry at me back in '98. I want to apologize for what I did, but my memory's not clear on what I'd be saying sorry for."

"No, you didn't do anything. It wasn't like that at all." Charlotte looked down at her hands. "It's actually a bit stupid, thinking about it now."

"Still, I'd like to know, if you're willing to tell me. Since I've moved back, I don't want to leave anything unsaid."

"I'll tell you, but you need to remember this was how I felt years ago. A completely different lifetime. I moved past it. I don't hold anything against you now. That's important."

"I understand," Adeline said, trying to keep her voice calm and prevent any of the annoyance from leaking through. "I think I need to know, so there's nothing lingering between us."

"It was right after Pete died, so I couldn't ... I was a complete mess. I was barely able to get out of bed in the days following the accident. When I finally had the strength, a week after that fateful day, I heard you were gone. Some folks were talking about you, saying nasty thing about you, rude things about your mama and her family, too. There was talk that y'all'd made a deal with the devil and that's why Elijah made it out of the mine alive when others didn't. I know it's all hogwash, those rumors. At the time though, I'm ashamed to admit I believed them. I needed something to tell myself, to explain why Pete died and Elijah survived." She looked at Elijah. "I didn't want you dead, I just—"

"It didn't seem fair."

"No, it didn't." Charlotte cleared her throat and focused back on Adeline. "My emotions were all over the place. Deep down, I was furious that you were able to get away when I couldn't. Everywhere I looked I was drowning in memories; I was jealous you'd gotten a fresh start."

"You were jealous? Why?" Adeline jumped when a door slammed upstairs, but quickly returned her attention to her host. "You could've left too. No one was stopping you. You—"

"Had lost the love of my life, the man I thought I'd marry, and was suddenly a single mother to a one-year-old. I guess you don't remember me getting pregnant when we were in school."

"You're right. I forgot Thomas was born at the start of senior year." Adeline shook her head at Elijah when his eyes widened at the revelation that Thomas was a potential suspect. She needed him to stay quiet. "I guess leaving wouldn't be as easy as I make it sound. I'm sorry you went through that."

"It wasn't your fault. These things happen. Tragedies come and go, with no rhyme or reason. I know that now. I hope what I said, about how angry I was at you back then, hasn't kept you awake at night or anything."

"It did a little. I mean, people I know keep dying, and no one knows why. It's hard not to think there's something unnatural happening."

"If I believed in that kind of thing, I'd agree with you. I think the folks that have died were attacked by a coyote or a rabid dog with the way they were ripped apart. I can't understand how there'd be any other explanation even though some folks are suggesting they were murdered. I just can't think of how or why a person would do something like that to such nice people." She shook her head. "Three deaths in a month is a lot, though. Hell, the last funeral I went to before Sandra's was for Irene Blevins."

"Irene Blevins is dead?" Adeline began to experience heartburn at the news.

"She died just after Easter. Didn't anyone tell you?"

Adeline's brow furrowed. "That doesn't make sense."

"Why not? She was older, and she smoked cigarettes like she couldn't breathe without them," Elijah said.

Irene hadn't been on his suspect list, but she assumed it was due to the woman's age, not because she was dead. "It doesn't make sense because Dale Blevins told me that his mama was asking about me, wanting to know what I've been up to. Last I checked, the dead don't talk." She furrowed her brows. "If Irene's dead, why's her son acting like she's not? Why lie to me about that?"

"I had to get you to trust me," a voice called from the entryway.

The trio turned to see Dale Blevins standing in the hall. He stepped into the doorway, a gun aimed at Elijah. Adeline froze and her stomach clenched.

"Dale, what the fuck are you doing?" Elijah asked.

He ignored the question and continued to talk to Adeline. "If I'd just asked you about your life you might've thought I was flirting with you or something. I figured it'd be easier to get you to tell me what I wanted to know if I said my mama asked."

Charlotte gasped and covered her mouth with one hand. She sputtered, searching for words.

Adeline ran through her conversations with Dale over the past month. He'd asked where she went after she left Evarts, if she was married or had kids. He had been fishing for information about her life, trying to find out if she and Elijah were the last Coburns, and she hadn't realized it. She'd been so focused on remembering how he'd looked or acted towards others at the funerals that she hadn't cared about what he'd said to her. She hadn't felt this stupid in a few years.

"And I thought you were just trying to make conversation. I guess I should applaud you since your ploy worked."

"Not completely. Not yet." He gestured towards the door with his gun. "Let's go."

"Math ain't your strong suit," Elijah said. His voice shook slightly but he quickly covered up his fear by lowering his timbre a bit. "There's three of us and one of you."

Dale looked behind Charlotte and smirked. "You might want to count again." Thomas Lennox stormed in through the other door, also wielding a gun. "How do you think I knew you were here?"

"*Thomas Peter Lennox. What in the hell is wrong with you?*" Charlotte yelled. "Go put your daddy's gun—"

"He's not my father. He acts like he is, but—"

"Yes, he is. He didn't father you, fine, but he raised you. And he and I both taught you better than this. You put that gun back where you found it and—"

"Mama, this doesn't concern you. I have to—"

"The hell it doesn't! Put that gun away. Now!"

Thomas's voice wavered as he argued with his mother. Adeline saw his hands trembling around the gun. He kept glancing over at Dale while he spoke, as if he was seeking approval. His face had gone pale. He seemed terrified, which made no sense to her since he was the one holding a gun.

While mother and son argued, Elijah and Adeline faced one another. Elijah's posture was tense, and he kept looking to her for a signal to spring into action. He was tall and strong compared to the armed men in the room. He could easily overpower Dale, the larger threat. Of course, Adeline could also use her witchcraft to subdue both Dale and Thomas. There was a chance of something going wrong, though, and she didn't know how anyone in the room would react to her using her magic. Someone could be injured or killed if she didn't carefully consider what move to make. She had to wait for the perfect moment.

Lucy Radassi's death was still fresh in her mind. When she blinked, she either saw the woman's body sprawled on the pavement or falling in slow motion off the balcony.

She didn't know how involved Thomas was in Dale's actions, but Charlotte was innocent in all this. Adeline didn't want either Lennox to die, and she certainly didn't want Charlotte to lose her son, even if he was Dale's accomplice.

"All right, I'll go with you," Adeline said, cutting off the argument between Charlotte and Thomas.

"Not just you. Elijah, too."

"Fine. We'll go with you." She stood up and her brother did the same. They waited with their hands at their sides, trying to look as non-threatening as possible. "No need to threaten anyone."

"Adeline, don't do this." Charlotte shook her head frantically and looked ready to cry. "I don't know what's going on, but—"

"We'll get out of your hair now, Charlotte," she said, hoping her casual tone would keep the other woman calm. Her phone buzzed faintly in her pocket as it vibrated. She covered up the sound by pushing back her chair with her foot, which caused a loud scraping noise to echo through the silent kitchen. "Thank you for having us over."

"Tommy, let's go," Dale said.

The younger man's hands shook slightly as he aimed his gun at the twins and led them out of the house. Dale warned Charlotte not to call the sheriff unless she wanted Thomas to pay the price, then followed them out of the house.

Once outside, Thomas bound Adeline and Elijah's hands with some rope that Dale handed him, then told them to walkover to a beat-up truck. The siblings were forced into the backseat as Dale got into the driver's seat and turned the engine on.

"Go with it. Just trust me," Adeline whispered to Elijah as she was getting settled into the vehicle. He nodded once in understanding.

She tried to subtly pull her phone from her pocket, but the movement caught Thomas's attention so she gave up on that idea for the moment. Elijah sat stock-still next to her but kept glancing over as they drove through town. The truck took several turns, but soon enough they were heading into the woods.

"Where are we going?" Thomas asked.

"Old hunting cabin; it's been in the family for years," Dale replied. "I saw people at the Coburn house, so we can't perform the ritual there."

"You didn't say anything about a ritual." The teenager's eyes were wide and he looked around in a panic. "You said all I had to do was—"

"I know what I said. That was the original plan, but plans change. Get over it. The cabin's secluded. No one'll notice the noise or be able to find us."

"Or, you could not perform this ritual at all. Just a thought," Adeline re-marked.

He ignored her and kept driving.

CHAPTER 23

— · —

Adeline couldn't discern whether Dale was intentionally trying to prevent her and Elijah from being able to orient themselves. Once they were outside the boundary of Evarts, he took several seemingly random turns down rural roads. Perhaps more disconcertingly, he also pulled over a few times to choke out a series of loud, painful-sounding, hacking coughs into a blue handkerchief before starting to drive again.

As the roads transitioned from paved asphalt to loose gravel to dirt, the ride grew bumpier. At one point when they hit a particularly rough stretch of road, Elijah could've sprung forward and snatched Thomas's gun from his grip, but the moment passed too quickly for him to act.

Far too soon for Adeline's liking, the truck came to a stop, and Dale ordered Adeline and Elijah to get out. The second she stepped out of the backseat, she heard him click off the safety of his handgun. She glanced over her shoulder to find it aimed directly at her back.

"Don't get any smart ideas."

Adeline knew fear was the sensible response in that moment. They were in the middle of nowhere with an armed killer who'd already murdered three people and was threatening her and her brother. Instead, she had to fight the urge to yell or light Dale on fire. She couldn't remember the last time she'd been this infuriated. How dare he kidnap her and threaten her brother? How dare he kill Sandra and Derek and Wyatt? Her hands shook with rage, which Dale mistook for fear, judging by the satisfied light in his eyes.

She looked away. In front of her stood an old cabin, the exterior stained and battered by weather and the passage of time. The planks of wood showed initial signs of rot. Aside from alight breeze rustling a few branches of the surrounding forest, the area was silent.

No animals scurrying through the vegetation. No insects buzzing about or chirping in the underbrush. The unnatural quiet caused the hairs on the back of her neck to stand on end.

"Beware the silent woods," she muttered to herself, repeating part of Siobhan's cryptic warning from last week.

Adeline closed her eyes to center herself and took a deep breath. Her magic thrummed within her, and the power of her ancestors was still within her reach. They hadn't left Harlan County.

With her Gift at the ready she had an advantage and plenty of options to keep Elijah and herself alive. All she had to do was destroy the ropes binding their hands and they could flee into the woods. Yet, freeing themselves and running off into unknown woods, unarmed and disoriented, wasn't the best plan. Dale would chase after them. Even if they escaped today he was likely to make another attempt tomorrow or the day after; he'd come too far in his dark magic practice to give up because a victim ran away. She vowed to herself the murders would end tonight; she just needed to get her bearings, and some answers, first.

"Let's go. Inside," Dale said, interrupting her thoughts. He gestured towards the door of the cabin with his gun.

Adeline glared but said nothing as she walked into the building. The cabin was mostly one large room with two doors along one wall, each leading to bedrooms. In the main room, the only furniture pieces were a worn-out brown couch slumped in front of a fireplace, and a cheap plastic table by the door. Windows covered one wall, and one of the glass panes was cracked, another broken entirely. A thick layer of dust covered everything, including the fireplace, and the floor creaked below their feet with every step they took. Scrawled across the walls were iterations of the sigil she'd seen at the three crime scenes: an arrow shot into a crudely drawn heart of the mountain.

"I should thank you, Adeline." Dale closed the door of the cabin, trapping Adeline and Elijah inside with him and Thomas. "You made things easier for me—for everyone, really—when you moved back."

"How'd you figure that?" she asked as she sat down on the ancient sofa. As she expected, it let out a loud creak and a cloud of dust flew into the air.

"I've been looking for you since March and figured I'd failed. You didn't come back after your daddy died; I wasn't sure if Elijah's death would be enough to get you here. Hell, I wasn't even sure if you were still alive. I'd nearly given up hope on this whole thing. Then, I saw you and that guy you were with, the pretty boy, coming out of the Gas'N'Go a few weeks back. I didn't believe it was you at first—thought my mind was playing tricks on me—so I asked Tommy here, and he said I'd seen none other than Adeline Coburn in the flesh. The prodigal daughter had returned."

Adeline looked at Thomas, who wouldn't meet her gaze and shuffled his feet. He muttered something about not calling him "Tommy" before walking out of the building.

"You almost gave up hope on what, exactly?" If Dale had been looking for Adeline for over six months, then he'd been planning these murders for at least that long. He'd been plotting since before his mother or Clay Dunn had died. How much of his short life had he spent working towards this end? "You stormed into Charlotte's house with a gun and kidnapped us. We don't know what any of this is about. Why were you asking about my life? What do you need Elijah and me for? What's happening?"

"You have to die. You both have to die." His tone was matter-of-fact. "I don't want to do it, just like I didn't want to have to kill the others, but—"

Adeline's body went cold at his admission. Between his behavior and the sigils scrawled on the wall his guilt was clear but hearing him admit to the murders so casually cemented it. She skipped past anger and fear straight to horror upon remembering the crime scenes. The brutality of their deaths was impossible to forget.

"Others?" Elijah's voice trembled. "You're saying that you killed Sandra Russett, Derek Green, and—"

"Yes, I had to. Their sacrifice, your sacrifice, it's the only way to bring my father back. Your deaths will help me resurrect him." His eyes were wide, and he had a frantic energy about him.

"Your father's dead. He's been dead for sixteen years," Adeline said as gently as she could while attempting to sound sincere. She didn't want to agitate him, but she refused to treat his claims like they were sane or rational. "Nothing you do can bring him back."

"You don't know what I know. Halloween's tomorrow: the veil between the living world and the realm of the dead will be thin enough for him to pass through. I've found things, uncovered secrets about life and death, that you wouldn't believe."

"And you don't know what I know," Adeline said. "It's a big world, and I've seen more of it than you. No matter what you might've read, what lies someone might've told you, the dead don't come back. If it were possible, raising the dead, don't you think someone else would've done it by now?"

"They've tried, but I'm the only one with the conviction to follow through. The folks who failed didn't want it badly enough. I know what you're doing. You're trying to talk me into letting you go, into stopping this. I've already started the ritual—nothing will stop me from seeing it through."

"I think reality and the basic rules of life and death will."

"She said you'd say that, the vampire who sold me the spell book," he muttered.

"A vampire sold you a book of spells that you're gonna use to resurrect your father?" she asked slowly. She filed his comment about a female vampire away for later to investigate.

"Don't try to make me sound crazy! I'm not crazy. It took me years to find it, and lots of failures, but I finally found someone on the dark web selling genuine books on how to cast spells that can raise the dead," he said. "And I know the book's authentic because I used it to kill the others."

Dale started to cough again, pulling out his handkerchief to cover his mouth. A reddish-blackish stain had begun to spread across the blue where he'd coughed up blood.

"You don't look so good. You should go see a doctor," Elijah said.

"Only because the ritual ain't complete. I tried to finish it last night, while you were asleep, but it didn't work. You had a guest I didn't expect. The spell's specific so it failed when there were three people inside the building instead of just two. But once I'm done, when the ritual is complete, I'll be in perfect health again. And I'll have done what no one else has ever accomplished. Thomas!" he shouted and the teenager shuffled back into the room. "I need to get a few things for the ritual. Watch them."

He turned his attention back to his captives. "Don't try to run. Tommy'll shoot you. And even if you get past him, I know these woods like the back of my hand. I'll find you. No one's coming to save you." He stormed out of the cabin.

Dale's engine sputtered to life before the cabin's occupants heard the truck drive off. For a few minutes, the cabin was silent as Adeline tried to form a plan. Thomas was outnumbered but visibly on edge, and people didn't make rational decisions in that state. She didn't know what role he'd played in everything Dale had done and couldn't determine what kind of force would or wouldn't be justified to use against him.

"What's in this for you?" Adeline asked the boy after several minutes of silence had passed. "Dale's said what he wants, as crazy as it sounds, but I don't know how you got tangled up in all this. And you don't seem like you want to be here."

"Because I don't. I saw him leaving Ms. Russett's house covered in blood after I snuck out to see ... someone. He told me to get home before the sheriff showed up, because he didn't want to get me in trouble. Then, he started asking what I knew about Mr. Green and Mr. Dunn, since they came into the Gas'N'Go often. I didn't know he was – He told me—"

"Were you there when he killed them?"

"No. He said he was bloody outside Ms. Russett's place because he'd tried to save her. I thought everyone was lying about her being murdered. Nothing exciting ever happens here, so I figured they were exaggerating, making a better story. My mama kept saying a wild animal killed them. I didn't know Dale was murdering folks until he came to the gas station, acting like he was high, and said he'd killed Wyatt. And you two were next. I – You really think I'd kill someone?"

"You pointed a gun at me less than an hour ago and helped Dale kidnap us, knowing he wants to kill us. You're a kid, but you don't get to stand there and act insulted. You didn't help before, but you're helping him kill us now."

"Addy, you're making things worse," Elijah said, watching Thomas's face grow redder and his glare become more hate-filled.

"Good. I'm not trying to be helpful. If we die, he'll have the same blood on his hands as his murder-buddy. He doesn't get to pretend he's innocent in this."

"What am I supposed to do?" Thomas yelled. *"Dale could kill me.* He already threatened to. He said he'd kill my mama if I didn't do what he said. I don't want you to die, but I – This," he gestured wildly at their surroundings, "helping him, it's my only option."

"No, it's not. You're being forced to help him. You can—"

"I'm done talking to you." He stomped over to the door and ripped it open, storming out of the cabin.

"What the hell's wrong with you?" Elijah hissed at Adeline as the door slammed shut behind Thomas. "This is a shit situation, but you're not making it any better by provoking him like that. He's got a gun. What if you'd pissed him off too much? He might've shot you!"

"No, he wouldn't have. He can't stop his hands from shaking around that gun. Every time Dale mentions the ritual, that kid looks ready to piss his pants. I needed to know how much he's involved and if we need to save him too. I also needed him to get angry and storm out." She reached into her jacket pocket and pulled out her phone. The movement was awkward with her hands bound, and it took a few tries. She had some battery life, but no reception. "Not that having my phone's helpful right now."

"You were expecting a signal? All the way out here?" He raised an eyebrow.

"What can I say: I'm an optimist." She surveyed the room. "We've got to find our own way out of this. Thank the ancestors we're still in Harlan County."

"Really?"

"Yup. I can feel my Gift, and the ancestors. It's like this warmth spreading through my body." In another situation, the constant presence of the ancestors might have been comforting.

"I can't hear the hills, though. They've been silent since last night. Actually, since you returned from visiting Mary."

"That's odd." The hills didn't seem fickle to her, but them abandoning Elijah at a time like this could only be described as such. "Speaking of Mary, why didn't you go to her in the first place?"

"What?"

"Before I came back, the hills were talking to you. Crops were failing, animals were dying. You knew something was wrong and kept calling me. You could've gone to Mary for help or guidance, but you didn't. Why not? Sure, you hadn't seen her in a few years, but you still could've—"

"The last time I saw her was after you left Kentucky, to keep my promise to you. When I told her you left and I didn't stop you, she told me to get out of her sight and that she never wanted to see me again."

Adeline sputtered for a moment. "Why'd she say that?"

"I don't know. I wasn't in the position to argue and wasn't gonna stay where I wasn't wanted." He shrugged. "Use your Gift, get us out of here, and ask her. Truth be told, I'm surprised you've held off from using your magic this long. I kept waiting for it back at Charlotte's."

"Too many things could've gone wrong if I'd tried a spell and it didn't work exactly the way I wanted."

"Why didn't you do anything during the drive here, or after we'd gotten out of the truck, then? Why aren't you using your Gift now to get us the fuck out of here?" He gestured with his bound hands. "Break apart these ropes and let's run before he comes back. I'll make sure Thomas doesn't stop us. What's the problem?"

"I want to have a better plan than untying these ropes, taking off into the woods, and hoping for the best. Us escaping isn't enough. You can escape and run for your life, but I have a responsibility to stop what Dale's doing. Dark magic's not my area of expertise, so I don't know what he's capable of with the power he's tapping into."

"And he doesn't know what you're capable of, or that you're a witch. He blamed his failed attack last night on Jakob's presence. We have the element of surprise."

"That's exactly my point. He doesn't know I have magic—that's our secret weapon right now. But you can only take someone by surprise once. The element of surprise is our biggest advantage, and I'm not wasting it on something that might fail."

"Maybe you haven't noticed, but Dale's in bad shape. He's pale as shit and coughing up blood. He won't be able to put up a fight if you unleash your magic on him."

"Dark magic's killing him from the inside out, but I don't know how strong he is despite that. When he's not hacking up blood, he seems pale but healthy. My magic's not endless. I don't know how long I'd be able to hold him off for, and if I fail, we die."

"If we just sit here, we'll die."

"No, we won't. We're getting out of these woods alive. I just don't know how yet. Let me think."

The cabin fell silent.

"When this is over, remind me to tell you that I was right," Elijah muttered.

"Fine. We shouldn't have stopped at Charlotte's. We should've gone home. No one predicted that Dale had help or that Thomas, of everyone in town, was his reluctant accomplice."

"No, not about that. I was right about Paul not being involved. I told you he wasn't."

"It's not like I wanted him to be an axe murderer. You wouldn't say why you were so adamant that he wasn't, so I had to explore the possibility. I don't suppose you want to explain why you knew he was innocent now? We've got time."

He fidgeted in his seat and looked away. He seemed more upset by her question than by their abduction or possible impending death. She was about to ask him again when the door swung open. Dale had returned. Thomas walked in a few steps behind him with hunched shoulders, muttering.

CHAPTER 24

— • —

Dale didn't speak to Adeline or Elijah as he walked over to the aged table in the corner. His face had grown paler in the hour or so that he was gone. He was out of breath as he set a thick, burlap bag down and started emptying it.

His back hid what he was doing from view, but when he turned around, Adeline spotted three large glass jars lined up next to one another. Each jar contained an unknown liquid with a specimen floating inside it. Adeline forced herself to keep her breakfast down as she identified Sandra's lungs, Derek's liver, and Wyatt's kidneys.

She felt the urge to scratch Dale's eyes out at the organs being displayed like sick trophies. Beside the three jars in use, he'd set out a fourth, smaller jar. It contained liquid, but nothing was suspended in it.

Dale walked out of the cabin and returned a few moments later, dragging something large and heavy behind him. The shape was covered in a plastic tarp, and was large enough to be a human body.

Fred Blevins' decomposing body.

Adeline gagged on the stench that filled the cabin and felt Elijah heave next to her. With some help from Thomas, Dale dragged the body into a separate room and closed the door, blocking that room off.

"I'm sorry about having to do this," Dale said softly after he'd finished setting up his gory display. "I wish there was another way."

"No, you're not. Or you wouldn't be doing it at all," Adeline said, looking out the window behind Elijah. She refused to look in Dale's direction, unsure of what she'd do or say if she had to look at him.

"You don't understand. I didn't want—"

"Save your bullshit for someone who cares," she said through gritted teeth. "Don't try to justify what you've done. Three people are dead because of you and—"

"Four, actually."

"No amount of – Four?" She turned to him. How could the Guardians have missed a victim? The crime scenes weren't subtle. The idea of a fourth, unidentified victim out there disturbed her.

"Clay Dunn's accident wasn't an accident. I caused the crash that killed him. When he brought his truck into the garage to get his engine looked at, he told me all about the life insurance he got through his job. That policy made him worth more dead than alive. It seemed like fate. I needed a Dunn dead, and Joan would get the insurance money no matter how he died, so I tampered with his brakes a little. No one thought anything of it when he crashed during a storm. But it didn't work; his death didn't count. I thought it was because his body got too mangled in the wreck, but it was 'cause Wyatt was still alive. The ritual only works with sacrifices without other close kin and in the right order. It's why I'd been so desperate to find you." His expression shifted as any trace of remorse left his face.

He pulled a vial of black powder from his pocket and poured it into an opaque bowl, followed by a red substance. He lit a match and dropped it into the bowl, causing black smoke to rise. An uncomfortable sensation crawled up Adeline's spine, like she'd touched something slimy or disgusting with her bare hands.

"I don't suppose one of you wants to volunteer for the ritual?" he asked. "Make it easier on me?"

Adeline and Elijah stared at him.

"If you don't choose, I will. Both of you are gonna die. Here. Today. The only question left is who dies first." He grinned maliciously as he rolled the vial between his hands. "It's poetic, in a way, you two being twins and all. You were born together, and in the grand scheme of things, you'll die together."

"I ain't volunteering, but what happens to the one who doesn't get sacrificed?" Elijah asked.

"I'll shoot them. It'll be quick and painless, like I tried last night. The idol I left at your door was supposed to kill one of you in your sleep so I'd only have to deal with whoever was left, but it failed because you had an extra guest. It wasn't strong enough to kill two people."

"And to the sacrifice?"

"I'll take them outside so they don't have to see the other die. I'm not cruel. Tonight, I'll perform another spell on them. I need something of each person who let him die. Sandra donated her lungs since I couldn't have Jeff's, Derek gave his liver, and Wyatt offered his kidneys." He pointed to the room where he'd taken his father's body. "Now, all I need's a heart. Who's it gonna be?"

Neither of the twins spoke.

"Can I go back outside now?" Thomas asked.

"No, stay by the door. They might try to run." He looked at the Coburns. "The sun goes down in a few hours. I'll let you two talk about it, but like I said: if you don't choose, I will."

When his words didn't prompt a response, he headed towards the room where his father's corpse waited. As he opened the door, Adeline spoke.

"Can I ask you something? Why bring your daddy back? Other than him being your daddy, I mean."

"The day he died, my life went to shit. Last time I was happy, last time my mama acted like a mother, was when he was alive. He died, she turned into this hateful shell, and I was alone in every way that matters. I wasn't supposed to end up as a mechanic in bumfuck nowhere Kentucky, barely getting by. When he's alive again, when I've set things right, I'll get the life I'm supposed to have."

Adeline was tempted to argue that Fred's death wasn't the only reason his life turned out the way it did, but she knew it wouldn't do any good. "Why are we last?"

"Huh?"

"You planned this out. We're your last sacrifice, and I'm guessing there's a reason for that. Why'd you save us for last?" She cleared her throat. "Since you say I'll be dead soon, I'd like to know."

"The sacrifices had to be in a specific order. I realized that after my attempt with Clay Dunn. Jeff Russett was the first one to escape the collapsing mine, so Sandra, as his proxy, had to die first. I didn't understand why at first, but then Sandra's death made me stronger. Derek was next, and with his death, the spell became stronger, so killing Wyatt was easy. The Coburn sacrifice has to be last because Elijah was the last man to get out of the mineshaft alive. He's the one who left my daddy down there to die." His gaze turned to Elijah. "Do you even remember leaving him behind to save yourself?"

"I didn't leave anyone to die."

"*Bullshit.* Yes, you did. No one would shut the hell up about it for years afterwards, about how you were the last man out. When the dust settled and they went in to collect the bodies, they told my mama he could've made it if he'd gotten a little closer to the surface, if you'd dragged him out with you. Instead, he got trapped underground, buried alive, and left to suffocate. Because of you!" His face grew red and his breathing heavy. "The others had no idea. They didn't know why they couldn't move, couldn't run, couldn't speak, as I cut into them. Why the pain seemed unending as I ripped them open. When I carve out your heart, I want you to know exactly why." He took a step forward. "I should just—"

"So much for giving us until sundown," Adeline cut in. She'd formulated a plan of what to do if Dale didn't wait until sundown, as he'd promised, to kill them. Her plan would probably end with someone being maimed, but it was better than waiting to die.

"Oh. I'll give you until then." He placed the bowl down on the table. "I'm a killer, but I'm not a liar. A few hours won't change anything."

"You'd be surprised the difference an hour can make."

"I wouldn't get too hopeful if I were you. Like I said, no one's coming to save you."

"Who said I'm expecting to be saved? I'll save myself."

"Don't make this harder than it has to be. I liked you as a kid; you were my favorite babysitter. I don't want to kill you, but I have to. Just, can't you die without making me feel guilty about it?"

"Oh, I'm sorry I'm making you feel bad about plotting to kill me," she sneered. "That must be so hard for you. I should sit here and wait to die. I wouldn't want you to experience regret over murdering six people."

"Addy—"

"What are you gonna do when it fails? What happens when this ritual you're obsessed with doesn't bring your father back?" She sat back and looked around the room before meeting Dale's eyes again. "Think about that while you're preparing for your stupid little ceremony."

Dale glared before walking into the other room carrying a few items with him. He left the organ jars behind as he ordered Thomas to watch them.

A minute later, a horrible, putrid stench started to waft through the building. Thomas moved as far away from the closed door as he could and turned green, while Elijah and Adeline started gagging.

***

Adeline waited about ten minutes before she stood up from the couch. Dale was distracted by his ritual preparations, which presented her with an opportunity she couldn't ignore. Her movement startled Thomas, who reached for his gun.

"I'm just stretching my legs." She held up her bound hands. "That sofa ain't the most comfortable and my behind was starting to go numb."

She walked back and forth in front of the couch a few times before Thomas relaxed and put his gun away. She walked over to the table where the stolen organs and Dale's other implements were laid out. She studied the contents of the table. Every few seconds, her eyes would drift towards Sandra's lung or Derek's liver, but she tore her gaze away as soon as she realized what she was doing.

Next to the only empty jar, intended for either her or Elijah's heart, was Dale's small vial of black powder. A strange thing happened when she drew closer to the mixture of salt, coal dust, and dried blood. Something in it was calling to her, asking to be unleashed. She ignored it, refusing to be tempted by dark magic. In front of the vial rested a folded pocket knife.

Stealing a glance at Thomas, she saw he was watching Elijah. As slyly as she could, she picked up the knife and wedged it between her left wrist and the rope binding her hands together. Out of the corner of her eye, she saw Thomas turn his attention to her. She picked up the first thing her hands touched.

"Put that down or I'll—"

"What damage do you think I'll do with," she looked down at what she was holding, "an old can of paint?"

"I don't know and I don't care. Put it back and sit down."

"Fine." She put the paint down.

Without another word, she returned to the sofa. Using her back to block the boy's view, Adeline showed her brother what she'd taken. The confusion on his face gave way to understanding. She unfolded the blade but then closed it.

Cutting through the rope could take a while and using magic wouldn't, but she needed to test a theory first. She hadn't been able to sense Dale's use of dark magic until it was focused on her last night, and she didn't know if he could sense ancestral magic. She doubted it since he hadn't realized his attack last night failed because of her protection spell, but she had to make sure.

She turned so her feet were firmly planted on the floor and closed her eyes. She tried to listen for a gust of wind, a bird call, anything coming from outside the cabin. After a minute or two, the faint sound of wind blowing, almost too quiet to hear, registered in her ears. With a deep breath, she envisioned that same breeze rustling a tree branch, causing it to tap against the side of the cabin. Three short taps, followed by three longer taps, ending with three short taps: S-O-S in morse code. She opened her eyes to see a tree branch tapping against the window.

"What are you doing?" Elijah whispered.

"Testing a theory," Adeline said. "If Dale comes out here, make it look like we're arguing over which one of us is gonna die."

She kept her attention on the room Dale had disappeared into. He didn't come out, which she interpreted to mean he couldn't sense smaller spells being performed. Adeline pushed her luck a little further and made the wind stronger so it rustled more trees and caused more branches to knock against the windows and siding of the cabin. Some air came through the broken window and blew dust and ashes from the ancient fireplace across the floor. Thomas looked spooked by the sudden wind, but Dale still didn't appear. She pushed a step further. Instead of a slight breeze, she envisioned a strong gust of wind from a powerful thunderstorm. It blew the front door of the cabin open, causing it to bang against the wall.

Dale came out of the backroom and looked around. "What was that?"

"Gust of wind blew the door open," Thomas said.

"No, that wasn't wind. I thought I felt – Go outside, check the perimeter." He watched the Coburns until the teenager returned and said there was nothing and no one outside. "Must've been the wind after all." He walked back into the room and closed the door behind him.

Adeline handed Elijah the knife, which he quickly unfolded and began to cut with, and slowly began to use her magic to pull apart the fibers of her rope. It was made out of some form of hemp, which made it easier to work with since it was a natural fiber. She did it slowly, matching Elijah's pace as he cut. The combination of Dale's work in the other room, the creak of the floorboards as Thomas shifted his weight around every few minutes, and the groan of the sofa every time the twins adjusted their positions was loud enough to mask the sound of Elijah cutting through his bindings as Adeline unraveled hers.

"You could go home, you know," Elijah said, watching Thomas. "You shouldn't see what happens to us."

"You're only saying that because if I leave it'll be easier for you to run away. Besides, once I get home, my mama will call the sheriff on me."

"She won't turn in her own kid. I've known her for a long, long time. If you tell her Dale forced you into this, she'll believe you because she'll want to. And, like Dale said, we won't get far like this." He held up his bound hands, but didn't raise them high enough for the fraying to be visible.

A loud, hacking cough came from the other room as Dale pulled the door open. "He's not gonna free you," he said as soon as he finished coughing, "no matter how much you try to convince him. Not if he wants to keep his mama safe."

"I didn't ask him to free us. Did you, Addy?"

"Nope. All you said was that Tommy should go home to his mama before he gets scarred for life. He's a child, after all."

"I'm not just some kid." Thomas made a gagging noise. "What's that smell?"

"My father's body ain't in the best shape—I mean, animal blood only does so much—but that will soon be remedied," Dale said as he picked up the jars containing Sandra's lungs and Derek's liver. He walked back into the room where he'd been working, closing the door behind him.

Adeline leaned to the side to lookout the window behind Elijah. The sky was starting to darken. Sunset wouldn't be for at least another hour, but time was running out. She was a few fibers away from freeing herself.

"Eli, we should talk about what happens now." She nodded behind him so he'd turn to look outside. "The sky's getting darker."

"Addy, I'm not – We're not talking about this."

"Look at me." He refused to meet her gaze. "I'll wait, but we don't have long. Look. At. Me." When he finally met her eyes, she glanced down at her hands and his eyes followed. She'd finally unraveled her bindings. "It's gonna be okay. Trust me." Thomas was standing with his back towards them. She leaned forward to whisper to her brother. "Go outside and to the right. Don't stop running until you see a car to flag down, or I catch up to you. I'll be right behind you."

He shook his head in disbelief. "I'm not—"

"I need you to trust me." With her hands free, she placed a hand over Elijah's bindings and snapped the ropes with ease. "Everything's gonna be fine. Okay?"

He nodded. "Okay."

Adeline bent down and grabbed a handful of dust and ashes from the floor. They would have to suffice, since she didn't have anything else. She cleared her throat. "Thomas, can you come here?"

When he was within a foot of her, she opened her hand and blew the dust into his face. "You're very tired. Sleep."

The boy's eyes began to droop as he swayed on his feet. Elijah caught him before he fell to the ground and laid him on the couch. "Now, we run?"

"Yes, go. Now," she said, pointing to the door. "I'll be right behind you."

He rushed over to the door, the floorboards groaning underneath his feet with every step. He glanced back at Adeline before exiting the cabin.

Adeline began to count in her head as she walked towards the door, stopping every few steps until she was outside. It took her one hundred nineteen seconds to reach the door. She ran outside and to the left, moving as fast as she could. Elijah would be pissed at her for lying, but she needed to make them both harder to find. With Thomas incapacitated, Dale could only follow one of them once he noticed their absence, giving the other a greater chance at finding safety.

A shout echoed through the trees as she ran. With the daylight starting to fade, the woods began to appear far more sinister as the shadows around her elongated. The lack of ambient noise from birds or insects made the eerie silence in the area, broken only by her own breathing, far more unsettling.

When she could no longer see the cabin over her shoulder, she stopped to catch her breath and get her bearings. Her occasional morning runs were nothing compared to running for her life.

"*Adeline! Elijah*," Dale called in a sing-song voice. "There's no point in running! I know these woods inside and out."

Adrenaline coursed through her veins and she knew she had to start running again. She looked behind her to make sure Dale wasn't close enough to see her.

Adeline took a deep breath and felt a powerful, soothing force surround her. There was a deafening crack behind her, followed by two slightly quieter cracks. Three large trees, two dogwoods, and an oak fell to the ground five yards from where she stood. As they landed on the forest floor, they blocked the path she'd just run down.

Whether the trees falling were an act of nature, intervention by the ancestors, or her own Gift exploding out of her, she wasn't going to waste the advantage.

She continued running and didn't stop until she heard birds chirping, insects buzzing, and the other normal noises of the woods.

When she stopped, she spotted a light off in the distance. It was at least half a mile away and seemed to be coming from up a hill. The trees looked more familiar than the ones surrounding Dale's cabin.

During the first thirteen years of her life, she'd spent a lot of time in these woods with her mother and Elijah. This stretch of forest was southwest of Mary's home, but far closer than she'd expected to find herself. Being close to Mary's meant she was closer to the ancestors and the source of her magic. Finally, some good luck. Her Gift was strong here; Dale would be easier to stop.

Somewhere in the darkness behind her, there was rustling and the sound of tree branches being pushed out of someone's way. A twig snapped. A voice shouted something that sounded like her name.

Dale was chasing after her. At least Elijah would make it somewhere safe. She started to run once again.

"*Enough running,*" a woman's voice echoed in her head. "*This is not something you can outrun.*"

CHAPTER 25

— • —

It had been twenty years since Lilah Coburn died, but her daughter hadn't forgotten her voice. The warmth of her words, the way words like "something" always had an extra twang. It was impossibly, inexplicably Lilah.

Adeline couldn't hear movement coming from the foliage behind her. Hopefully, Dale was no longer on her trail. She knew she needed to keep moving, but the voice transfixed her and her legs wouldn't move, no matter how many times she told herself to run.

"Mama?" she asked, her voice shaking. Elijah said Harlan sounded like their mother when the hills spoke to him. If the voice was Harlan, why was Harlan talking to her now, and not Elijah? Was the stress of running for her life causing her to hear things? Was this some trick of Dale's to prevent her escape? Or was some piece of Lilah's spirit trying to save her now, the way Elijah said the voice saved him down in the mines in 1998?

"It is time to stop running. You have spent far too long fleeing rather than fighting."

As she caught her breath, she felt invigorated. Her Gift, once a slow, steady thrum below her skin, was now a loud storm begging for release. Adrenaline explained some of the sensation, but her magic seemed poised to explode out of her at any moment.

Adeline stood in a small clearing. The sun had fully set, and the resulting darkness made it difficult to distinguish certain details of her surroundings. With such little light, she couldn't see very far. Continuing to run was an option, but she no longer knew which direction she was heading. Every tree in front of her looked identical to the forest of trees behind her.

Dale had been chasing her since dusk. For all she knew, he was still on her heels, tracking her deeper into the woods. Even if he wasn't following her exact path, he was in the vicinity. The idea of running all night concerned her. The voice she'd heard, whether it was truly the hills or a stress-induced hallucination, was right.

She couldn't run forever. It was time for her to fight.

The dark magic Dale was harnessing was killing him from the inside out. As the dark forces he'd called on had stolen his vitality over the past three weeks, he'd grown weaker and paler. He could barely last five minutes without coughing up blood. He might've died already. He could've dropped dead in the middle of the woods while chasing her and she wouldn't have known.

But if he hadn't died yet, he was a threat. If he was still alive, still chasing her and still intent on sacrificing her or Elijah in a doomed attempt to resurrect Fred Blevins, she'd do whatever it took to stop him. She had to, to protect her brother and to get justice for Sandra, Derek, and Wyatt.

Thomas Lennox was unconscious inside the cabin, unable to wake for another hour at least. Elijah, if he'd followed her instructions, was a safe distance from where she stood. She would've come across signs of any other people or cabins in the area. She was alone in this part of the woods with the killer she'd been tracking for nearly a month. She didn't need to worry about collateral damage or accidentally harming an innocent bystander.

A noise came from the woods behind her, the sound of branches being moved aside and she turned around. She'd face Dale head-on, no matter the outcome.

More rustling, followed by footsteps and then heavy breathing, came closer until Dale pushed himself through the trees. He stopped at the edge of the tree line, bent over and panting.

"When I find Elijah, I'll kill him in front of you. Slowly. Then, I'm gonna carve your heart out and, unlike the others, make sure you feel every second." He let out a cough and expelled something dark onto the dirt.

"I don't think any of that's likely to happen. You look like you're fixing to keel over."

He straightened his posture and looked at her. That crazed look in his eyes, the fanaticism he'd had when talking about resurrecting his father, was gone. Now, his gaze held darkness, a burning hatred. The sheer malice Adeline saw didn't look right on his face. She couldn't reconcile the murderous man before her with the little boy she'd once known, the sociable facade he'd put up, or the man driven mad by grief.

He sneered and pulled something out of his pocket. "Too bad for you, I've got a little pick-me-up right here."

Adeline took a deep breath and waved a hand towards one of the trees behind her. Keeping her witchcraft a secret was pointless now, and she wouldn't fight for her life in the dark. A tree was set ablaze, and the light illuminated the clearing enough for her to see what he was doing. The object in Dale's hand was the vial of black powder he seemed to favor. Some of the dust slipped between his fingers and fell to the earth.

Dale had pulled his arm back, but froze when the tree caught fire. He stared for a moment at the tree that was burning but wasn't damaged by the fire. "You – How'd you do that?"

"Witchcraft. Those stories about my mama and her family had some truth to them."

"No, it's not. You didn't recite a spell or use an amplifier. You didn't set up an altar. You—"

"I said I know lots of things you don't know. Or did you think dark magic was the only kind of magic out there?"

Dale's eyes lit up. "So that's why she said I should've killed you, first chance I got. It makes sense now."

"Why *who* said you should've killed me sooner?" Adeline was struck by a sinking feeling. He'd mentioned getting a book of dark magic spells from a female vampire. Estelle wanted her dead for killing Robert in Seattle. Had Dale stumbled upon the dark grimoire by accident, or had he been lured to it?

He ignored her question. "It doesn't matter anyway, you being a witch. Your little tricks are nothing compared to my power." He opened his palm and released the dust he'd been clenching in his fist.

It blew towards Adeline. She twitched her finger, and a gust of wind blew into the clearing and scattered the powder. A second, stronger gust passed over Adeline and hit Dale with its full force. He stumbled back a few steps and barely kept his footing. When the wind died down, he was glaring at her.

"Are you done? I don't want to have to kill you, but if you don't stop what you're doing, that's what's gonna happen." She really didn't want to kill him.

"Ha! You think you can kill me? You?"

"I don't have to. You're already dying. Nothing's free, especially magic. If you think otherwise, that's because your bill ain't come due yet." Dale was going to die. He wouldn't die peacefully or painlessly, as punishment for his foray into dark magic. It was as inevitable as the sun rising each morning. "Do you even realize what you've done?"

"Yes, but it had to be done! My dad—"

"You think you're the first person to lose someone? There's lots of people out there with dead daddies, dead mamas, hell, even dead babies. What makes you so damn special? I've lost people, too, and more than you have I'd reckon. You don't see me running around, chopping folks up 'cause of it!"

"Just because you're too weak to act, doesn't mean—"

There was rustling among the trees. Dale stopped mid-sentence and turned towards the noise. There was more movement in the foliage, but no one came running into the clearing, nor did any voices call out from the darkness. Adeline felt a prick on the back of her neck, the unsettling sensation of being watched.

Dale shook himself from his stupor and glared at Adeline. "Making the wind rustle some leaves ain't gonna be enough to stop me."

"And that black dust in your hand ain't enough to kill me. I'm surprisingly adaptable." Adeline raised her left hand in front of her and rotated her wrist so her palm faced outward. A gust of wind passed through the clearing, following the motion. For a second, she could see an iridescent sheen in the air as it pushed him backwards.

He fell to the ground with a groan, then muttered something. Adeline's legs weakened for a brief moment. She let out two coughs that rattled her chest before subsiding. The impact of his spell struck her and passed within a handful of seconds. She took a step backwards, surprised at how quickly it came and went.

"This upstart believes he has the strength to challenge our own? The mere suggestion is laughable." Adeline heard her mother's voice echo in her mind. *"And to invoke such darkness here is a grave insult. One he must pay a steep price for."*

Standing up, Dale poured more of the dust mixture into his hand. "This dust killed not one, but two men twice your size." He threw it in her direction and began chanting.

The language wasn't English or Latin, so Adeline couldn't identify the words. She planted her feet firmly on the ground about shoulder-width apart and raised her hands so she was holding them directly in front of her, like she was bracing herself against something. As if it ran into an invisible barrier, the black powder stopped in mid-air, lingering in space for a few seconds before falling to the ground in the three piles. One was salt, another coal dust, and the smallest was flakes of dried blood. A humming emanated from the coal and called to something within her blood. It wasn't just coal; it was Harlan coal.

Dale stopped chanting, bent over, and started coughing. Blood and phlegm mixed as he spat onto the ground, but he stood at his full height again once he was done. "Just because I can't hit you with it doesn't mean I can't use it to hurt you. We could've done this the easy way. I wasn't gonna make your death hurt. Then you had to ruin everything by escaping."

Any sympathy Adeline might've had for Dale had vanished while she was running through the woods. "You didn't really expect me to sit there and wait to be murdered, right? How delusional are you?"

He didn't deign to respond. Instead, he picked up a fallen twig from the ground and began to chant. The air began to smell like burning plastic as he formed a fireball. Once it was bigger than his hand, he threw it at her.

She ducked out of the way, and it vanished. He picked up another twig and repeated his chanting. Steadying herself, she raised one hand and caught the second fireball. She blew on it and the fire went out, leaving behind a burned, blackened husk of wood. She tossed it aside.

Dale created another fireball and let this new one grow until it was roughly the size of his head. Once again, he flung it at her. She had to use two hands to catch it, but quickly doused the flames. She threw the wood back at him. It landed on the ground a few inches from his foot. "Are you done?"

"I don't – Why – You shouldn't be able to do that," he shouted as he looked around frantically. There were no more twigs or branches to use as fuel for another fireball.

With a surprising amount of swiftness given his current state, Dale rushed towards Adeline as if to tackle her. She stepped out of his path at the last second and he fell. As he got to his feet and attempted to grab her, she pushed him to the other side of the clearing with wind generated by her Gift, where he fell once again.

"I'll ask again. Are you done? Because I can keep going for as long as you want to keep this up."

"What are you?" he gasped out.

"A witch," she said, "with an obligation to fulfill. I have to stop the darkness you've brought here from spreading further. I'd apologize for that, but you don't deserve it given what you've done."

She raised one hand. Some of the coaldust and salt mixed together and blew across the ground until it reached Dale. Roots began to grow out of the soil, wrapping around his feet and ankles, keeping him in place.

He barked out another spell and a small flame appeared in his palm. He tried to burn the roots, but they showed no sign of damage and continued to wind their way up his legs. They grew until they were just above his knees.

"How are you doing that? It's my dust, it's only supposed to work for me. *Everything I read said that.*"

"You didn't read enough. That's why I'm stronger than you. Well, one of many reasons." More roots burst out of the ground and started to grow upwards, winding towards his arms. "You made a mistake when you chose salt and coal dust as your ingredients."

"The dust contains my blood."

"Do you know why the dust works? How it works? Or did you just read the spell, throw the ingredients in, and hope for the best?" Adeline took a step towards him. "Your dust is a sick perversion of normal spellcraft, spellcaft that's been around for generations. Salt binds the spell together. Your blood represents a sacrifice, which powers the spell. You used coal dust to ground it, and that's your mistake." She stopped about a foot away from where the roots were trapping him. "You see, coal dust comes from coal. Coal is of the earth and you used coal that was dug right here in Harlan County."

"So?"

"My blood runs deep in these mountains and hollers, much deeper than yours does. Your family's been here for three, maybe four, generations. Mine's been here in one form or another for much longer. I've got roots buried so deep in this place it would take an act of God to unravel them. Some might even say those ties make me a child of the hills. No matter what you call it, nothing on or of the land can harm me. The holler protects its own."

"The land's protecting you? Bullshit. It's dirt and trees. It can't do shit." Dale shouted something in an unknown language. The branches wrapped around his torso splintered and fell away, cutting up his arms. "There's power you'll never understand at my fingertips."

A dark substance oozed out of the cuts on his arms and landed on the roots that trapped his legs. The roots began to smoke and crack. "A human heart's all I need to resurrect my father. After I take yours, I'll be able to do what everyone called impossible. I'll tear your heart out with my bare hands if I have to!"

He broke free and took a step towards Adeline as she took a few steps backwards. Instinctively, she called upon her Gift, and the wind picked up. Rather than a hearty gust of wind blowing into the clearing and pushing Dale away, the wind began to encircle her. He rushed towards her, but the column of air acted like a forcefield, preventing him from getting close enough to touch her.

The wind was so loud in her ears that Dale's labored breathing was barely audible over it. Branches and leaves swirled in the air around her as strands of her hair blew this way and that. Adeline had never experienced a hurricane, but she imagined being in the eye of the storm was similar to what she was seeing and feeling now.

Dale was undeterred by his continued failures to reach Adeline. He continued attacking, searching for a way through the wind barrier. He stopped every twenty to thirty seconds to cough, expelling more blood each time. Adeline watched him cough up blood for the eighth or ninth time and began to wonder how much longer he'd stay standing. He was fading, and fast, but he wasn't dead yet and seemed prone to sudden bursts of strength and energy. Somehow, the man dying before her eyes was still a threat.

Adeline knew what needed to be done. There was only one way to stop Dale's plans from coming to fruition. She could feel the storm of her power churning inside her, begging to be released. She took a deep breath and closed her eyes, then reached for her Gift and focused it into the soil near his feet.

A heartbeat passed. Then, a massive bolt of lightning struck the dirt a few centimeters in front of where Dale was standing. The current hit the ground and instantly traveled up his leg and into his body. He collapsed to the ground as soon as it hit and started to let out shallow, panicked breaths. Adeline dispelled the wind surrounding her and, after a moment of pause, rushed over to where Dale laid.

"I just – I wanted to see my dad again." He was paler than she'd ever seen him, and the contempt in his eyes was gone. His breaths were coming in fast, shallow gasps.

"I know. And I'm sorry." She bent down and placed a hand on his shoulder.

He started wheezing. "Am I dying? Is this what it feels like?"

"I think so."

"You didn't have to kill me."

"I told you magic comes at a cost. Even if that lighting hadn't struck you, the dark magic you've harnessed would've killed you. Did you think you could do everything you did and then just walk away when it was over? Go back to a normal life?"

"I don't ... want to die." Each word appeared to exhaust him.

"No one ever does."

He rasped out a few more ragged breaths.

Adeline watched Dale Blevins' heart give out in the middle of the woods, under the night sky. Relief washed over her when his chest stopped rising and falling, followed by a wave of sadness.

She'd stopped the killer, but at a cost. Dale wasn't the first person she'd watched die. He wasn't the first person she'd killed indirectly with her Gift, but his death wouldn't have happened at all if he hadn't delved into dark magic. He was only twenty-two.

There was more movement in the trees, and she got to her feet. Thomas couldn't have awoken yet, but Dale could've had other accomplices. She braced herself for another fight as two figures burst into the clearing.

CHAPTER 26

— • —

T ree branches, leaves, and other debris from the windstorm surrounded Adeline. With her Gift, she lifted a large, heavy branch into the air and sent it flying towards the two figures approaching from the edge of the tree line. One ducked out of the way, while the other was knocked to the ground by the debris.

"Adeline. You can relax. It's Jakob." He stepped further into the clearing with his hands out to show he was unarmed.

Behind him, his companion let out a groan as they got to their feet. When Adeline locked eyes with them, she recognized Dylan Bartley.

"Remind me never to sneak up on you," Dylan said, brushing her hands off on her jeans. "If I wasn't gonna be sore tomorrow, I'd be impressed."

"Thanks, I think." She looked at Jakob. "How'd you find me?"

"Your signal's hard to miss." He pointed to the burning tree behind her before his eyes landed on Dale's body. "He's the one? My guess was Troy."

"No, it was Dale here. He thought he'd solve all his problems if he resurrected his father." Not wanting the whirlwind of emotions she felt to be obvious, Adeline faced the burning oak tree. She smothered the flames with a thought and a wave of her hand. "I need to find my brother."

"He's fine. We found him like an hour ago, running through the woods. He said you were somewhere behind him. Wasn't expecting you to be four and a half miles away, running in the opposite direction," Dylan said. "The light show made you easy to find eventually."

"Not to be rude, but why are you here?"

"Ask your partner. He came to us, asking for help. He's not an easy guy to say no to when he wants to be persuasive."

"You didn't check in, so I figured something happened," Jakob said with a shrug. "I couldn't search the woods without a little help. She's right about your light show. The wind and lighting and all was more than a little impressive."

"Thanks." She cleared her throat. "We should – We need to get back to the cabin. There's still a body to deal with."

"Is that what that stench is?" Dylan asked, wrinkling her nose.

"You can smell the rot all the way out here?"

"Werewolf, remember? I've been tracking you by scent since we found your brother. The rotting corpse was noticeable five miles out. Follow me." She turned to walk away. "Unless one of you wants to stay with this corpse while we handle the other body."

Roots began to grow out of the ground and encase Dale's body. Within a minute, vegetation completely covered it and the man slowly sank into the ground.

"He stole from us. His body now belongs to us."

"Guess that's not necessary," Jakob said.

***

Adeline and Jakob followed Dylan back to the cabin. She cut a straight path through the trees, unlike Adeline's serpentine escape route. The building soon came into view. Adeline walked up to the door.

The werewolf grabbed her arm to stop her before she pushed it open. "Someone's inside. Alive." She tilted her head to the side. "Asleep, but alive."

"Yeah, that's Thomas."

"Thomas?" Jakob asked.

"Remember that skinny kid from the gas station? The story's too long to get into right now, but Dale forced him to help kidnap us. I knocked him out with magic. He's not a threat."

"And you're sure of that?"

"The only reason he's here is because Dale threatened to kill his mama if he didn't do what he said." She pushed her way into the cabin.

Thomas was asleep on the sofa, in the same position Elijah left him in. The various jars and equipment were still on the table. The bedroom door was thrown open and the decaying odor of a dead body filled the room. The stench was so strong that Adeline struggled to breathe.

"I've got the kid. You two deal with ... the rest," Dylan said as she threw Thomas over her shoulder in a fireman's carry.

"Did you call the sheriff?" Adeline asked Jakob.

"You know we can't. This would take too much explaining. A murder scene looking like 'cult shit' is one thing, but the organs alone complicate things. If normal humans saw what's here it'd cause a huge problem."

"Fire it is, then." She glanced around, her eyes landing on the jar containing Wyatt's kidneys. "I'd feel better if we could give Sandra, Derek, and Wyatt their organs back. My mama claimed the dead can't find peace with pieces missing."

"They aren't gonna haunt us over that."

"I wouldn't blame them if they did." She tore her eyes away from the jar. "I don't suppose you have a lighter?"

"I don't, but I've seen you start fires with nothing. Do you even need one?"

"I don't need one, but it makes this a touch easier." She bent down and touched the floor. "I call upon the strength of my ancestors. Fire is cleansing. Allow the flames to purify this place."

A small flame erupted next to the sofa and the fabric caught fire. "We should go."

Jakob followed her out of the building. "You had to say something to start the fire and fix Elijah's lawn, but you didn't say anything when you destroyed that cursed skull. You were creating bolts of lightning and windstorms, but you didn't say a spell for that either. Why?"

"Oh, I don't have to speak a spell to cast it. If I wanted to, I could do everything unspoken. The reason I don't is because it freaks some people out to see someone do witchcraft and not know what spell was cast. People fear what they don't know, and if they can't tell what magic I'm doing, they start thinking I'm cursing them or something."

"Makes sense. Our world's not as messy as the human world, but it's not free from misconceptions either."

"Our world, huh? You've never called it that before. At least, not around me." Her curiosity about Jakob's past hadn't subsided in the slightest. Stopping a murderer had taken priority over the past few weeks, but she hadn't forgotten about the enigma he presented.

"I know you've worked out by now that I'm not human."

"I had suspicions; just coming out and asking 'are you human' is rude."

"It varies from person-to-person." He paused for a moment. "I'm—"

"Don't tell me. I want to work it out for myself." She cut him off. "I can rule out the four factions around here. Not dead, so not a vampire. Not a woman, so not a vila. You wouldn't be so awkward with Dylan if you were a werewolf. And you're not a witch because of the questions you've asked about my Gift, plus you have some knowledge gaps about witchcraft." She nodded to herself. "That leaves dozens of other options. I love a challenge."

She followed Jakob as he wound through the trees. When she turned back after a few minutes, smoke was already rising into the night. He led her towards a spot a quarter mile from the cabin where his truck waited next to two others. A bunch of people were standing around the cars.

Elijah seemed agitated, arguing with someone leaning against one of the vehicles and pointing in the cabin's direction. The person he was talking to seemed relaxed and pointed over Elijah's shoulder when he stopped for breath.

He rushed over as soon as he saw Adeline, completely ignoring whatever the werewolf he'd been talking to had said. He wrapped his arms around her and she relaxed into the embrace. Safe. They were both finally safe. He stepped back and looked her over.

"You said you'd be right behind me. You lied."

"I knew you wouldn't leave if I told you I planned to run off in another direction," she said. "Lying was the only way."

"I saw someone carrying Thomas like a sack of potatoes, but no sign of Dale. Is he—?"

"Dead. Our ancestors' magic runs deep here, and they're not willing to give up their foothold. Dark magic's not enough to kill a Harlan witch."

"Thank God for that. I can't lose you too."

***

Jakob, Adeline, and Elijah couldn't agree on what to do with Thomas Lennox. No one wanted to leave him alone in the woods unconscious, but they couldn't bring extra attention to themselves. His mother might've reported him missing despite Dale's threats.

"How much did he know?" Jakob asked Adeline as they stood in front of his truck. Thomas was asleep in the backseat. "About Dale's plan and the supernatural?"

"I don't know. Dale mentioned spells and witchcraft in front of him and talked about resurrecting his father in front of him in the cabin. Thomas might've thought he was crazy or might've believed him. And I don't know what Dale might've said before today."

"He also mentioned vampires," Elijah added. "Said a vampire online sold him the grimoire he was using, but didn't give a name."

"Don't need it. Something he said later told me all I needed to know," she said. "I'll fill you in later, Jakob. Back to Thomas."

"Any chance you can make him forget the whole thing?" Jakob asked.

"In theory, but it would be like taking a chainsaw to his brain," she said. "We're not talking about erasing one memory from an otherwise normal day. He has other, older memories connected to what happened today, like finding out Dale killed Wyatt or seeing him outside Sandra's house covered in blood."

"Why didn't he tell anyone about that?"

"Not the point. I'd have to alter multiple memories, and the more I modify, the more we risk that it could permanently alter his brain."

"If you make him forget everything, he won't remember holding us at gunpoint, which will be a problem when his mama or the sheriff demand an explanation," Elijah said. "He'll look more guilty if he can't remember."

Adeline considered the options for a few seconds. "Here's my suggestion. We head towards the Lennox house. When we finally have cell reception, I'll wake him up. We'll say Dale hit him over the head and we escaped. He'll call his mother to let her know he's okay, and we'll take him home."

"Will he buy the story?" Jakob asked.

"He'll want to."

"Well, that's better than nothing." They got into Jakob's truck and he started the engine.

Adeline held her phone in her hand and checked for a cell signal every few minutes. When she finally had service, she told the others and ignored the log of missed calls and voicemails. She rested a hand on Thomas's forehead and spoke. "Wake up."

He let out a groan before cracking one eye open. He blinked rapidly a few times before sitting up. "What – Where am – What happened?"

"Oh, good, you're awake," she said, feigning relief. "We're safe. You're safe. Dale hit you over the head with something and you passed out. Elijah got loose and freed me. We grabbed you and ran out of that creepy cabin."

"Who's he?" He was staring at the back of Jakob's head.

"I'm a friend of Adeline's. She called me once she was out of the woods."

"Dale didn't take my phone," she said, holding it out to the teen. "Call your mama. She's probably worried sick."

"Why'd you help me? You yelled at me and said I had blood on my hands."

"I thought I was gonna die and freaked out. I know you didn't have a choice. Call your mother; let her know you're okay."

Adeline could barely make out the conversation Charlotte was having with her son, but the woman was audibly crying. She could only imagine what had gone through the woman's head all day when her son had vanished with a murderer.

When Jakob pulled up in front of the house, Charlotte, her husband, and the sheriff were all waiting at the door. Charlotte burst into tears when Thomas got out of the car.

"Someone want to tell me what in the hell happened today?" Sheriff Hopkins asked as everyone watched the tearful reunion between the teenager and his mother. "Charlotte calls me and says Tommy here was kidnapped. I get here, and she says he helped Dale Blevins kidnap the two of you at gunpoint. Now you three come back with a man I've never seen before, all chummy, and Dale's nowhere to be seen."

"I only went along with it because he said he'd kill Mama if I didn't do it," Thomas cried out.

"Went along with what?"

"Help kidnap Elijah and me," Adeline said.

"Why would Dale want to kidnap you?"

"His mama's death did something to his head," Elijah said. "I don't think his mind's been right in awhile. He thought he could bring his father back if he sacrificed some people. It's why he killed Sandra Russett, Derek Green, and Wyatt Dunn. He said their deaths were the key." He paused. "I know it don't make sense, but that's what he said."

"He was trying to raise the dead?"

"He said he was. He went and dug up his daddy's body too," Adeline said with a grimace. "Like Eli said, his mind wasn't all there."

"Where'd he take you? How'd you get away?"

"An old cabin out in the woods. It might've belonged to a relative of his. He tied us up, locked himself in a room with his father's body to do something, and left Thomas to watch us. Then, he got all paranoid about Thomas letting us go, so he hit him over the head. While he was distracted, we were able to free ourselves. Elijah threw Thomas over his shoulder, and we ran out of there. Eventually, my phone had a strong enough signal that I was able to call Jakob. He was in the area visiting a friend."

"The cabin, was it east or west of here?"

"East." She turned towards where the cabin was. A column of smoke was rising up through the night, illuminated by the moon. "About si – Do you see that smoke? It's coming from right about where the cabin was. Or at least, I think so. It's hard to tell in the dark."

"I suppose I should go see what that fire is about. Might be Dale trying to cover his tracks," Hopkins said as he walked over to his cruiser. "I'll stop by to-morrow, ask my other questions. All of you, including Mister Good Samaritan over there," he gestured to Jakob, "better stay in the county for the time being."

The sheriff drove off. After an awkward goodbye with Thomas, Charlotte, and Zachary Lennox, Elijah got into his truck with Adeline and drove off as well, with Jakob behind following them.

CHAPTER 27

— ◦ —

A deline's car was parked in the same spot she'd left it in that morning when she and Elijah had gone to see Joan. Another vehicle, a faded blue pick-up truck, was beside it when Elijah, Adeline and Jakob arrived.

Elijah and Adeline were exiting his truck when the driver of the pick-up got out of his vehicle and stormed over to the driver's side door. Before Adeline could greet Paul Lee, or ask why he was there, the deputy's mouth was on Elijah's.

They broke apart after several seconds. "I was so worried! I heard the call over the radio, about you and Adeline being kidnapped and—"

"Paul, um, I didn't — I mean I haven't—" Elijah looked over at his sister and then back at Paul.

"Paul's the person you've been seeing," Adeline said.

"Yes, for the last two and a half years. I said I was seeing someone, but I—"

"Never said it was a woman. Actually, come to think of it, you always said 'we' or 'they' and never anything else. Well, this explains why you kept acting weird whenever I asked about your girlfriend. And why he made some comments about you that made it seem like you two knew each other pretty well."

"I didn't want to tell you over the phone. And then you stopped by unexpectedly, and I couldn't find the words that morning to tell you I'm gay. Then, people started dying and — Please say something."

"If you're happy, then I'm happy for you. And you seem happy. I reckon this explains how you knew Paul wasn't the one murdering people either."

"I was a suspect?" Paul asked. "I don't even — *Sandra was ripped apart.*"

"Addy thought you might've been using dark magic," Elijah said. "Witches are real. Magic, vampires, werewolves, all that crap's real."

"And you're not supposed to tell people that," Adeline cried out.

"You can't, but I can. I'm not bound by the supernatural laws you told me about." For a moment, Jakob looked uncomfortable, but the moment passed as Elijah gestured between the two Guardians. "They were investigating the murders because they were supernatural, not because of cults or whatever they said."

"So, witches killed Sandra, Derek, and Wyatt?" Paul asked in disbelief.

"It wasn't witches, it—"

"Can we take this conversation inside?" Jakob asked. "I spent all day tracking you two down after you went and got yourselves kidnapped. I don't know about you, but I'm beat."

They went into the house, where Adeline and Elijah sat down with Paul and explained some Coburn family history, as well as what happened with Dale Blevins.

***

An hour after they returned to the house, after Elijah and Paul went upstairs, Adeline was making herself some coffee when Jakob walked into the kitchen.

"Is this the part where you say 'I told you so' about leaving without back-up?" she asked, not turning away from the coffee pot. "I'd like to remind you that no one ever would've predicted Thomas Lennox got mixed up in the murders."

"I planned to bring it up tomorrow. Saying it tonight would make me feel like a huge dick, considering the day you've had," Jakob said, leaning against the counter. "You said you'd explain how you knew vampires were involved in the killings?"

"Like Eli said, Dale mentioned somewhere in his ramblings that he bought a spell book from a female vampire on the dark web." She turned to face him. "Later, in the woods, he said something to the effect of 'she told me I should've killed you first.' Estelle's the only female vampire I can think of who'd want me dead."

"She didn't admit as much to Alexei, apparently, but she confessed she recently 'off-loaded'—her words—several books in her collection and heavily implied to him knowledge about the local murders. Alexei claims he called you earlier, and when you didn't answer he called me, which I ignored. I called him back while you were filling Paul in on everything."

"For his sake, I'd better have a voicemail from him. I got a missed call from someone before everything happened, but not a message." She crossed her arms. "I'm not saying I don't believe him, but—"

"It's awfully convenient he said that now, when everything's over." He nodded. "As for the rest, you don't strike me as impulsive, so why'd you put yourself at risk?"

"We're gonna need something stronger than coffee, if you really want to know." She walked over to the liquor cabinet and opened it with a spell. "Whiskey or bourbon?"

"Surprise me."

"I wanted to talk to some of the suspects, the unlikely ones. Charlotte was low on the list, and seemed like the safest bet. Catching up with an old classmate wouldn't raise eyebrows. Elijah came with me, but insisted we visit Joan first. Visiting her put things into perspective, and he talked me into coming back here."

Adeline handed him a glass of bourbon and then poured herself a bigger glass. "On the way back, I got a call from Seattle. My former boss's boss, or rather his assistant, was trying to get me back in Washington, to get my account of what happened to Lucy Radassi, the girl who died on my last assignment there. My old boss talked me into quitting so they wouldn't have to fire me, which would reflect badly on them, and they didn't even bother hearing my side of the story before giving me the 'quit or get fired' ultimatum."

"And that call pissed you off so much that you ran off to get kidnapped?"

"It wasn't the call itself. It wasn't even that Gabriel, the boss's boss who had fired me, was essentially demanding my presence in Seattle. Shane, the paper pusher who called, made it sound like the inquiry they're doing was so important, more significant than anything here, but he got her name wrong. Lucy died the day after the fall equinox, but they don't remember her name. Maybe I'm a good person or maybe I'm not, but I value life enough to know the names of people I've killed or couldn't save."

She took a swig of her drink. "He couldn't be bothered to learn her name and after that conversation, I didn't want to come back here and have nothing to do to keep myself from thinking about her."

"What happened to Lucy? I know she died, but you've never said how," Jakob said.

Adeline gave him the rundown of what happened. Who Lucy was, why she and Dominic had been looking for her, and finally what happened when Dominic wouldn't back down and kept trying to force the rusalka into coming with them, followed by Lucy's death and Dominic blaming her for it. She ended the story explaining how she'd left Seattle a few days later.

"That's such bullshit. Steve'll back you up, give you an excuse to stay here if they try to force the issue before you're ready."

"Shane tried that. I informed him that the ultra-powerful and scary Moranaa Dessis took an interest in our murder investigation. I 'forgot' to mention that interest was due to dark magic's involvement."

"The order mentioned magics, plural. Which implies they're interested in ancestral magic too."

"I hope not. I've got enough problems." She took a sip of her drink. "Anyway, since I mentioned the Moranaa Dessis, the Alliance will be off my back for at least a month. The whole organization's scared shitless of them."

"That's not suspicious at all." He looked her in the eye. "Don't tell me you're hoping to transfer back there."

"Absolutely not. I don't miss it. I left Kentucky because Elijah made me, and because I was scared of being trapped here, of dying like my mama did without ever seeing the world. I didn't care I was cutting myself off from my ancestors and the source of my power." She sighed. "I'm too old to be in denial about who and what I am. I can't leave now, and I don't want to."

"And so, you have stopped running." Harlan, using the voice of her mother, sounded serene, and a tad smug.

"So, you should definitely ask me to dinner, if your flirting last night was serious," she said.

"It was, but tonight didn't seem like the time to mention it again." He looked her in the eye. "You'd say yes then?"

"Yeah. Though, I should warn you, I can only blame half of my issues on being a witch."

"Yes, because I'm so well-adjusted over here with my PTSD, borderline alcoholism, and laundry list of other issues. You're not the only one that's a little fucked up."

Adeline was about to ask what he meant, but a loud yawn overcame her, and she realized how exhausted she was. She went upstairs to go to sleep, remembering at the last moment to plug her dead cellphone in to charge.

***

When Adeline woke up the next morning, her fully charged phone showed four voicemails, all from the night before, and several missed calls. Her old partner, Dominic, had called three times but left no messages. One voicemail was from Tatiana Petrova, one was from Gabriel Reynolds, and two were from unknown numbers.

With a sigh, she tapped the icon to start listening to the messages. She had a feeling most, if not all, of them would anger her.

"Hello, Adeline. This is Alexei Sokolov," Alexei said. "Please call me as soon as possible. I have learned something quite troubling from one of my sisters and believe your life to be in danger."

"He made an attempt after all. Ain't that a surprise?" She moved on to the next message.

"Hi, Adeline. I know you probably don't want to hear from me," Tatiana's voice said. "I was doing a reading for a client late tonight, but I got interference from the great beyond concerning you. Your destiny still lies in your birthplace, and it seems you are now on the path that will lead you there. Yet, when I sought to divine more, everything was obscured. I felt you should know, even if you may not wish to."

"What the hell am I supposed to do with that?" she muttered to herself.

She didn't know what to make of Tatiana's claims, nor did she want to consider what her destiny could be or the implications of the seer being unable to see anything about her future. The idea unnerved her as much as Astrid, the Norn's daughter, claiming her foresight was blocked.

She moved onto the next message.

"Adeline, this is Gabriel. I understand from my aide Shane that you're unwilling—"

She deleted the message without listening to the rest. She wasn't in Seattle, Gabriel had no authority over her, and she wasn't in the mood to deal with his bullshit after last night. She tapped the icon to listen to the final message.

There were a few beats of silence before a man cleared his throat.

"Hello, Adeline. At least, I hope this is Adeline Coburn's phone and not some random number. My name is Oliver Radassi. I'd like to talk to you about my sister Lucy's death. Please call me back at this number when you have some time to talk."

Numbly, Adeline listened to the message. When it was over, she put her phone back in her pocket without calling him back. Oliver deserved answers about his sister's death, and he would get them, but not today.

EPILOGUE

— • —

Three days after surviving her confrontation with Dale Blevins, Adeline drove out to visit her aunt Mary. She made the long trek up Brodens Mountain to where her family lived. To her surprise, she didn't run into anyone on her journey.

When she reached the clearing, about two dozen people milled about. The atmosphere was somber. She stood there for a moment, torn between coming back tomorrow or staying to talk to her aunt. Before she could decide, Mary spotted her and walked over.

"You're back."

"I said I'd come back so we could talk after the killings stopped, and they have. The killer—"

"Is dead. Struck by lightning, unless I'm mistaken," Mary said. "At least, it felt like you were creating lightning three nights ago. Don't start beating yourself up over it. All you did was defend yourself."

"I used to babysit him. It's a little hard – Never mind." She glanced around. She received sad smiles from a few people as they went on their way. "What's going on? If now's a bad time to talk, I'll come back."

"It's a sad day, but it's good that you're here. Edith's with the ancestors now."

"Edith's dead? Did what happened, the dark magic, cause it? You and I felt pain coming from the land; could she feel it?"

"No, she couldn't. Edith wasn't a direct descendant of Adeline Broden, but we are. Her health had been declining for a while. That's why she was so happy you came to her party. She knew she didn't have long left." Mary wrapped her arms around her stomach. "We buried her this morning. Her death means it's important you and I talk things over. Today."

"She just died. We don't need to talk about anything serious today." She turned to head back to her car, but Mary grabbed her wrist, stopping her in her tracks. The grip wasn't painful but Adeline couldn't easily pull away.

"No, we do. There's no point in waiting." She called her sons. "If anyone wonders where I've gone, tell them Addy and I are talking. We'll be inside."

Keeping her grip on Adeline's arm, she led them over to her house and opened the door. Adeline sat on the sofa and waited for her aunt to speak.

"I don't really know where to start. There's a lot we need to discuss."

"While you think it over, there's something I want to ask you," Adeline said. "Elijah told me something interesting a few days ago. Did you tell him you never wanted to see him again after he told you I'd left Evarts?"

"I did."

"Why would you say that to him?" Adeline crossed her arms. "He didn't force me to go; I wanted to. He supported my decision. You had no right to be mad at him, or at me for leaving. Until the day I came up here with Jakob, I hadn't seen you since the day we buried Aunt Eve. And between my mama dying and Eve, I saw you twice."

"I kept my distance, which was a mistake in hindsight, because I wanted to let you mourn Lilah without thinking I wanted to replace her. I worried that thirteen was too young for me to tell you everything you needed to know, and I figured you'd come see me when you were ready to learn more. When you were done with school and finally had time to devote to your Gift. Then, the wrong twin hiked up here and said you were gone, with no plans to come back. He didn't understand the devastation your absence would cause, and was excited for you. So, I told Elijah to leave before I did something I'd regret."

"What are you talking about? What devastation? You didn't need me here. No one did. No one's ever needed me to stick around."

"The ancestors did, and still do. You're—" Mary cut herself off. "When you've told people you use ancestral magic, how do they respond?"

"Surprise, mostly. Hell, some folks didn't believe me. One coven even tried to convince me that ancestral witchcraft's a myth, since we're rare among magic users." She rolled her eyes at the memory.

"We're not rare. We're dying out."

"We can't be dying out. I'm here. You're here. Your sons—"

"Didn't inherit the Gift from me or their daddy. Most on this mountain don't have the Gift. Edith did, but she's gone." Mary paused. "I don't know how many of us are left, worldwide, but in this coven—When Lilah died, there were six of us left: Edith, Norma, Eve, my mama, myself and you. Then, Eve died. We didn't want to put too much pressure on you, knowing one day you'd be the only one left. You were just a kid."

"I'm not a kid now."

"No, you're not. Norma and I have a lot to teach you before we join the ancestors, and far less time than I wanted."

Adeline leaned forward. "What do you mean, you don't have much time?"

"You weren't here for sixteen years; we could've taught you plenty in that time and we can't get those days back."

There was no use dwelling on the past. The only direction they could go was forward. "Where do we start?"

"With me coming clean about something. A few things actually. While I've never outright lied to you, I've lied by omission. For example, your job working for the Chancellor."

"You don't like the Chancellor, you don't think I should be working for 'the government.' What else is there to say?"

"I don't like it because it gives the Chancellor and all of them the illusion that they have some authority over us, and they don't," Mary said. "Ancestral witches aren't bound by their laws and they've always known that. You didn't know, and I knew you didn't know. Didn't you think it was odd that you hadn't heard about the Arcane Codex, the Chancellor, any of it, until after you left? You weren't told for the same reason you didn't learn about the French government: it's irrelevant to your life."

Adeline had found it odd when she had first left, but chalked it up to the coven being skeptical of outsiders. "If we don't have to follow their rules, why allow Guardians up here? Why play nice?"

"In case I needed help finding you. If I told them to kick rocks, they wouldn't be inclined to help us look for you."

Adeline's thoughts raced, not only about what this meant for her future but also how her ignorance had shaped her past decisions. "Okay, what else haven't you told me?"

"I've purposefully not asked you certain questions until now because you were preoccupied with your murder investigation," she said. "Give me a moment."

She walked over to her kitchen and rifled around in one of the drawers before returning to her seat holding a pen and paper. "Think about how strong your Gift was when you were eighteen, compared to now."

"It's stronger now, but I'm older. I've got more experience and knowledge."

"And that plays a role, but it's not the only reason. Since you came back, have you – Did you cast a spell, but it was stronger than you intended? Or maybe there was one you didn't mean to cast at all?"

Adeline remembered a few incidents, including breaking Elijah's coffee pot. "Once or twice. I was gone for so long. I-I thought I just didn't know my own strength."

"No. It's because you're accessing a larger amount of power than back then." Mary drew a circle on her paper. "Let's pretend this circle symbolizes the power of all the ancestors when your mama died." She drew a second, larger circle. "And this is it now."

"The second one's bigger. There are more ancestors."

"That's not the only difference." Mary drew lines, splitting the smaller circle into six sections and the larger one into three sections. "The collective strength of the ancestors is split amongst those of us on this side of the veil. When Lilah died, that was Eve, Edith, Norma, my mother, myself, and you. Now, there's three of us. You, Norma, and I each get a third of it."

She drew a third, even larger circle. "Once Norma and I join them, it's gonna look like this." She wrote Adeline's name in the center of the circle. "It'll be all yours."

"And why leaving was so taboo." Her eyes widened. "Part of why I wanted to go so badly was because everyone told me not to, but no one would say why."

"It didn't use to be taboo. One of Adeline Broden's daughters left when she married her husband. Others moved to avoid becoming collateral damage in one conflict or another, but that was back when there were more of us." Mary paused. "Over the last few centuries, people have also forsaken the ancestors by joining other covens. Many, many more have died. Our numbers have dwindled. To maintain balance, our power only survives as long as one of us is here, binding the ancestral realm to the land. There has to be a living descendant here; otherwise, there's nothing connecting the ancestors to the area. If the line is broken, if the only ancestral witches are the ones in the ground, all that power, the strength of dozens of witches who've lived and died over hundreds of years, would be released. Magic's energy, and all that energy has to go somewhere."

"Where?"

"Our ancestors didn't think to record it, or the writings were lost." She shook her head. "Just like none of the journals we have explain why we use our ancestors as the source of our magic, why we don't draw from the stars like ordinary witches."

"We're ancestral witches, and we don't know why?"

"No one among the living. I don't suppose you've met anyone capable of talking to the dead over the course of your wandering."

"One, but she'd run away screaming if she saw me," Adeline said. "I met her through work, and she'd think I was trying to kill her."

"Another reason why I'd suggest resigning from being a Guardian. Our role is to maintain balance, not police the actions of others. What are you guarding anyway?" Mary asked, before waving off her answer. "I think we've gone over enough family and coven history for today. Now, tell me how you created that lightning. I want to know how you understand what you did, so I can determine how helpful or useless your other mentors were."

ACKNOWLEDGEMENTS

There are a lot of people I owe a huge "thank you" to for helping make *Magic &* *Murder in the Holler* a reality. Writing a book isn't a solo effort, and I wouldn't have been able to publish this story without the talents and support of countless people.

First and foremost, I want to thank my parents for always supporting and encouraging me. I also want to thank my sister, Elana, for not only giving me the nudge I needed to sit down and write this book, as opposed to talking about it, but also for her support every step of the way. This story would still be all in my head without her. I want to express my gratitude to my friends, Danielle and Lianna, for listening to me ramble (and sometimes vent)about the ups and downs of the writing while I was working on this book.

A heartfelt thanks to my beta readers, Julianne B., Sarah Irwin, Mara Heath, Samantha Wong and November H. Tuppen, for their thoughtful and constructive feedback which helped strengthen the narrative.

This book wouldn't be the same without the fantastic editorial feedback from Erin Young and Emmaline Eble, as well as the amazing cover design by Ashton M. Smith of Ashton M. Smith Designs. They helped bring this story to life.

ABOUT THE AUTHOR

— · —

S ara J. Lilienfeld is a lifelong fantasy reader, often spending days getting lost in books. She began writing in her early teens and quickly because drawn to stories about community and discovering magic in unexpected places. She lives in the DC metropolitan area with her two cats, Gin and Whiskey. In her "day job" she works in finance.

Connect with Sara:

www.saralilienfeld.com

www.ingramcontent.com/pod-product-compliance
Lightning Source LLC
Chambersburg PA
CBHW050012120726
47903CB00006B/1741